Dear Readers,

Many years ago, when I was a kid, my father said to me, "Bill, it doesn't really matter what you do in life. What's important is to be the *best* William Johnstone you can be."

I've never forgotten those words. And now, many years and almost 200 books later, I like to think that I am still trying to be the best William Johnstone I can be. Whether it's Ben Raines in the Ashes series, or Frank Morgan, the last gunfighter, or Smoke Jensen, our intrepid mountain man, or John Barrone and his hard-working crew keeping America safe from terrorist lowlifes in the Code Name series, I want to make each new book better than the last and deliver powerful storytelling.

Equally important, I try to create the kinds of believable characters that we can all identify with, real people who face tough challenges. When one of my creations blasts an enemy into the middle of next week, you can be damn sure he had a good reason.

As a storyteller, my job is to entertain you, my readers, and to make sure that you get plenty of enjoyment from my books for your hard-earned money. This is not a job I take lightly. And I greatly appreciate your feedback— you are my gold, and your opinions *do* count. So please keep the letters and e-mails coming.

Respectfully yours,

William Johnstone

WILLIAM W. JOHNSTONE

TRIUMPH OF THE MOUNTAIN MAN

BATTLE OF THE MOUNTAIN MAN

PINNACLE BOOKS
Kensington Publishing Corp.
http://www.kensingtonbooks.com

PINNACLE BOOKS are published by

Kensington Publishing Corp.
850 Third Avenue
New York, NY 10022

All Kensington Titles, Imprints, and Distributed Lines are available at
special quantity discounts for bulk purchases for sales promotions, pre-
miums, fund-raising, and educational or institutional use. Special book
excerpts or customized printings can also be created to fit specific needs.
For details, write or phone the office of the Kensington special sales
manager: Kensington Publishing Corp., 850 Third Avenue, New York,
NY 10022, attn: Special Sales Department, Phone: 1-800-221-2647.

Pinnacle and the P logo Reg. U.S. Pat. & TM Off.

First Pinnacle Books Printing: April 2006

10 9 8 7 6 5 4 3 2 1

Printed in the United States of America

TRIUMPH OF THE
MOUNTAIN MAN

1

Once a week, a Sugarloaf hand rode into Big Rock, Colorado, to pick up the mail. Lost Ranger Peak brooded over the town, its 11,940-foot summit covered by a mantle of white year-round. Often the journey proved to be nothing more than an excuse to spend an hour or two in the Bright Lights saloon. With the exception of Sally Jensen's sporadic correspondence with a few old school friends, scant mail ever came to the home of the fabled gunfighter, Smoke Jensen. On a fine morning in late April, then, Ike Mitchell, the Sugarloaf foreman, expressed his surprise when Smoke Jensen announced that he reckoned he would be the one to ride into Big Rock.

Ike hastened to relieve his employer of the burden. "No need to trouble yourself, Mr. Jensen. One of the boys can make the mail run."

"No trouble, Ike. I really feel like I ought to go." Smoke brushed at his reddish blond hair and gazed across the pastures of the Sugarloaf with his oddly gold-cast eyes. "There's some little—something—nagging me to make the ride into town."

Ike chuckled behind a big, work-hardened hand. The wings of gray hair at his temples waved in a light breeze. "Needin' a little time away from Miz Sally, eh?"

"Not exactly, Ike. Though I'll admit I would enjoy a good card game and a few schooners of beer with friends."

With a knowing wink, Ike encouraged Smoke. "You'll have time enough for that, like as not. Not many people know where the Sugarloaf is, let alone how to reach it by mail. Enjoy your day, Mr. Jensen."

"I will Ike. Anything I can bring you from town?"

Ike removed his black, low-crowned Stetson and scratched his head. "The missus could use a bottle of sulphur elixir to treat the young'uns for spring."

Smoke involuntarily made a face at the memory of that medical treatment. It had not been one of the things he missed when separated from his family and taken in by Preacher. "I'll get it, then. Only, don't tell your brood who it was brought it."

Amorous meadowlarks whistled to prospective mates as Smoke Jensen rode over the wooden bridge that spanned the Elk River. and entered Big Rock. He kept his Palouse stallion, Cougar, at a gentle walk. In spite of the chill in the air, the sun felt warm on his shoulders. He had left his working chaps behind, and wore a rust-colored pair of whipcord trousers, a green, yoke shirt and buckskin vest. Around his narrow waist he carried his famous—or infamous, according to some—pair of .45 Colt Peacemakers. The right-hand one was slung low on his leg, the left in a pouch holster high on the cartridge belt, the butt pointed forward. Several writers of dime novels, Ned Buntline included, had made such a getup known to millions as a "gunfighter's rig."

Smoke looked on it as a practical necessity. The same as the .45-70-500 Winchester Express rifle in the saddle scabbard. While not expecting trouble, Smoke had learned long ago that it paid to come prepared at all times. As his legendary mentor, Preacher, had said, "It tends to increase a feller's life span."

* * *

"Morning," Smoke greeted a teamster who struggled with the ten-up team hauling a precarious-looking load of logs on a bedless, cradle wagon. The man gave a wave as Smoke rode on.

Farther into town, the streets became more populous. Women in gingham dresses and bonnets, their shopping baskets clutched in gloved hands, clicked the heels of their black, high-button shoes on the boardwalk of the main street. Horses stood, hip-shot, outside the saddle maker's, the bank, three saloons and the general store. A couple of empty buckboards rattled in from another direction, while one was being loaded by a harassed-looking teenager in a white apron. A typical Saturday in Big Rock, Smoke allowed. He nosed Cougar toward the hitch rail in front of the general mercantile. There he dismounted and climbed to the plank walk.

Inside the store, Nate Barber, the owner, greeted Smoke warmly. "Not often enough we see you, Mr. Jensen. You sure picked a day for it. Got near a whole mail bag full for you."

Smoke raised a yellow-brown eyebrow. "That so? I wonder what the occasion might be?"

"Catalogue time again," the postmaster/merchant advised, then added a familiar complaint. "Those mail order outfits are going to be the ruin of stores like mine."

Smoke nodded and went to the caged counter, behind which ran a ceiling-high rank of pigeon-hole boxes to hold the mail. His, he noted, bulged with envelopes. Barber went into his small post office and bent to retrieve a stack of bound, soft-cover volumes. "Here you are, Mr. Jensen. I'll get those letters for you, too."

Smoke went quickly through the catalogues. He found the latest *Sears* issue for Sally, another for musical instruments by mail order, and one for himself, from a saddle and tack manufacturer. That might prove useful, he reasoned. Anything made of leather eventually wore out, and no manner of patching could salvage it in the end Some of the breaking saddles used on the Sugarloaf had begun to look rather shabby. If the prices were lower fo this outfit in San Angelo, Texas, than in Denver, he migh order four new ones. Among the correspondence he found a creamy, thick envelope of obvious high quality addressed to him in a rich, flowery script that denoted that the writer had learned his letters in a language other than English. The return address was Rancho de la Gloria, Taos, New Mexico Territory. Don Diego Alvarado, Smoke recognized at once.

Smoke had come to know Diego Alvarado several years ago, when he had been in New Mexico briefly on a cattle-buying trip. The gentlemanly, reserved Don Diego was the grandson of an original Spanish grandee, who had the patent of the King of Spain for roughly a thousand acres of high, mountainous desert to the west of Taos. His father had retained title to the land through service to the Mexican government after independence and had added to the family holdings. Steeped in the traditions of his ancestors' culture, Alvarado was a superb host who loved to entertain. Smoke had soon discovered that Diego's facade of reserve quickly vanished with a glass of tequila in one hand and a slice of lime in the other. The "little feast" put on for Smoke and his hands had turned out to be a three-day extravaganza of food and drink. They had paid for their lavish keep before leaving, however. Smoke and his men had joined the *vaqueros* of Rancho de la Gloria in fighting off a band of renegade Comanches who swarmed up out of the Texas panhandle.

Barber interrupted his speculation. "Need any supplies today, Mr. Jensen?"

"No, Nate, I didn't bring a wagon along. Say, do you happen to have any of that sulphur elixir?"

Nate Barber nodded. "Just happens I do, now that I bought out old Doc Phillips's stock from the apothecary shop. How many bottles?"

Smoke chuckled. "Ike's got six youngsters out there. Might as well make it two bottles."

"Sure thing."

The merchant produced the corked, seamless glass bottles and wrapped each in paper. Smoke noticed that the packaging material appeared to be printed pages. "Advertising your place now, Nate?"

Nate glanced down, then smiled as he cut his eyes to Smoke. "Nope. Discarded catalogues. Some folks find 'em a bother and toss 'em away."

Smoke nodded his understanding, paid for his purchase and took his mail and the medicine along. Outside, he stowed it all in his saddlebags, swung into the saddle, and directed Cougar toward his next stop. Monte Carson would no doubt be downing his twelfth cup of coffee about now.

"Smoke! How'er you doin'?" Monte Carson bellowed as Smoke entered the office portion of the jail. Smoke and the sheriff had been friends for many long years, ever since the time when Smoke foreswore the dangerous life of a gunfighter-for-hire and stood back-to-back with Monte to rid the streets of Big Rock of some mighty nasty gunhawks and saddle trash. They had done a fair job of cleaning up all of Routt County for that matter. Smoke Jensen wore a badge for the first time in his life then, and had done so often since. Not that Smoke had been an outlaw in the truest sense of the word. He had never stolen anything, nor had he taken money for killing a man. Yet, it was always a close thing for a gunfighter to prove self-defense in a shoot-out. Being fully and permanently on the side of the law had a good feeling. Smoke had Monte to thank for that.

He poured coffee for himself and used the toe of one boot to hook a captain's chair over by a rung. Seated, he faced Monte. "Well, Monte, I came in on the mail run."

"You expectin' somethin' important?"

"No, but it appears I got it anyway." He went on to tell Monte about the letter from Don Diego Alvarado.

"Why don't you open it up and find out what it is?" Monte asked. "Might be an invite to the wedding of one of his sons."

Smoke shook his head. "I doubt that. Last I heard, Alejandro was already married. Xavier is down in Mexico at some seminary, studying to become a priest. Pablo would be a mere boy in his teens. Lupe could be only eight or so, and Miguel was born not three years ago."

Always curious, Monte prompted his friend. "So? Open the dang thing up and get a look."

"I will. But, being it's near noon, I thought you'd like to join me for a schooner or two of beer and some of Hank's free lunch over at the Bright Lights."

Monte grinned and, coming to his boots, nodded his head in eagerness. "You buyin'?"

"Of course. Although I wouldn't want it to be considered bribing an officer of the law. I don't want to be a guest of the county for even half an hour."

Monte reached for a drawer. "Well, then, hang a deputy's badge on yer vest and we'll call it a treat among brother lawmen. You know I'll bend heaven and earth to get a free beer."

They laughed together as they left the office. It was a short enough walk, only across the street, Smoke left Cougar tied off in front of the jail. The bar of the Bright Lights was crowded when they entered, so they took a table near the back of the room. The resinous odor of fresh sawdust perfumed the saloon. Smoke and Monte ordered beer and then built sandwiches of thick-sliced country ham, Swiss cheese, and boiled buffalo tongue, all on home-baked bread. They added fat dill pickles and hard-boiled eggs to their plates and carried them to where they would sit.

After taking a bite and chewing thoroughly, Smoke asked Monte about the town. The lawman responded eagerly.

"Let me tell you about these two drifters who tried to rob Nate's general mercantile," Monte began around a bite of his huge sandwich. "This happened about a week ago. They went in with bandannas pulled up over their noses and six-guns out. Well, Nate had no mind to try to stop them. One of the saddle trash growled at him about giving up all the money. Nate did, and put it in a paper bag, like they asked. The one who took the bag must have had a sweet tooth, 'cause right then he spied a jar of rock candy on the counter. Like a kid who only gets to town once in six months, he set the bag full of money aside and made for that jar. He stuffed his shirt pockets full of candy, and the ones in his vest, too. Then he grabbed up the cash and started to back out the door with his partner.

"What he didn't know," Monte went on, fighting back laughter, "is that he set that paper sack on top of the pickle barrel. It was a new, unopened one, but the lid had sprung. The bottom of the bag got soaked, and the weight of the money caused it to fall through. Coins went ever which a way. Right then, Nate grabbed up his shotgun while the robbers gaped at the fluttering bills that still fell from the sack. He had 'em disarmed and hands in the air when a passerby saw what was happenin' and came over to get me."

Smoke joined Monte's chuckles. "They don't make desperados like they used to. That all the excitement you've had?"

"Nope. Mrs. Granger had another baby, her eighth. Her husband swore he thought they were both too old for that to happen. A boy. That makes five boys and three girls."

"And all living?" Smoke inquired.

"Yep. By some miracle. Oh, yeah, how'd you fare out at the Sugarloaf in that thunderstorm middle of last week?"

"Not bad. Barely a shower there."

Monte frowned. "Might lot more around here. A regular goose-drownder. The Elk River went over its banks all along the valley. We had tree trunks and driftwood floating down Tom Longley Street for two days."

Smoke bit, chewed, and swallowed before remarking "I thought it looked a mite damp along there."

"'Damp' don't get it by about three feet, Smoke. Had some of the merchants writin' to the governor to ask for help in cleanup and repair. Hell, any fool knows the government ain't got any money. Only that they take from the people in taxes."

Smoke nodded agreement. "And I remember the time when a decent man wouldn't ask for a handout when he could make do for himself."

Monte put on a poker face. "But I reckon times they are a-changin'. It's gettin' too civilized around here."

Smoke slapped a big palm on one thigh. "Don't get me started on that. Any other urgent news?"

"Only that my chief deputy, Sam Barnes, was sparking the young widow Phillips last Sunday at the church box supper social."

"You mean the pretty young thing that some gossips are saying put old Doc Phillips in an early grave?"

"The same. A man's shy some gravy for his grits when he brings one home that's not half his age. Mind, I don't know about their home life and have no desire to speculate. She's a looker, though."

"That she is, Monte." In silence, they returned to their food.

Ace Banning paused to extinguish a quirley before he entered the bank in Big Rock. Few people remained in the lobby this close to noon. The bank would close in five minutes, according to the oak-cased wall clock that hung on the far wall. He waited behind a weighty dowager at one teller cage, and when his turn came, he asked for change for a twenty-dollar gold double-eagle. All the while, his eyes shifted, taking note of the layout of the establishment. Would they shut the vault at noon? He doubted it. There were two armed guards. That made Ace think of his friends waiting outside.

Shem Turnbull and George Cash lounged in front of the Bucket O' Suds saloon, two doors down from the bank. As noon neared, the street began to clear of people. Most of the shops closed over the dinner hour. Carefully they eyed passersby. Many of the men were armed. Those who were going home would be no trouble. Already a line had formed outside the eatery on the corner, and those would have to be closely watched. Shem turned to George.

"We shoulda brought another gun. Three fellers is not enough to carry this off."

"Oh, I don't know, Shem. They won't be expectin' anything, and their minds will be on their dinners. Ace can handle it real good."

"Not without a little help from you," Ace Banning declared as he walked up to his friends. "Shem, I want you inside with me. There's two armed guards. We've got only a minute, so let's move."

Smoke Jensen downed the last of his second schooner of beer, pushed back his chair, and dug in his pocket for a cartwheel dollar. "I'll walk over to the office with you, but then I have to head right back. I've got three mares who are due to foal at any time."

"You never opened that letter from Alvarado," Monte complained good-naturedly.

"That's right. I'll have to read it when I get home." Then reading his friend's expression, he added, "I'll let you know what Don Diego wrote about."

They had reached the tall, double doors with the painted glass inserts when the sound of a gunshot came from the direction of the bank. A woman's scream followed. Smoke turned that way at once, to be stopped when Monte laid a hand on his shoulder.

"I'll take care of this, Smoke. No need for you to stick your neck out."

Smoke cut his eyes to his friend and growled, "Even if I want to?"

Monte shook his head. "Not this time."

He set off for the bank. Monte made it halfway down the block before the outside man saw him coming and fired his six-gun from the lawman's blind side. The bullet struck Monte in the chest. Deflected as it punched through a rib, the slug cut a path through his lung from front to rear and buried itself in the thick muscle of his back. Shock took Monte off his boots. At once, Smoke started for him.

"Watch it, there's one over there somewhere." A pink froth formed on Monte's lips, and his voice came out far weaker than he expected.

Smoke reached his friend, his .45 Colt in hand, and glanced in the direction Monte pointed before the sheriff lost consciousness. Smoke saw his man instantly. A cruel grimace distorted the outlaw's mouth as he raised his revolver for another shot at the lawman. Smoke fired first. His round pinwheeled the man, punched through his sternum and tore apart his aorta. Charged up on adrenaline and action, he bled to death before he hit the boardwalk.

Kneeling, Smoke examined his fallen friend. Monte's face had grown pale, with a tinge of green around his lips, his breathing shallow and rapid. Smoke could hear a faint gurgle. If that bastard's killed him . . . he thought in a flash of anger. The thought came to him then. The first shot had been muffled; it had to have come from inside the bank. At once, he started that way.

It began going wrong the moment they entered the bank with bandannas tied over their faces. The employees and customers of the bank had no doubt what the masked men intended. Shem Turnbull headed for the teller cages, and Ace Banning shoved through the low swinging gate in the wall that divided the lobby from the working area. At once, the tellers raised their hands. Shem gestured with his gun barrel.

"That's right, keep 'em up until I tell you otherwise.

You, get a money bag and start filling it," he told the nearest teller.

Ace concentrated on the portly, balding man in a glassed-in cubicle. "Step out here and come over to the vault. We want all the hard money and all the greenbacks you can load in those sacks."

Rosemont Faulkner knew better than to make vain protests about the robbers not getting away with it. He left his desk and hastened across the floor to the door of the vault. There, instead of stooping to load the bank's precious capital into a canvas money sack, he swiftly grabbed the heavy door and gave it a hefty swing. It clanged shut, and he spun the dead bolt wheel. Defiantly he put hands on his hips and spoke with relish.

"That's a time lock. It won't open again until eight o'clock tomorrow morning."

That's when Ace Banning, already strained beyond control by the presence of two armed guards who were presently out of his sight, lost it.

"You bastard!" he screamed as the hammer fell on a cartridge, and Ace shot the bank president through the heart. A woman behind him began to scream. He spun on one boot heel and strode to the tellers.

"All right, Shem, grab everything they have and let's get out of here."

Two minutes went by with the outlaws holding bags in one hand and tellers stuffing them. Then a loud report came from outside. Ace nodded to the door. "That's George, let's go."

Quickly they reached the door, and Shem Turnbull flung it open. They stepped out into the presence of an angry Smoke Jensen.

"Hold it right there," Smoke growled.

Two men stood before him, crowded into the open double doors of the bank. Each held three bulging canvas bags. They also gripped identical Smith and

Wesson .44 Americans. Smoke followed his command with sizzling lead. Ace Banning dropped flat as the Colt in Jensen's hand bucked. The slug slammed into the pane of the bank door, and it shattered; shards flew inward to the chorus of screams from the three women inside. Ace fired wildly as the musical tinkle of glass sounded behind him.

His slug flew between Smoke's outspread legs. Already the last mountain man had moved his point of aim and triggered a shot that took Shem Turnbull in the thick meat of his side. He clapped a hand against it and discharged his Smith and Wesson. The .44 bullet cracked past Smoke's left ear and struck the bannister post of the balcony across the street. Smoke moved then, as Ace fired again. His third shot struck the prone Ace Banning in his shoulder, snapped the collarbone, and bored down into his lung.

At once, Ace began to gag and fight for air. His hand went slack on the revolver, and it dropped from his fingers. Smoke Jensen changed position again and fired a safety shot. Due to the small target, it gouged the back of Ace Banning. He cried out as the slug plowed along his spine and entered his right buttock. Beside him, Shem fired again.

A hot crease burned along the outer point of Smoke's left shoulder. Twisting with the impact, Smoke lined up on the bank robber and fired again. His bullet ripped into Shem's middle and punched a hole in his liver. As massive shock stole over him, he sagged back against the wall and released his hold on the money bags and six-gun. Slowly, he slid down to a sitting position. Peacemaker leading the way, Smoke Jensen walked up to them and kicked the gun away from Ace, then Shem. Years of experience told him that both would die within an hour. One of the bank guards came to the door.

"Go get Doc Simpson," Smoke commanded the astonished man.

Ace groaned and looked up at Smoke. "Th-thank you, mister. Ah—who—who are you?"

Smoke kept it cold. "I didn't send for the doctor to treat you. You'll be dead before an hour's gone by. And, I'm known as Smoke Jensen."

Greater misery washed over the pale face of Ace Banning. "We—ah—we didn't think you were still alive. And a lawman at that."

His last sentence did not make much sense to Smoke, so he ignored it and replied to the first. "Your mistake."

Dr. Hiram Simpson entered the outer treatment room of his office wiping his hands on a towel. "Let's take a look at you, Mr. Jensen."

"First tell me, how is Monte?"

Doc Simpson sighed tiredly "It was close. I had to clean the wound channel first off. Then, when I got the bullet hole plugged, and closed the two holes in his lung, the Almighty musta smiled on me, 'cause the lung reinflated. He's healthy. he should heal that up in good time. I've given him enough laudanum that he will sleep through to evening. That should aid the healing process. But, the bullet is lodged in the thick muscle only a fraction of an inch from his spine. After having to open his chest to work on his lung, no one can go in there after it right now."

"When can you?"

Doc Simpson read the strain in Smoke's voice. "Provided the sheriff heals as expected, I'd say someone could operate within six weeks, if that lead don't shift and paralyze him in the meantime."

"That could happen?"

With a hesitant nod Simpson replied, "I'm not a master surgeon, but right or wrong, it is taught in medical school that foreign objects in the body can shift under certain circumstances. That's why I don't want to operate on him. I'll send for a special surgeon from Denver."

That information did not sit well with Smoke. While Dr. Simpson worked on him, he kept at the physician to give a more accurate description of what damage had been done to Monte Carson. He remained dissatisfied when the doctor cut the last piece of tape and handed him two laudanum pills.

"Take half of one of these now. If the pain persists, take another half every six hours."

"I don't think I'll be needing them, Doctor," Smoke informed him, handing back the medicine. "How much do I owe you?"

"The county will pay for it. You were working as a deputy at the time."

With that settled, Smoke shrugged into his bloodied shirt, put on his vest and hat and headed to the door. It would be a long, uncomfortable ride back to the Sugarloaf.

2

Halfway back to the Sugarloaf, Smoke started to regret his rash decision to reject the opium-based medicine. He also thought darkly about the morning's events. Why did it have to be Monte Carson who caught that bullet? Although Monte had the constitution of an ox, he was nearing sixty. People didn't heal so quickly then. Smoke knew from experience that a lung shot often led to pneumonia, which more often killed the victim than the bullet itself. In his moody thoughts, Smoke castigated himself for not having gone along with Monte. Better still, gone in his place.

No, Smoke admitted to himself, Monte had too much pride. It would have robbed him of his self-respect to acknowledge that age might be slowing his gunhand, delaying the proper read of a situation. Yet, the results spoke for themselves. Monte lay unconscious in the small infirmary off Doc Simpson's office. Smoke had a slight bullet burn on his shoulder. They had both gone about it wrong. Admitting it did not mollify Smoke in the least.

Once he had turned Cougar into the corral, in the hands of Bobby Jensen to cool him out, Smoke took the mail to the main house. Sally greeted him with a spoon dripping melted lard in one hand. "Hello, handsome. I'm fixing a batch of doughnuts. My, what a lot of mail."

"Yep. There's a *Sears* catalogue for you."

Sally clapped her hands. "Oh, goody, I get to buy things."

Smoke answered her with a sidelong glance. "No, you don't. And a letter from a woman named Mary-Beth Gittings."

"Who?"

"That's what it says. I'll give it to you inside."

Seated at the kitchen table, Smoke distributed the mail into neat piles. While Sally chattered on and added more lard to the heated deep skillet for the doughnuts, he turned his attention to the intriguing letter from New Mexico. He opened it to find a disturbing difference in his old friend. Instead of the usual bubbling enthusiasm of this jovial grandee, who so loved to entertain, it was a gloomy account of growing difficulties. High in the Sangre de Cristo range of the Rocky Mountains, things were not right, Don Diego Alvarado informed Smoke Jensen. He went on to illustrate:

"There is an Anglo named Clifton Satterlee, who covets all of the land around Taos. He is powerful and wealthy. He has a hacienda outside Santa Fe and is believed to have the ear of many of his fellow Anglos in the territorial government. It is also said that he has many interests and much influence in the East. He has surrounded himself with some most unsavory men, who aid him in achieving his goals by any means necessary. Amigo," the letter went on, "there have been some incidents of violence. Men have been driven out, Anglos as well as Mejicanos."

Absently Smoke reached to the plate holding the doughnuts. He let go of one quickly enough the moment he touched it. "They're hot," Sally reminded him with a laugh.

Smoke went back to the letter for the final paragraph. "No one here seems capable of dealing with the man. So, forgive my presumption in asking this, old friend, but I feel that I must appeal to you to come out here and get the feel of what is going on." Only reluctantly, it seemed to Smoke, did Don Diego add his personal difficulties. "I, myself, have lost some cattle and the lives of some of my vaqueros." His missive concluded with some of his usual flourish. Smoke put it aside in thoughtful silence.

They rode up quietly, five beefy, hard-faced, tough men, and tied off their horses to a stone-posted tie rail outside the high-walled hacienda on Calle Jesus Salvador in Taos, New Mexico Territory. Beyond the wall they could see the red tile roof of a Spanish colonial style, two-story house. Nestled in a large valley, surrounded by the Sangre de Cristo range, the residence had an air of peacefulness. That was quickly broken when the leader, Whitewater Paddy Quinn, spoke to his henchmen.

"Remember, we ain't here to break him up, just to get him to sign."

One of the thugs, a man named Rucker, responded with a snigger. "Right, boss."

"Sure, I mean that, Rucker. Not a bruise. Now, let's get in there."

Quinn stepped up to a human-sized doorway inset in the tall, double gate, and raised a large brass knocker. The striker plate bolted to the portal gave off a hollow boom as he rapped it. He kept at it until a short, swarthy servant in a white cotton pullover shirt and trousers opened the door. "*¿Sí, señores?*"

"We're here to see Mr. Figueroa."

"*¿Qué? Lo siento, no hablo Ingles.*"

Paddy Quinn struggled to put his request into Spanish. *"Es necesario a hablamos con Señor Figueroa."* His grammar might not be perfect, but he conveyed the idea.

Figueroa's majordomo brightened. *"Ay, sí! Vengan."* His leather sandals made soft, scraping noises as he led the visitors across the cobbled courtyard to the main entrance.

Through a wrought-iron gate and a pair of tall double

doors, a tunnellike passageway led to a lushly planted open square. A large saguaro cactus filled one corner. In the center, a fountain splashed musically. Standing beside it was a slim gentleman of medium height, his white hair combed straight back in two large wings from his temples. He wore the costume of another age, tight, black trousers, trimmed with gray stripes along the outer seams, matching cut-away coat with gray lapels. His shirt was snowy, with a blizzard of lace and a wing collar. Calf-length boots had been burnished until they shone like polished onyx. From beyond him, practice scales on a piano tinkled from an open, curtained window. He turned at their entrance, and a dark scowl quickly replaced the smile of welcome he had prepared.

"You are not welcome in this house," he declared.

Paddy Quinn put a wide smile on his Irish face. "Sure, I'm sorry you see it that way, Mr. Figueroa. We will try to be brief, we will. I have come to arrange for the sale of this property to Mr. Satterlee."

Figueroa glowered at him. "Then you have come on a mistaken mission, señor. I have no intention of selling."

Beaming happily, Quinn ventured to disagree. "Oh, yes, you do."

"No, I do not. I have told you that five times before. I have not changed my mind. Now, leave or I shall send for some of my retainers."

At that, Paddy Quinn gave a signal to two of his henchmen. They crossed the space separating them from Ernesto Figueroa and grabbed the elderly gentleman by the arms. Quinn gestured toward the open window. With little effort, they frog-marched him to the lace-curtained window from which the music came. Quinn came up behind and shoved Figueroa's head through the opening. The scales had given over to a piece by Mozart now, played by a sweet-faced little girl.

"A nice girl, your granddaughter, she is," Quinn observed. "Lovely, innocent, vulnerable. You'd not be wanting anything to happen to her, now would you?"

A shudder of revulsion passed through Figueroa a moment before the thugs abruptly swung him around to face their leader. He fought for the words. "You wouldn't dare."

Quinn gave him a smile. "You're right, I would not. But I cannot account for every minute of my men's time. Come, señor. You will be more than generously compensated, an' that's a fact. You can take your lovely, expensive furniture and possessions elsewhere, anywhere you wish, and live to see her grow to womanhood. And a lovely figure she will make, it is."

Wincing from the painful grip on his arms, Ernesto Figueroa remained defiant. "What will happen if I still refuse?"

Paddy Quinn's face changed from beaming benignity to harsh evil. "Then I will let my men have their way with her and kill her before your eyes. But not you," he went on. "We'll be leaving you to live with what your stubbornness caused. Think about it, bucko."

Ernesto Figueroa hesitated only a scant two seconds before his head sagged in resignation and he made a hesitant gesture to indicate he would accept. Paddy Quinn handed him the papers and even produced a travel pen and brass inkwell so the defeated man could sign.

After due consideration, Smoke Jensen decided to go to Taos. His reasoning was simple. The foaling season, from February through April, was over and the first of May not far away. Besides, he owed Diego Alvarado. He left the hands busy with the new colts and went to talk it over with Sally.

"I expected this since you first told me what the letter contained. I'll not beg you to stay here, Smoke. I know better, and you would be disappointed in me if I did. How long do you expect to be gone?"

Smoke considered it. "Ten days. Two weeks at the most."

Sally's chuckle held a hint of irony. "I've heard that before. How are you going to travel, Smoke?"

"I'll take the Denver and Rio Grande south to Raton, then go by horseback through the Palo Flechado Pass to Taos."

A light of mischief glowed in Sally's eyes as though she particularly liked the thought that burst on her. "That sounds easy enough. I think I'll come with you; it will be nice to see Don Diego again."

Smoke shook his head rejecting the idea. "Who'll run the ranch and look out for Bobby?"

"Ike can run the ranch, and Bobby is grown enough to bunk with the hands and take care of himself."

Smoke remained unconvinced. "Think about what you just said."

"About Ike running the ranch?"

"No. About Bobby. He's thirteen, Sally. Do you remember what our others were like at that age?"

Fresh worry lines formed on Sally's forehead. "Yes . . . unfortunately I do."

"I think you should reconsider."

Sally stood in silence a long two minutes, leaning shoulder-to-shoulder with Smoke. "All right, you win this one. I'll be realistic and not start to worry until three weeks have gone by."

"Nice of you," Smoke jested, giving her a swift hug. "I will write you when I reach Taos."

"Send a telegram instead. It will get here sooner."

"All right."

"Now, let me ask only one thing. What are you going to do when you have to keep your promise to that boy about taking him along on one of these trips?"

Smoke affected a groan. "I'll figure that out when the time comes. Now, dear wife, will you pack me something suitable to wear at Diego Alvarado's?"

With an impatient twist to his lips, Clifton Satterlee gazed from the narrow window of the mud wagon stagecoach that rattled and swayed along the narrow dirt roadway that led from Santa Fe to Taos. "One would think," he muttered under his breath, "that since our nation has conquered this country, the government would put down proper paving stones." If they did not reach the relay station soon, he swore he would leave his breakfast on the floor of the coach. Across from him, his chief partner in C. S. Enterprises, Brice Noble, sat beside Satterlee's bodyguard, Cole Granger. To the increase of his discomfort, Satterlee realized that Granger actually liked this trip. He seemed to thrive on the discomfort. Suddenly Clifton's stomach lurched, and a fiery gorge rushed up his throat. He turned sideways and hastily flung aside the leather curtain.

"Oh, God," Satterlee groaned as he thrust his head out the window. With explosive force, he vomited into the rising plume of dust that came from under the iron-tired right front wheel. He could feel Granger's amused gaze resting on him. Damn the man!

When he recovered himself, Clifton Satterlee crawled limply back inside. Cole Granger held out a canteen for him, which he took eagerly and he rinsed his mouth. Then Granger extended a silver flask. "Here you go, Mr. Satterlee. It's some of your fine, French brandy."

Irritation crackled in Satterlee's voice. "It's cognac, Cole. C-O-G-N-A-C."

Hastily, Satterlee seized the container and swallowed down a long gulp. Immediately his stomach spun like a carousel. Then the warm, soothing property of the liquor kicked in, and his nausea subsided somewhat. From outside, above on the box, came a welcome cry.

"Whoa, Tucker, whoa, Benny, whoa-up, Nell. Wheel right." He called out the rest of the team, and the momentum of the stagecoach slackened.

Satterlee addressed the rest of the occupants. "About damned time. You know, that little upset of mine has left me ravenously hungry. Or maybe it is the cognac." He took another swig.

Cole Granger checked the stage itinerary. "There'll be a meal stop here, Mr. Satterlee."

Brice Noble looked balefully out the window. "I certainly hope the food will be better than we had this morning. That must have been what caused your discomfort, Cliff."

Satterlee nodded his gratitude for his partner's cover-up of his motion sickness. He hated any sign of weakness, as did Noble. Clifton Satterlee studied his partner. A man in his late forties, ten years senior to himself, Brice Noble had a bulldog face with heavy jowls. For all his youth, Noble was completely gray, his hair worn in long, greasy strands. Shorter by three inches, Noble weighed around one hundred seventy pounds and had the hard hands of a working cowboy, although Satterlee knew he had been a wealthy man for a long time. Brice had never given up his habit of carrying a brace of revolvers, in this instance, Merwin and Hulbert .44s. Satterlee knew only too well how good he could be with them. His pale blue eyes had a hard, silver glint when angered.

For his own part, Clifton made certain he never infuriated Brice. Even at six feet, two inches with longer, once stronger, arms and barrel chest, Satterlee readily acknowledged that he was no match for Noble. He sighed as he glanced down at the beginnings of a potbelly. He would have to get out and do more riding, Satterlee admonished himself. Although a lean man, Satterlee's left armpit felt chafed by the shoulder holster he wore there, and more so from the weight of the .44 Colt Lightning double-action that fitted it. Recalling its presence brought a laugh to the lips of Clifton Satterlee. He had not had occasion to draw it in anger or even self-defense in the three years since he bought it.

"What's funny, Cliff?"

"I was thinking about my gun, Brice. Do you realize I have not used it, except for practice, in the past three years?"

Noble nodded to Granger. "That's what Cole is here

for. But, I can tell you I'm looking forward to whatever food they have for us."

With a shriek of sand caught between brake shoe and wheel, the stage jolted to a stop. The station agent brought out a four-step platform with which the passengers could dismount. "Welcome to Española, folks. We've got some red chili, chicken enchilada and beans inside for you."

"Sounds good," Cole Granger told him with a big smile.

Clifton Satterlee saw it differently. "By all that's holy, don't you have any white man's food?"

"Nope. Not with a big, fat Mexican cooking for me. She cooks what she knows how to."

Satterlee appealed to his partner. "Do you know what that will do to my stomach, Brice?"

"Fill it, no doubt." Then, to the agent, "Do you have any flour tortillas?"

"Yep. An' some sopapillas with honey to finish off with."

Stifling a groan, Clifton Satterlee instructed, "I'll start with those."

Inside, over savory bowls of beef stewed with onions, garlic, and red chili peppers, corn tortillas stuffed with chicken, onions, black olives, cheese, sauce, the driver and guard joined in demolishing the ample food laid out for the occupants of the coach. Satterlee morosely doused the fried dough in an amber pool of honey. After devouring four of the sopapillas, he spoke low to Noble.

"I want you to stay a few days, up to a week, in Taos. Look around, make contact with our people. Make certain they are getting things done. My wife and I will return to Santa Fe two days from now."

Brice Noble chewed on the flavorful cubes of meat. He washed them down with beer that had been cooled in the well. "What do you propose doing next?"

"Our people have to accelerate their efforts. We need

that timber and damned soon. Our whole lumber business depends upon it. Go after those blasted savages."

Smoke Jensen stopped in on Monte Carson the next day, before he took the afternoon train south to Denver, where he would change for the run to Raton. He could have taken the AT&SF to Santa Fe, but he wanted to catch what word there might be running up and down the trail. Monte was awake when Smoke entered the infirmary. His skin held a pallor, and his response when he turned his head and saw Smoke was weak.

"Smoke, good you came. Maybe you can talk sense to the man."

"What's that about?"

"That croaker, Simpson, says I have to stay here for two, maybe three weeks. Then some kind of operation by a doctor from Denver."

Smoke nodded. "You've got a bullet in you, Monte. I'll tell you what he probably won't. It's near your spine. There's the chance . . . for permanent injury."

Monte cut his eyes away from Smoke. "Damn. If that happens, I won't be fit for anything. Old before my time and stove up. Not a fittin' end."

"No," Smoke agreed. "At least you would be alive."

"You call that *alive?* Ask me, it'd be nothin' more than livin' hell."

Smoke decided on a change of subject. "I came to tell you what was in that letter from Don Diego."

That brightened the lawman somewhat. "Really? What did the old grandee have to say?"

Smoke's fleeting frown framed his words. "There's trouble brewing out in the Sangre de Cristo. Some feller named Satterlee has it in mind to build himself a little empire. According to Don Diego, he's not shy about the sort of persuasion his men use to get what he wants. Alvarado's lost some stock and some cowboys. He asked if I'd come take a look."

"And are you?"

Smoke nodded. "Leavin' today, Monte. Train to Raton, then trail it from there. But, I feel bad about leaving you here all bunged up."

Monte tried to make little of it. "Not much happens in Big Rock anymore. My deputies can handle it."

"After that list you gave me yesterday, and what we ran into, I'd say your 'not much' is a bit of an exaggeration." Smoke tipped back the brim of his Stetson. "Well, I have to get to the depot. Look out for yourself, Monte. And do what the doctor says."

Monte scowled, then gave a feeble wave. "Watch yer back trail."

Smoke turned for the door. "I have a feelin' I'm going to have to."

3

On the train south, Smoke Jensen settled into his Pullman car with a copy of the Denver *Dispatch* and sat in the plush seat that would become part of his sleeping berth. The editorial page contained the usual harangue about the lawlessness of the miners and smelter workers. Someone named Wilbert Clampton had a piece on the subject of temperance. According to him, Demon Rum was soaking the brains and inflaming the passions of the lower classes. Until Denver banned liquor, the depredations chronicled elsewhere in the newspaper would only continue and increase. A moderate man in his drinking habits, Smoke could not find the energy to get worked up over Clampton's cry for abstinence. After twenty minutes and a dozen miles had gone by, Smoke put the paper aside. Immediately he noticed an attractive young woman seated in the same car.

She smiled in his direction with her eyes as well as her lips, then dabbed at her mouth with a dainty square of white linen. Her heart-shaped face was framed by a nest of small, blond curls. That and her expensive clothes added to her allure. Fiercely loyal to his beloved Sally, Smoke made only the lightest of passing acknowledgment to her discreet flirtation. The rail carriage swayed gently as the train rolled through the high mountains.

Up ahead, Smoke knew, his two horses, a sturdy pack animal and Cougar, would be comfortable in padded stalls in a special car. The expense of such travel conveniences had grown steeply over the past few years. Yet, he could afford it. Blooded horses brought good money. Far more so than cattle. Smoke went back to his newspaper.

There was talk again of building a canal across Central America to speed ship passage. More for cargo, Smoke knew, than passengers. With the nation linked from coast to coast with steel rails, the hazards of a sea voyage could be easily abandoned for the more secure railroads. At least with the James gang out of business, there seemed little possibility of robberies like those of the past. After completing the speculations on a canal, Smoke reached into an inner coat pocket and removed a twisted tip Marsh Wheeling cigar and came to his boots.

When he walked past the young woman, on his way to the vestibule for his smoke, she spoke in a melodic, honeyed voice. "Good day."

Smoke touched fingertips to the brim of his hat. "Yes, it is."

He had barely gotten in four satisfactory puffs when she appeared in the doorway to their car. With a hesitant smile, she came forward. "Excuse me. My name is Winnefred Larkin. Forgive me if this sounds too brazen. But, I'm traveling alone, you see, and I wish to ask you if you would be so kind as to escort me to the dining car later this evening."

Smoke hid his smile behind his cigar. "Not at all, Miss Larkin. My name is Jensen, Smoke Jensen. I would be delighted to be your escort."

"Thank you. I am so relieved. Smoke . . . Jensen. What an odd name."

"It's sort of a handle other folks hung on me. My given name is Kirby." *Now why did he say that?* Smoke wondered. He hated that name.

Winnefred made a small moue of her pretty lips.

"Then I shall call you Smoke. First call for dinner is at five. Or is that too early for your liking?"

"Yes, it is, a bit," Smoke allowed.

"Would seven be better?" Without conscious intent, Winnefred appeared coy.

"Perfect. I'll present myself to you then," Smoke replied, working out of himself a gallantry he rarely had cause to display.

"Then, I shall leave you to your cigar. And again, my sincerest thanks."

When Smoke Jensen entered the dining car with Winnefred Larkin on his arm, it turned heads all up and down both sides of the aisle. They made a striking couple. Smoke led her to a vacant table and seated her, then drew up his own chair opposite. A rather recent addition, these rolling restaurants had been designed, like the sleeping cars, by George Mortimer Pullman. They had proven quite successful, much to the chagrin of the Harvey House chain of depot-based eating establishments. Smoke examined the menu, printed in flamboyant style, bold black on snowy white.

"What sounds good to you?" Winnefred asked after a few silent moments of study. "Everything seems so strange to me."

Smoke nodded understanding. "I gather you are from the East, Miss Larkin? When one gets this far west, the larder on these dining cars is stocked from locally available food for the most part. See? There's rainbow trout listed, though I don't know what *amandine* means. Bison tongue, elk steak, and beef stew."

"Please, make it Winnie. And, *amandine* means the fish is done with an almond and lemon sauce. Quite the rage in Philadelphia. Perhaps you would choose for the both of us, Smoke?"

Never a fancy eater, Smoke Jensen concentrated to select something that he believed would please Winnie and yet not be too out of his ordinary fare. He selected cold, sliced bison tongue in a mildly hot sauce for an appetizer, then followed with elk steak, new potatoes and peas, cold pickled lettuce and hot bread. Winnie Larkin seemed enchanted with the choices. Their waiter, a large, smiling, colored man in a short, white jacket and black trousers, suggested a bottle of wine. At Smoke's insistence, Winnie made the selection.

For once it all turned out right, and even Smoke enjoyed the meal. Cut from the rib eye, the elk steak was juicy and tender. The California claret went well with it. Fortuitously, Smoke had asked that the cook withhold the green peppercorn sauce from the meat. It was rich and thick, and to the way Smoke thought, if a piece of meat was poor in quality, one could dump all the sauce in the world on it and not make it the least bit better. This time it was decidedly not needed.

While they ate, Winnie kept up a light, fanciful banter about her travels in the West. She found New Orleans charming, Texas rough and exhilarating, Denver a cultural oasis in the midst of near-barbarism. Now she looked forward to Santa Fe. She had heard somewhere that the territorial governor had written a most popular book.

"Yes," Smoke informed her. "It's called *Ben Hur.* Surely you have read it?"

"Oh! Then General Lew Wallace is *Governor* Wallace? And, yes, I have read that book. It is so . . . uplifting."

When she learned Smoke was involved in breeding blooded horses, she waxed ecstatic over her childhood desire to have a papered horse. All her parents had, Winnie lamented, were a pair of plodding dray horses. She spoke of riding lessons as a girl in her teens and how she still longed to own a Thoroughbred of her own.

Smoke quickly disabused her of that ambition. "I don't raise Thoroughbreds. They are for racing and fancy shows back east. Mine are Palouse and Morgans and Arabians. Those of lower quality I sell to the army as remounts. Arabians are show horses, but a lot of military officers want, and can afford, them for parade horses. The Morgans are great for carriages as well as saddle stock. Since the Nez Perce have been forced onto a reservation, their breed, the Palouse, has all but died out. I am trying to recover it."

Winnie looked entirely helpless. "Oh, dear, that sounds incredibly complicated. It must be rewarding to see all those horses thriving, though."

"Yes, it is, Winnie. I used to raise cattle. They are stupid, intractable animals. They also eat a lot and are vulnerable to the harsh winters in the mountains. Horses aren't much brighter, but they survive better and do useful work. Did you know that wolves are the smartest animals in the wild?"

Winnie shuddered. "Wolves? How awful. They're killers."

"No. Not how you mean. A wolf will not attack a human, even a child, unless cornered or they believe their young to be threatened. They have a structured society, with strict rules and a pecking order. They care for their pups until they are able to fend for themselves. They even have intricate tactics for hunting."

"See, that's what I mean. They are relentless killers."

Masking a flare of impatience with a straight face, Smoke tried to explain. "Wolves prey on the weakest animals of a herd. By doing so, they improve the breed. You might say that what I do for horses by record keeping and selective breeding, they do by instinct."

Tiny frown lines appeared on Winnie's high, smooth brow. "I've never heard anything like that before."

"Not likely that you will. People have been badmouthing wolves since the Middle Ages. Wolves are the most misunderstood animals on the frontier. I have counted up to eight in one pack running on my ranch, and I have never lost a foal." He paused, then produced a rueful grin. "Of course, I wouldn't want one living under the same roof with me. They are still wild animals."

Winnie's eyes grew wide. They went on talking amiably

through dessert and coffee. Gradually the car emptied of occupants. The waiters began to clear the tables and turn down kerosene lamps. Only a balding, portly man and his buxom wife remained when Smoke stood and went around the table to help Winnie from her chair. Smoke had noticed earlier that the fusty busybody had been giving them a jaundiced eye throughout the meal and had even restrained her husband when he made to leave earlier. With a silent snigger at those with nothing better to do, he pushed the incident out of his mind, took Winnie by the elbow and escorted her to the door.

They found their Pullman bunks made up and ready. Smoke and Winnie said their goodnights, and Smoke went on back to the smoking car for a cigar. He struck up a conversation with a man near his own age about the severe storms of the previous winter. When their stogies had burned down to short stubs with long, white ash, Smoke excused himself and went on back to his bed.

A shrill scream punctured the peaceful silence of the sleeping car.

It seemed to Smoke Jensen that he had only just laid down his head, yet light streamed around the pull-down shade as he opened his eyes to the continued wailing that came from up the aisle.

"She's dead! She's dead! My God, it's horrible. Blood everywhere."

Smoke swiftly pulled on his trousers and boots, shrugged into a shirt and slipped a .45 Colt Peacemaker into his waistband. A middle-aged woman stood in the aisle, hands to her pasty white cheeks as she continued to shriek. Smoke reached her in four long strides. He took her by one shoulder and shook her gently.

"Who is dead? What do you mean?"

She pointed with a suddenly palsied hand, and her voice quavered. "In—in there. Th—the y-y-y-young woman you took to dinner last night. W-w-we h-had an arrange—

arrangement for breakfast this morning. Only her Pullman was still closed. I called out, then looked in." This time she covered her face and spoke through broken sobs. "Her—her eyes were staring right at me, but I could tell they held no life. Sh-sh-she's covered with blood." Suddenly she broke off and stared with horror at the hands of Smoke Jensen, as though expecting to see splashes of crimson.

Speaking firmly to maintain control, Smoke directed, "Sit down over there. I will go get the conductor."

He returned three minutes later with a worried man in a dark blue uniform trimmed with silver braid. At Smoke's urging, the conductor looked in the closed Pullman. He recoiled in aversion. "Lordy, what a sight. When did this happen?"

Smoke shook his head. "I don't know. The woman over there found her about . . ." He plucked his watch from the small pocket in his trousers. "Four minutes ago. Her screaming woke me up."

By then, a crowd had gathered, and Smoke noted five heads poking out of curtained bunks. The conductor examined them with disapproval. Then he waved the people away with small shooing motions as though dispersing a flock of chickens.

"There has been an unfortunate accident. Everyone who does not have a seat in this car, please leave. Those who belong here, take your seats and remain there." Then he turned to Smoke. "You'll likely want to get into your coat. Then I would like to talk to you at length. I'll send for the train crew to take care of the body."

Wise in the ways of trail crafts, Smoke knew how many bits of information could be gained from a study of all signs. "No, I don't think that's a good idea. I want to get a thorough look in there before anything is moved, including Miss Larkin."

Face twisted with distaste, the conductor responded indignantly. "We can't just leave a—a *dead body* lying here. People will blame the line."

Smoke spoke firmly, convincingly. "You can leave it until a peace officer examines the area around her."

"But that won't be until Walsenburg. And, oh, dear, everyone on the train will have to be questioned."

"As to your first observation, that is not necessarily so. Come with me, I have something to show you."

Still dithering, the conductor followed along in the wake of Smoke Jensen. At Smoke's bunk, he reached in and retrieved a small leather wallet from his valise. He used his back to block view of it from the rest of the car and opened the fold. The silver shield of a deputy U.S. marshal shined up at the conductor.

"I have jurisdiction in Colorado. In as much as you have a mail car on this train, I also have jurisdiction over any crime that occurs on it, if I choose to exercise it. What I would like you to do is lock the doors to each car and contain the occupants while you put this train on a siding somewhere along the line, close to here, then have your express agent use his key to send ahead to Walsenburg that you have an emergency and are on the siding and identify which one. That's when we can conduct our own investigation."

Testily, the conductor removed his visored cap and scratched at a balding spot on the crown of his head. "That's a tall order, Marshal—ah—"

"Jensen. Smoke Jensen."

"*Jesus, Mary and Joseph!* You're *the* Smoke Jensen?" At Smoke's nod, he went on in a rush. "I'm Martin Stoddard, folks call me Marsh. I'll try to do everything I can to see that you get what you want. We'll put men out once we've stopped to watch and make sure no one tries to get away from the train."

"Good thinking, Mr. Stoddard—er—Marsh. I'll naturally come with you. We will need to set up a place to question everyone. Say the smoking and bar car? But first, I want to take a look at the body."

* * *

Rail coaches squealed and jolted to a stop beyond the southernmost switch of a siding. The switchman threw the tall cast-iron lever that opened the switch and signaled to the engineer. Huge gouts of black smoke billowed from the fat stack as the engineer reversed the drive and the big wheels spun backward. Slowly the observation platform on the smoking car angled onto the parallel rails of the siding and swayed through the fog. With creeping progress, the other carriages followed. When the cow-catcher cleared, the mobile rails slid back to the normal position. The train braked.

At once, members of the crew dismounted. Armed with rifles and shotguns taken from the conductor's compartment, they took position to observe the entire length of both sides of the train. From the express car came a short, slender, balding man with a green eye-shade fitted to his brow. He carried a portable telegraph key with a length of wire attached. Smoke Jensen and Marsh Stoddard joined him at the base of a pole. The express agent nodded toward the upright shaft.

"I ain't gonna try climbin' that. Not a man of sixty, fixin' to retire."

Smoke turned to him. "Do you have climbing spikes and a belt in the express car?"

"Sure do."

"Fetch them for me, will you, please," Smoke requested.

Quizzically, the grizzled older man cut his eyes to Smoke. "D'ya mean you can do Morse code?"

Smoke nodded. "Among my lesser accomplishments I did happen to learn it. I may be a bit rusty, but I can manage. If need be, I'll have you write the message out for me in dots and dashes and simply follow along."

"Now that's a good ida. 'Sides, you'll need the identity code for Walsenburg."

"It is WLS, isn't it?" Smoke asked.

Surprise registered on the old-timer's face. "Wall I'll be danged, you do know something about it after all."

'hen he cut Smoke a shrewd look. "What about the ain signal?"

"I'll bet it's DLX."

"Right as rain; Daylight Express." Nodding eagerly, the xpress agent started for the car. "Be jist a minute."

While Smoke Jensen fitted himself with the climbing ear, the agent wrote out the message, as dictated by 1arsh Stoddard, in plain English and handed it and the ey to the last mountain man. Smoke ascended the pole ith ease. He settled himself comfortably at a level with he wires and fastened the bare ends of the lead to the roper one. Then he tightened the wing nut that fed ower from the battery pack slung over one shoulder nd freed the striker. Eyes fixed on the message form, moke tapped out the words.

After two long minutes acknowledgment came back long with a question. "DLX whose fist is that(q) It is not ,b(x)"

Smoke sent back, "No(x) Eb did not want to climb the ole(x) This is US Marshal Smoke Jensen(x)"

That brought a flurry of questions. "What is a marshal loing on the train(q) What is the nature of your emer-ency(q) How long will you be delayed(q)"

Smoke's reply must have electrified them. "There has een a murder(x) Notify the law in WLS(x) We will be t least two hours(x)"

With that Smoke detached the lead and descended he pole. "Now, Marsh, I suggest we set up to question he good folks on this train."

Naturally enough, Smoke Jensen began by questioning he people from the car where the murder had occurred. Ie had passed through ten of them, including the still ipset woman who had found the body, when he came ace-to-face with the nosey dowager from the dining car. Mrs. Darlington Struthers—Hermione—proved to be a voman of strong opinions and downright regal conde-

scension to those she considered her inferiors. With
small, gloved fists on her ample hips she stood before the
table where Smoke interrogated the passengers.

"I will tell you nothing, young man. The very idea that
an upstart the likes of you can commandeer this train,
halt it on a siding and pry into the affairs of its passengers
is a matter I shall have my husband take up with the directors of the line. Darlington Struthers has considerable
influence, as I am sure you shall learn to your regret."

Smoke eyed her with ice glinting off the gold flecks in
his eyes. "Are you quite through? This is a murder investigation. You will please answer my questions, or you will
spend a few days at the tender mercies of the sheriff in
Walsenburg."

Hermione's face grew bright red. "The nerve . . ."

"I assure you it is not nerve. Now, where are you seated
in relation to the dead woman?"

"You are not the law, and I do not have to answer your
questions."

Smiling, Smoke produced his badge folder. "Oh, but
I am. Deputy U.S. Marshal. First, let me say that your eva-
sions and bluster make you sound more like the guilty
party than a mere fellow passenger. With that in mind,
let me ask again: Where are you seated?"

Testily, Hermione Struthers answered. Smoke asked if
she had seen or heard anything unusual during the
night. Her face took on the expression of a dog passing
a peach pit when she snapped her answer in the negative. Smoke tried another tack.

"Well, now, I might be just a hick lawman from the high
lonesome, but I do have some smarts about me. From
where you would have been in your bunk, it is impossible
not to have heard any sounds of struggle. And believe me,
from the looks of that Pullman berth, there was considerable struggle. Even the window shade is torn."

"I am a sound sleeper."

Smoke could not resist the barb. "A little too much
claret, eh?"

Indignation rose to balloon the face of Hermione Struthers. "I am a teetotaler, I'll have you know."

Smoke considered her stubbornness. She knew something, of that he was sure. Yet, he could not use force to learn it. And right now, his guile was wearing thin. "So, you heard nothing. Did you see anything, anyone around there?"

"I am not in the habit of spying on others."

I'll bet you're not, Smoke thought silently. "Hmm. We'll let that pass for the moment. If you heard nothing and saw nothing during the night, what about early this morning, when people began to rise for the day?"

"Again, nothing. Not the least thing."

"Very well. You may go, ma'am. But I may want to talk to you again."

Hermione turned to the door and spoke over her shoulder. "Do as you will. You will get nothing from me." With a smug, tight expression she opened the portal and stepped across the threshold.

That's when Smoke Jensen launched his final arrow. "Oh, so there is . . . something?"

Outside in the vestibule between the smoking car and the rearmost Pullman, Hermione Struthers unloaded her bile on Marsh Stoddard, her voice loud and cawing. "Mr. Conductor, there is something you should know about that so-called marshal in there. To my certain knowledge, he is the last person to have seen the late Miss Larkin alive. They were carrying on scandalously in the dining car."

4

For two blistering minutes, Hermione Struthers belabored Marsh Stoddard with a highly fanciful account of an imagined torrid liaison between Smoke Jensen and Winnefred Larkin. What she lacked in imagination, she made up for in viciousness. She concluded with a demand, hot with vehemence.

"I insist that you put this train in motion at once and proceed on our way. I'll have you know that my husband is an associate of the president of the line and well known to the board of directors. I intend to bring your dereliction to the attention of Mr. Struthers. Your future employment may depend upon your prompt obedience."

Stoddard tipped the billed cap to her and spoke softly. "Somehow I doubt that."

"What did you say?" Hermione demanded.

"I said, I don't doubt that."

"As well you shouldn't. I shall return to my car, and I want immediate entrance." She started for the vestibule steps.

Stoddard hurried to intervene. "I wouldn't do that, ma'am. One of the crew might take a potshot at you."

"What do you mean?"

"Marshal's orders, ma'am. All vestibule doors are to be

ept locked, and no one is to leave the train until the
iller is unmasked."

Hermione's face drained of color. "But I have already
old you. *He* is the murderer. That false marshal in there."

Stoddard kept a tight rein on his expression. "Very
vell, ma'am, I'll take care of it right away. First, come
vith me and I will see you to your car."

Stoddard came back and entered the smoking car.
That damned woman. Claims you are the killer. Once
he's got her steam up, she'll blow it off to everyone who
vill listen, and a good many who won't."

Smoke considered that a moment. "That could com-
plicate matters a little."

"D'you have any more of an idea of who it might be?"

"None, so far. But I am convinced that officious old
nen knows something she's not telling. I think I'll have
er back in here after I've gone through all the others.
Bring the next one, if you will, please."

During the next three-quarters of an hour, Smoke inter-
iewed the train's porters and every one of the passengers,
vith the exception of four people. Those who had come
rom the car that housed Hermione Struthers cast ner-
ous, suspicious glances at Smoke when they thought he
vas not watching them. So much for the old bag. Finally,
ne of that group blurted out his apprehension.

"Mrs. Struthers says she has positive proof that you are
he killer."

"Well, Mr. Paddington, tell me this. When's the last
ime you saw a Poland China sail past overhead?"

Paddington looked confused a moment, then angry.
That's all stuff and nonsense. Ain't never been a Poland
China that could fly."

"That's my point. You can believe whatever that woman
ays the day pigs start to fly. Now, would you tell me if you
aw or heard anything out of the ordinary during the
ight?"

"Uh—uh well, nothing you'd call unusual, all considered."

"Meaning what?"

"Ain't unusual for young folks to do some sparkin' on a train at night. They think it's romantic."

That grabbed Smoke's attention at once. "And you saw something like that?"

"Yes, I did. I didn't see 'em actually clingin' to one another like soul mates, but I reckon that had come right before." Again, Paddington paused irritatingly.

"Before what?" Smoke pressed.

"Jist before I saw this young man leave our car. He come from down the direction of that poor young woman's berth."

"Could you recognize him?"

For once, Paddington did not hesitate. "Not for certain. His head was all in shadows. An' he seemed in a hurry. I was gettin' up to visit the slop jar an' he like to knocked me back into my bunk."

Smoke listed physical characteristics in an attempt to spark memory. "Was he tall? Short? Heavy? Thin? What did he wear?"

Paddington mused on it. "He was about my height, five-nine, slightly built, I'd say, and had a suit on. Seemed to me the shirt was of two colors, dark and light."

"Could that have been black and white?"

Surprise wrathed Paddington's face. "Say, yer right, marshal. It sure could have been."

"Are you aware that in very low lamplight, or moonlight, blood looks black?" There had been a lot of blood.

"Ohmygod! If only I'd seen his face."

Yes, if only, Smoke thought with disappointment.

That had been fifteen minutes earlier, and Smoke was now ready to start on the last four. He ruled out the first to enter at sight of the man. He was short, fat and wore spectacles that would rival the bottom of a wine bottle. Smoke questioned him anyway.

No. No one had passed through the chair car where he

had been trying to sleep. He had heard nothing. At least not until some woman screamed bloody murder early in the morning. Could hear her clear up in his coach. Smoke excused him and asked Stoddard to bring in the next.

A slender man in his early twenties entered the smoking car. He had shifty eyes, and his palms were notably wet and unexpectedly cold when Smoke shook his hand. Smoke let him sweat in silence for two minutes after giving his name.

"Now, Mr. Reierson, in order to save time, we'll start this off the hard way. I am a deputy U.S. marshal, empowered to investigate the murder that happened on this train last night. I'm going to ask you some questions and I expect truthful answers."

"Why, of course. Any——" Reierson's voice caught. "Anything I can do to help."

While Smoke went through his routine questions, Reierson developed a nervous tic at the corner of his left eye. His trepidation increased the harder Smoke probed. More so when Smoke pointed out that his answers did not hold up with the observations of others.

Reierson tried bluster. "That's preposterous. I know where I was and what I did. They must be mistaken."

Smoke rounded on him suddenly, his voice a soft purr. "No they aren't. You did it, all right. What I don't know is why. What made you kill that lovely young woman?"

"I didn't! Y-you're falsely ac-accusing an innocent man."

"No, I'm not, Reierson. You did it, right enough. How did it happen? Did she resist your demands? Struggle? Maybe claw at you with those long fingernails?"

His face alabaster with fright, Reierson made to bolt for the door. Smoke Jensen reached him in two swift strides. He grabbed Reierson by one shoulder, spun him around and shoved him into a chair. Panicked, the pathetic specimen of a craven killer groped under his coat and whipped out a small, four-shot, "clover-leaf" pocket revolver.

"Yes, I killed her, goddamn you. And I'll kill you, too."
Sobbing in frustration, he fired wildly.

Smoke Jensen was a lot faster and much more accurate.

Stoddard burst through the vestibule door. "What happened?"

"He confessed. After he drew a gun on me. I'll write up a complete report and you can give it—and the bodies—to the law in Walsenburg."

Soft music floated through the huge dining room of a hilltop mansion outside Taos, New Mexico Territory. A string quartet in formal black sawed away at an opus by Brahms. Clifton Satterlee sat at the head of a long, shining, cherrywood table that would easily seat eighteen. A wide strip of white linen ran the length of the ruddy, glowing surface. Brice Noble sat to Clifton Satterlee's right; to his left, Clifton's wife, Emma. Noble's wife, Mildred, sat to her husband's right. At the far end were Patrick Quinn and a young woman of his acquaintance, Lettie Kincade. The other women at the table would have been scandalized and highly offended if they knew that until ensnaring the attentions of Quinn, Lettie had been the inmate of a deluxe Santa Fe bordello.

Soft, yellow light from three silver candelabra flattered the complexions of the older women, smoothing out wrinkles, while it put a light of naughty mischief into the pale blue eyes of Lettie Kincade. Cole Granger stood in front of the high double doors that gave into a high-ceilinged, vaulted corridor. Dinner had concluded and the last of the dishes cleared away. At a sign from her husband, Emma stood and addressed the other women.

"Ladies, I suggest that we retire to my sitting room for coffee and sweets. If you gentlemen will excuse us?"

Clifton nodded blandly, and all of the men came to their boots as the women left the room. When the side door closed behind them, Satterlee turned to the butler.

"Pour cognac around, if you will, Ramon, then you are excused."

Soft clinking followed while Ramon Estavez poured from a crystal decanter into three glasses. When he finished his task and lighted cigars for all three, he soundlessly departed from the room. Satterlee lifted his glass in a toast and mockingly paraphrased Shakespeare.

"We grow . . . we prosper. Now, gods, stand up for bastards." They all laughed and drank; then Satterlee continued. "First, let me announce that my lovely Emma will be returning to Santa Fe with me the day after tomorrow. Now, Mr. Quinn, we would appreciate a report of your progress."

Rising, Quinn set aside his cigar. "The Bar-Four now belongs to C.S. Enterprises, it does. So does the Obrigon ranch. We completed papers on the Suarez ranch this morning. Two stores on the Plaza de Armas now belong to your development company, with three others likely to fall in line within two days more, an' that's a fact."

"Thank you, Paddy, my friend." Satterlee beamed.

"Ah, but there's more. The title on the Figueroa hacienda cleared the territorial land office late this afternoon."

Satterlee shot to his feet in enthusiasm. "Splendid."

"Here-here!" Brice Noble chimed in. "Though I must say, it was a blasted expensive undertaking. It cost a fortune to buy that mansion. Why not simply kill the old man? After all, the granddaughter could not inherit. The territorial government would appoint an executor to manage it until she reached her majority. And then"—he gestured widely—"through our connections in Santa Fe we could have gotten it for a song."

Satterlee countered that at once. "To use our bought politicians on so trivial a matter would have unduly compromised them. The time might come when we need their influence much more. Now, let us move on to the next phase of our agenda."

* * *

Railroad workers rolled a movable loading chute in place at the door to the stock car that held the horses Smoke Jensen had brought along. The last mountain man stood by patiently as a man led Cougar down the ramp onto solid ground. Smoke had been surprised by how much Raton had grown since he had last been in the northern New Mexico town. Low adobe houses now sprawled out for a good mile from the more settled part of the community near the depot, each with its familiar picket fence of ocotillo cactus rods. Smoke abandoned his reflections when Cougar let out a shrill squall and swayed drunkenly, unaccustomed to not having the surface below his hooves in constant motion. Smoke hurried to the heaving side of the big Palouse stallion.

"Easy, boy. Whoa, Cougar." To the depot worker he added, "He'll get his legs back in a bit. Don't try to walk him around right now."

When both animals had recovered, Smoke saddled them, then strapped the large panniers on the packsaddle. The sudden thought hit Smoke that in the years past, he had never needed a packhorse to accompany him. Nor had he dragged along all the comforts that the pouches of the panniers now contained. He would have laughed at the wrought-iron trestle, cast-iron skillet and Dutch oven, three-legged grill and cooking utensils. A coffeepot and a small, lidded skillet had been all he had ever needed. *Yet, when the years go by,* he mused with regret, *one's needs change.* Mounted on Cougar, Smoke walked his way toward the main intersection, where he would take the east-west trail toward Taos. With the Santa Fe and Denver and Rio Grande both passing through Raton, the usual entrepreneurs and hustlers had flocked into the burgeoning city. Hawkers with carts stood on street corners, touting their wares. Hundreds of people thronged the streets. A low haze of red-brown dust hovered at first-floor level throughout. Stray dogs yapped at the hooves of his packhorse, and the animal snorted its irritation and flicked one iron shoe. A yellow bitch yelped and slunk off. As he passed a saloon, a loud shout attracted Smoke's attention.

"Hey, let me go!" A young man stumbled out onto the street, as though propelled by eager hands.

Following him came three scraggly ruffians who spread out across the thoroughfare. To Smoke they had the seedy look of low-grade wanna-bes. The one in the middle raised an arm and pointed in a taunting manner. "Yer wearin' a gun, you little shit. Now yer gonna have to use it."

With a start, Smoke Jensen recognized the speaker as Tully Banning, a two-bit gunfighter more renowned for the number of his back shootings than he was for face-to-face shoot-outs. In the next instant, as he reined in, Smoke realized that the challenged youth could not be more than fifteen. A beardless, frightened boy. Smoke quickly sized up the two louts with Banning. What his read gave him he did not like. The boy did not have a chance. Smoke stepped right in the middle of it.

"Banning! Tully Banning."

Banning turned only his head. "Who th' hell wants to know?"

"That's not important. What I want to know is why you don't pick on someone your own age or older?"

Banning uttered a string of curses, and concluded with, "Maybe you'd be interested in taking this punk kid's place. If so, I'll deal with you first, then kill Momma's little boy anyway."

Smoke pulled a face. "I don't think so. Keep your stray curs off me while I step down so I can accommodate you."

"You've got that, old man."

Old man? Smoke never thought of himself as old. He climbed from the saddle and tied off Cougar and his packhorse, Hardy. Then he walked out to stand beside the youth who had been challenged. "Step out of the street, son. You didn't ask for this, and there's no reason you take any harm for it."

With an expression of mingled relief and frustration, the sandy-haired boy angled off the street to stand by

Smoke's horses. Then Smoke looked up at Banning. "I'm ready any time you are."

Tully Banning's shoulders hunched, and his right hand twitched; but he did not go for his six-gun at once. It had been a signal, one old and familiar, to his companions. The challenged individual could be expected to focus his attention and anticipation upon the challenger. That's the way it had worked for Tully Banning time and again. So, when the cheat and sneak made the little jerk and arrest movement, his henchmen immediately drew their revolvers.

One small miscalculation marred their perfect ambush. Although the trio had often heard of the exploits of Smoke Jensen, none of them had ever met with him face-to-face. Now that they had, it was entirely too late. Smoke expected some sort of dirty work, so he readied himself accordingly. When all three louts drew, Banning last of all, Smoke already had their demise planned.

Drawing with his usual blinding speed, Smoke killed the one on the left first. Then he swung past Banning in the middle to take on the right-hand gunhawk. The poor soul never had a chance. He did get off one wild shot that split the air high above the head of Smoke Jensen. Then the hammer of Smoke's .45 Peacemaker fell, and a hot slug ripped into the ruffian's gut. It burned a trail of agony through his liver before it ripped out a piece of his spine and tore a hole in his back. Rapidly dying, he went to his knees as Tully Banning attempted to level his six-gun.

To his horror, Tully Banning saw the calm expression and faint smile of the man facing him an instant before flame and smoke spewed from the muzzle of the Colt and a wrenching agony exploded in his chest. Staggered, he took two feeble, uncertain steps to the right and triggered his piece. Banning's slug kicked up dirt between the wide-spread legs of Smoke Jensen.

Then Smoke shot again. Another terrible hammer blow smashed into the chest of Tully Banning. His legs went out from under him, and he dropped on his backside in the dusty street. Dimly he heard the shouts of amazement from the onlookers who had assembled well out of the line of fire. This couldn't be happening. The trap had always worked before. It would take the best gunfighter in the world to best the three of them, Banning's spinning mind fought to reject his mortality.

Blood bubbled on his lips as he asked weakly, "Who are you?"

Smiling that ghost of a smile again, Smoke Jensen told Tully Banning, who turned even whiter before he died. Suddenly, the freckle-faced, sandy-haired boy appeared at Smoke's side. "I didn't recognize you, Mr. Jensen."

"Don't reckon they did, either."

"You sure saved my life. Uh—my name's Ian MacGreggor. Most folks call me Mac. It's an honor to meet you. And, thank you, thank you for getting me out of that fix. They never gave me a chance to say no."

Smoke nodded understanding. "Their kind never do. And, they never, ever pick on anyone capable of defending themselves. Remember that."

"Yes, sir, I will. Thank you again."

It took Smoke Jensen an uncomfortable fifteen minutes with the town constable to explain what he had accomplished in two seconds. Given the assurance it would be recorded as self-defense, Smoke at last got on the trail to Taos.

Thick-foliaged palo verde trees made silver-green smoke clouds against the horizon of red earth and cobalt sky. Cattle grazed on the sparse grass of Rancho de la Gloria. Throughout the prairie lands, from Texas to Montana, cattlemen talked of cows per acre. Not so here. Don Diego Alvarado had learned at his father's knee to think in terms of acres per cow. In future times, the elegant Diego Alvarado often told himself, irrigation would make this harsh desert into a veritable garden place. Not in his lifetime, though. So he did not share his dream with his friends and fellow ranchers. His vaqueros knew of it, and believed him. Three of them had been given the assignment of tending a herd of two hundred that grazed through a high meadow on the north end of the ranch property.

They found their work peaceful and pleasing. Not far off lay a connected chain of *tanques* where the beasts would water and they could take their *almuerzo*. Each had a cloth bag in his saddlebag, provided that morning by his wife, that contained a burrito—beans and onion rolled in a flour tortilla—a savory tamale, and fresh, piquant chile peppers to add flavor and spice. Arturo had even brought along some cornmeal sugar cookies baked by his wife. Arturo Gomez and Hector Blanco had promised their younger sons they could bring lunches and join the men at the tanks, the lads taking a noontime swim. That would get them out from under their mothers' feet. The older boys all tended goat herds during the day and could always find ways to get cool and wet. As a newlywed, Umberto Mascarenas, the third vaquero, only dreamed of the day when he would have sturdy sons like his companions. He looked up at the sound of pounding hooves. Could it be the *niños* already?

Caught unaware, Umberto Mascarenas did not hear the first gunshot, or any of those that followed. A bullet struck him in the right side of his head, an inch above his ear, and blew out the other hemisphere. He pitched from his horse in a welter of gore.

"Git them other greasers," a harsh voice shouted.

More gunfire sounded across the plateau. Arturo Gomez returned fire with his Obrigon copy of a .45 Colt and had the satisfaction of watching an Anglo *ladrón* spill from his saddle at the third round. Then pain burned the life from him as three bullets struck him in half a second. To his right, Hector Blanco dismounted and drew his rifle. The Marlin cracked sharply, and the hat flew from another rustler's head. Hector shot again, and the thief threw up his hands and fell backward off his mount.

By that time, the reports of the weapons had registered on the dim brains of the cattle. They reacted at once and broke into a shambling run. Controlling the cattle became the primary objective of the rustlers, yet one took the time to ride down on Hector Blanco and steal his life with a bullet through the brain. Then the killer galloped ahead to join the others in a V-shaped formation in front of the stampeded herd and direct it off Alvarado land toward a waiting holding pen in a blind canyon.

Twenty minutes later, the horrified and grief-stricken sons of Arturo and Hector found the bodies of all three vaqueros. The Whitewater Paddy Quinn gang had struck again.

5

An hour short of sundown, with long, golden and carmine shafts of light spilling through the canyons, Smoke Jensen made night camp on a bluff above the Canadian River. He staked out his horses to graze and prepared a fire ring. Then he gathered dry windfall and laid a fire. With seemingly calm indifference to his surroundings, he went about setting up his cooking equipment. Constantly, though, he kept his ears tuned to the sound of soft footfalls that grew steadily nearer. Smoke's surprise registered on his face when the source of that noise came up within thirty feet of the campsite and hailed him.

"Hello, Mr. Jensen. It's me, Mac."

Smoke looked up from the task of slicing potatoes into a skillet to study the gangly youth. Mac's shoulders were broad and his arms long, the promise of a fair-sized man when he got his growth. He was slim, though, and narrow-hipped, and with that boyish face, he looked a long way from reaching that maturity. Smoke motioned him in.

"Howdy, Mac. What brings you along?"

"Well, Mr. Jensen, I wanted to thank you again for saving my life. Really, though, I sort of got to thinking. I wondered if—if you'd welcome me to ride along with you. Seein' we're headed the same direction, that is."

So much earnestness shone from his freckled face that

Smoke had to turn away to keep control of his laughter. He fished an onion from a pan of water and began to slice it onto a tin plate to add to the potatoes. "Now, what direction would that be?"

"Why, to Taos, of course."

Smoke feigned doubtfulness. "I'll have to think on that one. But, step down. Least you can do now is share my eats. I've got some fatback, taters, and I'll make some biscuits."

Memory of the boiled oatmeal, twice a day, that had sustained him between his home and Raton prodded Ian MacGreggor. "Gosh, you sure eat well, Mr. Jensen."

"Call me Smoke, Mac."

Caught off balance by this, Mac gulped his words. "Yes, sir, ah, Smoke."

"Now, to eatin' well, it's only common sense. In this climate, a man has to use up his fresh stuff right at the start. By the time we reach Taos it'll be spare enough." Smoke turned his attention to the food for a while, then asked, "You have family in Taos?"

"No, sir, I'm leavin' home for good. I'm my pap's third son, so there's nothin' for me around the farm. We have a little dirt-scrabble place over in Texas. Whole lot of Scots folks around Amarillo. The farm'll go to my oldest brother, Caleb. Dirk is hot for workin' on the railroad. Wants to be an engineer. The apprenticeship and schoolin' costs money, so there was not much left for me."

"Then, I gather you are looking for work in Taos?"

"That's right, Smoke. I heard there was plenty work being offered out Taos way. There was even a notice in the Amarillo paper. A man named Satterlee. He's lookin' for cowhands, timber fallers, all sorts of jobs."

Smoke's frown surprised Mac. "Ah—Mac, I don't want to disappoint you, but do you know anything about this Satterlee?"

"No, no I don't. What's the matter?"

Smoke did not want the boy to go bad. He seemed to have some promise. So, he told Mac what he knew of

Clifton Satterlee from the letter sent by Diego Alvarado. As he spoke, the youngster's eyes grew big, and he produced an angry expression. When Smoke concluded, Mac shook his head.

"I sure don't want anything to do with someone like that. Sounds like he's puredee crook." Then he took on a sad expression. "But now I've burned my bridges, what am I gonna do to make a livin'?"

"Taos is growing. And I have a friend. A man who owns a large ranch. Do you happen to speak Spanish? His name is Diego Alvarado; he's a real Spanish gentleman."

Mac nodded enthusiastically. "Sure do. Learned it from the sons of our hired hand. I growed up with them."

"Then, if Don Diego takes you on, you'll have lots of use for it. All of his ranch hands are Mexican."

Mac frowned. "I don't know much about cows. We planted mostly hay, sold it to the ranchers, put in some wheat, corn. Pap wanted to try watermelons. They grow real good in Texas."

"As I recall, Diego has some fields down by a creek that runs behind his house which he uses to irrigate them. He grows several kinds of melons, as well as corn, onions, beans, chile peppers, and a little cotton. He provides nearly all the needs for the entire ranch."

"How—how big is this place?"

"Three or four thousand acres, I'm not sure which."

Mac looked at Smoke in awe. "That's the biggest spread I ever heard of. All we have is a quarter section."

Smoke took pity on Mac, though not much. "Diego has more land under irrigated cultivation than that. I'm willin' to bet he could use an experienced farmer."

Over their meal, Smoke worried around another idea in his head. When Mac offered to wash up after supper, Smoke poured a cup of coffee and spoke his mind. "If Diego has no need for a farmer, there might be something else you can do. Something for me. Though it might prove risky."

New hope bloomed on Mac's face. "Anything, so long as it's legal, Smoke."

"I assure you it's that. Don Diego asked me to come out and take a look at this Satterlee's operation. I could use some help in doing that."

"How can you poke into something crooked? That's a job for the law."

Smiling, Smoke produced his badge and showed it to Mac. "So happens, I'm a deputy U.S. marshal. What I have in mind is that if Diego does not take you on, you go ahead and take that job with Satterlee. Only, don't break the law yourself. Look around, keep your ears open. See what kind of sign you cut on his operation. Then, make arrangements to report anything you learn to me. You'd get regular deputy marshal pay, provided by the U.S. Marshal's Office. That should give you a good stake after the job is over."

"What about the risk you mentioned?" Mac asked soberly.

No fool this one, Smoke reflected. "If you are caught, Satterlee or one of his henchmen will try to kill you. Or at least hurt you pretty bad."

Mac cut his eyes to the six-gun in the holster on his hip. "I ain't as fast or accurate as you, Smoke. An' I never caught on to the trap of those three in Raton. But I am good with a gun."

"You'll have to be. What d'you say?"

"Okay. I'll do it."

Smoke looked Mac levelly in the clear, blue eyes. "Done, then. But you may not live to regret it," he told the boy ominously.

A refreshing spring shower had brightened the yellow bonnets of the jonquils and purple-red tulip globes in the wide beds planted at the front of the main house on the Sugarloaf. A rainbow hung on the breast of the Medicine Bow Mountains to the northeast. Sally Jensen gave up on her industrious dusting program at the clatter of narrow, steel-tired wheels on the ranch yard. She removed the kerchief which covered her raven locks, abandoned her smudged rag and straightened the apron as she walked to the door. She opened the portal to an astonishing sight.

A woman, vaguely familiar, and four children sat on the spring-mounted seats of a sparkling, brightly lacquered carriage. The three boys, their soft, brown hair cut in bang-fringed pageboy style, wore manly little suits of royal blue, Moorish maroon and emerald green, with identical flat-crowned, wide-brimmed hats. The small girl sat primly beside her mother, in a matching crushed velvet cape and gown of a puce hue, feathered bonnets to match. The young males quarreled loudly and steadily among themselves.

Sally took three small steps to the edge of the porch. She paused then as she put a name to the face, remembering the letter she had received three days earlier. Mary-Beth Whipple. No, Sally corrected herself, her married name was Gittings. Obviously when Mary-Beth had written asking to make a brief visit, she had taken for granted that the answer would be yes. How typical of Mary-Beth, Sally thought ruefully.

"Sally, dearest," Mary-Beth burbled happily as she reined in.

"Mary-Beth?" Sally responded hesitantly. "I—didn't expect you so soon."

Mary-Beth simply ignored that and gushed. "It's so good to see you again. You have no idea how much I've missed my dear schoolmate." She raised her arms and flung them wide to encompass the whole of the Sugarloaf. "We're here at last."

"Uh—yes, so you are. Won't you come in?"

"Of course. Right away. Can you get someone to take care of these dreadfully stubborn animals?"

For a moment Sally wondered if she meant the snorting, lathered horses or her three sons. The volume of their altercation had risen to the shouting stage. Sally recalled her school chum only too well. The daughter of a wealthy New England mill owner, she had always been a petulant, spoiled young woman. One who proved woefully empty-headed. Sally had been compelled to drag Mary-Beth's grades upward at the Teachers' Seminary. Worse, she absolutely, positively refused to eat meat. Yet those were not her only eccentricities, Sally recalled as Mary-Beth spoke again.

"These abominable horses, of course. They have made our journey from Denver absolutely miserable. So tedious. Well," she declared, releasing the reins and standing upright in the carriage. "We're here now. And we can look forward to not having to deal with these fractious creatures for a whole month."

A month? Sally thought sinkingly. *That* was Mary-Beth's idea of a brief stay? "I'm afraid we're not . . . prepared for such a long stay."

Mary-Beth's face clouded up, and she produced a girlish pout. "But, we simply must. My husband is doing businessey things in Denver, and it is frightfully boring."

"But . . . my husband is not here. He has been called away."

"Oh, bother the men. They are all alike. Born to neglect. I sometimes regret that I gave birth to even a single male. Little Francine here is all my life."

Her words chilled Sally, who instantly saw the confusion and hurt in the expressions and suddenly flat eyes of the boys. For all of that, Sally's inborn hospitality compelled her to welcome them. She opened her arms in an inviting gesture. "Come on in, then. I'll fix coffee. And I have a sponge cake. Your boys will like that, I'm sure."

Three bright, happy faces shined out on her. "Cake, yah!" they chorused.

Inside, with the boys gulping down slice after slice of the cake Sally had planned to have for herself and Bobby for supper, Mary-Beth returned to her earlier topic. "Ever since you described this heavenly place to me, I've dreamed of visiting. And we simply must stay the whole month. Grantland will be tied up in dull meetings every day for a full thirty days. Lawyers have such a dreary life. Besides, Denver is so depressing, with its heavy pall of smelter smoke hanging over everything. And, such rough, unlettered people swarming everywhere, with absolutely no control over them." Mary-Beth paused and looked at her cup.

"Actually, I prefer tea. Could you arrange to have tea from now on?"

Sally curbed her temper. "I have some tea. When it's gone, it's gone."

Mary-Beth reached over and patted Sally's forearm. "Fine, dear, I understand." She looked over to where her sons had started to squabble noisily over the last slice of cake. "Boys, you go outside with that. You've eaten quite enough. It will spoil your supper."

Grumbling, the three little louts jumped from the table and trudged outside. Mary-Beth picked up again. "At what hour do you serve dinner? We are accustomed to eight."

"Well, Mary-Beth, we are accustomed to six. If you'll pardon me, we will stick to that schedule." Gloomy images of a month of this flashed through Sally's mind.

Bobby Jensen first encountered the newcomers when he came up to the main house from the foaling barn where he had been mucking out stalls. He went directly to the wash house, where he had laid out clean clothes before beginning his task, to clean himself of the stink of blood, manure and horse urine. Bobby had barely eased himself into the big, brass bathtub and shuddered in pleasure at the feel of the warm water when he heard a sound like rats in the rafters. He looked around and saw nothing, so he went to his ablutions. The sound came again.

Bobby paused in the vigorous scrubbing of his hands and arms and let his gaze slide from corner to corner. Again he could find no source. He ducked his head of white-blond hair below the surface and began to lather it when he came up. The rustling persisted. Bobby rinsed his hair and pushed up on one arm.

"Who's there?" When no reply came to his demand, he gave careful examination to the interior for a third time, then returned to his bath. When he was satisfied with his degree of cleanliness—he had not washed behind his ears—Bobby climbed from the tub and stepped under the sprinkler can nozzle attached to a length of lead pipe. Lukewarm water cascaded down on the crown of his head and his thin shoulders when he pulled a chain attached to a spring valve. While he rinsed, he caught sight of furtive movement over by the chair where he had laid his fresh clothing.

A small, pale white hand reached slowly around the obstruction of the chair and headed for the parrot bill grip of Bobby's .38 Colt Lightning. Bobby took three quick steps toward the hidden person and called out in as hard a voice as he could muster.

"Get your hand off my gun."

Suddenly, a boy somewhat smaller than Bobby popped up behind the chair. His appearance would have made Bobby laugh if he were not so angry. He wore a funny blue suit, with a big old flowery tie done in a bow under his chin, and had hair only a few shades more yellow than Bobby's, done in a sissy cut. Ribbons tied the bottoms of his trouser legs just below the knees. Full, bee-stung lips that were made for pouting formed a soft, Cupid's mouth. He screwed those lips up now and spoke in a snotty, superior tone.

"You can't have a gun. You're only a kid. Besides, nobody has a right to have a gun, except a policeman. And even they shouldn't have them. My mother says."

Although naked as a jaybird, Bobby immediately snapped out his verbal defense. "The hell I can't. Smoke Jensen gave me this six-gun himself. I've got a rifle, too."

"Liar. My mother says no one has the right to a gun. That they are the most evil things on earth."

Bobby bristled further. "You're the liar. You ever hear of the Constitution? Smoke taught me real good. There's a part of it that says, ' . . . the right of the people to keep and bear arms shall not be infringed.' So there."

Mary-Beth's eldest, Billy, narrowed his eyes and balled his small fists. "Think you're one of those dirty, back-shootin', coward gunfighters like Smoke Jensen?"

That proved too much for Bobby. He swiftly closed the distance between himself and the other boy and gave his antagonist a two-handed shove to the chest. Rocked off his heels, twelve-year-old Billy stumbled backward. Bobby came right after him. Another push and Billy went sprawling out of the wash house. Bobby watched the other boy flail in the dirt a moment, then turned back and shrugged into his trousers. He came out of the building as Billy scrambled to his feet.

Billy made the mistake of swinging the moment he saw Bobby. Young Jensen ducked and threw a punch of his own. It smacked Billy under the left eye. He cried out at the pain and then rushed Bobby. Bobby side-stepped and tripped Billy. At once, the older boy dropped down on his knees, astraddle the small of Billy's back. Bobby began to drub his opponent on the shoulders. Billy made squealing, yelping sounds and kicked the toes of his boots against the ground. At last he found purchase enough to thrust upward and throw Bobby off of him.

"Damn you, you don't fight fair," Billy sobbed, his dirt-smeared cheeks streaked with tears. He dived on Bobby before the older boy could get up.

From there their fight degenerated into a lot of rolling around in the dirt. Bobby got a couple of good punches to Billy's ribs. Then he clouted his opponent on the ear, which brought a howl of agony from Billy. Bobby wrestled himself around on top and began to drive work-hard-ened fists into Billy's midriff. All pretense of toughness deserted Billy, and he began to wail in a pitiful voice.

"Help me! Momma, help me! Get him off, get him off."

The sudden commotion reached the ears of Sally Jensen and Mary-Beth Gittings where they sat on the porch, sipping at cups of jasmine tea. Mary-Beth's face went blank, then white a moment, and she clutched at her heart. Half rising, she put her cup aside.

"I think that's Billy. Whatever could be happening?"

Sally listened to the uproar a moment and picked out Bobby's voice. "Yer a liar and a trespasser. Git the hell outta here."

Dryly she remarked to Mary-Beth, "I think he has met our youngest. We had better go see."

Together they headed in the direction of the wash house. The sight they saw made Sally Jensen ache, though inwardly she burned with pride for her adopted son. Bobby Jensen remained astride Billy Gittings, pounding him rhythmically. Billy was getting his tail kicked right properly. One eye showed the beginnings of a splendid mouse, and his nose had been bloodied. He sobbed wretchedly with each punch Bobby delivered. She could not let that go on, Sally realized at once. She hurried to the boys.

"Bobby, you stop that at once. Get off Billy this instant." Embarrassment filled Sally Jensen as she dragged Bobby Jensen off Billy Gittings.

Mary-Beth Gittings harbored entirely different emotions. Her voice became accusative and filled with indignation. Her son and Bobby each gave his version of what had started the fight. Her face red, she turned with hands on hips to lash out at Sally.

"Billy is correct. No one has the right to own a gun except the police. I would certainly never allow a child of mine to have one."

Bobby remained defiant. "Then why did he try to steal mine?"

Surly, though in control of his sobs and tears, Billy answered truculently. "I was gonna take it away from you and do what's right and give it to Mother."

Sally stepped in. "Bobby is correct. Taking another

person's property, whether you think he has a right to it
or not, is stealing. There will be no more of that around
here. Now, both of you go in there and get yourselves
washed up. You're a couple of mud balls. And shake
hands and try to be nice."

Thoroughly mollified, Bobby put out a hand. "My
name's Bobby, what's yours?"

"Billy," the other boy answered, still offended. Then
he drew himself up. "William Durstan Gittings. But you
can call me Billy."

They released their grip and turned away from the
adults. With an arm around each other's shoulders, they
walked toward the bath that awaited them. Sally
breathed a sigh of relief, only to learn that Mary-Beth
had not finished.

"One thing you must accept, dear Sally. My son was
right in what he did. He certainly did not deserve anything like the beating he got."

Sally groaned inwardly at the thought of the ensuing
month, saddled with this now former friend.

In a large, adobe mansion outside of Santa Fe, Clifton
Satterlee and four of his associates from back east sat in
a sumptuous study, two walls lined floor to ceiling with
books in neat rows on their shelves. Long, thick, maroon
brocade drapes covered the leaded glass windows, with
the usual wrought-iron bars covering them from outside.
A small, horseshoe-shaped desk occupied the open
space directly in front of the limestone casement. That
was where Satterlee held court. The tall back of a large,
horsehair-stuffed chair loomed over his six-foot-plus
height. He wore a blue velvet smoking jacket and open
front shirt of snowy perfection, riding trousers and calf-
length boots. His guests clothed themselves with all the
formality of eastern evening wear. Brass lamps provided
illumination, and the yellow rays of the kerosene flames
struck highlights off the cut crystal decanter and five

glasses on a low table around which the visitors sat. The topic of conversation had turned to their plans for the conquest of Taos and its environs.

"We already have a good foothold," Satterlee reminded his associates. "C.S. Enterprises has the timber rights to a thousand acres on the eastern slopes of the Sangre de Cristo range. By selective cutting, we can clear a way to allow passage of the logs we harvest from the land currently held by those Tua vermin. We can pass them off as coming from our legally held property."

Durwood Pringle cocked an eyebrow. "Do you think that will fool any inspectors the Interior Department sends out here?"

"Of course, they are the same kind of trees. We will continue to log off the eastern slopes so that an inspector will see cutting activity. And, we will have ample advance warning of any surprise visit. Besides, when it comes to the local officials, we have already bought them."

Pringle still lacked assurance. "Yes, but are they *honest* politicians?"

Satterlee snorted in impatience. "What do you mean? We paid them off, didn't we?"

"I understand that, Clifton, old fellow, what I mean is that an *honest* politician is one that once he's been bought, he stays bought."

They shared a good laugh at this levity. Then Satterlee moved on to the next subject. "The merchants and residents of Taos remain stubborn for some reason. Although we have added to our cattle holdings recently with two hundred head from the Alvarado ranch."

A frown creased the forehead of Durwood Pringle. "That's excellent, Clifton. But what we want to know is what is being done to encourage these reticent merchants in Taos to sell out?"

Clifton Satterlee took a long pull on his cognac and produced a warm smile. "Have no fear, Durwood. That is being taken care of as we speak."

6

Bright orange tendrils of flame coiled through the black night sky over Taos, New Mexico. The intensity of the inferno paled the thin crescent of moon and dampened the starshine. A horse-drawn fire wagon, its bell clanging frantically, sped through the streets. Men in light blue cotton shirts tugged at the suspenders of their bright yellow, water-proof, oil-skin trousers. A cold hand clutched their minds as one. The worst possible disaster had actually happened.

"Where's the blaze, Cap?" a late arrival volunteer fireman asked of his captain.

Captain Taylor pointed to the south. "Couldn't be worse, Clem. The lumberyard is on fire."

Seconds later, their red-and-black lacquered fire engine stormed down the street toward the lumberyard, which had become an orange ball. The chief of the volunteer fire department, Zeke Crowder, directed them to the south side of the block-square enterprise. Flames and showers of sparks shot fifty feet into the air. Zeke Crowder studied this condition with a grim expression. After several seconds, he called his captains together.

"We've got to keep this from spreading to other buildings. Remember what happened in Albuquerque last year. Three blocks in a row wiped out by what started as a small fire in a restaurant kitchen."

"How do we go about it, Chief?" Fire Captain Taylor asked.

Chief Crowder produced a thoughtful expression. "Even though most of these buildings are made of adobe, they all have palm thatch roofs. Dry as it is, if sparks land in that, fire can sweep through as fast as the scorpions and other critters that live there. We have to knock down the flames now to keep that from happening. If we don't, we'll lose half of Taos."

"How we gonna git it done?" another captain persisted.

Chief Crowder did not hesitate. He gestured to the twelve-foot adobe walls that surrounded the lumberyard. "We need to knock down these walls, make 'em fall inward and blow out the flames. Parker, go to the general store. That's the only other source of dynamite in town. Oh, and you might send someone out to the mines. They'll have some. But hurry."

Captain Taylor stated the obvious. "Don't we have to get Mike Sommers' permission to blow up his walls?"

"Yeah, if we can find him. I haven't seen him at all." Chief Crowder paused a second, then directed Taylor. "Find Hub Yates, Mike's foreman. I need to talk to him anyway."

Five minutes later, Capt. Don Taylor returned with Hubbard Yates. "Hub's not seen Mike, either, Chief."

Quickly, Captain Crowder explained the situation to Yates. He concluded with an appeal. "We have to get someone's permission to knock down these walls."

Yates shook his head. "I don't know if I can do that or not."

"If you can't, I do have the authority to do it anyway. Only thing is the city could be charged with the cost of rebuilding. But, if we don't do it, like I said, we can lose half of the town."

Hub Yates looked at the towering column of sparks. "Go ahead, then. I'll take the chance and speak for Mike."

"All right. Don, come with me. We're going to set charges on both sides of the walls. The stronger ones on the inside. You take a crew that knows explosives and put them to it. And tamp them solid. We want to upend those adobe blocks and drop them inward. The blast should help blow out the flames, too."

While volunteers and onlookers alike labored at the long pumper rails, other fire fighters directed inadequate streams of water onto the burning stacks of raw pine and fir. Steam rose in gouts. The core of the fire glowed a dark magenta. Don Taylor and his men took cases of dynamite as they arrived and prepared charges. A shout of alarm rose when the roof of the building nearest the blaze caught fire from sparks and began to burn lustily.

At once, Chief Crowder directed the three hoses of one company onto the new hot spot. Hissing in protest, the flames slowly died. "Keep on wetting that one down," Crowder directed. He sent two runners to instruct the other fire rigs to do the same.

"Why are you giving up?" a bystander demanded.

"We're gonna lose the whole she-bang, that's for certain. All we can hope for is to keep it from spreading."

"I still say you oughta keep on fighting."

Crowder eyed him coldly. "You're not wearing this coal scuttle on yer head, either. Hell, you're not even helping. I'd keep that mouth buttoned up tight, if I were you.

After half an hour, Captain Taylor reported to the chief. "We're all set."

"Then let her rip!"

At a signal from Taylor, fuses were ignited. The solid thump of explosions rippled along the walls, working outward from the center. Thick clouds of dust billowed and obscured the fire. With a muffled rumble, the tiers of adobe blocks leaned inward and began to fall. The initial blasts had dampened the flames considerably. Now, the four-sided curtains of disturbed air from the falling walls snuffed much more. The feeble streams from the hoses began to gain ground. From the far side a cheer went up.

Chief Crowder began an inspection tour of the fire site. He found that through some fluke, the building front had only been slightly charred. Taking two firemen with him, he picked his way gingerly through the smoldering coals and mounds of ash. Near the rear of the store portion, where the fire had been far hotter, he came upon a huddled mound. Crowder brushed at accumulated ash with a gloved hand and revealed a human shoulder.

"Give me a hand here," he commanded.

His firemen bent to the task. Shortly, they recovered and revealed the severely burned corpse of the owner. A sickeningly sweet odor wafted up from the seared flesh. One of the fire fighters, who had eaten mutton for supper, turned away and abruptly lost his supper. Fighting back his own rush of nausea, Chief Crowder issued yet another command.

"Get Doc Walters over here right away."

In midmorning of the next day, a visibly troubled Dr. Adam Walters found Zeke Crowder in his saddlery shop. The volunteer fire chief sat at a bench, shaping strips of leather into the skirt of yet another of his excellent saddles. A steaming coffee cup rested to one side. He looked up as the bell over the door jingled and the doctor entered.

"'Morning, Doc. What news on Mike Sommers?"

"Nothing good, I'm afraid, Zeke. That's why I'm here. I also asked Hank Banner to join us. He should be along shortly."

"The sheriff? What for? Mike died in an accident, didn't he?"

"No. The fire was not an accident and Mike did not die from it."

Right then the bell jingled again, and Sheriff Hank Banner entered. "Howdy, Adam, Zeke. Now, what was so all-fired important, Doc?"

Dr. Walters sighed heavily. "Maybe we should all have a cup of coffee at hand. I brought along some medicinal brandy."

He remained silent while Crowder poured. Then the physician added brandy to all three mugs. He sighed heavily again before he made his revelation. "Mike Sommers was murdered. He had been shot twice. Once in the chest and once in the head. Whoever started that fire figured he would be too badly burned for us to find that out."

"Any idea who might have done it?" the sheriff asked.

Dr. Walters hesitated. "I think you could guess the name I'd give you. Mike told me only last week that he had been approached with an offer to buy him out. He refused. Then three of the ruffians who have been moving into town of late roughed him up some on Saturday night. Now, this fire, and Mike is dead, killed by someone working for Clifton Satterlee, or I'll eat my medical bag."

With a grunt, the sheriff raised a restraining hand. "Be careful about unsubstantiated accusations, Doc. You know that particular gentleman would not hesitate to haul you into court on a slander suit."

"But dang-bust it. What can we do about this? About everything?"

Again Hank Banner urged caution. "I must admit I share your suspicions that Satterlee is behind all that has happened, including the fire and the murder of Mike Sommers. But, I have no proof. Get me something positive and I'll fling him in jail so fast his boots will take a week to catch up. You know, every day I see more hard cases moving into town. I've a feeling this is about to come to a head."

* * *

Beyond the first line of trees that screened a small clearing beside the steep, winding grade that formed the eastern up-slope to Palo Flechado Pass, Moose Redaker, Gabe Tucker, Buell Ormsley and Abe Voss watched two riders walk their mounts past their observation point. When the pair, a young wet-behind-the-ears kid and an older man, had ridden well out of hearing range, Moose Redaker elbowed Buell Ormsley in the ribs.

"Didn't I tell you? When I first seed them, I knew that bigger feller was Smoke Jensen. We're lookin' at better than five thousand dollars re-ward on the hoof."

"You sure those flyers are still in force?" Abe Voss, the cautious one, asked.

Moose had a ready reply. "They ain't been tooken up, have they?"

"That don't mean someone will pay up after all this time."

"Sure they will. And even if they don't, killin' that holier-than-thou gunfighter will be pure satisfaction in itself." Moose Redaker beamed at his companions. "He's done collected too many bounties that should have been ours by rights. 'Sides, it'll do a whole lot for our reputation, now ain't that so, Gabe?"

Gabe Tucker showed a grin of crooked, green-fringed, yellow teeth. "Right as rain, Moose. Hey, how'er we goin' about this?"

A shrewd light glowed in the eyes of Moose Redaker. "These flyers all say he's wanted dead or alive, right?" He paused and put a hand to his wide chin, which hung below a lantern jaw. "Do any of you hanker to manhandle a live and kickin' Smoke Jensen?"

Buell Ormsley scratched at his fringe of ginger hair that surrounded his bald crown. "Not this lad. My momma never raised no idiots."

"She come mighty close," Moose Redaker jibed. "Yep, I reckon we'd do best to jist shoot him in the back and haul his body up north, Montana way."

Buell Ormsley squeezed his bulbous nose. "Won't he get to stinkin' a lot, we do that?" He had a valid point.

In his usual manner, Moose had an answer. "Not if we go by train and ice him down."

Abe Voss rubbed his gloved hands together. "Then, let's get at it."

"Don't be in such a hurry. We gotta do up a plan first."

"What about the boy?" Gabe Tucker inquired.

"Kill him an' leave him for the buzzards," advised Moose.

Ian MacGreggor had dropped back to tighten a loose cinch and relieve a swollen bladder. His horse stood stubbornly sideways in the trail as he tried to mount it. When he swung aboard, he got a quick glimpse of four grim-faced men riding toward him at a fast pace. Swiftly, he turned the animal's head and put spurs to its flanks. Behind him, the evil quartet put their mounts into a gallop. Rapid reaction by Moose Redaker prevented Abe Voss from firing a shot at the boy and revealing their presence for certain. As it happened, they might as well have shot anyway.

When Mac came within hailing distance of Smoke, he called out a warning. "Look out, Smoke. Four hard-looking guys headed our way." Then he reigned smartly to the side and disappeared behind a large boulder.

Redaker and his crew of ne'er-do-well bounty hunters crested a rise that had separated them from their quarry and found the boy gone from sight. The four of them faced a lone Smoke Jensen. Had their combined intelligence been anywhere near average, that fact might have given them more than a little pause to consider. Since it was not, they blundered on, drawing their six-guns as they came. Smoke waited patiently. The moment the first eager lout came within range, Smoke cut him down with a round from his Winchester Express rifle.

Abe Voss flew from the saddle, while still far out of

revolver range. His companions could only curse. The deadly accurate rifle spoke again and a 500 grain .45 slug sped downrange. Moose Redaker had accurately gauged Smoke Jensen's intentions and ducked low at the precise moment. A fraction of a second later, the bullet cracked past in the space formerly occupied by his head. The distance had decreased, which lent encouragement to the bounty hunters. Gabe Tucker jinked to the left and rode into the meadow to that side. He sought to flank Smoke Jensen and get in a good shot. He made it half the distance to his goal when an invisible fist slammed into his right side and knocked him out of the saddle. He hit in a shower of broken turf and rolled to a halt faced away from Smoke Jensen. The burning pain began to fade to the numbness of shock.

On the other side of Moose Redaker, Buell Ormsley angled toward the cluster of boulders. He watched as Smoke Jensen swung the muzzle of the Winchester toward Moose Redaker. When the express rifle bucked in Smoke's grip, Buell swung the nose of his mount back toward the last mountain man and let fly with two fast rounds.

At first, he thought he had hit his target. Smoke Jensen reared back in his saddle and then bent forward. With a start, Buell realized that Smoke had merely put the rifle back in its scabbard. Jensen came up with a six-gun that looked right at him. A wild cry of denial and fright blew from Buell Ormsley's thick lips as Smoke Jensen fired.

At a range of some thirty feet, the bullet had not the power to kill, but it did hurt like hell when it punched through the leather vest Ormsley wore and broke a rib. Reflex action sent him out of the saddle and onto the ground. He landed hard. More pain shot up his spine when his rump made contact with the soil. Temporarily out of the fight, he fought a wave of dizziness. Dimly he saw Moose Redaker close within killing distance of Smoke Jensen.

Smoke remained calm as he waited out his opponent. The only one still astride a horse, the scruffy-looking hill trash presented the only challenge Smoke could see. Both men fired at the same time, and their slugs missed. Smoke's by so narrow a margin that a hot line burned along the rib cage of Moose Redaker. Moose yowled and fired again. The slug punched through the side panel of Smoke's vest. That brought an instant response.

Another .45 round spat from the Peacemaker in Smoke's hand. This one struck Moose in the chest with stunning force. Redaker reeled in the saddle and tried to put his own six-gun into action. A dark red curtain seemed to descend behind his eyes, and the world grew hazy. At last he triggered his Smith American. The .44 slug screamed off a rock and disappeared in the direction of Taos. Then the ground seemed to leap up and smack Moose in the face. He died wondering how that could happen.

Buell Ormsley scooted over the ground toward his dropped six-gun. He had quickly discovered that he had sprained an ankle in his fall from the horse. Buell reached the weapon while Smoke scanned the other three for any sign of continued resistance. Carefully he raised it, and sighted in on the broad back of Smoke Jensen. He eared back the hammer of the Merwin and Hulbert .44 and sighted again. Buell heard the beginning of a loud report from a revolver close by an instant before an intense light washed through his brain, as the off side of his skull flew apart in gory shards.

Ian MacGreggor rode out onto the trail, smoke still curling from the barrel of the old Schoffield Smith .44 in his left hand. "He was gonna back-shoot you, Smoke."

Smoke masked his surprise and produced a grateful grin. "You done good, Mac. Saved my life, that's for sure. I'm beholdin' to you."

With sincere modesty, Mac made small of it. "You'd a done the same for me."

"Thanks all the same. I wonder if it's worth the effort

to take this trash along and see if there's a bounty on any of them?"

"D'you think there might be?" Mac had not considered such a possibility.

"Never know." Smoke searched the body of Moose Redaker and found the aged, out-of-date posters depicting his own face. Also a letter signed six years earlier giving a commission to one Albert Redaker to seek out wanted miscreants under the auspice of the sheriff of Denton County, Texas. "Still don't mean they're free of any head money."

"I—ah—if it's all the same, I'd just as soon not have them along for company." Smoke noticed that Mac looked a little gray-green around the mouth.

"First time you killed a man?"

"First time I ever shot at one," Mac admitted.

"Take it from me, Mac, it don't get any easier. Only your reaction to it changes. We'd best cover them with rocks and mark 'em so the nearest law can find them."

Back at the Sugarloaf, little Seth Gittings, Mary-Beth's middle boy, had become a particular burden for Sally Jensen. Every bit as much a brat as his elder brother, he chose this afternoon to leave off the severe biting of his fingernails long enough to bite Bobby. His little jaws proved exceptionally strong as he crunched down on Bobby's left forearm. Bobby instantly felt a jolt of hot pain run up his arm and spread in his chest. He wanted to cry out, to even shed a few tears of agony. Yet he shut his mind to such childish things and sought to remedy the situation.

His hard right fist cracked into the side of his tormentor's head. Seth let go with a yowl and an instant flood of tears. "Ow! Owie! Billy, Billy, he hit me. He hit me," quickly followed.

Bobby immediately pursued his advantage. Chin on his chest, shoulders rolled like Smoke had shown him, he waded in. Fast, solid rights and lefts rained on the chest and exposed belly of Seth Gittings. The ten-year-old back-pedaled and flailed uselessly with his stubby arms. Bobby changed his target and felt a flood of satisfaction as blood gushed from Seth's nose. He continued to whale away on Seth until Billy arrived. At once the twelve-year-old took up for his brother and joined the fray in the form of an attack on Bobby Jensen's turned back.

It staggered Bobby for a moment. Then, determined not to be deterred until he had taught them a lasting lesson, Bobby put his back to the outer wall of the bunkhouse and forced them to come at him from the front. His superior size and strength soon began to tell. First Seth, the cause of the altercation, gave up. He ran off, whining and crying, to find their mother. Billy battled on. The pain of his bite had been forgotten. Bobby never gave it thought until droplets of his own blood splashed in his face. Then he shook his arm in the astonished face of Billy.

"See this? See what that brat little brother of yours did to me?"

Stunned by this evidence, Billy gave off fighting with Bobby. "Yeah, he does get sorta wild at times. Bit the hell outta me once."

Bobby, too, stopped exchanging blows. "What did you do?"

"I whipped his butt."

"What do you think I was doin'?"

"Yeah, but he's my brother."

"So? It's me he bit this time."

"Yep, I guess so. Uh—you oughta get that fixed, Bobby."

Quickly as that, the two boys dissolved their animosity. They had their differences amicably ironed out when Mary-Beth Gittings, led by a wailing Seth, and Sally Jensen descended upon them.

"What is the meaning of this, you monstrous, vicious little wretch?" she snarled at Bobby Jensen. Even her son looked shocked at her vehemence. Then she rounded on Sally Jensen. "Sally, you simply must punish that unruly boy."

Mutely, Bobby held up his arm to show the tooth marks and the blood that ran from them. Always slow to anger, Sally suppressed a hot outburst and spoke sweetly. "Since it was two on one, and Seth obviously bit Bobby, perhaps your little darlings share some of the blame."

To the surprise of the Jensens, it was Billy Gittings who came to the defense of Bobby. "He bit me, too, Mother. Remember?"

Mary-Beth pulled an expression of horror. "The very idea!" Thus dismissing her son's revelation, she turned on Sally and snapped, "Seth would never do a thing like that. My precious children are learning such terrible, ruffian ways out here on the frontier. This—this cast-off child of yours is nothing short of a savage. If it weren't so intolerable in Denver, I would return at once."

Oh, do, please do, Sally thought to herself.

7

On a hill overlooking Taos, New Mexico Territory, Smoke Jensen halted to consider their course of action from this point on. He turned to Ian MacGreggor. "We'll enter town from different directions. Remember, Mac, when you see me, you don't know me. Later, when this is over, I will definitely introduce you to Diego Alvarado."

Somewhat sobered by the shoot-out on the trail, Mac nodded thoughtfully. "I can understand that, Smoke. Only, how do I make contact when I learn anything important?"

"If there is time, send a letter to Paul Jones, care of general delivery in Taos, giving a time and place. If not, break off from Satterlee's men and ride like the wind for town."

Mac pulled a dubious expression, but answered easily. "Sounds simple enough. Why Paul Jones?"

"More likely to slip past anyone Satterlee might have watching the mail."

Mac pursed his lips. "Yeah—yeah, that makes sense. Did you learn all of this to be a marshal?"

Smoke had to chuckle over that. "No. A lot I figured out on my own, some Preacher taught me, and the rest I got from lawmen like our sheriff back in the high lonesome. Monte Carson is mighty savvy about such things." For a moment, recollection of Monte brought a tightness to Smoke's chest. "Now, get on your way. I'll give you twenty minutes and then ride in."

Smoke watched Mac ride away and could not help but reflect on himself at that age. He had been rough-edged, a bit wild and woolly, and had lived about a year with Preacher. The old mountain man—some people called Preacher the *first* mountain man—had proven to be incredibly knowledgeable about every aspect of life in the high lonesome. He could lecture for hours on the habits, love life, construction skills and market price of the beaver. Add in religion and fighting techniques and he could do the same for a good seven Indian tribes. A complete fascination with such subjects soon smoothed the rough edges, calmed the wildness and trimmed the wool of young Kirby Jensen.

At fifteen, Mac's age, Smoke had received a special present from Preacher. It was a Colt, Model '51 Navy revolver in .36 caliber. With it came grueling hours of drill and instructions in how to load and accurately fire the weapon. He had also learned the speed draw that had made Preacher famous as the first gunfighter. That had not come without a price. More than a dozen times Smoke had discharged blank loads with the revolver still in the pocket. The accidental discharges had burned like hellfire and scarred his leg. Preacher had found it amusing.

Chuckling each time it happened, he had reminded young Kirby, "Boy, you've gotta be quicker on the draw before you work on quick on the trigger."

It had embarrassed the youth, but it made him work harder and become better. In later years, his speed and accuracy with a six-gun would excel even that of his mentor. If Mac was only a quarter as good as Smoke had become, he could for sure hold his own.

Pablo Alvarado, third son of Diego Alvarado, strolled into the cool interior of the Bajo el Cielo de Mexico cantina in Taos during the busy noon hour. The ever-present muslin sheeting dropped white bellies from the rafters, placed there to prevent unwelcome visits by the scorpions and other insects that inhabited the palm thatch roofing. Men lined the bar, gustily drinking down their cellar-cooled beer, while they munched industriously on plates of *taquitos*—rolled corn tortillas filled with roast, shredded goat meat and crisp fried. Others consumed small clay cups of *caldo de camarón,* a thick dark red chile-shrimp soup made of tiny dried shrimp, onions, garlic, tomato paste and hot chiles. All of them frequently dipped tortilla chips into bowls of fresh-made *pico de gallo* salsa, redolent with the aroma of chopped chiles, garlic, and fresh coriander. Nearly half of the patrons were Anglos. Pablo joined three vaqueros from his father's *estancia,* Rancho de la Gloria. He soon had a tall, slender glass of beer, called a *tubo,* in one hand. With his other, Pablo lifted a *taquito* from a plate.

His presence was immediately noted by a trio of scruffy saddle trash seated at a corner table. They bent their heads together and the leader, Garth Thompson, spoke in a low voice. "That's one of that stubborn greaser's sons. I think you two ought to arrange a little entertainment for him outside this place."

"That shines, Garth. What sort of party should we figger to throw?" Norm Oppler responded.

Thompson pursed his lips, then spread them in a nasty grin. "One that will leave him definitely hurting."

Hicky Drago, the third hard case, flashed a toothy smile. "Now that sounds like fun. Do we leave him alive and hurtin'?"

Garth showed his own teeth. "That's entirely up to you."

Both downed their drinks and came to their boots. They left the busy saloon without attracting any attention. Over at the bar, Pablo gestured to an old woman in a plain polka dot dress, her head swathed in a black rebozo. *"Una copa de caldo de camarón, por favor."*

Bearing a large, blue granite kettle, the seam-faced woman attendant came over and ladled out a cup of shrimp soup for the young *caballero*. Pablo took it and nodded his appreciation. *"Gracias."* Then he turned to the ranch hands.

"We will have to start back to the ranch after we've eaten. There seems not to be enough hours in the day."

"Especially to get the work done and for you to see Juanita, eh, *patrón?*" one of the cowboys remarked with a smile.

Pablo's eyes twinkled as he thought of his current favorite. "Juanita is . . . worth making time for. We are going to be married. She doesn't know that yet, but I do."

"¡Que romantico!"

Pablo chided him in jest. "Do not mock true love, Arturo. Some day it will overwhelm you."

"What, me? With a fat wife and three little ones?"

Garth Thompson watched them darkly as they laughed over that sally. He had been given his orders by Whitewater Paddy Quinn as to what to do about the family of the stubborn old fool, Diego Alvarado. The rancher refused to sell out, and his Mexican cowboys had already killed three and wounded eight of those sent to harass him. It was time to turn up the heat, Paddy had said. *So be it,* Garth mused. He watched while Pablo and the vaqueros downed a prodigious quantity of food and two glasses each of beer. Then they hitched up their belts and walked toward the door. Silver conchos along the outer seams of their pant legs sparkled even in the low light.

When they stepped outside, Garth strained to hear over the low rumble of conversation and laughter the challenge he expected. It came a moment later in an angry growl from Norm Oppler.

"Hey, watch where you're goin', greaser."

Smoke Jensen walked Cougar and Hardy down the broad eastern avenue that led to the Plaza de Armas in the center of Taos. Palo verde trees had been planted in circular basins all along the residential section. Their pale, wispy, smokey green leaves fluttered in a light breeze, like the fine hair of a young woman. Most houses sat well back from the Spanish tile sidewalks, presenting high, blank walls to the passersby. Some had built-in niches where flowers had been planted or religious figures installed. Red tile roofs peeked over the blue and green shards of broken bottles plastered into the tops of these ramparts. The last block before the central square had been overtaken by shops, restaurants and cantinas. Smoke reached the midpoint when a harsh voice called out insultingly.

"Hey, watch where you're goin', greaser."

A handsome, light-complexioned young man of Spanish/Mexican descent took a step back and spoke soft words of apology. Then the import of the insult sank in. His eyes narrowed, and his full lips twisted in offense. "What did you call me?"

"I called you a bean-slurpin', chile-chompin' greaser."

Smoke Jensen reined in to watch the exchange. The youth had a familiar appearance, though Smoke could not place a name with the face. Both men were armed, though the well-dressed Spanish youth chose to use his hands. With a suddenness that spoke well of his ability, he swung a balled fist that smashed into the jaw of the loud-mouthed saddle trash with enough force to knock him off his boots.

He hit the tile walk with a flat smack. At once the youth stepped over him. "I'll accept your apology for that insult and there will be no harm done."

"Like hell you will!" shouted the thug as he whipped out his six-gun and fired point-blank into the young man's belly.

At once the other Anglo cleared leather. His bullet cut a searing path across the small of Pablo's back. Smoke Jensen had time only for a hasty shout before his own hand filled with a .45 Colt. "Don't!"

Three dark-complexioned vaqueros with the youth only then reacted, spreading apart with shock and surprise on their faces. One drew a knife. The Colt in the hand of the seated hard case roared again. He missed his attempt to shoot the knife wielder through the chest. His slug bit flesh out of the vaquero's side.

"Drop the guns, both of you," Smoke demanded.

When the Anglo opponents refused to comply, Smoke tripped the trigger of his Peacemaker and shot the seated one through the shoulder, breaking his scapula. The smoking revolver in his hand flew from his grasp. His companion spun on one boot heel to face Smoke Jensen. He raised his six-gun to shoulder height and took aim as Smoke cocked and fired his .45 a second time. His bullet took the gunman in the center of his chest. Behind Smoke, Hardy whinnied in irritation. Shouts came from inside the saloon. The man Smoke had shot looked down at his chest with a dumb expression of disbelief as he staggered forward. Slowly he released his grip on his weapon. The revolver thudded in the dirt of the street a moment before the body of the dead assailant.

By then, the wounded one seated on the tile walk had recovered his Colt and threw a shot at Smoke that cracked past the head of the last mountain man to bury itself deep in an adobe wall across the street. Without a flinch, Smoke returned fire. Hot lead punched a neat hole in the upper lip of the shooter, exposing crooked, yellowed teeth. He went over backward and twitched violently for a few seconds.

During that time, the three vaqueros recovered their composure and rushed to the side of their fallen companion. "Pablo, Pablo, can you hear me?" one spoke urgently.

Pablo? Keeping his Colt handy, Smoke Jensen dismounted and crossed to where two of the Mexican cowboys kneeled beside their employer's son. "*¿Con permiso?*" Smoke addressed them in his rusty Spanish. "Is this Pablo Alvarado?"

Dark, angry faces turned toward him. "Why do you ask, *gringo?*"

Smoke answered simply. "I am a friend of his father."

The surly one produced a sneer. *"Ay, sí.* And I am the pope in Rome. What is your name, *gringo?*"

"I am called Smoke Jensen."

Surprise registered on the three faces. Embarrassment warred with it. At last, the angry vaquero spoke in an amiable tone. *"Tengo mucho vergüenza,* Señor Jensen. I should have known. No one else could have handled two gunmen so fast and so effectively. It is only that Don Pablo has been shot, and Ricardo, *tambien.* And it is forbidden us to carry our *pistólas* into town. We could do nothing."

"And naturally that bothered you. That I can understand. One of you had better go for a doctor." Smoke examined the wounded men. "Ricardo has only a scratch. Pablo is still breathing and he has a strong heartbeat," Smoke observed as he examined the young man. "But he still needs help right away, *inmediatamente, comprende?*"

The embarrassed one spoke up. "I am called Miguel Armillita. I will go."

"Good, Miguel. Another of you should ride to the ranch and tell Don Diego."

"Uh—there is a wagon with supplies," a young vaquero blurted.

Smoke spoke decisively. "Ricardo can drive that, after he is patched up. The other take a fast horse and head for Rancho de la Gloria."

The town marshal and the sheriff of Taos County arrived at the same time. Pablo Alvarado remained unconscious, and two of the vaqueros had sped off on their assigned tasks. An angry and shaken Garth Thompson, who had only now come out of the saloon, leaned against the outside adobe wall of Bajo el Cielo de Mexico scowling at Smoke Jensen. When the lawmen pushed through a crowd of the cantina's patrons, he spoke up in angry accusation.

"This stranger came along and shot two of my men for no reason at all. Shot the Mexican kid as well."

"I'll take that iron," the marshal demanded as he and the sheriff drew their weapons. "You've got some tall explaining to do, mister. Since this involves folks from outside town, I'll let you handle it, Hank. I'd better see to a doctor for young Alvarado."

Smoke looked up at them. "I've already sent for a doctor."

Hank Banner, the sheriff, spoke up then. "I'll take that gun, feller, seein' as how you've not handed it over."

Smoke complied, giving the sheriff both of his Colts, but insisted on waiting until a physician arrived. Miguel Armillita came with him and stood back, silent and respectful in the presence of such awesome authority as the marshal and sheriff. After the doctor had arranged to move Pablo to his office and bandaged Ricardo, and Hank Banner had taken Smoke Jensen off to jail, Miguel went to his horse and rode hastily off toward Rancho de la Gloria to inform Don Diego of this turn of events.

"Sit down and tell me something about yourself," Sheriff Banner invited as he gestured to a chair beside his desk. "Do you regularly go around shooting men without the least provocation?"

Smoke Jensen declined the chair for the moment. Being uncertain as to which side the lawman happened to be on, he did not use his real name nor did he show his U.S. marshal's badge, nor did he use the cover name he had given to Ian MacGreggor.

"Let's get one thing straight first, Sheriff. I did not shoot Pablo Alvarado. My name is Frank Hickman, and I do go around shooting people who shoot friends of mine."

Banner looked skeptical. "You are a friend of the Alvarados?"

"I am."

Now the sheriff leaned forward, his expression turned hard. "Why is it I don't believe you?"

Smoke gave him a cool, indifferent look. "I could give you a couple of reasons."

Banner did not give in. "Try me."

A frown momentarily creased Smoke's forehead. "You could be one of those folks who dislikes people of Spanish or Mexican origin and is unwilling to believe any white man could be friends with them. Or, you could be one of those lawmen who has taken some consideration from a powerful man."

Banner clenched his fists and made to swing on Smoke. Smoke raised a staying hand. "Sit down, Sheriff I apologize for baiting you that way. What is it you want to know?"

"Everything that happened out there. Start from the first."

"I was riding into town when those two provoked a quarrel with Pablo Alvarado. At that time, I didn't recognize Pablo, it has been quite a while since I last saw him."

Banner still had not lost his suspicion. "People don't often change that much."

"They do if they were ten the last time someone saw them."

"Ah—yes, yes, that makes sense. Go on."

Smoke Jensen related the events surrounding the shooting of Pablo Alvarado. Then he described what he did. When he concluded, the two men sat a long while in silence. At last the sheriff spoke up.

"So you intervened in defense of Pablo Alvarado? He was armed, I saw that."

"The one who shot him first didn't even call him out, he just drew and fired away. The other one tried to back-shoot Pablo."

"Yes, you said that. I think I understand. What I don't follow is why you stepped in at all."

Smoke sighed out his irritation. "Because I have a big problem with sneaks and back-shooters. Both of them drew on the boy. Pablo's men were unarmed. I could do something about it, so I did."

"Sheriff?" a squeaky voice called from the open doorway.

Smoke looked over to see a boy of ten or eleven standing there, his head crowned with a thick thatch of sandy brown hair. His gray-green eyes sparkled with intelligence above speckled cheeks and a wide, generous mouth. Oblivious of Smoke's scrutiny, the lad concentrated on the lawman.

"What is it, Wally?"

"Doc Walters says Pablo Alvarado is con—con—awake now. He's ready to make a statement. But you have to come over to Doc's office."

"Thank you, Wally." Banner flipped a nickel to the boy and cut his eyes to Smoke. "I think you should come along. If Pablo can identify you, I'll be satisfied with your account of what happened."

Well, the Frank Hickman name was out of the barn with this, Smoke thought with irritation. He smiled evenly at Banner. "Whatever you say, Sheriff."

Dr. Adam Walters had his office and infirmary on the entire second floor above a men's haberdashery and a women's clothier. Smoke Jensen followed Sheriff Hank Banner up the steep flight of stairs and through a white-painted door. The odor of ether and carbolic acid hung heavily in the still air of the interior. Dr. Walters greeted the men with surgical tools in hand, which he scrubbed at energetically.

"Pablo got lucky this time, Hank. It was a clean, through-and-through shot to the side. Missed his intestines and liver. He got just a scratch across his back. I cleaned the wounds, closed and sutured them. I'd say he's a sure bet to recover. He's awake now and asking for you. Oh, who is this?" The last accompanied a nod toward Smoke Jensen.

"Says he's a friend of the Alvarados."

"He can come in, then."

They found Pablo Alvarado propped up on pillows, the sheet and quilt folded down to his waist. His bare middle was swathed in bandages. He looked up as they entered and broke out a big smile. "Smoke! You came like Poppa said you would. Sheriff, it's good to see you."

Smoke Jensen cut his eyes to the lawman and saw genuine affection for Pablo shining in his. Banner gave him a puzzled expression. "Smoke?"

"I'm afraid I wasn't entirely truthful with you, Sheriff. My name is Smoke Jensen.

"The hell. *The* Smoke Jensen?"

"The only one I know. I needed to find out whose side you are on before letting out too much."

Banner nodded. "Everything I've heard about you argues to that. It's a pleasure to meet you. Now, excuse me. What do you have for me, Pablo?"

"I know those *ladrónes* who shot me, Sheriff. They run with the gang led by Paddy Quinn. They didn't give me a chance. They just drew and fired on me."

"How did Smoke Jensen get involved?"

Pablo frowned. "I'm not sure. I was down by then. What's certain is he saved my life. Smoke is an old friend of my father."

Banner remained skeptical. "That may well be, but not every card is on the table as yet. I'll keep Smoke around until everything is straightened out."

"In jail?" Pablo demanded.

With a shrug, Banner replied. "Where else?"

8

Late in the afternoon, Don Diego Alvarado, accompanied by Miguel Armillita, arrived at the jail. He stormed in and confronted Hank Banner at his desk. The pencil line of black mustache on Diego's upper lip writhed with his agitation.

"What is this that you have my good friend, Smoke Jensen, in jail? I insist that you release him at once."

Banner remained obstinate. "Now, why should I do that? Two men have been killed. Your son has been shot."

"First, because Smoke is a valued friend. I will vouch for him. And because I sent for him to look into the matters we have discussed. Clifton Satterlee owns the judges, half of the legislature and nearly as many lawmen. If not for you and Marshal Gates, there would be no one opposing him."

Hank Banner came to his boots. "Then he's as free as a bird, *amigo*." Taking his keys, the sheriff went to release Smoke Jensen.

Diego greeted Smoke with an energetic *abrazo*, then turned to Banner. "His *pistólas*? I am sure he will have need of them."

His weapons restored, and with the assurances of Diego Alvarado as to the honesty of Hank Banner, Smoke Jensen at last showed his badge and covered the reason for being in Taos. "I have to ask you to keep this an absolute secret between us, Sheriff."

"You have my word on it. And I wish you luck. Whatever happens, let me advise that you had better not operate outside the law."

"Sheriff, in my world, I've found it wise to always shoot the bear before the critter could wrap arms around me."

Banner eyed him narrowly. "What does that mean?"

Smoke cheerfully mixed his metaphors in his reply. "When a feller is dealing with a rattler, he doesn't pay much attention to any rules that protect the snake."

"I . . . see."

"I hope you do, Sheriff. Now, Don Diego and I have a lot of catching up to do."

Diego went first to see his son. Then he directed Smoke around the town to proudly show off the improvements that had taken place in the absence of the last mountain man. He waved an arm expansively at an adobe building with a second story of clapboard siding. A large bell stood in the bare yard outside.

"We have a new school now. A *secondary* school, amigo. In my modest way I contributed to its construction and established an account in the bank, to which others contribute, to provide pay for the teachers." Diego frowned slightly. "There are only four qualified ones now. The other three are volunteers from among the merchants. Alejandro teaches Spanish when he can get away from the *rancho*. It is all very exciting, no?"

"Of course it is. How is Alejandro and all your other children?"

"Healthy, thanks be to God. To my way of thinking, living in town robs a man of vigor and his years. My next to youngest, Lupe, who is eight, still breaks the thin spring ice from the *riachuelo* to swim, like her brothers before her. *Gracias a Dios,* she will live a long life. I, myself, have fifty-two years."

"I don't believe it, Don Diego," Smoke spoke truthfully.

Diego Alvarado looked far from fifty-two, more like a young forty. His full mane of longish, black hair showed only thin streaks of gray at the temples, and his face remained unlined, save for the effects of sun, wind and cold. Trim and fit, he could not weigh more than a hundred fifty pounds, Smoke estimated. He wore his *traje corto* on a five-foot-nine frame with an elegance that made others appear common and shabby.

Dressed all in brown today, his cordovan sombrero sat his head at a rakish angle. The bolero jacket, adorned with small, silver conchos, rode the midline of a scarlet sash around his waist, above flared-cuff trousers, with wide gussets of satin in matching color to his girdle. A snowy shirt, with lace-trimmed pleats, appeared above his vest. His string tie stood out in starched erectness, rather than the usual limp droop. All together he represented a fine rendering of the man Smoke had known ten years earlier.

"I saw all the new houses to the east," Smoke remarked.

Diego looked unhappy. "Yes. So many children being born and so few jobs on the ranches. They come to town to work in the fine homes of the rich *gringos* and Mexicans, and to make more babies."

Smoke shrugged. "Nature has a way of doing such things. What else is new since my last visit?"

"Come, I will show you. We have a *teatro*, an opera house. Opened last year. At last I can hear my beloved music. Handel, Mozart, Bach. And, of course, the classic Spanish composers. We will stop by the theater first. Then we shall stop at La Comida Buena for something to eat before heading to the ranch."

Seated at a rickety table in the Bloody Hills road ranch outside Taos, Whitewater Paddy Quinn listened in stony silence to the report of his lieutenant, Garth Thompson. Two men killed. Gunned down, according to Garth, by a saddle tramp who looked to be about forty or so. Impossible. He said as much to Garth.

"No. Norm Oppler and Hicky Drago weren't exactly the fastest and best," Garth advised. "I didn't see the shooting myself. I came out of the saloon after it was over. Like to have knocked me out of my boots. He must have called them out with a gun already in his hand. Don't see any other way."

Quinn's eyes narrowed in curious speculation. "Now I'm wonderin', what was it they were doin' to get themselves killed?"

Garth Thompson studied the toes of his boots, uncomfortable with that question. "Young Pablo Alvarado came into the cantina and joined with some of his vaqueros. That Miguel Armillita was amongst them. You know the one?"

Paddy Quinn nodded. "Him that gives those disgusting bullfight demonstrations, is it?" At Garth's nod, he went on. "Bloody damn barbarian, says I. Sure an' cows is for givin' milk and eatin', not for bloody sport."

"You've got to kill a cow to eat it, don't you?" Garth brazened out.

Quinn sighed and cut his eyes to the ceiling. "An' that's a fact, Garth me boy.

"When this Armillita kills a bull, he gives the meat to the sisters at the mission to distribute to the poor. So it's not a waste."

Quinn cocked an eyebrow, and anger lines formed around his mouth. "Yer talkin' like you approve of that deviltry, is it now?"

Thompson hastened to regain the respect of his superior. "No-no, it's only the man's courage that I admire. It takes a lot to stand out on the sand, with nothing but a cloth in yer hands, in front of a half a ton of raging animal that has two-foot-long horns."

A twinkle in the eyes of Paddy Quinn betrayed his true opinion, contrary to that which he spoke. "Cowards, the lot of them greasers."

Secure in his position once more, Garth Thompson hazarded a barb. "Would you do it?"

Quinn did not hesitate. "Hell no! D'ye think me a bloody fool?" Of a sudden, his mood grew serious again. "Still, I want to know what those two were up to."

Garth swallowed. "You said to put pressure on Alvarado. So I sent Oppler and Drago to pick a fight with Pablo. They did, and they shot him, but he didn't die."

"Something has to be done about the shooting of our boys. This stranger has to be taught a lesson, made an example of, don't ye see?"

"I'll send Luke and Grasser to keep an eye on him. I heard before I left town that the sheriff let him out of jail. Seems he's a friend of the Alvarados."

Fire and ice warred in the black eyes of Paddy Quinn. "Sure an' I'd not lose any sleep if something happened to old man Alvarado. Maybe you oughta get together enough of our lads to have a go at the both of them."

Garth Thompson gave a steady look at his boss. Paddy Quinn had a deceptively cherubic Irish face. He was always smiling, even when he killed a man. He was big for a victim of the potato famine, standing 5'10", with about 158 pounds behind his belt. His ears and nose were small, his mouth wide only when he smiled. A shock of glistening black hair hung over a high forehead. Without his brace of .45 Colt Peacemakers and the .38 Smith and Wesson he carried for a hideout, he could easily pass for a shopkeeper. Garth knew better, though.

When on the prod, the fit, trim, hard-muscled Quinn virtually exploded into violent mania, calmed only by a frenzy of bloodletting. Odd, Garth speculated, that Quinn of all people would object to the violence and spectacle of bullfighting. But, then, the man who had hired the gang had a fondness for pussycats. No telling, Garth thought in dismissal of his reflections.

"Where do we wait for them?"

"Here to begin with. Then it depends on what Luke and Grasser report. Get on it, then, bucko."

* * *

Smoke Jensen recognized the type the moment Luke Horner and Charlie Grasser tied off their horses at the tie rail outside the saloon across the street from La Comida Buena. As always, Diego Alvarado had shown impeccable taste in his choice of a place to eat. Contrary to usual Mexican custom, the thinly sliced steak turned out to be remarkably tender. It had been marinated and then quickly grilled over charcoal. The *carne asada* had come to their table on platters that held beans and rice, along with a bowl of freshly made *pico de gallo*. The salsa of tomato, onion, garlic, chile peppers and chopped cilantro was hot enough to blister the mouth of anyone of lesser fortitude than possessed by Smoke Jensen. He heaped it on everything and chewed with obvious enjoyment. Formal dinner, Smoke knew from experience, would come at around nine-thirty that night at the ranch. It would be preceded by a steady flow of tequila and beer, and served with fine wines from Pedro Domecq, a winery located in the high central valley in the Mexican state of Aguas Calientes. His pleasure diminished when the two hard cases arrived. He nodded to the street, and Diego paused in his mastication to look over his shoulder.

"See that pair? That's more trouble on the hoof, or I miss my guess."

"*De veras.* That's true, my friend. Though they are obviously—how you say?—small fry."

Smoke produced a wry expression. "Where the fingerlings swim, the bigger fishes are close behind."

Worry clouded the face of Diego Alvarado. "Do you think they came to finish with Pablo?"

With a negative shake of his head, Smoke gave his surmise. "No. I think whoever sent the first two has someone else in mind."

"Meaning you?" Diego prompted.

"Yes. And perhaps you. Well, old friend, let's finish up. We don't want to disappoint them."

* * *

Smoke Jensen would have liked to follow, and perhaps question, the two hard cases. Proddy, and eager to impress his boss, Luke Horner didn't give them the chance. He leaned against an upright four-by-four post that supported the canopy over the saloon front across from the restaurant where Smoke and Diego had eaten an early supper. Luke swiveled his head constantly, alert for a sight of the familiar figure of Diego Alvarado. When the subject of their surveillance appeared suddenly outside the restaurant, Luke turned his head away and alerted his companion.

"Grasser, there they are. Right across from us. I say we can take them right now. You game?"

Charlie Grasser came upright in the chair made from a small barrel and peered across at the two men. "I'm not so sure, Luke. Didn't Garth say that feller was faster than greased lightning?"

Luke remained unimpressed. "So what? He caught the boys unaware. There's two of us, an' he can't be all that fast. That old greaser won't be able to shoot very well. I think we oughta do it."

So saying, he pushed away from the post and stepped out into the street. Not nearly so eager, Charlie Grasser separated from his companion and did the same. Luke jabbed an extended left forefinger toward Smoke Jensen, his right hand already on the butt of his six-gun. "Hey, Mister, you killed two friends of mine. I don't take kindly to that. I'm here to make you pay for it."

With that, Luke Horner pulled his Colt.

Smoke Jensen bested him anyway. The .45 Peacemaker appeared in his hand as if by magic, the hammer fully cocked. As the muzzle leveled on the center of Luke's body, Smoke triggered a round. The bullet struck Luke at the tip of his breastbone. He jolted backward and bent double. The barrel of his Colt had not yet cleared the holster. To the surprise of Charlie Grasser, Diego Alvarado had drawn with nearly equal speed.

Don Diego's Obrigon cracked sharply, and the slug chewed a nasty trough across Grasser's left shoulder, after breaking the collarbone. Charlie howled at the pain. To his right, Luke struggled feebly to free his six-gun and get off a shot. Alvarado's .45 spat another chunk of hot lead, which missed Grasser only because he had spun to his left to distance himself from the fight. Diego cocked the Mexican-made weapon again as Grasser made his first long stride toward the welcome void of an alley.

Dying on his feet, Luke Horner managed to draw at last and distracted Diego Alvarado momentarily when he sent a bullet speeding toward the fastidious rancher. It missed, and the air filled with the hiss and crack of hot lead. Smoke Jensen fired a safety shot into the top of Luke Horner's head, which blasted the second-rate gunfighter off this earth for all eternity. By then, Charlie Grasser had found the safety of the alley and sped off to inform Garth Thompson.

A scant minute later, Sheriff Banner arrived and took in the body of Luke Horner. "Shootin' snakes again, Jensen?"

Smoke tipped back his Stetson. "You might say that. One got away."

Diego Alvarado stepped forward, replacing his three expended cartridge casings. "I wounded him. Too bad he could run faster than I could shoot."

"Do either of you think you could identify him?"

Both men nodded, and Diego spoke. "Oh, yes. He'll have his left arm in a sling. I am positive I got him in the collarbone."

Hank Banner listened to their account of how the shoot-out had begun and left them with another admonition. "Remember, you make good and sure that they force the action every time. I'd not like to lock up a friend . . . friends," he amended.

* * *

On the road to Rancho de la Gloria, Smoke Jensen and Diego Alvarado discussed the possibility that there would be another personal attack upon them. Diego weighed all Smoke said about these sort of gunhawks and offered a prophesy.

"You are probably right. But, Satterlee has so far kept it rather quiet. He does not seem ready to force the issue. I think it will be some time before any more of his *ladrónes* come after you or I."

Five minutes farther down the trail proved how wrong he had been.

A fine Andalusian, the horse ridden by Don Diego Alvarado shied a fraction of a second before a plume of white powder smoke spurted upward in a thicket of mesquite that had been cut and stacked for burning. In the next fraction of a second, a bullet cracked past so close to the rancher that it clipped the sombrero from his head. Half a dozen more rounds came from the ambush site.

To Diego's right, Smoke had already fisted his .45 Colt and returned fire. He drubbed Cougar's flanks with his round knob spurs and started away from the hidden gunmen, only to find the way blocked by more of their kind. In a swirl of dust, Smoke Jensen released his pack-horse, Hardy, and charged the obstruction.

9

Men cursed and fired blindly at where Smoke Jensen had been only moments before. They next saw him as he burst through the fog of dust and powder smoke and blazed away at point-blank range. Two men left their saddles in rapid succession. A third yelped a second later and clutched at his suddenly useless right arm. The rifle he had been holding dropped from his grasp, the small of its stock shattered by the bullet that had smashed his shoulder socket.

Smoke did not stop there. He whirled and disappeared into the miasma, to pop out on the flank of the mesquite barricade, flanking the ambush. One hard case sensed the presence of Smoke Jensen and whirled to fire his weapon. That way, he took the bullet from Smoke's Colt full in the face. He went over backward with a soft grunt. Beyond the dying man, Smoke saw Diego at the opposite end of the hiding place. Alvarado placed his shots carefully, wounding three men. As soon as they could recover enough of their difficulties, they hastily abandoned the fight. With their desertion, the ambush began to quickly dissolve.

But not before Garth Thompson snapped off a round that nicked Diego Alvarado in the fleshy part of his left upper arm. Diego squinted with the pain that shot through him and coolly pumped a round into another of the outlaws. Garth's hammer dropped on an expended cartridge, and he rose in his stirrups.

"Break off! Pull back, boys. Scatter," he bellowed.

Garth's head spun in confusion over the ferocity and speed of the reaction of their targets. It had not been a fluke, or a sucker call, that had downed Oppler and Drago. Whoever this master gun happened to be, he was fast and mean as a hell hound. The man beside Garth fired again at Diego Alvarado and put spurs to his mount. Garth quickly joined him.

At once, Smoke and Diego joined up and went in pursuit of two of the hard cases who had chosen the roadway as the easiest route of escape. Diego hailed Smoke with a big smile on his face. "We have them trapped between us and the ranch. They will not get far, *amigo.*"

"Might be, but will anyone be expecting them?"

"We are close enough that the shots will have been heard. Someone will be watching. It is too bad the others got away."

Smoke thought on that. "Not for long if we get to question these two."

They picked up the pace then. Within ten minutes they rode through the low scud of red dust stirred up by the hooves of the horses ridden by the fleeing men. Moments later, the sound of gunfire came from ahead, and the pursuers urged their mounts into a gallop. At that ground-eating pace, Smoke and Diego soon saw the backs of the two outlaws. One was on the ground, drawn up in a fetal position. The other, his horse shot out from under him, used the fallen animal as a breastwork.

Although wounded, he fired over the saddle at unseen adversaries as Smoke Jensen closed the gap between himself and the member of the Quinn gang. When Smoke and Diego came into clear view, whoever kept the outlaw pinned down ceased fire. In the silence that followed, the hard case heard the hoofbeats behind him and turned to see Smoke and Diego less than twenty feet away. All resistance left him, and he laid down his revolver and raised his hands.

"I'm givin' up. Don't shoot me."

"Seems as how you tried like hell to do just that to us," Smoke growled.

His feeble protest would echo down the halls of the future. "I was jist followin' orders. Nothin' personal, you understand?"

Smoke snorted in contempt. "When someone throws lead at me, I take it right personal, y'hear?" Smoke dismounted as Alejandro Alvarado showed himself, along with three of the vaqueros.

Beaming, Alejandro extended a hand. "It is good to see you again. Poppa said you would come."

"He made it sound irresistible. Let's take a look at the fish you caught."

Roughly they searched the outlaw, supervised by Smoke Jensen. Two knives, a stubby-barreled Hopkins and Allen .38 Bulldog revolver and a .41 rimfire derringer appeared from the voluminous clothing of the miscreant. For reasons known only to himself, Smoke found that amusing.

"Looks like whatever you lack in skill, you make up for in sneaky armament."

"Who are you, mister? You tore through our ambush like a bull through a corral of steers."

"Folks call me Smoke. Smoke Jensen."

"Awh . . . dog pucky. That ain't fair. It jist ain't fair. How was we to know you were around here anywhere?"

"Chalk it up to bad luck. Now, my good friend here, Don Diego, and I would like to know who you work for?"

Defiance flared in his eyes. "You'll never hear it from me."

Smiling, Smoke Jensen taunted the injured man. "I'll hear it when I want to. Although I don't think I really need to. Don Diego has told me all about your boss, Whitewater Paddy Quinn."

Ever so slightly, the gunman's eyes narrowed and tension lines sprang up that did not come from the bullet wound in his thigh. He pressed his lips tightly together. Smoke shattered the man's newfound resolve with one terse, ominous sentence.

"If he won't confirm that, Alejandro, kill him."

That broke the last of his bravado. "Yes—yes, you're right, goddamn you, Jensen. And when Paddy Quinn finds out what you done to us, he'll be down on you like stink on a skunk."

Dryly, Smoke answered him. "I can hardly wait."

"Amigo, we still have a league to ride to the *estancia*," Diego reminded Smoke.

"Then, we'd best be going. I trust you can deal with this mess, Alejandro?"

"*Sí.* Any day, Smoke."

They left Alejandro to clean up after the ambushers and to send vaqueros to town to deliver the dead and living one to the sheriff.

Smoke Jensen was met by the entire Alvarado flock. The youngest, a totally naked toddler of two, crawled up on Smoke's knee and patted him on the cheek. Horrified by the overly familiar conduct of her infant son, Señora Alvarado, Lidia rushed forward to pluck the squealing boy from his perch and apologized effusively to Smoke for the social gaffe. Smoke laughed about it and patted the youngster on the top of his head.

"But, you are a *caballero*," Lidia protested. "You should not be bothered by the prattling of children."

Smoke smiled to show his sincerity. "He's no burden, Doña Lidia. I remember my own at that age."

Lidia Alvarado gave him a surprised look. "But they are all grown, yes?"

"All but one my Sally and I adopted not long ago. He has thirteen years."

"A burdensome age. I will leave you gentlemen to your tequila and old campaigns." With that, Lidia exited, her giggling youngster on her hip.

Diego took up the subject of most interest to both men. "Let me tell you what I believe is behind Clifton Satterlee's determination to secure all of the land for twenty miles around Taos. It is greed, plain and simple. Somehow he has found a way to make a profit out of land that sells for twenty-five cents an acre, due to its poor quality of soil. In its natural state, nothing much grows here, except for cactus and mesquite. Perhaps he has learned, as I have, of the value of irrigation. I do not believe that is the case. He means to plunder the land and leave it desolate.

"There is gold in the mountains. Not much, but enough to attract a greedy man. There is also the cattle that I and others raise. The price of beef is going up, now that it has been made more tender and palatable to the eastern taste. Satterlee's entire assets, at least those I have been able to discover, are not worth more than one hundred thousand dollars. The sale of our cattle would increase his holdings by ten fold. There is five times that value in the timber on the Tua reservation. Although the land is protected by your government in Washington, treaties have been broken in the past and will be again, given enough money changes hands."

Smoke smiled warmly. "You don't put much trust in the United States government, amigo."

"No more than I did that in that of Ciudad Mexico. Politicians are . . . politicians. It is the nature of government to become more intrusive, more controlling of people's lives and their property. Yours, ours now, perhaps less than many others. But who knows what the future may hold? Satterlee is a law unto himself. Therefore, I believe that he is not so much empire building as empire looting."

Smoke gave that some thought. "That's a strong accusation. Why would he want to acquire the town of Taos?"

"It is the seat of power in this part of New Mexico. We are far removed, by mountains as well as distance, from the government in Santa Fe. Our governor is a good man. I regret that I cannot say the same for some of those around him. Recently there was an affair that is being called the Lincoln County War. Governor Wallace offered amnesty to those of both sides. Secretly, some of those in power put out the word that certain among the combatants were to be killed upon their surrender. It seems that their continued existence would prove an embarrassment to some of our politicians.

"But, I digress, old friend. You are here to determine exactly what it is Satterlee intends, and if it is illegal or harmful to the best interests of the people, to put an end to it." Diego paused to refill his clay cup with tequila. He prefaced his next words with a low, self-deprecating chuckle. "That sounds remarkably like a politician, does it not? Forgive me, you came here of your own accord. If I have burdened you with too great a load, it is only because of my great concern."

Smoke shrugged. "If you'd put too much on my plate, I'd be riding out now."

"It's the people I am concerned about. Many of those who live around Taos work for me, or have sons and daughters who do. And Alejandro has business interests in the town. Then there are the Indians. Did you know that they rose up one time and slaughtered all the Spanish living around here? They are capable of doing so again. Now, let us go in to dinner. Fernando has roasted us a whole small pig. It will make excellent *carnitas de puerco.*" Diego added in explanation, "One of those traditional dishes that happened by accident the first time. Someone accidentally dropped chunks of pork into boiling oil. By the time they were fished out, the meat was crispy on the outside, juicy and tender inside. I'm sure you will enjoy it."

Smiling, Smoke emptied his cup of the maguey cactus liquor. "Anything Fernando cooks is an equal to my Sally's best efforts. I'm sure I'll like it."

Later, after the sumptuous meal, Smoke retired to a guest room for the night. As he lay on the comfortable bed, his thoughts strayed to the High Lonesome and to Sally. He fell asleep with visions of her in his mind.

Around noon the next day, Sheriff Monte Carson rode up to the main house on the Sugarloaf. He brought with him two dispirited, hang-dog youngsters atop a mule he led by a long rope. Seth and Sammy Gittings, although looking contrite, to Sally Jensen's expert eye managed to reveal their confidence that they would escape punishment. Monte reined in and greeted the two women who were picking spring flowers to brighten the interior of the house.

"Mornin', Miz Sally. Mornin', ma'am. These two belong to someone out here? Least they say they do."

Mary-Beth looked up with apprehension and surprise. "Why, they are my sons. Where did you find them?"

"In town, ma'am."

A fleeting frown spread on Mary-Beth's forehead. "Seth, Sammy, didn't I tell you not to leave this place? It is wild and dangerous out there."

"There's more to it than that, ma'am."

"Why, what do you mean—ah—Sheriff?"

"I caught them in the general store, stealin' horehound drops from a jar."

Predictably, Mary-Beth sprang to the defense of her sons. "That's not possible. My sons never steal."

Monte nodded to the boys. "Unlike these two, I never lie, ma'am."

"They don't lie, either."

"Oh? Then they are the sons of Johnny Ringo, and he and his gang will come get me if I don't let them go?" Monte maintained a straight face as he related the wild tale the boys had spun.

Shocked, her shoulders slumped with defeat, Mary-Beth Gittings resorted to a woman's best defense—tears. She dropped her bouquet and covered her eyes with both hands. Her body shook with sobs.

"Whatever am I to do? My hus-husband is nearly always away on business. And when he is home, he spoils the children abominably. I feel so helpless. Someone tell me how to deal with these things?"

Unconvinced by her performance, Monte snorted in disgust. Sally, equally dubious, smiled sweetly. "It's simple," she spelled out for her guest. "First, you talk to them and explain that what they did was wrong. That such behavior by children or adults is not tolerated by society."

"What do I do then?"

"Excuse me. I'll be right back and tell you."

Sally went into the house and directly to one corner of her kitchen. Then she returned, one hand held behind her. "Now comes the part that has the most positive effect. You yank down their britches and smack the hell out of them," she concluded, revealing the thin willow switch she had held behind her back.

Monte Carson whooped with laughter. "Now, that sounds like jist the thing. I'll haul them down and you do that, ma'am. You do that right now."

Dohatsa tugged at his forelock and looked down at his moccasin-clad feet in the manner his people had been taught since the Spanish first came. He was not conscious of his hand extended with palm up. The small bag of coins that dropped into it felt heavy indeed. It made Dohatsa glow inwardly.

"That's me good lad, Dohatsa. Now you go back to yer mud houses and stir up some mischief for me, won't ye now?" Paddy Quinn grinned at the young Tua warrior.

With another nod, Dohatsa tucked the money behind the wide, yellow sash that he wore over his shirttail and loincloth. Then he turned and trotted off toward the distant Tua pueblo located north and a bit west of Taos. Whitewater Paddy Quinn turned his horse and walked away in the opposite direction. He had other errands to perform.

There was that fat, stupid policeman in Taos who must be paid his monthly stipend, who reminded Paddy of another lawman he'd known, the reason Paddy had decided to come to America. Dead policemen, even a white pudding of a bobby in Dublin town, raised quite a row. In Boston he had quickly learned that the fine art of bribery got one far more benefit than did muscle. Not a copper, it had seemed, that wasn't on the take. Inevitably, Paddy had encountered the exception to the rule. A lad from the old sod at that. John Preston Sullivan. Which was what had brought Patrick Michael Quinn to the West. No doubt Sullivan still searched the alleyways of Boston for him. Ten years to the day and Quinn was now the boss of the largest gang of cutthroats, highwaymen and robbers on the frontier. Which reminded him that Garth Thompson and some of the lads had something on for later that afternoon. Sure ought to stir things up a mite.

Smoke Jensen rode at ease alongside Diego Alvarado. The hacienda had put out flankers and two men on point for protection even here on his own huge ranch. Those visible rode with their rifles across their thighs, and were in sight of others farther out. It had been so, Don Diego had explained, since the first raid by the rustlers. More likely, Smoke reckoned, it had been so since the first Alvarados came here in the fifteen hundreds. He suggested the possibility.

"It was like this the last time I visited, if I recall correctly."

"Yes, *los Indios* were raiding."

Cougar whuffled softly, and Smoke popped his next question. "And in your father's time?"

Diego chuckled, a low, throaty sound. "There was a war. We had you gringos to combat, if you recall."

"And your grandfather?"

"The revolution against the Spanish. My family fought for Mexico."

Smoke waved at the vaquero bodyguards. "So this arrangement is nothing new?"

"I thought not to make you uncomfortable. This is a cruel, wild land. Most unforgiving. Not all of the danger comes from two-legged foes. Tell me, my friend, did you come to any conclusion as to how to deal with Satterlee?"

A smile crinkled Smoke's lips. "I slept too soundly. Too much tequila, I suppose. I'm not accustomed to much strong drink. Beer is more my style."

Diego appeared intrigued by this. "For a man who does not drink much, you show a lot of machismo, amigo."

Smoke avoided a response by a study of the distance. Up ahead, he saw a flock of sheep, herded by half a dozen small boys ranging from ten to twelve. It made him think of Ian MacGreggor. "Diego, I have a friend who is looking for work. He speaks Spanish and rides well. But . . . he's a farmer's son. I promised him I'd ask you if you had need of anyone like that on the ranch."

Diego considered that a moment. "Enrique Toledo is growing old. His bones ache him. Perhaps he would welcome a younger assistant. When would this young man want to start?"

"After I've taken care of this business with Satterlee."

Diego cocked an eyebrow. "He is secretly involved in this?"

Smoke pulled a droll face. "In a manner of speaking. He is looking into some things for me. I haven't seen him in a couple of days."

Drawing a deep breath, Diego made his decision. "I will suggest something to Enrique. I am sure he will welcome the idea of help."

10

A large mesquite bush toppled down a rocky slope to block the road, located twenty miles outside of Taos. Its sudden appearance did not rattle the driver of the Butterfield stage that ground its way along the narrow, rutted trace. He hauled in on the reins and worked the brake with his booted foot, the long wooden lever operated by an angle iron that jutted from the underside. Too late, he realized the purpose of the fallen bush.

Swarming out of defiles and crevasses, a dozen men in the colorful, loose clothing and braided headbands of the Pueblo Indians closed around the coach. They wore high-top moccasins and long, black hair. All of them carried rifles or revolvers at the ready. With eyes keen and knowledgeable, the driver sized up these Indian highwaymen and reached a quick conclusion. He shared it in a whisper with the express guard.

"Injuns don't rob coaches."

At once, the shotgun rider brought up his short-barreled L.C. Smith 10-gauge and discharged a round. The shot splattered the shoulder of one pseudo-Indian, who howled involuntarily and cursed in English.

"I tol' you so," the driver hollered as he reached for his six-gun. "Ain't one of them's an Injun."

An arrow thudded into his chest and skewered his

heart. He folded sideways as the six-up team came to a halt before the prickly branches. Two revolvers cracked, and the guard dropped his shotgun. Blood spurted from his shattered shoulder. "I don't believe a thing he said," he babbled.

They killed him anyway. While two of the Quinn gang held the headstalls of the lead team, another ambled his horse over to the coach and grunted in his best imitation of an Indian. "You get out. Put up hands. Give money. Much money."

"Make fast, squaw," another demanded of a hefty dowager who whimpered and jiggled as she climbed from the stage.

Quickly the outlaws gathered the valuables from the passengers while others released the draft team. After securing the strongbox, the members of the Quinn gang rode off, scattering the stage horses ahead of them. That left the frightened, demoralized passengers to fend for themselves. One of them, a portly man in a green checkered suit, expressed the astonishment of them all.

"Well, I never. Indians actually robbing a stagecoach. We have to get to the way station and find help."

Her cheeks ashen, the dowager suggested, "Someone should go on to Taos."

"Lady, we're on foot. It's too far to Taos. We'll find someone at the relay post with a horse. Then we'll report these Indians to the law."

On a low knoll, beyond his palatial hacienda outside Santa Fe, shaded by an ancient cottonwood, Clifton Satterlee watched the convolutions of an attractive young woman. Martha Estes was his house guest, the daughter of one of his business associates. That did not serve as a deterrent for Satterlee, whose lust guided him. His wife had decided to return east and visit her family, so he knew himself to be free to pursue and conquer the lovely Martha. To do so, he had set forth on a subtle seduction.

From her position, where she exercised her horse, Martha Estes studied Clifton Satterlee from under the brim of a rakishly cocked, feminine version of a man's top hat. The bright green, crushed-velvet head adornment with its scarlet feather contrasted nicely with the red cape and riding skirt of the same material. She had become well aware that Satterlee was engaged in a skillful seduction, and it amused her. But why all the elaborate preamble, when all he need do was ask?

He needn't have given her pearls, or the promise of a luxurious house in Taos. She would have happily fallen into bed with him on the afternoon of her arrival. Her loins ached and throbbed with desire. Clifton represented power, raw, naked strength, and the willingness to employ it. Martha had hungered for him since her eleventh year, when he and her father had become associated in some slightly shady enterprises. Now, eight years later, her craving had not diminished. If anything, it had grown to unbearable dimension. She abandoned her musings to give Clifton a cheery wave and rode up to join him.

"You are a magnificent horsewoman, Martha."

"Thank you, Clifton. It is one of my . . . lesser accomplishments." She lowered long, silver-blond lashes over cobalt eyes in a coy invitation.

"Let's proceed on, shall we? There is a charming little place I want to show you."

"We'll picnic there?"

"Yes, my dear Martha. And while away the hotter part of the afternoon. The natives call it *siesta,* and I heartily recommend it."

Half an hour's ride brought them to the reverse slope of a larger knob. There stately, ancient palo duro trees shaded a trio of deep tanks which had formed in depressions of solid rock. Martha clapped her hands in delight. Clifton Satterlee dismounted and helped her from the cumbersome sidesaddle. He held the heavy picnic basket while Martha spread a blanket. He came to kneel beside her then, and put out their repast. Martha's eyes sparkled as she took in the elaborate fare.

"Is that really a *paté de fois en brochet?*"

"Yes, it is, Martha. Goose liver at that. And we have sliced ham, roast beef, pickled tongue. Oh, so many things."

Martha Estes affected an insincere pout. "You'll make me fat and unattractive."

Clifton patted one gloved hand. "Never, my dear. Many men are strongly enamored of full-figured women. I am, myself, I have to admit. Though I will say that you wear svelteness to perfection."

A trill of pleased laughter came from Martha. "You flatter me shamelessly. Um, I am hungry. A morning's ride always stimulates my appetite."

"I brought wine," Clifton offered.

"How thoughtful. I hope you brought a corkscrew."

Clifton produced the tool with a flourish. "I thought of everything."

Martha began filling her plate while Clifton opened the bottle. Then he availed himself of the splendid viands and poured wine for both of them. Sunlight sparkled off the clear water of the tanks. Overhead, cactus wrens twittered in domestic harmony while they sought grubs to feed their young. After some thoughtful chewing, Martha brought up the subject of the house in Taos.

"When do I get to see my house in Taos?"

"Soon. Within three days, I should think."

"Wasn't it once owned by a Mexican family?"

"Yes, it was. A family named Figueroa. They named a price I could hardly refuse."

Affecting a jaunty swagger he did not recognize as his own, Ian MacGreggor pushed through the glass-beaded curtain that formed the entryway of Cantina Jalisco, in Taos. Half a dozen hard-faced men had gathered at one end of the bar. They drank beer from glazed clay pots.

Even to Mac's untutored eyes, they all appeared to pay deference to a burly, barrel-chested man at the center of the group. Mac walked up near them and ordered a beer. The bartender took in the six-gun at Mac's hip and served him without question. Mac lifted the foam-capped container in salute to the Irish-looking, beefy man and pulled off a long swallow.

It nearly choked him, but he did not let on since he felt all eyes turned to him. After another swallow, he walked closer to the hard cases and addressed the man in the bowler. "Might you be a gentleman known as Paddy Quinn?"

Eyes narrowed, Whitewater Paddy Quinn fired a question of his own. "Who might it be that is askin', is it now?"

"I'm known as Mac. Ian MacGreggor."

Quinn smiled. "A fellow celt, as I live and breathe. It is said that the clan MacGreggor defended Queen Mary and the faith. Would ye be of those MacGreggors?"

Mac tilted his beer pot to Quinn. "Aye."

"And for what is it ye'd be wantin' Paddy Quinn?"

"I hear you are hiring gunhands for a man named Satterlee."

Paddy held up a cautionary hand. "Sure an' we don't be mentionin' certain names in so public a place. Say, rather, that I be hirin' for mesel', ye should."

"Well, then, for yourself?"

"What if I be? You don't look dry behind the ears."

Mac eyed Quinn levelly. "You have heard of Billy Bonney?"

That gave Quinn a good laugh. "Sure an' it's a lot of horse dung if yer tryin' to pass yerself off as Billy the Kid."

"No, I'm not. But, Billy was not yet dry behind his ears when he killed his sixth man. I'm not in his class, but I'm good with a gun."

"Are you now? Suppose we go out behind this place and you show me."

"I'm not calling you out, Mr. Quinn. All I say is that I am fast and I hit what I shoot at."

Quinn stepped forward, away from the bar, and patted Mac on one shoulder. "Nah—nah, don't fash yerself, lad. I was thinkin' of whiskey bottles, or better still beer bottles. They make smaller targets. One o' me boys could throw them up, say two at a time, and you draw and break them both before one hits the ground."

When there had been money enough for powder and lead to make reloads, Mac had practiced at that often enough to feel confident. "I think I can do that."

"Come along, then." Quinn turned to the bartender. "*Oye,* Paco. We're gonna take some of your empties out and make little pieces of glass out of them."

Paco shrugged. "Whatever you say, Señor Quinn."

Behind the saloon, the gunmen stood to one side, except for one, who reached to a stack of wooden cartons and extracted two beer bottles. He faced quarter front to Ian MacGreggor. Paddy Quinn gave his instructions at Mac's side. "When I nod, Huber there will throw the bottles in the air. You draw and fire at will."

With that, Quinn stepped behind Mac, so the youth could not see him give the signal. Not hesitating for a second, Paddy nodded to Huber. Two beer bottles sailed into the air. The moment they came into Mac's line of sight, he made his move. Before the two containers reached the apex of their arc, he had his six-gun halfway out of the holster. His first shot blasted a bottle to fragments a heartbeat later. The second clear glass cylinder seemed to hover at the peak, then turned to a bright shower of slivers as a second bullet struck. The gun was back in Mac's holster before Quinn could recover from his involuntary blink.

Quinn scowled, unconvinced. "Try that again."

Mac did, with the same results.

"One more time, lad."

Both bottles broke this time before either had reached the apex. "B'God, it's fast ye are. Only one little thing, there is. I wonder how you would perform if the target was shootin' back at ye?"

Mac considered that a moment, then decided to answer with a cleaned-up version of the truth. "A friend of mine and I were jumped on the way here to Taos. Four men. I killed one of them, and Joe took care of the others."

Quinn cocked an eyebrow. "Who'd you say that was?"

"You wouldn't know him. Joe Evans, from over Texas way, where I come from."

"He your age?"

Mac kept his gaze cool and level. "No, sir. He's older. Around twenty-five."

"Would he be lookin' for the same thing you came after?"

"No, sir, Mr. Quinn. He rode on to Santa Fe."

"Well, then," Quinn boomed with a hearty clap on Mac's shoulder. "It looks like we got us only one more good gunhand. You'll do, young MacGreggor. At first, I'll be puttin' you with someone more experienced. At least until ye get yer feet wet, so's to speak. You'll be paid sixty dollars a month. Ammunition bought for you. Later, there'll be a share of any spoils we bring in. Now, then, go settle up with wherever ye've been stayin' an' meet us ten miles out on the road to Questa."

Their rumps sore from unaccustomed hours in the saddle, two frightened and wounded survivors of the Butterfield Stage Line robbery trotted their borrowed mounts into Taos in late afternoon. They asked for directions to the sheriff's office and for water to drink in that order. Next the two men stopped at a public horse trough and refreshed their flagging animals, industriously working the pump to bring up fresh for themselves. The sheriff's office came next.

"Sheriff," one blurted as they stumbled through the door. "The stage from Albuquerque got robbed outside town about twenty miles. We were on it. Owens here took a nick in the shoulder. All I got's a scratch. But the guard and driver are both dead. It was Injuns done it, sure's you're born."

Sheriff Banner had strong doubts that the Tua, or any of the Pueblo Indians, had taken to robbing stages. "You got a good look at these highwaymen?"

"That's what we just told you, Sheriff. Long black hair, head bands, floppy clothing. Swarthy skin and mean as hell. Oh, they was Injuns right enough."

Banner remained unconvinced. "What way did they ride when they left?"

"To the west."

"Toward San Vincente?"

"What's that? We don't know the area."

"It's a pueblo and mission out that way. But the San Vincente Pueblos are even more peaceful than the Tuas."

"They talked funny English and rode bareback," Owens added helpfully.

"Anyone can talk funny and ride bareback. Did they speak any Spanish or Indian tongue?"

Owens cut his eyes to his companion. "Nope. Come to think, all they did speak was English."

Banner rubbed his hands together in satisfaction. "Well, gentlemen, I think you have been had. Sounds to me like white road agents done up to look like Indians. At last, that's the way I'm going to look into it." Banner turned to the door and called out. "Wally, come in here."

Wally Gower, who had been lurking outside the door to learn any gems of news he could sell to the editor of the Taos *Clarion*, popped around the door frame and darted to the sheriff's desk. "Yes, sir?"

"Dang you for a rascal, Wally. But this time you can be of some good use. I want you to ride out to Rancho de la Gloria. Ask for Smoke Jensen and tell him to please come in. Say I have something interesting for him to look into."

"Yes, sir. I'll do it right now."

"Good. There'll be two bits in it for you."

"Gosh. That much? I never get more than a nickel."

"You will this time. There's a lot of trouble brewin' out there. Now, get along."

Wally Gower led an ideal life for a kid. He was footloose and, for the most part, unsupervised. His father had been injured in a mining accident several years ago in Colorado. While his father remained unable to work and stayed at home to care for the seven children, his mother did custom alterations and general sewing for Señora Montez, the fashionable Spanish lady who owned a large women's clothing store in Taos. When school let out for the summer, Wally gleefully abandoned studies, shoes, and often shirt, to hang around town doing odd jobs for the money it brought in for the family. A lot of his time went to swimming with friends at the many *tanques* outside the town, or in pulling slippery rainbow trout from the icy creeks fed by snowmelt in the Sangre de Cristo range. He liked it most when the sheriff had something for him to do. The lawman paid better than anyone else. Wally was glad he had a pony he could use for this present assignment.

It was a small, shaggy mustang and only partly broken to saddle. But Wally loved Spuds with all his heart. He went to the small stable house behind their adobe home and saddled Spuds. He led the snorting half-wild animal from its stall, plucked a parsnip from last winter's garden and fed it to Spuds. Chomping pleasurably, the pony ground the pungent root vegetable into a mash which it swallowed. Wally put one bare foot in the stirrup and swung aboard. He angled Spuds toward the alleyway behind the Gower home. Had it been anyone else atop the little horse, it would have exploded into crow hops and sunfishing that would have unseated any but the most expert horse breakers.

Wally trotted toward the western edge of town and the trail southwest to the Alvarado ranch. He reached the scattered fringe of small, poor Mexican adobe homes when he found out that life in Taos had drastically changed for the foreseeable future.

Three hard cases leaned against a low adobe wall, with two split rails atop. When Wally approached, the lean, tallest one eased upright and stepped into the road. He raised a hand and spoke in a low, menacing voice.

"Whoa-up, sonny. Where do you think yer goin'?"

A quick thinker, Wally invented something he hoped would be believed. "Out to where my paw works."

"Where's that?"

"Uh—the Bradfords' B-Bar-X."

Eyes narrowed in accusation, the clipped words challenged Wally. "He ain't come through here since we've been here."

"Oh, no. He goes out before dawn."

"Well, there ain't nobody goin' out of town from now on without our say-so."

Wally pulled another appeal from his ingenuity. "Bu—but my paw will beat my tail if I don't bring him his coat. He's got night guard tonight."

A nasty sneer answered him. "That's your problem, kid. If you're smart, you'll do what you are told. You go on back now, get lost and tell that sheriff friend of yours nothing."

"Yes, sir. I suppose you're right, sir."

Being a plucky lad, Wally turned on the first side street, cut his way through several blocks and went directly to Hank Banner's office. He made his report with wide-eyed excitement. Hank listened to him with a growing frown. Then he made a suggestion that appealed to the adventurous nature of the boy.

"Well, then, why don't you ride out the other side of town?"

"Sure enough, Sheriff. Right away."

Wally dusted out the door and swung into the saddle. He drubbed bare heels into the flanks of Spuds and started for the east end of town. He made it half a mile out of Taos this time. Four of the biggest, meanest-looking men Wally had ever seen in his eleven years blocked the entire road. A line of people on foot, in wagons and on horseback had formed in front of them. The surly fellows allowed free entry to town, but denied departure to all except for the poorest *campesinos* and mission Indians. Patiently, though with mounting apprehension, Wally waited his turn. He tried his "taking a coat to Paw" story again and was again turned back.

On his own, Wally tried the south road out of town. This time he believed he had it all figured out. When he saw an angry-looking farmer and his family headed back for town in a wagon, Wally hailed them and asked if the road was closed.

"Why, yes, son, how did you know?" the wife asked.

Wally worked his shoulders up and down. "I got turned back two places already. What is goin' on?"

"Some bad folks up there, boy," the farmer told Wally. "Best thing for you to do is turn around and go back now."

Wally scrunched his freckle-speckled button nose. "How far to where they are?"

Scratching his head, the farmer figured on that. "Quarter mile, maybe a little more. Beyond that bend yonder."

"Thank you, sir," Wally replied politely.

He turned Spuds' nose to the west and cut across a field in the direction of Pacheca Creek. Keeping constantly alert, Wally looked to the threat on his left as he progressed through a corn field and into a pasture beyond. He did not see the men who he now knew to be nothing more than outlaws, so he felt confident they could not see him. A line of cottonwoods and aspen marked the course of the creek. He pulled up inside the screen and leaned down to pat Spuds on the neck.

"You're gonna get cold, Spuds. So am I. We gotta swim our way around those fellers. When we git outta the crick, I'll rub you down and dry off, then we'll cut to the southwest and head for the Alvarado spread." Wally reached in his hip pocket and produced another parsnip, which he fed to Spuds.

Dismounting, Wally led his pony to the creek bank and stepped gingerly out on the sand and pebble-strewn streambed. They stayed in the shallows for a while, the water frigid and hip-high on Wally. When he gauged they had come close to being opposite the hard cases, he urged Spuds out into the current, and they both swam past, gooseflesh forming under Wally's shirt.

When he reached a spot he considered safe, Wally swam cross-current until he gained footing. Spuds reached solid underpinning first and surged forward past the boy's slim shoulders. Wally stumbled behind. On the bank at last, boy and beast stood shivering.

"That was colder than I thought, boy," Wally admitted through chattering teeth. "Gotta strip and warm up."

With that he pulled off his wet clothes and threw himself down on a sun-warmed rock. Before long, the chill subsided, Wally's eyelids drooped and he fell into a light sleep.

11

Nearing the end of the first week's visit by the Gittings, tension hung over the Sugarloaf. Normally a direct, outspoken person, Sally Jensen repressed her instinctive reaction to Mary-Beth's feather-headedness and the constant misbehavior of her undisciplined brood. As a result, Sally's old friendship with Mary-Beth was in conflict with her good sense. Put simply, Sally knew she should firmly demand that they leave.

Especially when Seth and Sammy had escaped their deserved spanking for stealing the candy. Oh, Mary-Beth had switched them—two half-hearted whacks on buttocks that had not even been bared. Both boys shot sneers at Sally and laughed openly over the lightness of their punishment as they walked away. That had been two days ago, and the situation seemed to worsen by the hour. From the direction of the corral, a boy's voice, raised in anger, reminded her of that.

"Stop that! Stop it, damn you, Seth, Sammy. Those foals can be hurt real easy."

It was Bobby's voice. Sally wondered what devilment the Gittings boys had gotten up to this time. If it was serious enough, she would find out right soon. She had asked their foreman, Ike Mitchell, to keep an eye on the rebellious boys, and to take matters into his own hands if need be. Since he had been successful on earlier occasions, she also implied the same to Bobby.

The boy was more than capable of taking responsibility for himself. He could act in a responsible manner toward others as well, Sally reasoned. Bobby's voice once more cut through her self-examination. "Hey, what are you doin'? Quit that."

Then came a long silence. Sally's apprehension rose.

Bobby Jensen came upon Seth and Sammy Gittings at the small corral outside the foaling barn. There the mares and their newborn could exercise away from the rest of the herd. Both of the younger boys had taken it in mind that it would be funny to watch the reactions of the small horses when they pelted them with rocks. Bobby looked on in shock and anger as two missiles struck a stalky-legged foal and it ran off squealing in terror to find its mother. The building rage pushed out the disgust Bobby felt. He stepped in at once, voice raised to a strident shout.

"Stop that."

Seth and Sammy looked blankly over their shoulders at Bobby, and the younger boy stuck out his tongue. As one, they hefted fresh rocks and hurled them at another colt. Bobby's voice deepened with his outrage.

"Stop it, damn you, Seth, Sammy. Those foals can be hurt real easy."

"Oh, yeah?" Seth challenged in a quiet voice. "Says who?"

Sammy added his opinion. "Yeah. 'Sides, it's funny when they make that noise and run around."

Bobby's voice grew low and menacing. "You stop that or I'll make you hurt like you've never hurt before."

Seth sneered. "No you won't. Mother won't let you."

With that, both Gittings boys turned and chucked stones at Bobby Jensen. One struck his left shoulder with enough force to hurt, though it merely angered him more. He tried once again to end their assault. "Hey, what are you doin'. Quit that."

Laughing, the boys threw more rocks. For a moment, while he dodged the fresh onslaught, Bobby thought of pulling his six-gun and blasting the both of them to oblivion. A satisfying, warm rush washed through him. Then he remembered what Smoke had taught him. Only a coward settles something with a gun that he can handle with his fists. Accordingly, Bobby rushed the smaller boys and threw Sammy to the ground. Seth leaped at him and swung a fist that contained a healthy-sized stone. It struck Bobby on the forehead and split the skin.

Blood began to run down through one white-blond eyebrow and into Bobby's left eye. He ignored the discomfort and shot a fist to the nose of Seth Gittings, who dropped the rock, screeching his agony. Bobby grabbed the front of Seth's shirt with both hands and hurled him to the ground. He stood over the supine boys a long, silent minute while they whined and sniveled. Satisfied that the incident had ended, Bobby turned away and started off to clean up his cut and patch it. Another rock, hurled in defiance, decided Bobby that he would report the situation to Sally after all.

Sally Jensen looked with mounting fury at the rising lump on Bobby's forehead and the court plaster he had stuck on the cut. "That cuts it, damnit!" Although she rarely swore, Sally thought the situation called for it.

Bobby Jensen looked at her with clear, wide eyes. "What are we going to do?"

"You are going to stand back and make the accusation. I am going to take care of what has needed doing for a long time." She crossed to the stove corner and brought out her willow switch, then moved to the door to the hallway and called into the depths of the house. "Mary-Beth, come here right away."

When Mary-Beth arrived, she took one look at the

limber willow wand, and her cheeks lost color. A hand flew to the corner of her mouth. "Oh, no. Not again. Not my boys."

"Oh, yes, Mary-Beth, dear. Take a look at Bobby's forehead. Seth attacked him with a rock. Smashed him in the head, then threw another that bruised him between his shoulder blades. You are coming with me right this minute and put an end to it."

Sally took a firm hold on Mary-Beth's left wrist and literally pulled her to the outside kitchen door. With Bobby at her other side, Sally strode to the foaling barn. They rounded the corner in time to see Seth connect with another of the frightened, tormented foals. Sally did not temper her words.

"You will stop that this instant, you little monster."

Impudent defiance shone in the eyes of Seth Gittings. "We don't have to, do we, Mother?"

Sammy let escape a revealing statement. "Yeah, you said we could do anything we wanted."

Shocked to the core at last, Mary-Beth stammered a partial denial. "I—I said no such thing. I said you could do anything you wanted, so long as it did no harm to others."

Seth whined in protest of his innocence. "We didn't hurt anyone. All we did was tease the little horsies some."

Bobby could contain his outrage no longer. "Then you turned on me and threw rocks at me. When I pushed Sammy down, you hit me in the head."

Sally advanced on the boys. At the last moment, she whirled to Mary-Beth. "Either you do what is necessary, Mary-Beth, or I will do it for you."

Faced with such determination, Mary-Beth came forward and took the willow switch from Sally. She started after Sammy first. His small face took on an expression of horror, and he tried to back away, arms extended, palms outward to ward off imagined blows.

"No, don't. You can't hit me with that. Poppa wouldn't like that. No, Mother. Please."

Without a word, her lips set in a grim line, Mary-Beth yanked down Sammy's trousers and bent him over one knee. Then she laid on with a dozen good, hard, swift blows. He howled, shrieked and wailed, tears flowed freely from his eyes. When she had finished, she put him on his feet again.

"You, young man, will not leave the house for the next three days. Now, Seth, it's your turn. You are old enough to know better."

"You can't do this! I won't let you," Seth screamed in utter panic. *"No, Momma, please!* You can't, you can't."

A wild light glowed behind golden lashes as Mary-Beth spoke wonderingly, more to Sally and herself than to the boy. "You know, I just discovered that I can indeed."

In a thrice, Seth received the same treatment as Sammy. Only this time his mother delivered fifteen strokes before ending it. A very satisfied Sally Jensen looked on. When Seth again stood before her, still blubbering, she had further admonishment for him. "If you ever, ever again use a weapon on an animal or another person, whether it is a rock or a knife or, God forbid, a gun, I will beat you to within an inch of your life. Now apologize to Bobby this instant."

"Alejandro will round up those among my vaqueros who can shoot the best," Diego Alvarado told Smoke Jensen.

Ten minutes after Wally Gower arrived at Rancho de la Gloria, Smoke Jensen and fifteen vaqueros rode out for town. The boy kept station close beside Smoke, his chest puffed with pride. They soon came upon several disgruntled people who had been turned back from town, and from them learned more details of the roadblocks.

"Beats all hell," one long-faced rancher observed. "There was six of them when we made to enter town. Told me an' the boys to turn about and high-tail it for home. Said that the town was closed 'til further notice. Who can do a thing like that?"

"From what I've heard," said Smoke Jensen, with a nod toward Wally Gower, "it's Whitewater Paddy Quinn."

A glower answered Smoke. "That no-account. Claims to be foreman for some outfit called C.S. Enterprises. Common outlaw, you ask me."

"I think you have the right of it, sir," Smoke agreed.

They rode on, allowing the horses to walk only when they began to retch and grunt from exertion. In that manner, they made it to a point where they could observe the roadblock from a distance. Smoke studied the activity, noting that people no longer queued up to attempt to leave town. Smoke sent Wally back beyond range and turned to the Mexican cowboys.

"First things first," he told them. "We're going to take out these *bandidos*, then move around to each road entering town and do the same."

"Do we kill them, Señor Smoke?" Bernal Sandoval asked.

Smoke eyed him levelly. "We're not here to kiss them, Bernal."

"Muy bien." He turned to his companions. *"Adelante, muchachos."*

Smoke led the way as they charged down on the outlaws ahead. With weapons at the ready, they closed in a cloud of red dust. Quinn's men turned at the sound of pounding hooves, and the one in the center of the road shouted a challenge.

"Rein in and turn around. Nobody gets into town today. This is your last chance. Do it now or you'll be hurtin'."

With a firm tug on Cougar's reins, Smoke halted first and took careful aim. He intentionally shot the hard case in charge through the left shoulder. The man grunted and raised his own six-gun. It barked loudly, but without effect. Smoke had given him his chance, and he had not taken it. So the last mountain man put a bullet through the chest of the outlaw. At once the gunman's underlings opened fire.

Not lacking in courage, the vaqueros sent a storm of hot lead into the rank that partitioned the road. Slugs from both sides whipped and cracked through the air. More dust churned up, to mingle with powder smoke and obscure the view. From the midst of the haze, a man screamed. Another called for help. Alejandro silenced him. Two vaqueros cursed in Spanish. Another ragged volley rippled across the hilly ground. Then, on the far side of the melee, a horse sprinted free. Its rider cried out in near hysteria.

"Get out before they kill us all!"

Within five seconds, the roar of gunfire dwindled to silence. The dust blew away on a stiff breeze, and the vaqueros began to slap one another on the back and congratulate themselves for the easy victory. Smoke Jensen gave them a couple of seconds, then called them together.

"We'll go on to the next. Alejandro, you take half our men and come at them at an angle; we'll take them head on. No time to waste until we clean out all of these skunks." He beckoned to Wally and the boy joined him expectantly.

Yank Hastings had been with the Quinn gang for three years. He had seen the scruffy rabble of low-grade highwaymen and rustlers turned into a finely tuned force, not unlike an army. At the constant goading of Paddy Quinn and Garth Thompson, they had cleaned up their collective rag-tag, unwashed appearance. They had practiced with their weapons until they had reached a proficiency unheard of among most common bandits. Every man now took orders without questioning them, obeyed to the letter or died trying. They robbed banks like precision machines; they learned the skills of intimidation to add to their ability to use force; those most skilled at it stole cattle by the whole herd, rather than

wenty or thirty had at a time. It made Yank Hastings
proud to be among their number.

That was why it shocked him, then, when two of the
gang ran down on their barricade on the Taos-Raton
road on frothing horses. Their eyes wide with panic, they
shouted that an attack was imminent.

"A bunch of Mezkin cowboys hit our roadblock jist a
while ago," one blurted out "They shot hell outta Cort
an' Davey and lit out after us toward here."

"Yeah. They'll be here any minute," his companion
assured.

Yank had started to calm them and discredit their
fears when a bullet cracked overhead. He looked beyond
them with a stunned expression.

Alejandro Alvarado and seven vaqueros raced
toward the roadblock at an oblique angle to the road.
It had been Alejandro who had fired at Yank. Hastings
holstered his six-gun and drew his rifle. He was not
about to let this jumped-up "Mezkin" get the better of
him. He worked the lever to chamber a round and felt
a stunning pain in his hand as a bullet struck the small
of the stock. Fingers numbed, he dropped the weapon
as he stared in disbelief while seven more vaqueros, led
by a white man, stormed toward them along the road.
The air filled with deadly bees as the attackers blazed
away at Yank and his men. He had to do something,
and fast.

"Everybody dismount. Josh, take the horses back. The
rest of you get in those rocks. Hold your fire until you
have a sure target."

Quickly the men spread out to take positions of at
least partial cover. Undeterred, the riders came on.
Return fire spurted from the muzzles of guns in the outlaws' hands. From a peaceful, quiet afternoon, the world
had swiftly changed into a place of noise, fury, and
death. The fighting intensified. Suddenly, a whole swarm
of Quinn's hard cases appeared over a low rise and
charged toward the attackers.

* * *

Smoke Jensen watched the approach of the reinforcements and made a quick decision. He turned aside and cantered back a hundred yards to where Wally Gower had hunkered down in a pile of boulders. He leaned forward and spoke urgently to the boy.

"Wally, I want you to ride like lightning back to where we cleaned out that first roadblock. Then skedaddle into town and go to the sheriff. Tell him what we are doing and to get some men here right now."

"Yes, sir, I can do that."

Wally sprinted off on his pony before Smoke could wish him good luck. Smoke turned back to the battle that had developed in his absence. The vaqueros appeared to hold their own. They kept moving, making difficult targets of themselves. Smoke located one outlaw, who had climbed high on the rocks and now took careful aim with a Winchester at Alejandro Alvarado. Smoke settled Cougar with a pat on the neck and sighted in on the exposed target. When he had what he wanted, he gave a sharp whistle and shouted to the hard case.

"Over here!"

Obligingly the man turned, so that Smoke caught him in the upper left chest with his first round. Quickly Smoke cycled the action of his Express rifle and fired again. A shower of volcanic rock chips formed a plume behind the thug after the bullet exited along the midline of his body. He flopped back down and lay still. Smoke sought another target. He had no lack of them, he soon discovered.

Outlaws milled everywhere. The new arrivals had been slow in taking to the rocks. Diego's vaqueros made a good harvest among them. Bodies sprawled in the grotesque postures of the dead and dying. Smoke saw another man seeking a vantage point high in the rocks. Quickly he raised his Winchester. The discharge of a heavy .44 revolver close by caused Cougar to flinch and side-step at the moment the weapon fired. A torrent of dark, red-brown, porous rock exploded in the face of the gunman.

His sharp cry of pain sounded over the tumult of battle. Smoke levered a fresh round into the chamber and felt the hot breath of a bullet kiss his cheek. Unflinching, he raised the sights into line and shot the author of that close call through the breastbone. Smoke made a quick count. They had taken a hefty toll of the gang. The advantage of numbers had shifted to their side. Only one vaquero showed signs of having taken a wound. And that, Smoke noted, seemed slight. Smoke was about to call to the Mexican cowboys to rally and storm the rocks when more of the outlaw gang closed in, led by Garth Thompson.

Santan Tossa kneeled at the edge of the sacred sand painting and examined the evidence. Someone had come again to the kiva and stolen several of the religious articles stored there. The footprint of the culprit was distinctive. Much wider than usual, longer also, it served as a signature. Santan Tossa knew to whom the splayed foot belonged. He and several others had been most vocal about raising up the entire male population of the tua pueblo and striking at the outsiders who had invaded their land. And he thought he knew who it was that they worked for.

There was a white man, a round-eye, named Satterlee. This would be the one. He had come to the pueblo to talk the elders into giving him permission to cut trees, a whole lot of trees, on their land. It had been refused, of course. Many of the trees were very old, older than the memories of the Tua. So old as to have shaded the Anasazi, those mysterious dwellers of the time of legends. Santan Tossa had noted the glow of greed in Satterlee's eyes as he had looked upon the sacred amulets, bracelets and necklaces in their niches. Now, fully half of them had disappeared. How much, he wondered, had Dohatsa taken to become a thief?

No matter the reason or the reward, this required help from outside the pueblo. Although he didn't like it, Tossa knew he must take his findings to the white lawman in Taos. He was powerless to investigate anyone not of the pueblo, but the sheriff would know how to go about it. Thus decided, Santan Tossa made a quick examination of the remainder of the kiva and exited through the hole in the roof. He went directly to the small corral on the southeast side of the compound and caught up one of his ponies.

Tossa rode the short three miles to the low adobe wall that surrounded the outsider town of Taos. There he went directly to the sheriff's office. To his surprise, he found it empty. He would wait. Now that he had committed himself to this course, he might as well see it through. While he bided his time, Tossa reflected on conditions at the pueblo.

Theft of the religious objects had been a shock to those who knew—and not all did—and also a source of much justified anger. As a tribal policeman, he kept his own counsel, but Santan Tossa did not question the rightness of his suspicions. Some of the hotheads among the young warriors had been most vocal in demanding retribution against the whites, whom they felt certain had stolen the object. Particularly Dohatsa, who had called a meeting of his warrior society in the kiva the previous night. After the meeting would have been an ideal time to steal the missing items. Santan Tossa had attended the gathering, although he had not been made to feel welcome. Now he recalled what had happened. . . .

Firelight flickered off the bare, bronze shoulders of Dohatsa as he addressed the Puma Society members. "Brothers, we all know that precious articles of our religion have been stolen. It is clear to me who is responsible. It is white men. Not the Mexicans, not even the Spanish before them, would touch any of our holy relics. They considered them heathen and forbidden. Their lust was for gold not silver. So they discounted even the value of our most treasured works.

"I know that somewhere, our sacred squash blossoms and shells decorate the body of a white woman, maybe more than one. We must ask our mothers and sisters who work in the houses of the whites to look for them. Only they must do this carefully and quietly. And caution them not to say anything of this to anyone."

A young warrior raised a hand in protest. "Our women have never seen the sacred objects. How will they know what to look for?"

Dohatsa produced a wicked smile. "We will describe them, only not tell of their meaning and purpose. When they are found, we will move silently and swiftly. Our knives and lances will taste white blood. Not a one of the guilty shall live."

Santan Tossa could not keep silent. "If you do such a thing, outside the pueblo, you will bring much trouble to us."

Dohatsa turned a scornful sneer to Tossa. "What do you know? A policeman? You have already sold yourself to the whites. This is the best way."

Santan Tossa knew better. He believed it to be wrong that night. . . .

And he believed it today as he awaited the return of Sheriff Hank Banner. More so for knowing now that the thief had been Dohatsa.

12

Another five minutes and they would be as dead as King Sol, Smoke Jensen thought to himself as the fresh wave of bandits rolled toward them. He took time to aim carefully and knocked another outlaw from the saddle. Still they came. Around him, the vaqueros from Rancho de la Gloria made the switch from a near victory to furious defense with smooth unconcern. Their expressions did not change as they pumped round after round into the advancing gang members.

Truth was, Smoke realized, they seemed to enjoy it. With a violent forward surge by the gang, little more than two dozen yards separated the contending forces. Any time now Smoke and the vaqueros would have to break and run or be annihilated. The outlaw leader sensed it also.

With a triumphant whoop, he urged his men on. They closed the gap by five yards. Suddenly a stutter of shots erupted behind them. It rapidly grew to a ragged volley. Confused, fully half of the bandits turned about. Smoke Jensen seized the moment to charge.

"At them! *¡Cuchillos y machettes!*" he yelled, calling for knives and the deadly long blades used for chopping jungle and high grass.

"Yiiiiiiii!" several vaqueros shouted in unison.

With bared blades in one hand, revolvers in the other, reins between their teeth or looped over the large, flat pommels of their saddles, the Mexican cowboys broke clear and thundered down on the astonished Anglo outlaws. The appearance of keen-edged steel unnerved many among the gang. They would gladly face down four or more blazing six-guns, but the thought of deep, gaping wounds, of severed limbs, or decapitation filled them with dread. Pressed from both sides, they abandoned all effort at resistance and fled in panicked disarray.

In no time, the posse led by Sheriff Banner and the vaqueros joined up. The field had been abandoned by Quinn's rogues so swiftly that the wounded had been left behind. Smoke and the sheriff rode among them. None of them appeared capable of further fight.

"It's over," the sheriff opined.

Smoke did not share Banner's confidence. "For now."

Back in the sheriff's office, Banner showed surprise to find Santan Tossa waiting. "It is good to see you, Santan. May I ask what brings you to Taos?"

"I wanted to check in. See what is going on in town."

Banner sensed the young Tua policeman's hesitation and decided to change the subject. "Oh, by the way, this is a very famous man among my people. His name is Smoke Jensen. Smoke, Santan Tossa, one of the Tua tribal police."

A smile bloomed on the dark copper face of Santan Tossa. To Smoke's surprise, he spoke excellent English. "Smoke Jensen. I have heard much about you. You have fought our brothers among the Kiowa, the Cheyenne, the Sioux, Blackfeet and Shoshone. But you were always fair. You've had a lot of run-ins with white men also. I had some of your exploits read to me by one of our people who understands English better than I do."

Smoke gave him a deprecating grin. "All lies, Santan. If I had shot at, let alone killed, as many men as the dime novels say, there would be an ammunition shortage in the country to this day."

They laughed together. When the sheriff joined them, the tension eased some. Banner decided to get to the point. "Now, what is it that brought you here?"

"We have had some thefts at the pueblo. Religious articles." He went on to explain about the stolen objects, and the desecration. He did not reveal the possibility of an uprising.

"Do you have any suspects?"

Tossa shook his head, looking unhappy. "Yes, I do. It had to be one of our own who entered the kiva. No Mexican or white man could get away with it. The one I think took the relics is Dohatsa. I think he stole them for a man named Clifton Satterlee."

"But why?"

"To cause trouble between our two people. I think he wants us to do something that will result in our being driven out. Satterlee wants the land. The trees most of all."

Smoke, who had listened with intense concentration to the conversation, looked up then and spoke what was on his mind. "I suggest that it might be time for me and this young man to pay a visit to Satterlee's hacienda in Santa Fe. Who knows what we might spook him into doing?"

Sheriff Banner snorted and shook his head. "That's it exactly. Who knows? I don't like it. There's too much can go wrong. But, I suppose there's no other choice. Be careful, Smoke."

Smoke gave him a curt nod. "Now that I will do."

Rapid, strident notes shivered brassily from the bell of a sliver-plated trumpet. The short, thin, dapper mariachi who played it had a pencil line of mustache that writhed above the mouthpiece as he articulated each tone. To his right, a big man with a huge bass guitar plucked the strings with gusto, rhythmic vibrations that directly strummed the heart. To the trumpeter's left, a standard guitar and two violins played out the melody. Under their wide-brimmed *charro* sombreros, three of the quartet sang lustily. The song was "Sonora Querrida." Clifton Satterlee looked with pride over the milling guests at his hacienda outside Santa Fe. Seated at the table on the palm frond shaded dais with him, his three partners and several of his eastern connections ate and drank to their hearts' content.

Across the patio, on which some of the guests danced to the music, two small, barefoot boys, dressed in loosely fitted white cotton shirts and knee-length pants, turned a spit over a large bed of oak and piñon coals. Their eyes shone with the excitement generated by the fiesta that swirled around them. Steam and smoke rose from the fat and juices that dripped off the split side of beef the youngsters tended. The aroma of the roasting flesh kept everyone in a constant state of hunger. Large, glazed clay bowls of beans were emptied and promptly refilled. Others of delicate saffron rice, mixed with onions, green peas and tomatoes, suffered deep inroads. Mountains of freshly made tortillas, both flour and corn, disappeared with regularity. Beer, tequila and bourbon flowed freely. The happy laughter of women tinkled from every quarter.

Obviously enjoying all of this, one huge-bellied, overdressed man with pink pate showing through thinning hair leaned toward Satterlee and patted him on the forearm. "I have to hand it to you, Cliff, you know how to throw a party. All of this must cost a fortune."

"Not at all, Findley. Labor is cheap. Back when the Spanish, then the Mexicans, ruled this land, the law had it that when a man owned the ground, he owned everything on it. That included villages and the people in them. Of course, he was required to provide a livelihood for the peons, see that they had a roof over their heads, food to eat, even paid a small amount of money. The patron had responsibility for their well-being, but to all intent and purpose, they were his property. When I took over, they had nowhere else to go, so they stayed. I provide and maintain their houses in the village, employ them to run the stores and the cantina. I even support their church, although it is the Popish Roman rite."

"Rather like slavery," Findley Ashbrook said with a chuckle.

Satterlee affected shock and abhorrence. "Heaven forbid, Findley. They are nothing of the sort. After all, they get paid. Ten dollars a month is tops."

"You crafty devil," burbled Quinton Damerest, a burly man with a hang-dog face seated beside Findley Ashbrook. "You've gotten around that demagog Lincoln and his emancipation, damned if you haven't. I admire you for it. Is that how you intend to log out lumber way out here, ship it all the way back east and sell at a profit?"

Satterlee nodded, sipping from a clay mug of beer. "Precisely, Quinton. Once we have the workers living in company houses, buying only from the company store, getting their work clothes from the company commissary, just like my peons here at Santa Fe, then we wait until they are deeply in debt to the company and cut their wages by half, then half again. Before long, they'll also be making only ten dollars a month, like these Mexican peons."

Findley Ashbrook spoke up next. "What says they have to stay here?"

"The law, Ashbrook my friend, the law. We'll be their employer, and also the local law. If they try to get away from here, we'll take them in front of our tame justice of the peace, get an easy conviction for some trumped-up charge, then slap them and their whole family into jail. A little of that and they'll see the light, have no fear."

"What about the unions?" Findley asked darkly.

Satterlee smirked. "They'll never get a start here. If they try, or if they organize a strike, we have Paddy Quinn and his men to take care of such annoyances." He nodded to a slender, young, boyish-faced individual at one of the trestle tables, helping himself to another plate of *carnitas de puerco, carne de res barbacóa* and all the fixings. "You see that one over there? He is a prime example of what I'm talking about. He looks like a baby, but Patrick Quinn assures me he is one of the fastest, most accurate gunhands he has ever witnessed."

Eyes wide, his cheeks gone pale, Quinton Damerest spoke in an awed tone. "Is that William Bonney?"

Satterlee chuckled indulgently. "Not at all, Quinton. He calls himself Mac. A Texas boy named MacGreggor. But he's hell-fire with a six-gun. I've seen him in action."

Unaware that he had become the topic of conversation on the dais, Ian MacGreggor went about filling his plate. He had grown up on the spicy foods of the Southwest. The barbecued beef, with its hot, sweet, red sauce and the carnitas with the wide variety of condiments were among his favorites. He had consumed two plates so far. He could eat at least that much more.

"A growing boy," his mother had often said in mock irritation.

Well, it was true. For the last two years he had always felt hungry. At least being with the Quinn gang had that advantage. The food was good and plentiful. It had surprised Ian when he had been told he would be going along with a part of the gang to act as bodyguards at a fancy do put on by the Big Boss, Clifton Satterlee. The prospect excited him. He would get a chance for a close-up study of the man. He might also overhear something useful to Smoke Jensen. His plate loaded, Mac picked up a squatty clay pot of *jugo de tamarindo*, the savory extract of tamarind pods sweetened with honey and cut with water.

He could have had all the beer he wanted. No one would have questioned him. But he felt it wiser to remain alert and sober. His wisdom proved itself fifteen minutes later when Cole Granger rode in on a lathered, foaming-mouthed horse. Granger knocked the dust from his clothing and came directly to where Mac sat chewing industriously at his meal.

"Where's the boss?"

"Mr. Quinn? He's over there with the 'important' people on that platform," Ian responded between bites.

Granger was abrupt. "Thanks."

Mac sensed something important came with Granger. "Hey, what's up?"

Cole Granger made an all-encompassing gesture. "Big trouble. You'll find out soon enough."

With a sigh and a regretful backward glance at his abandoned plate, Ian MacGreggor drifted along behind Cole Granger. The latter stopped at the bottom of the three steps that led to the dais. There he waited to catch the eye of Paddy Quinn. Mac held back and turned away to avoid recognition. At last Paddy looked up and saw the agitated Granger standing on the edge of the tile patio.

"Sure an' what is it ye are lookin' so exercised over, Cole, me lad?"

"We've got some big trouble up in Taos, Paddy."

"Ouch, now, that's such fresh news, it is." Paddy had been hitting the tequila heavily. It showed clearly to an attentive Mac.

"No, really. We had the roadblocks busted up by a posse and some vaqueros who work for Diego Alvarado. About nine of the guys dead, some others near to death. Shot all to doll rags. An' I—well, I recognized someone fighting with the Mezkin cowboys."

"An' who might that be?"

"Maybe we ought to move away a bit before I tell you?" Cole Granger suggested, as he cut his eyes nervously to Clifton Satterlee and his partners.

Grumbling under his breath, Paddy Quinn grabbed a fresh shot of tequila and a lime wedge from the tray of a waiter and climbed from the platform. Ian MacGreggor had moved off, though not out of hearing. Granger led Paddy over by a palo verde. There he spoke in a low tone.

"It was none other than Smoke Jensen."

Shock and surprise registered on the face of Paddy

Quinn. "Th' hell. I thought him to be dead and buried long ago."

"Not so. He's taken a hand in what's goin' on in Taos."

Quinn looked grim. "I'll have to tell Mr. Satterlee."

He went at once to where Satterlee sat and asked to speak alone with him. Off the dais, the head of C.S. Enterprises listened while Quinn explained. From the thunderous expression that shaped Satterlee's face, Mac could tell he liked the news even less. At last, Satterlee spoke in a low tone.

"The presence of Smoke Jensen could prove a major threat. Quinn, I want you to select some men and do something about Jensen. And do it fast."

Riding side by side, Smoke Jensen and Santan Tossa felt the warm sun on their right cheeks and shoulders. Santa Fe remained a full thirty-five miles away. They would not reach the bustling territorial capital until the next morning. As they neared a steep saddle, Smoke noted a large red-tailed hawk, its wings extended, tips down-curved, riding stationary on the strong breeze that blew through the opening.

Abruptly a shrill squeal came from a small, young rabbit crouched on the ground. Frightened beyond endurance by the hawk that hovered above it, it broke cover and sent spurts of red dust from under its hind feet. Instantly, the hawk folded its wings and dived like an arrow. Legs suddenly extended, claws flexed, the red-tail snatched the tiny creature from the earth and soared away toward its lair. The pitiful cry of its victim faded as it gained distance. Smoke Jensen watched unperturbed. He never forgot that nature was indeed a harsh mistress.

Santan Tossa nodded toward the dwindling silhouette of the hawk. "The young of the red-tail will eat well today."

"That is so," Smoke allowed. "Tell me, Santan, how long have you been a policeman?"

Tossa smiled, his chin lifted somewhat in pride. "Four years now. Although I will admit that this is the first real crime I have had to investigate. Most of the time I deal with a few drunks, or a dispute over ownership of a horse. What about yourself?"

Smoke had no need to search memory. "I've worn a badge, off and on, for well over fifteen years. I've fought outlaws and cleaned the riffraff out of towns, protected people in the government, even looked into the murder of friends and a few strangers."

Tossa looked expectant of Smoke's answer. "Do you like it?"

Smoke gave a snort of laughter. "A whole lot better than bein' on the other side of the law. I've not run into many Indian policemen. The Sioux and Cheyenne don't have them."

Tossa shrugged. "They are still controlled by the soldiers and the Indian agents. We are on our own. We're . . . pacified." The word sounded bitter to his mouth.

That decided Smoke to change the subject. "Do you have a woman? A family?"

"I am too young to raise children. At least that is the way we Tua believe. The padres of the *iglesia católica* want us to marry young and have many children."

"But that is not the Tua way."

A broad grin spread across Tossa's face. "No. And in that way, we mystify them. A Tua man usually takes a wife when he has twenty-six summers—er—years. He is through with war and breaking wild horses by then. Ready to settle down, hunt and plant and provide for a family. It is a good way."

"I agree," Smoke conceded.

They rode along making infrequent and idle conversation. They came down out of the Sangre de Cristo at Española and rode on a ways. The sun slanted far to the west and highlighted red plumes to their backs. Smoke Jensen had kept notice of them for some five miles when he reigned up.

"Someone is following us."

Tossa nodded. "I noticed it, too."

Smoke cut his level, gold-flecked gaze to Tossa. "What do you think we should do about it?"

The Tua shrugged. "Find out who they are."

Cole Granger and the four men Paddy Quinn sent with him rode hard and fast out of Santa Fe, in an effort to reach the halfway point between the Satterlee hacienda and Taos before nightfall. As it happened, they arrived in Española only minutes before Smoke Jensen and Santan Tossa passed through. Granger, who had been the one to recognize Smoke in the first place, spotted the tall, broad-shouldered, firmly erect figure as Smoke walked his mount down the main street. In spite of three hundred years of settlement, roads remained sparse in this part of New Mexico. It did not require great genius for Cole Granger to figure out where Smoke Jensen might be headed.

"Him an' that Injun are on the way to Satterlee's."

Pete Stringer eyed him dubiously. "How you know?"

"Where else would he be going? He's in a dust-up with us and right off, he heads south. He's goin' to call out the big boss."

Stringer eagerly went for the obvious solution. "Then, let's take him out right here an' now."

Granger shook his head. "Not likely. The marshal here's hell on killings in his town. Even if we let Jensen draw first—which would be a terrible mistake—we'd wind up in jail, most likely charged with murder. We're gonna follow along. Pick our spot, then jump the two of them."

"What does the Injun have to do with it?" another of the hard cases asked.

With a squint-eyed stare, Granger spat on the ground. "Who cares? He'll be only another dead Injun."

At Granger's suggestion, they gave Smoke and Tossa time enough to cover five miles, then rode out, retracing

their hurried route to the small mountain town. The
outlaws pulled into sight twenty minutes later. To their
right, the sun floated over the western arm of the Sangre
de Cristo range. Long shafts of orange and magenta
light cast their features in unnatural colors. Dark, elongated shadows of horses and riders kept pace with them.
Their quarry dipped below the horizon, where the road
descended yet another three hundred feet to the more
open desert land that stretched to Santa Fe.

When Granger and his henchmen reached the grade,
the outlaw leader immediately discovered that the men
they hunted had disappeared. The first cold, portentous
inklings of extreme danger clutched the spine of Cole
Granger.

13

Fat, dumb and inattentive, four of the five hard cases who followed Smoke Jensen rode into a nasty surprise. Only Cole Granger hung back, acutely conscious that the missing men represented a threat that could not be ignored. Yet, had he warned the others, taken some sort of defensive position, Smoke Jensen and the Indian could have simply ridden off some unexpected direction and disappeared for good. Jensen was slippery as a greased eel. Somehow, Granger knew, he had to allow them to spring any trap they had planned. That happened far sooner than he had expected.

His underlings had ridden on ahead, and only now became aware that their intended targets could no longer be seen. "Hey," Pete Stringer called out. "Where 'n hell did they go?"

"I'm right here." The voice of Smoke Jensen came from beyond a jumble of rocks that masked the right side of the trail from the view of Granger and the others.

"And I am here," Tossa answered from the opposite side.

Four astonished saddle trash cut their eyes from one side of the trail to the other. On their left they saw the squat figure of a Pueblo Indian, powerful shoulder muscles bunched as he drew the string of a thick, stubby bow back to his cheek, an arrow nocked and ready. In the other direction, a hard-faced white man held a six-gun on them in a competent, steady grip. All at once a terrible reality had caught up with them.

Given the alternatives, they decided to do what, to them, seemed the only thing to do. All four went for their guns. The arrow made a ripping cloth sound as it left its perch, propelled by a seventy-pound pull. It made an eerie moan through the air before it penetrated the chest wall of one thug and buried half its length in his lungs and other vital organs. He didn't even scream before he fell from the saddle.

From the other side, a .45 Colt Peacemaker barked with authority, and a hot slug smacked solidly into the gut of Pete Stringer. Pete's arm jerked, and his one shot went wild, to scream off the rocks. Another bullet brought an immense darkness to shroud him until a tiny, bright pinpoint of light began to swell and Pete Stringer rushed off to eternity. Pete didn't hear the next shot, which clipped Handy Manson in one shoulder and sent him in wild flight down the trail toward Santa Fe. The third, stiff-legged jounce threw Manson from the back of his horse. He hit the ground hard, folded into a ball to moan and writhe in misery.

On the opposite side of the trail, the close quarters left no time to string another arrow. Santan Tossa leaped from the back of his pony and dragged the remaining outlaw clear of his horse. They landed with a thud, the Tua Indian on top. Brigand ribs cracked like brittle sticks under the impact of Tossa's knees. Orange sunlight flashed on the keen edge of the knife Tossa whipped out and pressed to the throat of the winded thug.

So much for making a plan based on Jensen's expected attack, Cole Granger thought quickly. The only *plan* that made sense was to get the hell out of here. He reined his mount around and put spurs to its flanks. Smoke Jensen rode into sight then and threw a shot at the departing Granger with little hope of it hitting meat.

At the forefeet of Cougar, the youthful desperado had

eyes only for the knife that threatened him. After a cautious, though nervous, shudder, he raised his gaze to the white man who calmly sat his horse, looking down with apparent dispassionate interest. That sight caused him to lose it entirely. He began to shriek and utter great sobs. Only gradually did Smoke manage to interpret what the sniveling thug tried to say.

"Please . . . puh-leeeze! Save me from this savage. Drag him off me. You're a white man. You can't let him kill me."

Laughing nastily, Smoke Jensen bent down and spoke softly. "I'll let Tossa skin you alive if you don't cooperate. You and your friend down there." He gestured toward the fallen Handy Manson.

"What do you want to know? What? What?"

"Who do you ride for?"

"I can't—I can't tell you. He'll—kill me if I do."

Coldly, Smoke taunted him. "And you don't think Tossa there will kill you if you don't?"

Face ashen, he cut his eyes away from both of his captors. "Oh, Jesus."

Iron tipped Smoke's words. "He can't help you. I might. If you tell me what I want to know. Who do you ride for?"

"Whi—Whitewater Paddy Quinn."

Relentless, Smoke pressed on. "And who does he work for?"

Shaking with terror born of the impossibility of his situation, certain he would die no matter what he said, the craven rascal gulped himself into a fit of hiccoughs. His eyes squinted tightly shut, and great tears squeezed out. "C-C-Clif—Clifton Sa-Sa-Satterlee."

Smoke Jensen cut his eyes to Santan Tossa and asked rhetorically, "Why am I not surprised?" He made a curt gesture, and Tossa released the captive. "Get the other one. We'll patch them up and take them along with us while we go have a talk with Satterlee. Then, on the way back, we can drop them off in Española. The law can lock them up for us there."

* * *

Seth and Sammy Gittings intermittently wiped at the tears that streamed down their dirt-grimed faces with the backs of their hands as they saddled two small Morgan horses they had decided to take for their escape from the Sugarloaf. Horror and a terrible sensation of rejection burned in their minds. She had done it again. Their rumps still stung from the hard, swift swipes from the willow switch.

Seth sniffled loudly and smeared his upper lip with the mucous that ran from his nose. Then he spoke both their thoughts. "It ain't right. What did it matter if that dumb ol' pig got squashed. It was fun rollin' rocks downhill into the pigpen and watchin' the mud splash up."

"Yeah, Seth. It wasn't our fault that baby pig was stuck in the muck and couldn't get away in time. Mother had no right to spank us. She's never ever done it before."

Seth nodded energetically. "Poppa wouldn't let her. Now she's done it twice. It ain't fair," he whined. "We'll show her. She'll be sorry when we're gone."

Abruptly a rooster bugled his welcome to the pending dawn. Both boys jumped and looked at each other with the shock of fear reflected in their eyes. The cock crowed again, and a fit of giggles erupted from Seth and Sammy.

Through his sniggers, Sammy admitted, "That cock-a-doodle scared me. I about peed my pants."

"What's new about that?"

"Liar! I ain't done it in a year now."

"Shut up an' let's finish."

Seth completed the fold-over tie-off of his cinch strap, grateful that his older brother's friendship with Bobby Jensen had allowed him to learn how to master the tricks of saddling a horse, and he had in turn taught them. He went to check on his little brother. Sammy, as usual, had made a mess of it. He began to undo the bulky knot.

"Not like that, stupid. Here, watch."

Quickly Seth adjusted the cinch strap, slipped the

leather end through the crosspiece and jerked it down. Next he hung a canteen over the saddle horn and added a cloth bag that contained some biscuits, split and smeared with apple butter, two pieces of cold, fried chicken and a hunk of cheese. An identical bundle already waited on his saddle. Through the barn window he saw a thin, gray line on the eastern horizon. It was time they left. Any more delay and they might get caught.

"Miz Jensen will be awake any time," he observed to his brother. "So'll the hands. We gotta go now and fast."

"Mother won't get up for hours," Sammy remarked.

"So what? We've gotta be way gone from here by then."

Both boys led their stolen horses from the barn and mounted up. Walking the animals to make the least amount of noise, they angled across the ranch yard and into the near pasture. Only then did Sammy notice the smooth, dark wood of a rifle stock in the scabbard on Seth's saddle.

"Gosh, what's that, Sethie?"

"Bobby's rifle."

"Why'd you take that; you don't like guns, do you?"

Seth had a wild gleam in his eyes. "Really, I think they're keen. Besides, we might need it. Mother says it is dangerous and wild out there." He put heels to the little Morgan and moved the beast into a trot.

Neither youngster had the slightest smidgen of horsemanship. Their thin legs bounced out from the sides of their mounts while their rumps banged up and down without even a hint about posting. By the time they had left the cleared fields of the Sugarloaf their thighs ached and their behinds knew more agony than any from the spanking. Tall fir, hemlock and pine closed around them, and the sky disappeared above a thick mat of branches. Stunted aspens reduced visibility to twenty feet on either side. Sammy grew round-eyed with apprehension. It did not decrease when they picked up a game trail.

Seth pointed it out. "Look, there's a trail. I bet it leads to that dismal little town, you know the one?"

"Big Rock?"

"That's it, Sammy. We'll follow it, okay?"

"Sure."

Seth took the lead on the narrow trace, with Sammy close behind. They remained totally unaware that they were going in the exact opposite direction from Big Rock. Or that they grew more lost with each step their mounts took. They also continued into the vastness, ignorant of the cool, amber eyes that watched them.

Slowly the muscular, tawny body roused itself, lifted its blunt, white muzzle and sniffed the air. With a surge of new interest, the wily old cougar smelled a fresh meal.

Diamonds of moisture sparked on the leaves of Spanish bayonet and tufts of saw grass as Smoke Jensen and Santan Tossa reigned in behind a low, sandy knoll outside the hacienda of Clifton Satterlee. Smoke nodded to their captives.

"We'll put them down and tie them to those mesquite bushes. Gag 'em, too."

Handy Manson had regained some of his former bravado. "You go in there after Clifton Satterlee an' you ain't comin' out alive."

Smoke gave him an amused expression. "You had better hope we do. Because no one is going to know where you are. Dying of thirst and hunger is a bad way to go, I'm told. So, hold a good thought for us, eh?"

"You—you ain't gonna leave us some water? Something to eat?"

Smoke appeared downright jovial. "Nope. You won't be able to make use of it anyway, what with a gag in your mouth and hands tied behind a tree."

After securing the prisoners, Smoke and Santan rode on into the warmth of mid-morning. Once out of hearing, Tossa asked of Smoke, "Do you think they will try to escape?"

"I imagine so."

"You do not seem concerned, Smoke."

"I'm not. The way I tied those knots, the harder they struggle, the tighter they'll become. Those two will still be there when we return."

"Don't they know a man can live five or six days without food and nearly as long without water, even in this desert?"

"I doubt it. Even if they do, it will take them some time to remember it. By then we should be back. In a case like theirs, fear can kill more likely than the doin' without."

Worry rode firm in the saddle on the back of Ian Mac-Greggor. A full day had passed since he had overheard the conversation between Cole Granger and Paddy Quinn. Four men had ridden out with Granger to "take care of Jensen," as Satterlee had put it. What had happened to Smoke? Pushing his concern to the back of his mind, he went about his assigned task of scanning the distant horizon. Motion caught his attention. He stared at the spot, and the dark silhouettes disappeared. He blinked and rubbed his eyes.

There they were. Two figures, clearly on horseback, headed toward the hacienda at a fast trot. Ian MacGreggor soon got the knack of looking slightly to the side of what he wanted to see, instead of dead-bang on. It let him decide that they were definitely both men. As they drew nearer, he determined that they did not resemble any of the gang he knew. What would strangers be coming here for? Mac turned aside and called down from the rampart that spanned the inner side of the high outer wall.

"Riders coming. I don't recognize them yet."

Another member of the gang repeated his announcement. Mac went back to a study of the approaching men. He could make out the color of their clothing now, and the style. Another dozen strides from the powerful shoulder muscles of their horses and Mac could make out their features. One of them appeared to be an Indian.

And the other . . . the other rider Mac suddenly recognized as Smoke Jensen. It struck Mac like a fist in the stomach: *Smoke Jensen.* In a flash he recalled Smoke's admonition that if they saw each other, they would not give any sign of recognition. He shouted down to the cobblestone courtyard again.

"They're both strangers. One of them is an Injun. The other is a white man."

"Will ye come on down now, lad, will ye?" Whitewater Paddy Quinn called to him.

"Yes, sir, Mr. Quinn."

Hoofbeats rang loud in his ears as the horsemen grew nearer. Mac clattered down the rickety ladder that gave access to the parapet and joined a cluster of other outlaws who had formed up between the main gate and the house. Mac heard Smoke and his companion rein in. After a pause, the large iron ring that served as a knocker struck the portal with a hollow bang.

Old Jorge Banderes shuffled to the small, human-sized door in the thick wooden gates and opened the viewing port. "*¿Sí, señores?*"

"We're here to see Señor Satterlee."

"*Lo siento,* señores, Señor Satterlee is not receiving anyone at this hour," the grizzled Mexican retainer replied.

"Tell him that Smoke Jensen is here. He'll see us, I'm sure."

Jorge scuttled off to deliver the message. While they waited, Smoke exchanged an amused glance with Tossa. Despite the age of the doorman, it took only three minutes. Jorge Banderes threw the bolt on the door and swung it wide.

"Come in, señores. Don Clifton will admit you to his salon now."

Smoke Jensen took a purposeful stride through the opening and cut his eyes to the gathering of hard cases. At once he saw Ian MacGreggor, then his gaze slid on without the slightest sign of recognition. Mac turned slightly as though to keep eyes on the Indian.

"We may regret this," Santan Tossa spoke in a whisper.

Mary-Beth Gittings entered the large living room of the Sugarloaf headquarters in a state of high agitation. Sally Jensen knelt on the hearth, removing ashes from the fireplace. Mary-Beth wrung her hands, and her face showed a puffiness unusual to herself. Sally noted her friend's perplexity at once.

"Mary-Beth, what is the matter?"

"I can't find them. No one has seen them this whole day."

"Who is it you cannot find, Mary-Beth?"

"Seth and Samuel. Your son says he knows nothing about them, only that his rifle is missing. Though I doubt his word on both counts."

Sally fought unsuccessfully to hold back a scowl. "That is entirely uncalled for. I resent the implication that Bobby would lie. It reflects on us as parents, and that is insulting."

Mary-Beth's face crumpled. "I'm sorry, Sally, dear. It's only . . . I am so worried. None of the hands have seen them. The boys are not at the corral, not in any of the barns, not in their room. I've been everywhere."

"Have you asked Billy about his brothers?"

"Yes, and he knows nothing either."

She could be mean, Sally considered, *and ask if Mary-Beth doubted her son's word also.* No, that would hardly do. "Ike Mitchell has a good eye for reading sign. I'll have him take a good look around and see what he can come up with."

"Would you? I'd be so grateful. I worry so whenever they are out of my sight."

Sally found that unsettling. "Even when they go to school?"

"Of course not, Sally. I'm not an over-protective mother."

Oh, no, not by half, Sally opined silently.

Sally left her task for later and, with Mary-Beth trailing along, went in search of the foreman, Ike Mitchell. She found him in the smithy, pounding on a newly forged iron hinge. He looked up as they approached and wiped sweat from his brow with the back of one forearm.

"Ike, have you seen the younger two Gittings boys today?"

"No, ma'am. That I haven't. Told the missus that not two hours ago."

"Well, Ike, they've gone missing. Would you please take a good look around and see if you can come up with anything that might indicate where they got off to?"

"Sure, Miz Sally. Glad to be of help."

Ike completed leveling the hinge, doused it in a tub of water and laid it aside to cool. Then he plunged both hands into another container of clean water and washed the charcoal smudges from his face. He rolled down his sleeves and started off to examine various parts of the headquarters ranch yard. Sally put a hand on Mary-Beth's arm.

"This is likely to take some time. Come back to the house and I'll make us some tea. We can let Ike work at his own pace."

Three-quarters of an hour later, a stern-faced Ike Mitchell presented himself at the kitchen door. Hat in hand, he knocked briskly. Although clearly uncomfortable, he presented his findings in a crisp flow.

"I reckon they done lit a shuck outta here, Miz Sally. I cut their sign west of the big corral. Tracks led northwest across the pastures. I followed them to the edge of tall timber. They kept goin'. Then I came back here and went over the stock. It appears they took two of the young Morgans, blankets and saddles, and high-tailed it early this morning. Don't look like they reckon to come back. We'd best get some of the boys together an' go after them."

"I should say so," Mary-Beth blurted. Then the realization of the danger her children might face struck her. "My babies!" she wailed.

Blunt as usual, Ike had the last word. "They ain't babies anymore, ma'am. They're horse thieves."

14

Jorge Banderes escorted Smoke Jensen and Santan Tossa into the high, curved-ceiling passageway that separated the main entrance of the house from the gardenlike atrium at the center. Smoke found it to be cool and dark. Everyone blinked when they stepped out into the bright sunlight that washed the tiled central courtyard. A burly man stood beside the central fountain, his face a square mask that failed to conceal the boiling anger beneath the surface. Although Smoke had not seen him before, he surmised this to be Patrick Quinn. Leave it to a two-bit, gunslinging thug to choose as pretentious a moniker as *Whitewater,* Smoke thought.

Smoke Jensen had seen real whitewater on the Rogue River and sincerely doubted that Quinn had the stuffing to ride on it under any conditions. Paddy Quinn took a single step forward and extended both arms, palms up. "The guns. I'll take them now."

Smoke scowled, and his eyes went cold and flat, narrowed slightly. "That'll be the day," he growled.

Quinn proved himself no fool to Smoke's reckoning when he did not choose to press the matter. "Suit yerselves. An', sure ye'd not mind if me an' a couple of the boys stood close at hand while ye have yer little talk with Mr. Satterlee, would ye?"

Smoke could not resist the opportunity to tweek his enemy. "Not at all, a-tall."

For a flash, Quinn's expression grew even more furious. His eyes widened and revealed black centers that glittered malevolently. With obvious effort he reined in his emotion. "Come this way, then."

Framed by lush vegetation, an attractive young woman took her ease on a white-painted, wrought-iron settee near one side of the patio. Her silver-blond hair and fair, peaches-and-cream complexion glowed in the leaf-filtered sunbeams. She smiled warmly at the visitors and greeted them in a musical contralto. "Welcome to Hacienda Colina del Sol. I am Martha Estes, another guest of Clifton's. I trust we will be together for dinner tonight?"

Always appreciative of a good-looking woman, Smoke spoke his regrets with sincerity. "I doubt that such a pleasure will be possible. We must meet with Mr. Satterlee and then attend to other urgent matters.

Now *here* was a man who could make her knees weak. Martha breathed deeply, expanding her firm, medium-sized bosom, and gave him a melting smile. "What a pity. I—ah—don't believe I caught your name?"

"It's Jensen, Miss Martha. Smoke Jensen."

Martha raised an ivory Spanish fan to her lips and spread it in an agitated motion. "Oh, my. A regular celebrity where I come from. An honor, Mr. Jensen."

"Thank you. Now, if you will excuse us?"

No such warm welcome awaited Smoke Jensen and Santan Tossa when they entered the presence of Clifton Satterlee. The master of the house turned from his affected pose of gazing out the tall windows of his library and spoke with a petulant, condescending tone. "Don't you find it a bit presumptuous to be calling on me like this?"

Although not entirely certain of the meaning of the word, Smoke considered "presumptuous" to be insulting. So he accepted that the best defense would be a good offense. "Not at all. But I do consider it presumptuous of you to have sent men to follow us and attempt to kill us. Likewise to put up roadblocks to cut off all commerce and other traffic into or out of the town of Taos. And I am sure my friend here, a tribal policeman from the Taos Pueblo, sees it as presumptuous of you to inveigle someone among his people to steal certain religious articles from their kiva."

Clifton Satterlee affected a hurt expression, colored somewhat by indignation, and undertook to talk down to them like foolish boys who had been caught in some schoolyard prank. "Oh, come now. That's all quite preposterous. You can't possibly believe I would deign to stoop to such brigandish endeavors? I am a man of influence and substance in the territory. What flightiness could bring you to believe that anyone in my employ might be responsible for the difficulties in and around Taos. Dismiss the thought, gentlemen."

With that, Satterlee took Tossa by one elbow and began to steer the both of them toward the door to his library. Smoke Jensen set his boots and did not move. "One minute, if you please, Mr. Satterlee. You have not heard the full extent of our complaints, let alone our opinion of your condescending, self-serving response."

Satterlee stopped, rolled his eyes heavenward and sighed heavily. "Then, I suppose I must."

"You may have influence, and this layout proves your substance," Smoke told him levelly. "But in my book, you are just a grasping, greedy, lying son of a bitch. If you continue to send your third-rate gunfighters to enforce your will and to harm the people around Taos, I will have no choice but to keep on putting them in the *campo santo. ¿Comprende?*"

With that, Smoke allowed himself and Tossa to be escorted from the presence of the great man. In the garden, Martha Estes gave them a light-hearted wave as they passed by on their way to the outside. At the tall, double doors of the main entrance, Paddy Quinn drew closer to Smoke Jensen and spoke heatedly, though softly, through a sneer.

"You're dead meat, Jensen."

Smoke gave Quinn a bleak, thousand-mile, gunfighter stare. "I'll remember that. I trust that you will?"

Riding away from Hacienda Colina del Sol, in the direction of Santa Fe, the two lawmen who had become friends on the ride south remained silent until well away from Satterlee's lair. Then Santan Tossa spoke what was on his heart.

"You really aren't afraid of Satterlee and his gunmen, are you, Smoke?"

Smoke held a moment before replying. "As a matter of fact, I am. Any man who faces death from so many enemies and says he is not afraid is a fool or a liar. But, knowing that, you can use that healthy fear to help you decide which enemy you are going to knock down first. Say you are facing three armed men. One is good, cool under fire and fast with a gun. Another is a common thug with a gun. The third is edgy and unsure of himself. Which one do you go against first?"

Tossa rubbed his lantern jaw, absorbed in thought. "You take the easiest one first, right?"

"You might think that, but it is absolutely necessary to get rid of the greatest threat first. So you go for the best gun. Take him out while you are fresh and unharmed. Then go after the weakest one, because he's likely to do something cowardly. Save the average feller for last."

Santan Tossa stared at his companion. "I would never have thought of that."

Smoke Jensen gave Tossa a smile that reached all the way to the crinkle lines at the corners of his eyes. "No one does, first time out."

"All right, I'll accept that. Now, I have one for you. Did you see that squash blossom necklace that Miss Estes was wearing?"

Smoke nodded. "Yes, I did. It's the most beautiful piece of its kind I've ever seen."

"It should be. It is one of the stolen sacred objects."

"You are sure?"

"Positive, Smoke. I have worn it in ceremonies a dozen times."

Smoke gave that only a second's reflection. "I think we ought to return later tonight and have a private talk with that young woman."

Santan Tossa stared in astonishment as they entered the outskirts of the territorial capital. Tiny Taos was the largest community he had ever seen. By the time they reached the business district of Santa Fe, which extended two blocks in all four directions from the Plaza de Armas, his head swam.

"So many outsiders," he gasped, then recovered himself. "Sorry. It is how we think of those who are not of the Pueblo people. And I have come to not think of you as an outsider, Smoke."

"I'm flattered," responded Smoke dryly. "We'll find a saloon and start to ask around about Satterlee."

"I cannot enter any place that sells the white man's crazy water—uh—liquor."

"That's right, you can't. What do you reckon to do?"

"There are signs in Spanish on the walls that tell of a *Charrida* ring. There I will find others of my Pueblo people. I will ask questions among them about Satterlee."

"Good idea. We'll meet—ah—there." Smoke pointed to a small restaurant on a corner at right angles to the cathedral. "Say, two hours before sundown?"

Tossa nodded and rode off. Smoke turned the other way and reined in outside an arcade formed of plastered adobe arches. From the cool shade created by the sidewalk overhang, the door of a cantina invited him. Smoke dismounted and handed Cougar's reins to a small, brown-skinned boy with big, shiny, black eyes.

"The livery stable, señor?"

"No. Take him into the Plaza *jardín* and get him watered. Then bring him back and tie him off here." He handed the boy a coin.

Eying the silver U.S. quarter dollar, the lad's face glowed. "*Gracias, señor.*"

Smoke touched him on a thin shoulder. "That is to insure he is here when I come out. You understand?"

"*Comprendo, señor. Muchas gracias.*"

Inside the cantina, Smoke stood at the bar, beside two white cowboys, and ordered a beer. He nodded to the men and their nearly empty *tubos.* "Buy you a refill?"

The older ranch hand smiled under a well-groomed walrus mustache. "Don't mind if you do. Thank you kindly. I'm Eric, this is Rob."

"Jensen," Smoke said shortly, then observed, "You two have the look of working stockmen."

Eric found that grimly amusing. "Working ain't the half of it. You must be new in these parts not to know that graze is so sparse we've gotta keep the cattle on the move all the time or they'll starve. Weren't half this bad in Texas. Used to be I could sit all night and play poker. Now I've got so many calluses on my butt I stand up to eat."

Smoke affected to consider that a moment, then put on a sorrowful expression. "Maybe I came out here on a snipe hunt?"

"How's that?" Eric asked.

"I got let out by the last outfit I worked for. There was this posting in our local paper about someone hiring out here. All sorts of jobs, including cattle work."

"What newspaper was that?"

"The Amarillo *Star,*" Smoke replied, using the name of Mac's source.

Eric nodded. "Don't want to pry, but what's the name of this man who can spend so much money to get hands?"

"Didn't give a man's name. Some outfit called C.S. Enterprises."

"Cliff Satterlee." Eric spat the name as though it had a foul taste. Then he turned fully to Smoke and gave him a long, cool study from head to boot toe. "You look to be a straight shooter. I figger you're on the right side of the law. So, if you don't mind, I'll give you some good advice. Were I you, Jensen, I'd steer as far clear of Satterlee, an' any of those around him, as I could."

Pleased with what he had heard, Smoke pressed his luck. "He's crossed horns with the law, has he?"

Eric nodded. "More'n once. Nothin' ever proved, of course. Money talks. Though it's said by more than one that Satterlee's drovers throw wide loops."

Smoke knew what that meant. In cowmen's talk, throwing a wide loop implied that a man rustled most of his stock, or at the least, claimed more than his share of unbranded cattle. "There's more?"

"Some fellers have died of a sudden," Eric confided. "Satterlee has him a so-called foreman, name o' Paddy Quinn, who's prone to be quick to use his Colts. The rest of them that rides for the brand are jist as proddy."

"What brand is that?"

Rob added his bit. "C-Bar-S. There's some say it stands for his ranch, Colina del Sol. But it's for Clifton Satterlee and his C.S. Enterprises, you can be damn sure. Leastwise, it's an easy brand to use to blot another one with a runnin' iron."

"Thank you, Eric, Rob. I'll sure keep distance between me and Satterlee." Smoke downed the last of his beer and strode to the bead-curtained doorway.

Outside, Cougar waited for him, the reins in the patient hands of the small boy. Smoke looked left and right and located another saloon only three doors down. He spoke to the boy. "You keep him here. I'm going to walk down to the Cinco de Mayo."

Surprise raised black eyebrows. "Walk? You are not a vaquero, señor, *¿es verdad?*"

"That's right, son. I guess you could call me *un ranchero, un hacendado.*"

"*¡Por Dios!* It is an honor to serve you, señor."

Smoke ruffled the lad's thatch of black hair and started off to continue his information gathering mission.

* * *

Santan Tossa sat on the top of the low, plastered adobe wall that separated the *callejón* from the performance ring at the *Charrida* plaza. Elongated, like a hippodrome or the Circus Maximus, the Mexican rodeo ground lacked the circular symmetry of a Plaza de Toros. To one side and in front of Tossa, a young vaquero from the San Vincente Pueblo leaned his back against the wall, one leg elevated, knee cocked, boot resting against the inner surface of the barrier. The youth longed to be a recognized *Charro,* but knew of the prejudice harbored by the Spanish-blooded Mexicans against anyone of pure Indian origins. Tossa understood this and used it to loosen the fellow's tongue.

"You will ride in the *Charrida* this Sunday?"

A glum expression darkened the wide, Indian face. "I will clean stalls, saddle horses, and maybe, just maybe, ride as a header—to set up the bulls for the *Charros* to rope. It is dangerous, but it lets people see what you can do. Another year . . two years, who knows?"

Tossa tried to be encouraging. "Chosteen, you will one day wear the *Sombrero Grande* of a *Charro*. This is part of the land of the White Father in Washington now. He will not let the Mexicans keep our people out of the *Asociacion Nacional de Charros.*"

Chosteen turned to him. "And why not? Its headquarters is in Mexico . . . the old Mexico. The white eyes' laws do not apply there."

With a shrewd expression, Tossa offered his bait. "If you worked for C.S. Enterprises, perhaps the *Charros* would accept you as an Americano."

Suddenly, Chosteen's features clouded. "I would rather work for Soul Eater. At last you expect Him to be evil." His eyes quickly narrowed as he thought of something. "Do you work for Satterlee? Are you here to try to get others to sell their Spirits to that outsider demon?"

"No—no," Tossa hastened to object. "I am interested

in him, only. We believe that he, or someone he used, has stolen sacred objects from our kiva."

Chosteen spat on the sand. "Then he is as evil as I have been told."

"You know something of this Satterlee, Chosteen?"

"I do." For the next twenty minutes the two Pueblos spoke earnestly and intensely about Clifton Satterlee.

When they concluded their talk, Santan Tossa made his way to an outdoor barbecue pit where a small calf, which had been crippled in the day's practice, had been dressed out and put on a spit to roast. He watched the small carcass turn for a while, his stomach rumbling, prompted by the aroma. Mostly his people ate sheep, or wild meat. Over the years as a policeman, Tossa's frequent visits to the white man's town had given him a taste for beef. He pushed temptation aside to ask among the Pueblo men about Clifton Satterlee. One lean, young man, not yet in his twenties, gave him confirmation of a suspicion of his own.

"I have heard it said that he wants the land where your pueblo stands. He would cut the trees. All of them. He would lay our Earth Mother bare and let the rains wash gullies and ravines in her breast."

"Is nothing sacred to these pale skins?" another asked.

The first to speak went on. "They care nothing for the land. There is more, always more, to be taken, laid waste and then move on to yet more. Their god is formed of those circles of gold that they treasure so much."

Yet another advised, "Do not speak ill of the white outsider, Satterlee. He is a dangerous man."

Through the afternoon, Tossa heard much the same, and more, from those he questioned. He reached the conclusion that none of them admired or trusted Clifton Satterlee, and that most feared him. He ate some of the roasted veal, wrapped in flat, cornmeal cakes, and seasoned by a thick sauce of chile peppers and garlic. Then he made his farewells and left to join Smoke Jensen.

* * *

Smoke Jensen had finished his first swallow of beer in the Cinco de Mayo cantina and had settled down to weighing up the other occupants when Ian MacGreggor pushed aside the strings of glass beads and entered the saloon. Mac ambled to the bar and elbowed a place beside Smoke. He ordered a beer and drank deeply before speaking in a low tone, his lips not moving.

"I have something important. We need to talk soon. And it's getting too hot for me here. There's nothing much for us to do and too much time for the others to ask questions."

Smoke did not look at the young undercover deputy when he replied. "Find some excuse to get away for a while. Ride out from the estancia and join us on the road to Taos. We'll be there early tomorrow.

"I can do it. And, Smoke, you're not going to believe what I found out." Lapsing into silence, Mac finished his beer, then turned away from the bar. Smoke stopped him with a hand on one shoulder.

"There's one thing you can tell me now. Which room is Miss Estes using?"

Mac frowned slightly. "She's not. Not in the main house, anyway. She has a small cabin outside the place, near the north wall. It's the one on the south end of a row of three."

"Thanks." Smoke released Mac and the young man walked out the door.

In every saloon and eating place Smoke Jensen visited, he encountered someone who had heard of either Clifton Satterlee or Paddy Quinn or both. Not until the fourth cantina he looked into, did he run into the first men to have anything good to say. In fact, they took immediate exception to Smoke even asking questions. Thrown from a blind spot, when he least expected it, a fist whistled past Smoke's head.

Smoke dodged it and spun on a boot heel. A hard-knuckled right fist drove up from waist level. Off balance from the missed blow, the pig-faced brawler caught Smoke's punch full in the gut. A loud grunt exploded from his lips. Eyes bulging, he bent double in time to take Smoke's swiftly upraised knee in the nose. Bright lights flashed in his eyes, to be swiftly followed by a blanket of blackness. He keeled over and struck his bloodied chin on the tile floor. At once, two others grabbed Smoke from behind and sought to yank him around.

Smoke Jensen set his powerful legs and twisted at the waist. One of the thugs went flying. The other hung on. *This shouldn't be happening,* Smoke thought. All he had asked was, "Anyone here know a feller named Satterlee? I hear he's hiring."

The others said nothing. Instead, they started swinging. They still remained silent as another one jumped into the brawl. Smoke rolled a punch off his shoulder and popped the hard case who held him under the chin. His eyes rolled up, he blinked and tried to kick Smoke in the crotch. Smoke turned slightly and hit him again. He gave a shudder and let go of Smoke to sprawl with his face in the urinal trough that fronted the bar in most Mexican saloons.

Right then the fight took on a far more serious tone as two of the Quinn gang went for their six-guns.

15

Smoke Jensen saw their moves from the corner of one eye. He filled his own hand with a .45 Peacemaker in a blur of speed. One cut-rate gunfighter had time to gasp in astonishment before a 230 grain slug smashed into his left shoulder and he went flailing into a table, which collapsed under his weight. His six-gun, only partly out of the holster, fell to the floor at his side. Already, Smoke had swung his Colt to bear on the second gunman.

That unfortunate fellow had time enough to pull his barrel clear of leather and began to level the muzzle on the midsection of Smoke Jensen. His misfortune came from that fact which caused Smoke to put a bullet through his heart rather than shoot to wound. The gunhawk slammed back against the bar and slid to a sitting position. It had all happened so fast that only now did the bartender react with a shout to his other customers as he ducked below the bar.

"Tengan cuidado! Los pistoleros."

A third gang member unlimbered his six-gun as Smoke swung his Colt that direction. He stopped the move instantly when Smoke raised his point of aim and the man could look down the black tunnel of the barrel. A thin curl of powder smoke rose from the muzzle. Smoke remained motionless while bar patrons dived for cover and the rest of the Satterlee partisans showed open, empty hands. A tense three minutes went by in which the only sound to be heard came from the wounded hard case. Smoke lowered his revolver only when the law arrived.

Face a fierce mask, the town marshal entered the saloon with drawn six-gun. He cut his eyes from the downed men to the bartender, and then to Smoke. "All right, who started all of this?"

No one seemed eager to reply, so Smoke Jensen holstered his Colt and stepped into the breach. "They did." He indicated the wounded gunman and the dead one. "First off, three of those fellers over at the bar took offense to something I said and threw punches at me. When I knocked a couple of them flat, those two drew on me."

A skeptical raise of eyebrow projected the lawman's mood. "And you just happened to be faster."

"That's right. I was . . . or should I say am?"

"Do you have a name to go with all that speed?"

"I do. Could we talk about it at your office, Marshal?"

"You'll get there soon enough, I'd say. What's wrong with here?"

Smoke nodded at the gang members. "There are— other ears. What I have to say is for you alone."

With a shrug, and another dubious look, the marshal turned to one of his subordinates. "Nate, take care of things here. You, mister, come with me."

The marshal marched Smoke Jensen cattycorner across the Plaza de Armas to his office. Inside, the lawman took a seat behind a scarred, water-stained desk. "If it hadn't been some of Clifton Satterlee's hirelings, you'd be answering questions from inside a cell. So, speak your piece."

Smoke dug into his vest pocket and produced his badge. "I'm glad to hear that, marshal. My name's Smoke Jensen. I'm a deputy U.S. marshal. At the request of a friend, I am here to look into Satterlee and his dealings."

"Who is this friend?"

"Don Diego Alvarado, of Rancho de la Gloria, outside Taos."

"It's about time," the marshal snapped. "Governor Lew Wallace will be glad to hear that Satterlee is being investigated. By the way, I know your friend, Alvarado, and m'name's Ambrose . . . Dave Ambrose."

Smoke Jensen appeared more amused than relieved. "Well, Marshal Ambrose, I'm not here to investigate Satterlee. My job is to eliminate him."

Marshal Ambrose had a sudden change of mood. He snorted with contempt. "Another hired gun hidin' behind a badge."

Smoke immediately put him straight. "Nothing of the sort. What I should have said is that Satterlee has broken several federal laws, or at least arranged for others to break some for him. I'm here to bring down his business and put him away for a good long time."

Ambrose shot Smoke a disgusted look. "What if he chooses not to cooperate? Hell, man, he owns the judges."

Smoke gave the marshal a cold, hard smile. "Then I'll just have to eliminate him."

A bloated, red-orange ball hung over the snow-capped peaks to the west. Cold air rising off the white mantle distorted it into the wavy shape of an egg. Dark, purple shadows lay across the ground. Sammy Gittings sat on a fallen tree trunk, tears sliding silently down his chubby, round cheeks. They were lost. They had wandered off the Sugarloaf and no one would ever find them. He knew it, no matter what Seth said.

Seth looked up now from the pile of dry wood he had gathered. "Don't just sit there. Help me. We need to get a fire started."

"What good will that do?" Sammy pouted. "We don't have anything to cook."

Seth stood, grubby hands on his hips. "You come down here and build a fire and I'll get us something to eat."

"How? You can't hit anything you shoot at."

"Shut up! Jist shut up. I'll get something this time."

A squirrel chattered alarmingly as it suddenly darted away through the tree limbs above. Seth looked up. "Maybe a squirrel."

Sammy made a face. "Ugh! They look like rats when they're skinned."

"Are you hungry or not?"

Sammy paused before replying to his brother. "Not that hungry."

"Then don't eat. I'll have it all."

Lower lip protruded in a pout, Sammy challenged Seth. "Won't either. I get my share. It's only right."

Seth started to laugh at his little brother, only to have it cut off by a harsh primordial cough. His face went chalk white. "What was that?"

Right then, the wily old cougar that had been stalking them uttered another hoarse hack, flexed its powerful hind legs, and with a strident snarl, launched itself. Sammy screamed at the sight of the tawny blur and fell backward off the tree trunk. Seth let go a yowl and scampered backward. He tripped over an exposed root and landed on his round bottom. His arm stretched out as he desperately searched the ground. His fingers found the cold steel of a rifle barrel, and he closed around it in desperation. The mountain lion missed Sammy by a foot when the boy toppled away from its spring and now whirled in the small clearing under large, overgrown branches. It lunged again at the terrified, smaller lad.

In that split second, Seth brought up Bobby Jensen's little .32-20 rifle and fired at point-blank range. By sheer chance, the slug hit the cougar in the right ear and plowed a ragged furrow through its brain. It leaped into the air and fell back dead. One needle-clawed paw twitched three inches from the soft belly of Sammy Gittings.

"You got him! You got him, Seth," Sammy shouted.

Unfortunately for the boys, the ferocious charge and odor of the puma thoroughly frightened the horses.

Neighing in terror, both animals slipped their insecure ties off and ran away. Only a haze of dust and pine needles marked their course as their rumps disappeared down the trail.

Seth stared after them in consternation. Sammy came to him then, wailing between great sobs. "What—are— we gonna—do? What are we—gonna do? We'll die out here all alone."

The moon would not rise until after midnight. It provided ideal conditions for Smoke Jensen and Santan Tossa to penetrate the security around the hacienda of Clifton Satterlee. Thanks to the information he had received from Ian MacGreggor, Smoke could pick the right place to scale the wall and be the least exposed to any of the watchers. The cabana occupied by Martha Estes was located close to the east wall of the compound, well away from the main house. Smoke had not come prepared to scale a high wall. Particularly he had not planned for the rows of jagged-edged, broken bottles that lined the top.

With gloves in place, moccasins on his feet, Smoke Jensen balanced himself on the shoulders of Santan Tossa. Cautiously, he reached up and felt his way between the blue ranks of dragon's teeth and found purchase. Smoke flexed his knees, then launched himself. He swung one leg upward to nudge against the outer row of bottle shoulders. He held on to the inside of the wall until his balance returned, then dropped the bite end of the rope around his neck to Tossa. Levering himself upward, Smoke went over the wall and dropped to the ground below.

Quickly he secured the loop of the rope to a post and gave the line a little tug. At once, it tightened and began to vibrate. On the far side, Tossa literally walked up the adobe palisade. In brief seconds he joined the last mountain man on the ground. Smoke pointed to a low, square adobe cabin to one side. A yellow square picked out a window, and indicated that someone occupied the premises. Silently, the two men moved in that direction.

Smoke eased to the corner of the building and peered around to take in the outer courtyard. Nothing moved, and he saw no sign of sentries. He beckoned to Tossa, and they went directly to the only door. Smoke put his ear to the panel and listened for ten long seconds, then grasped the latch, threw it and swung the portal inward.

Startled, Martha Estes looked up from the book she had been reading, her expression showing her to be a bit frightened. "Wha—what are you doing here, Mr. Jensen?"

"I've come to see you, ask a few questions, Miss Estes."

Martha took a deep breath, reaching up with her hand. "This is—rather irregular."

Smoke made a pacifying gesture. "I apologize for that, but I have learned something of importance that I want you to explain for me."

Martha gathered herself. "I—I'll try to help if I can."

"Good. What it is . . ." Smoke hesitated, then went on. "That squash blossom necklace you were wearing this morning. Where did you get it?"

"Why, Cliff—er—Clifton gave it to me. He has some other lovely pieces in the safe in the library."

Smoke eyed her levelly. "Are you aware that those are stolen property?"

Martha started an immediate protest. "That can't be. Clifton is a respected businessman, an enterprising investor."

Santan Tossa took over then. "Miss Estes, that necklace and the other items are religious objects, stolen from my people at the Taos pueblo. They are sacred to our kiva."

Martha's face twisted in a war between disbelief and outrage. "Why, that's—that's terrible. However could Clifton have gotten ahold of them? Perhaps he purchased them, not knowing their origin?"

Smoke Jensen shook his head. "I'm afraid not, Miss

Estes. Santan Tossa here is a tribal policeman, investigating the theft. All of his leads have taken him to Clifton Satterlee. For all his mighty reputation around Santa Fe, Miss Estes, Satterlee is not what he appears to be."

"But . . . my father is a business associate. Surely he cannot be involved in such nefarious schemes."

Deciding to ease her mind, at last for the moment, Smoke offered a suggestion. "To get away with what he is planning, Satterlee needs the cover of honorable, legitimate businessmen. By reflection, you see, it makes him seem the same. Your father is most likely one of those."

Martha became more agitated. "No matter how he acquired the jewelry, it is simply unforgivable that your sacred items not be returned."

She rose and crossed to a large, walnut armoire against one wall. There she kneeled and slid open a drawer. From it, she took the necklace. A look of anger had replaced her earlier confusion and shock. "Here, take this back and put it where it rightfully belongs."

A thought occurred to Smoke Jensen. "What will you tell Satterlee if he notices it is gone?"

"I'll think of something. We women have our ways." Martha smiled for the first time since they had entered the room.

Tossa accepted the silver and turquoise work of art and folded it into a strip of purple velvet. "Thank you, Miss Estes. I will keep it secret for a while that the necklace has been recovered."

"I thank you, too," Smoke added. "Now we'll say good night. It would be prudent if you did not let anyone know we have been here."

"Of course. Good night, Mr. Jensen."

Smoke built her a smile. "Call me Smoke."

Clifton Satterlee had stayed up late also. He paced the confines of his library, hands clasped behind his back. Thick, rich velvet drapes covered the leaded glass windows so that not a hint of light escaped. A small fire crackled in the beehive fireplace set into one wall. These early spring nights remained chill. Seated in a large, wing chair, his long legs sprawled carelessly across the Kermint oriental rug, Paddy Quinn sipped appreciatively at the Irish whiskey his employer had thoughtfully provided for him. At last, Satterlee stopped his measured tread, poured himself an inch of cognac in a snifter and sighed heavily as he turned back to his guest.

"Obviously the men I sent to deal with Jensen failed in their task. He knew too much when he came here to warn me. *Warn me!* What impudence."

Quinn waggled a finger at his boss. "Every rooster likes to make his cock-a-doodle-doo before he gets his head lopped off for the stew pot, he does. Ye ask me, Mr. Satterlee, this Smoke Jensen is runnin' scared. He was flexin' muscles he don't have. He's tryin' to buy hisself some time."

Satterlee sipped the liquor and breathed out its aroma. "Somehow I don't quite believe that. There's more to the man than we saw in this room today. Are you familiar with his reputation?"

Quinn dismissed that with a curt gesture. "Reputations amongst the gunfighting brotherhood are gen'rally tall tales blown out of all proportions, they are."

"Even your own?"

For a long moment Quinn studied Satterlee until he decided the remark had been made in jest. He responded then with joviality. "Far be it from me to disabuse anyone of my ferocious nature."

Satterlee smiled tightly. "The same applies to Smoke Jensen. He is dangerous. I want you to send more men, enough this time to get the job done."

"An' what is it ye have in mind?"

"I want them to follow and finish off that inquisitive Smoke Jensen and the savage he had with him this morning. Then they are to continue on to Taos and join in the blockade Garth Thompson is conducting."

Quinn looked uncomfortable with the news he had to impart. "It might be more of a task than you think. Some of the boys had a brush with Smoke Jensen in town this afternoon. They came out the losers. Two dead."

"Damn that man. Neither you nor I can afford his arrogance. Too much of it will make us look bad. Perhaps I will have to take care of this personally."

Sheriff Hank Banner thoroughly enjoyed getting together with Doc Walters and several of the Taos businessmen once a week for a few hands of poker. This particular night had been especially satisfying, considering the step-up in pressure from the Quinn gang. To top it off, Banner had played only with other men's money after the third hand. Matter of fact, he had come away from the table about twenty dollars to the good. Not bad for a dime ante, quarter limit game. His boot heels echoed hollowly on the red tile sidewalk as he turned the corner and started to cross the Plaza de Armas to his office. Two men suddenly stepped out of the well-tended shrubs to block his path.

One of them worked his mouth in a nasty sneer under a poorly kept mustache. "Goin' somewhere, Lawman?"

"If it's any of your business, I'm headed back to my office."

"Unh-uh. Oh, no."

"Nope, you ain't," the second man added.

So far, neither man had done anything serious enough to justify drawing a weapon, but Sheriff Banner sensed the very real menace they exuded. His hand twitched to close on the butt of his Colt. Right then, two more hard cases stepped onto the crushed rock path behind the sheriff.

"No, you're not goin' to your office," the first one said again. "We're gonna go have us a nice little talk."

He recognized them then. The one doing the talking was named Islip; the one with him they called Funk.

Drawing a deep breath, Banner mustered his nerve. "Were I you, I'd go have a nice talk with a bed, Islip. You're drunk. If you don't want to face a charge of disorderly conduct, clear out of my way and let me pass."

Grinning like an imbecile, Funk, the second gunhand, shook his head and tapped a forefinger on the center of the badge worn by Hank Banner. "Can't do that. We got our orders. You an' us is gonna have that talk, an' we're gonna reach an understanding."

At once, the two thugs at his back grabbed the sheriff and pinned his arms to his sides. With a smooth move, they lifted him off his feet and carried him toward the mouth of a dark alley that led off of the plaza on the north side. Once within its shadowy confines, they put Banner's boots on the ground and kept hold while the first pair caught up. Without preamble, Islip and Funk began to take turns, driving hard fists into the chest and stomach of Sheriff Banner.

After a little preliminary softening up, Abner Islip started speaking in a low, insistent tone. "You're gonna forget all about what's happenin' in Taos. No more backin' those who get crosswise of Mr. Satterlee. In fact, you're gonna take a nice little vacation. Go off and visit relatives somewhere, why not? Or go fishin'. I hear they've got some bodacious critters down in the Gulf of Mexico. A feller ought to try for 'em onest in his life, don't you think? Maybe you can take up lawin' in Georgia or Mississippi.

"Any way you want it, Sheriff, yer gonna shake the dust of Taos offen yer boots and clear the hell an' gone outta here by tomorrow morning."

Through the haze of pain, Sheriff Banner maintained his defiance. "You'll be in hell long before I do that, you and Funk, too."

Funk shoved his sweaty face in close to that of the lawman. "In that case, we've got other orders. We ain't to leave enough of you to do any fightin'."

With that, all four began to pound on the sheriff. Islip,

his hands growing sore, switched to the use of his pistol barrel. He viciously pistol-whipped Banner until he drove the sheriff to the ground. Then all four formed a circle and began to kick him. Mercifully, blackness swarmed over Hank Banner, and he did not feel the last dozen gouges to his ribs, belly and back.

Bare soles made hardly a sound as Wally Dower scampered along outside the closed and unlighted business fronts on the north side of the Plaza de Armas. In another five minutes he would have completed his final rounds. Only the cantinas remained open. He still had to go back and escort old Laro Hurtado to his house. He would be drunk of course. If he had any money at all, or could cage drinks from some of the vaqueros, he would be falling down, piss-his-pants drunk. Oh, well, his wife always gave Wally a big, silver Mexican dollar for his mission of mercy. It was only worth about a dime American, but it felt nice in his pocket. When he neared the alley entrance, he heard the soft thuds and grunts that forewarned him that someone was in a fight. Wisely, Wally held back.

After what seemed forever to the boy, the noises ended, and Wally heard the thump of boot heels fading in the distance, toward the opposite end of the alley. He edged closer and risked a quick peek down the alley. Nothing. No, that wasn't right. He saw a darker lump in the blackness of the passageway. Wally watched for a long while, then hazarded to step into the opening. Five paces down the path, he came upon the huddled form of a body. Wally bent and rolled the man by his shoulder.

At once his eyes went wide. It was Sheriff Banner. A low groan escaped from bloodied lips. Wally did not need prompting to know what to do. He came upright and sprinted from the alley, then settled into a dead run toward the office of Doctor Walters.

16

Their wounded captives in tow, neither the better for wear and tear, Smoke Jensen and Santan Tossa cantered along the wide, well-defined road between Santa Fe and Taos. The sun, slightly over the median, warmed their backs and chewed away at the last of a low ground fog that had given dawn a hazy, closed-in quality. They would reach Española by mid-afternoon. With the prisoners off their hands, they could make even better time. Smoke wanted to meet soon with Sheriff Banner and Diego Alvarado. The encounter with Clifton Satterlee had awakened several questions. He felt certain the lawman and the rancher could provide answers. Always conscious of his back trail, Smoke cast another glance in that direction as they crested a low swell.

Immediately, he saw dust where none had been before. His eyes narrowed in concentration. It could be two, three or even more riders. No doubt men sent by Satterlee or Quinn to carry out the threats of yesterday. Smoke turned back and made a gesture to Tossa.

"Behind us. We have company."

Santan Tossa's thoughts traveled the same trail. "You think they are men sent by Satterlee?"

"It wouldn't surprise me." Smoke thought a moment, eyes searching the surrounding terrain. "See that bend up there? I think we should wait for our friends around there, out of sight."

Tossa flashed a wide, white smile. "Who surprises who—er—whom?"

Smoke nodded and laughed. *A very bright young man, this Santan Tossa,* he thought. *He's improving his English by simple exposure.* "It's the best way to be in an ambush . . . be the ambushers."

The dust plumes had grown noticeably closer by the time Smoke and Santan rounded the curve in the road. Shielded by the swell of a sandy mound, they reined in and walked their mounts off the road to either side. In moments, the faint thud of hooves could be heard. Smoke slid his .45 Peacemaker from the right-hand holster. Santan readied his stout bow, a triangular, obsidian point bright in the midday sun. Closer now, the hoofbeats became a regular drum roll.

When the heads of the horses came into sight, the gunfighter and the Indian policeman made ready to fire. Immediately, Smoke Jensen checked himself. "Hold it!" he barked to Santan Tossa.

Much to his surprise, Smoke had recognized the pretty face of Martha Estes over his gun sights. His command had the effect of halting her as well. She blinked in astonishment at sight of the drawn weapons. Beside her rode her maid, a young Zuni woman, whose carriage indicated that she would be capable of taking care of the both of them. On her other side rode Ian MacGreggor.

Hand to her mouth, Martha reacted explosively. "Oh, I . . . you startled me, Mr. Jensen. This nice young man thought it might be you. We were trying to catch up."

"You caught us, all right. Well, Mac, what do you have to say for yourself?"

"I was riding out to meet you like we arranged. She came to the barn while I was saddling. Said she wanted to go with me. That's what delayed me."

Smoke gave Mac a sidelong squint "All night?"

"I couldn't get away last night. Ten of the gang rode

out on Quinn's orders. From what I overheard, they were to find you and kill you. The watch was doubled all around the hacienda. As it was, she—the lady helped me leave this morning."

"Yes," Martha verified. "I told the men at the gate that he was accompanying me on my morning ride."

Smoke nodded to the maid. "What about her?"

"Lupe always comes with me, unless I'm riding with Clifton."

"Humm. You're here now, you might as well ride along."

Martha put a bite in her words. "You're too, too kind."

Smoke removed his hat in a sweeping gesture and bowed low. "My pleasure entirely, madam." Then to Mac, "Let's you and me ride up ahead and you can tell me this news you have."

Martha leaned forward in the saddle to press her case. "Let me make something clear, Mr. Jensen. I gave a lot of thought to what the two of you told me, and I've decided to leave Clifton Satterlee. There isn't any way he could have obtained that jewelry lawfully, is there?"

"Not that I can see."

"I only wish I could have taken the rest."

Smoke smiled fleetingly. "We know where it is. We can come for it later. And . . . you are a welcome sight."

"Thank you. And I mean it, this time."

Smoke and Mac trotted on ahead while Tossa escorted the women. Mac's jaunty expression changed as the distance between the parties widened. "Smoke, Quinn is bringing all of the gang north to Taos. Mr. Satterlee has ordered him to blockade the town until the people give in and turn over everything to him. Quinn will leave later today, and Satterlee will come along after. Wants to be there to gloat, I suppose."

A frown creased Jensen's high forehead. "That don't sound good. Any talk of burning down buildings, killing people?"

"No. From what some of the gang said, I believe that

Satterlee wants it to look all legal and proper. At least on paper. There were a lot of really important people at a party I was sent there to bodyguard for. Everyone but the governor, and he did send a representative. When things started calming down, they all went inside for a meeting. They seemed mighty pleased to be in Satterlee's company. I got the feeling, when I heard about the siege at Taos, that if Satterlee had the papers all signed and in order, his friends in government would not ask any questions about how he went about getting folks to turn over their land and businesses."

Smoke nodded, well pleased. "You've got a good head on you, Mac. You'll not be able to go back now, of course. Just sort of stay out of sight when we reach Taos."

"Hey, I'm not worried. I can out-shoot near all of them. And, you'll need all the guns you can get on your side."

With a curt nod, Smoke sought to delay the inevitable. "We'll talk about it later."

Leaned back against rocks that reflected the heat of a hat-sized fire, Smoke Jensen listened while Martha Estes talked about her father. He was partners with Clifton Satterlee in a large firm that built houses back in the crowded East. Satterlee became involved because he had, or was going to get, large sources of timber. The lumber that came from the trees would be used to build houses. Some of them would be tenements, three or four stories, half a block deep, with limestone fronts.

Smoke didn't think there would be much of a demand for such expensive structures and said so. Martha informed him to the contrary. "Boats loaded with immigrants arrive at least three days of every week. Wealthy men will buy the tenements and rent apartments in them to the newcomers. With three or four to a floor, the profit will be enormous. The buyers won't mind paying twenty or thirty thousand for the buildings.

Clifton—Mr. Satterlee and my father will keep ownership of the land and receive a percentage for the use of it."

Considering that, Smoke scratched at an earlobe. When he spoke, his voice reflected the mystery. "Something seems out of kilter about that, but I can't put my finger on it. It's sort of like having one's cake and eatin' it, too."

Martha's eyes shined. "Exactly. Any time Cliff—er—C.S. Enterprises wants to raise the percentage, they can. After all, the owners can't move their buildings off the ground." The image gave her a new thought. "That does sound a little crooked—no—unethical, doesn't it?"

"I liked your first choice of words. That's what bothered me before. Those rabbit hutches could be held up for ransom. And, from what I've gathered about Clifton Satterlee, he'd be likely to do it."

Martha gave him a puzzled look. "Is he really as awful as you make him sound?"

"Worse, no doubt, Miss Martha. I've just learned that he plans to force everyone out of Taos and take over the whole town for himself. That don't sound like someone who would refuse to squeeze the suckers who bought those houses."

"But, my father . . ." Martha started to protest when a muzzle flash bloomed brightly and a shot crashed out of the darkness.

Orin Lassiter smirked, unseen in the darkness. They'd had some difficulty finding the camp. The small fire, shielded all around by large boulders, gave off little light. He and the others had ridden through Española without finding the men they sought. Lassiter did learn that Jensen and the Indian had come through town about three in the afternoon. They now had three people with them. Two women and another man. One woman appeared to be that sweet thing the big boss was sporting with. How could that be? he asked himself.

Then he put that behind him when he remembered

that two of the gang now languished in the jail at Española. He had immediately tried to see them. The sheriff had refused. Angry, he had stomped from the office to be given the only good news for the day. One of his men had informed him that they were only two hours behind their quarry. They had set out at once. Even so, it had taken them until two hours after full darkness to locate this place. The time of month favored them, Orin noted as he moved closer to the camp. The moon would not rise for at least four more hours. Conscious of the men to either side of him, he motioned them to greater silence when reflected firelight made their faces visible.

Then they were in position. Orin Lassiter raised his six-gun and fired at the figure of a man seated beside a woman at the base of a large, volcanic boulder. Dark, red-brown rock turned to powder six inches above the head of the man when the slug struck stone. Orin Lassiter watched as Smoke Jensen dived forward and took the woman with him. What he did not see, because it went too fast, was the big .45 Colt clear leather on the man's hip and snap in his direction.

He saw the muzzle bloom a split second before intense pain exploded in his left biceps as the bullet shattered his humerus. Dimly he was aware of the other boys opening up. The shock of his injury slowly numbed, and he remembered to move before another slug could find him. To his right, Baxter Young screamed horribly and clutched at a feathered shaft that protruded from his belly. Distantly, Orin heard the shouts as five of his men rushed the far side of the camp.

"Stay down," the man Orin Lassiter now believed to be Smoke Jensen shouted to the woman. A fraction of a second later, Jensen sprinted away from his exposed position by the fire.

Biting back his agony, Orin fired again.

* * *

"Stay down," Smoke Jensen commanded as he gave Martha Estes a shove on one shoulder. Before she could reply, he came to his boots and sprinted into the shadows away from the fire.

A revolver blasted from a few feet away, and suddenly another man loomed over her. Martha Estes looked up and stiffened when she recognized Orin Lassiter. He reached down to her. "Come on, you're going with me," he growled.

"No! Leave me alone."

Shock and pain ran through Martha as Lassiter slapped her with a solid, open palm. Her skin burned and tingled, and she could not prevent the sudden flow of tears that washed down her cheeks. Lassiter growled at her again. "Dry that up and do as I say."

Defeated, Martha raised a hand to be assisted upright. Automatically, Lassiter extended his left arm and immediately groaned at the new rush of agony. He spoke through gritted teeth as he holstered his six-gun. "Take my right arm."

She complied and hoisted herself to her high, black, narrow boots. At once, she heard the rustle of a full skirt that came from the darkness to her right. Lupe rushed at Lassiter with a knobby chunk of mesquite root held above her head with both hands. Hampered by Martha clinging to him, Lassiter could not completely dodge the blow. The hunk of wood slammed into his left shoulder, and he could not prevent the howl of agony that burst from his lips. Still aching, he pulled his good arm free of Martha's grasp and dropped the Indian woman with a hard right to the jaw.

Martha noticed the bloodstained shirtsleeve then, which evened the score somewhat for the slap. "He shot you—good."

Mustering his waning resources, Lassiter snarled at her. "Shut up, bitch."

Her courage nearly fully recovered, Martha risked a

further taunt. "Or you'll what? Kill me? Clifton wouldn't like that."

Her barb found its mark, and Lassiter only grumbled under his breath as he dragged Martha off into the night. He found another of his henchmen and jerked his head in the direction of the camp. "Go get that Injun woman and bring her along."

A flurry of gunshots alerted him to the fierce resistance his other men had met, and Lassiter let go a shrill whistle. The signal was picked up by someone nearer the conflict and repeated. A third man echoed the call. Heeding the signal, the outlaws broke off their fight and faded into the darkness. Lassiter led the way to the horses and saw to securing Martha and Lupe on dead men's mounts. Then they rode off into the darkness.

Ian MacGreggor counted the muzzle flashes and made note of their positions. Then he raised his .44 Marlin and pumped a round toward the black smear to the right of one red-orange blossom. The burning gasses ceased. To his left he heard the twang of a bow string, followed by the hideous shriek of the target. An outlaw staggered into the firelight, his hands clawing at the wooden shaft of an arrow that had sunk deep into his upper right chest. The Tua bow sang again, and he went down with a shaft through his heart.

Three men tried to rush at that point, overconfident that no bowman could launch arrows quickly enough to hit them all. How quickly they forgot about him, Mac thought as he took aim and began to fire as rapidly as he could cycle the Marlin and take aim. Smoke Jensen's .45 Colt opened up from Mac's right, and another hard case left the earth. Then Mac heard a piercing whistle, repeated twice more close at hand, and the enemy fire ceased. Mac fired once more and then listened to the fading sound of boots thudding in retreat. It was all over. At least for now.

* * *

Yellow fingers of light reached through the second-floor window of the infirmary maintained by Dr. Adam Walters. They brushed invisibly on the eyelids of Sheriff Hank Banner. The lawman blinked and then abruptly opened his eyes. For the first moments everything registered as a blurred mass. Gradually individual objects came into focus. His head ached abominably. After three minutes of silent effort, he discovered that he could not see clearly out of his left eye. Only impressions of light and dark, all of it fuzzy. At last, he tried to move his arms.

A loud groan, brought on by that effort, summoned Dr. Walters from his office and treatment room. "What do we have here?" he asked with forced joviality.

His old friend and poker adversary looked like hell. His left eye was swollen nearly closed by a huge purple-yellow-green mouse. His left arm was immobile in a splint, in hopes the fracture would mend properly. Another device, created out of necessity by the good doctor, tried to give some semblance of the original shape to a broken—no, mashed would be more apt—nose. It consisted of rolls of cotton batting shoved into the nostrils, with court plaster holding in place two pieces of broken-off tongue depressor. A white sea of bandage held broken ribs immobile. Both lips were split, made three times normal size by puffiness. Without consciously thinking about it, Dr. Walters spoke his thoughts bluntly.

"You look like hell, Hank. How many of them were there?"

"Four I'm certain of. Maybe five."

"And I oughta get a look at them, eh?"

Banner tried a grimace and flinched at the result. "Horse manure. Adam, they done tom turkey tromped the crap out of me."

Dr. Walters winced and spoke ruefully. "No kidding. I had to get you out of your trousers to treat your injuries, so I know for a fact." A loud groan came from his patient. "Did I embarrass you? If so, I'm sorry."

"No, Doc, it's just your winning bedside manner. What brought that sorrowful noise on was that I just added up the score. It left me with one tail-biting question. What in hell's gonna happen to Taos with me bunged up like this? And, worse, with Smoke Jensen off sniffing around Clifton Satterlee? Those hard cases are going to be back, you can count on it, and who's to stop them from shuttin' down this town right permanent?"

From the bed opposite him came the voice of Pedro Alvarado. Pedro had come in to have the stitches and drain tube removed from his belly wound and stay for overnight observation. "My father will send as many vaqueros as you need."

"That's mighty kind of you, son. But the way I see it, they got us all outnumbered at least three to one."

"You just lie back and rest, Hank. I'll have my girl"— he referred to Dorothy Frye, his sometimes nurse and record keeper as *my girl*—"bring you some broth. Though with the shame your mouth is in, I reckon you'll have to take it through a pipette."

"You're so full of encouragement and good news, Adam."

"Thank you," Dr. Walters said with more humor than he felt. Pedro might be encouraging, but for the life of him, the doctor did not have an answer.

Kyle Curtis, one of the Sugarloaf hands, reined in and raised up on his stirrups. He waved a gloved hand to draw attention from the searchers close at hand. "They're over this way. I can see 'em down in a draw about two hundred yards below me."

At once, the rider closest to Kyle drew his six-gun and fired three fast rounds into the air to summon the remainder of the search party. Faintly he heard cries of alarm when the last shot echoed away among the mountain peaks. Fully a dozen ranch hands, drawn by the sound, closed in on the shooter. Kyle Curtis then pointed the way to the missing Gittings boys.

When the youngsters saw them coming, they were overjoyed. Then a terrible thought struck Seth. They had taken horses without permission, and then lost them when the cougar attacked. No doubt they would be in for it now. And a worse paddling it would be than one that came from their mother. The idea of having their britches yanked down in front of all those men humiliated and shamed Seth beyond anything so far in his young life. Then a black lance of pure, boyish hatred thrust through him.

He was there with them. Bobby Jensen. How he'd sneer and make life miserable for them from now on. He swallowed back his outrage and looked up at Ike Mitchell, who led the search party.

"How—how did you find us?"

"Easy," Ike informed him as he bent forward and down from the height of his sixteen-hand Palouse horse. "We just backtracked those horses that got away from you."

Seth's eyes widened when he recalled how they had lost their mounts. "It was a mountain lion. He come at us and scared off the horses."

Ike narrowed his eyes and rubbed at his chin. "Somehow I doubt that. If he had much interest in comin' at you, you would be in his belly 'fore now."

"Nope." Pride swelled Seth's shallow chest. "I shot him dead. One bullet, right in his ear."

Bobby Jensen chose that moment to erupt. "You're a liar as well as a thief, Seth."

Seth shot out his lower lip in a pout. "I didn' lie, an' I'm not a thief."

"You took my rifle and those Morgans without permission. That's stealin'. Horse thievin' is still a hanging offense out here in the high lonesome. An' I brought along a good rope."

Real terror gripped both boys. His legs trembling, Seth dropped to his knees. Sammy flopped on his belly and bawled like a colicky baby. Seth turned to Ike Mitchell and beseeched him. "You can't do that. We're jist little kids. They don't hang children."

Bobby Jensen stung him with harsh words. "Like hell they don't. They tie a big sack of sand around your ankles so's to get the job done proper-like."

Ike had the last word. "Before we go back I want you two to show me this cougar. If it's like you say, I might put in a good word for you."

Face alabaster, the grime overlaying it became more pronounced as fat, salty tears began to stream down the face of Seth Gittings. Both brats had been thoroughly cowed by this revelation. All sign of rebellion was instantly banished. Heads hanging, they submitted without protest to riding behind two ranch hands, it being deemed that they did not deserve mounts of their own. Sammy cried and sniveled all the way back to the Sugarloaf. His butt made even more painful by the lack of support from stirrups, Seth regained some of his spitefulness.

He lost that quickly enough when the small party reined in outside the main house. Instead of rushing to them, wretched with worry over their disappearance, their mother remained in place on the porch, her face rigid with anger and affront. Slowly she raised an arm and commanded them.

"Come up here this instant."

Ike Mitchell dismounted and handed down the boys, one at a time. With dragging feet, they approached the steps to the porch. Mary-Beth Gittings gazed beyond them and met the eyes of Ike Mitchell. "We know that they took horses without permission, and that Seth, for some insane reason, took a rifle belonging to Sally's son. What else have they done?"

"They left the ranch, ma'am. By a good twelve miles. What I reckon is that they was fixin' to run away for good an' all. Now, about that rifle, ma'am. If they didn't have it along, they would have been cougar meat long before now. Before we started back here, I had them take me to where the cougar jumped them. He was there, all right. Dead with one shot to the brain. Seth, here, saved his brother's life and his own."

Sally's face remained fixed in stern disapproval. "But that does not excuse the terrible things they have done."

By then, Seth had preceded his little brother up to the second step. He gulped involuntarily when he looked up at her rigid features. His mother darted out one hand and closed her fingers tightly around his upper arm, so tightly he squealed from the pain it caused. Then she yanked him off his feet and stood him on the porch. She reached with the other hand for the willow switch Sally Jensen held, puffed down his pats and bent him over.

Seth got twenty-five lashes this time, and every one of them hurt more than he could stand. He was bawling by the fourth one, hoping to wring his mother's heart. He did not, and his humiliation grew greater when he heard some of the hands snigger.

17

Wally Gower took the reins of the horse ridden by Smoke Jensen. The moment the tall, rangy man stepped down from the saddle on Cougar, the boy piped up with the news he had been bursting to convey. "Did you hear that the sheriff got beaten up the other night?"

Smoke gazed down at the boy. "No, Wally—Wally is it?" The lad nodded and Smoke went on. "Tell me about it, Wally."

Wally went on to describe what he had seen of the attack, mainly the results. He concluded with an unhappy expression. "I didn't see any of them, so I can't say who it was. But Doc Walters and the sheriff say it was some of the Quinn gang."

"Where is the sheriff now?"

"Over at Doc's, Mr. Jensen."

"Then I suppose the thing to do is pay him a visit."

Wally trailed along, hopeful of being allowed inside. At the foot of the stairs, Smoke turned to him. "You'd best wait here, Wally. If the sheriff has any message for you, I'll bring it to you."

Disappointment clouded Wally's face. "Awh, I wanted to talk to him."

"Maybe later."

Up in the office, Dr. Walters took Smoke in to Sheriff

Banner. The man looked terrible, Smoke noted at once. "You look like you've been run down by a buffalo stampede," Smoke advised the lawman.

Banner made a sour face as best he could. "I feel like it, too."

"Tell me what happened?"

"First off, that stray, Wally Gower, saved my life right enough. I sure want to see him and thank him in person."

Smoke grinned. "He's downstairs, waitin' on word on your condition."

Hank Banner actually managed a smile. "Bring him up, bring him up. That boy's got him a double eagle waitin' for what he did. He come here right away and brought Doc to me. Hell, we'd jist finished playin' poker half an hour before. Next thing I know, I'm wakin' up in this bed, hurtin' like damn all. But I know who did it. Recognized two of em." Then he went on to identify the men and describe the beating he took before he lost consciousness.

Smoke Jensen listened with growing anger while the sheriff outlined the boot stomp he had received. When the lawman finished, Smoke spoke softly. "I'll go get Wally now. I don't think he needed to hear what you just told me."

Wally nearly wept when he saw the condition of the sheriff. But he was manly in fighting back the huge tears that welled in his gray-green eyes. "I'm sorry this happened to you, Sheriff. You're—you're the best man I know. *Please* get well."

"C'm'ere, Wally."

Obediently, Wally scuffed bare, callused soles across the wooden floor as he approached the bed. Hank Banner reached with his good hand and took a hinge-clasp leather purse from the table. He snapped it open and dug inside with thumb and forefinger. He withdrew a twenty-dollar gold piece.

"Here. This is yours. It's for saving my life."

Eyes huge with awe, the eleven-year-old gulped as he

stammered out, "Twen—twenty dollars? I can't—can't take that much."

"You've got to, Wally. It's a reward. That's right, ain't it, Smoke? No one can refuse a reward."

Smoke reached out and tousled the lad's sandy brown hair. "That's right, Wally. Buy your mother a new dress with some of it, if you want."

"Really? I can do that? Oh, boy!"

Doc Walters cleared his throat. "Time's up, Wally. You'd best scoot on and do something like that. You're gettin' Sheriff Banner all exercised."

"Thank you, Sheriff. Thank you, thank you." With that, Wally scampered from the room and thundered down the outside staircase.

"Now, I have some news for you, Sheriff," Smoke Jensen announced.

"Give it."

"Don't tax him too much," warned the doctor.

Quickly Smoke related what he had learned from Mac and told the peace officer that he had proof Satterlee had the stolen Tua religious paraphernalia. Finally he added the abduction of Martha Estes. The sheriff digested it a moment, then spoke brusquely. "That does it, then. Smoke; considerin' the shape I'm in, I want you to become undersheriff. Take over for me. And, you can have a free hand dealing with Satterlee."

Smoke hesitated only a second. "I'll agree to it, Sheriff. Provided I can make Santan Tossa a deputy."

Distress displaced the pain etched on the lawman's face. "But, he's an Injun. Oh, I know, they've been peaceable for more'n a hundred years and the Pueblos are civilized and organized. But . . . he'd have to carry a gun."

"Have any of your deputies been effective against Quinn so far? Tossa has killed at least five of them, and with a bow and arrow."

Banner frowned. "You've got a point. If the governor gets wind of this, he'll have a fit. Armin' an Injun is serious business. There's some places it's still against the law to provide a firearm to any Injun."

"But not here, I gather?"

Banner nodded. "That's right. Okay, go ahead and fit him out from the rack in my office. Then I'll swear the both of you in."

"Not today you won't," Doc Walters interjected.

Banner scowled. "C'mon, Doc. I'm feelin' fitter every hour. If this town is gonna get besieged, we've gotta move fast."

Smoke agreed with that. "Just so. First thing, I'm going to send to Diego Alvarado for all the gunhands he can spare. Then, can you give me names of men in town who are loyal to the local government and willing to fight?" At the sheriff's nod, Smoke went on. "I think it would be a good idea for Tossa to try to recruit some help from among his tribal police."

Banner's good eye widened. "You really like to flirt with wrath from above, don't you, Smoke? All right, Smoke. You're undersheriff, so it's your ball game, as that feller Abner Doubleday would say. Now, you can start by askin' Ezekial Crowder, Marshal Gates, Warren Engals . . ." He went on to name two dozen more.

Sighing heavily, Sheriff Banner lay back on the bed as Smoke Jensen left the room. Within seconds he lapsed into a deep, though troubled, sleep. Even with help from the Tuas and Diego Alvarado, he knew Smoke faced a terrible dilemma.

A small drum tapped a staccato rhythm, and smoke rose from the square opening in the roof of the Tua kiva. Santan Tossa handed the reins of his pony to his younger brother, who looked up at the tribal policeman with an expression of hero worship. He climbed the single rail ladder and washed his hands and face before taking the descending steps to the floor of the religious center. He saw immediately that a dozen young men had gathered, seated on the circular, shelflike ledges that ringed the domed, circular structure. At the altar, sweet grass, pine needles and sage gave off their pleasant aroma as they smoldered on a small bed of coals.

Using an eagle-wing fan, the gray-haired shaman wafted the thin, gray tendrils of pungent smoke over the empty altar. Silently, Santan Tossa approached and knelt before the medicine man. From his sash he produced the folds of velvet cloth and opened them.

"Grandfather, I have recovered one part of our stolen sacred heritage." Quickly he revealed the necklace.

For the first time since the theft, Whispering Leaves smiled. "You have done well, my son. Have you any idea where the . . ." Hope flared a moment in the old man's eyes. "The others might be?"

Torn nodded. "Yes. It is known to me."

"If he knows that, it is he who stole them," came the grating voice of Dohatsa from behind and to one side of Tossa.

Tossa whirled as he bounded to his moccasins. The muscles of his neck and arms corded. "You should guard your tongue, traitor."

Aware from childhood, as with all of them, that this was no place for anger or violence, Dohatsa did not respond to the challenge, merely shrugged and turned away. Inwardly, a striking sensation gripped his heart. Exactly how much did Santan know? He relaxed some as the soft words of the shaman came to his ears.

"This is not the place for hot hearts, Santan," he gently chided the younger man.

Santan Tossa lowered his eyes and nodded. "That is a true thing. I have come for another reason also." He turned to take in his fellow Tuas. "You all know of the gang of white outsiders who have tried to take our land. They work for a man named Satterlee. While I recovered the necklace from the house of Satterlee, I learned that the white gang is going to ring Taos, like the Spanish did our Pueblo in the first days of their coming. The gringos call it a siege. The purpose is to prevent anyone from entering or leaving, and to starve the people inside into surrender. The star man, the sheriff, has asked us for help. I am made a dep—u—ty of the star man. I want any who will join me to gather outside the kiva with their ponies. We must ride swiftly back to Taos."

His precarious situation forgotten in a flush of anger over this outrageous suggestion, Dohatsa snarled his challenge and contempt. "You are a fool, Santan Tossa. The white outsiders are using you. You will get no thanks from those people. And it is shameful that you ask we give any help to them."

"In other circumstances I would agree with you, Dohatsa. But this is different. These outlaw whites will only come here next. They want all the land, and they can take it if we do not fight."

Goaded by this, Dohatsa lost his composure and his reason. "You lie! Satterlee and his first warrior, Quinn, are our friends. I have spoken with them. To stop you, I will fight you."

Automatically, Santan Tossa's hand went to the unfamiliar butt of the six-gun at his hip. "Will you now? That is interesting. But, as Whispering Leaves says, this is no place for anger, or fighting. If I must fight you, I will. Wait for me outside this sacred place." He turned to the others. "Now, who will join me?"

Several among the young men of the pueblo made as though to come over, among them three of his tribal policemen. They hesitated, though, at a scowl from Dohatsa, who had begun to climb the ladder to the outside. Santan Tossa turned back to the shaman.

"Be patient, and hopeful, Grandfather. I will soon bring the rest of the sacred objects. With enough men, the white outsiders can be defeated, and I can go with my friends to get the holy dolls and the masks."

"Yes, Santan Tossa, but which outsiders are the real enemy?"

Tossa paused at the foot of the ladder. "Why, the gang led by the one called Quinn, of course."

With a mocking smile almost identical to the one worn by Dohatsa, Whispering Leaves nodded once. Santan Tossa continued out of the kiva. In a steady line behind him, the other young men followed. Tossa found Dohatsa waiting for him on the ground below.

"I will kill you if I have to," Dohatsa stated flatly.

"It is forbidden, you know that."

Dohatsa shrugged. "It does not matter. Take off that white man's weapon."

"Naturally."

While the other occupants of the kiva formed a loose circle around them, more men and a number of small boys of the pueblo gathered to watch. Santan Tossa untied the pegging string of his holster and slipped the buckle. He let the six-gun drop as he instantly launched himself at Dohatsa. The renegade had expected that and easily side-stepped Tossa. Dohatsa drove an elbow into the small of Tossa's back smashing him to the ground, his strength robbed by the burst of pain in his kidneys. Some among the onlookers cheered. At once, Dohatsa whirled and kicked Tossa in the stomach. Renewed agony exploded in the tender parts of Tossa's body. He gasped for air and fought to get purchase.

Failing that, he scooped up a handful of dirt and hurled it in the face of Dohatsa.

"There is no honor in that," shouted two of Dohatsa's partisans.

Fire erupted behind the eyelids of the traitor, and he clawed at his face. Tossa fought back the debilitating effects of the blows he had absorbed and came unsteadily upright. He took two shaky steps forward and engulfed Dohatsa in a bear hug. Flexing his knees, Tossa tried to throw his opponent.

Heavier by far, Dohatsa did not move at first. Then, slowly, his moccasins rose into the air. Tossa swiveled his hips and threw his enemy to the ground. Dohatsa did not land flat. He hit his head first and his shoulders next as Tossa landed on top of him. Now Tossa dimly heard men cheering him. A spectacular nighttime shower of stars filled Dohatsa's head. He fought to suck air into his restricted lungs. When his chest moved, he dimly heard the brittle snap of three ribs. Fiery torment seared his chest cavity. Tossa had greater strength than he had expected. If he did not break this soon, he would not fight on this day, let alone win. As though from a distance, he commanded his legs to rise.

When the soles of his moccasins rested flat on the ground, he flexed powerful thighs and heaved upward. Although the burden of weight upon him shot up into the air, Dohatsa failed to dislodge Tossa. When the wiry young tribal policeman came down, he buried one knee in the slightly paunchy gut of Dohatsa.

Sour bile and the remains of his morning meal erupted from Dohatsa's mouth, preceded by a heavy gust of air. His head swam and his limbs went slack. In desperation, Dohatsa rallied his flagging resources and went for the knife in his bright orange sash. When it came free, he made a swift slash at Tossa.

Nimbly, the young Tua avoided the blade and sprang to his feet. A quick kick sent the knife spinning brightly in the sunlight. Then Tossa had the arm pinned. He rolled the offending hand of Dohatsa over, palm down, and stamped on it with a moccasined foot until he heard bones crack. Howling, Dohatsa doubled up, nursing his injured extremity. Tossa stepped behind him and knelt. He took a large hank of black hair and yanked back the head of his enemy.

"I could, I should, cut your throat. Instead, what I want from you is the truth. Tell me all about our stolen sacred articles."

Dohatsa surrendered all of his arrogance, along with his resistance. He had been in the pay of Satterlee for nearly a month. He knew that his confession would mean certain exile, if not death, under tribal law. Shamefacedly, he turned his head to look at the man who had bested him. "What you accused me of before is true. I have taken money from the white outsiders, Satterlee and Quinn, for a moon now. It is I who stole the religious objects and gave them to Quinn. What he did with them I do not know."

Disgust at such betrayal twisted the face of Santan Tossa. He came upright and turned to address the gathering of Tua men. "You heard what this disgraced one said. Confine him somewhere until the Council can attend to his crimes. Now, who will join me? Come, it is a thing of honor. Without the help of the white lawman I would never have found the necklace."

Two young Tua men stepped forward. Three more joined them. Then half a dozen. One spoke for the others. "If you will have us, Santan Tossa, we will fight with you for the white men."

Before he left for Taos, Santan Tossa had acquired a force of twenty-eight.

Shortly before nightfall, Deputy Sheriff Sammy Jennings cantered up to the *case grande* at Rancho de la Gloria. The majordomo greeted him politely and hailed a boy to lead the lathered horse to the stableyard, to be cooled out, watered and rubbed down. He showed the lawman into the central courtyard.

Don Diego Alvarado sat there, on a white-painted, wrought-iron bench, smoking a cigar. He roused himself to welcome his visitor. Jennings made it short and to the point.

"I've come from Smoke Jensen, Don Diego. He is undersheriff in Taos now."

Jennings, an uncomplicated man, missed the sardonic note of irony in the grandee's chuckle and words. "My friend Smoke is coming up in the world. I gather that there is something of importance that I should know?"

"Yes, sir. Smoke sent me to tell you that the Quinn

gang intends to lay siege to Taos. Shut off the town and starve out the occupants. He asks that if it is possible you send as many vaqueros as you can."

"I can fill forty saddles within the hour. Will that do?"

Jennings swallowed hard. "Oh, Lordy, sure. Fine as frog's hair, señor."

"Excellent." He raised his voice and called to his eldest son. "Alejandro! Come out here and round up the vaqueros. I want forty of the best."

Alejandro appeared in a doorway of a room on the second floor. "What is it, Father? Have the rustlers returned?"

"No. We ride to Taos. Smoke Jensen has need of our firepower." He turned back to his visitor. "As I say, this will take an hour. You must be in need of refreshment. Come, I'll have Maria prepare food and get you something to drink." Steering the young deputy toward the doorway to the detached kitchen, Don Diego shouted ahead to his cook to fix some meat and cheese and tortillas. Also to have Pepe bring up three beers from the spring house.

After sending off his last messenger, Smoke Jensen settled down in the sheriff's office to a plate of beef stew from the corner eatery. This being Taos, the stew had potatoes right enough, but with tomatoes, onions, garlic and chile peppers instead of turnips, carrots and garden peas. The gravy was rich and thick, which he scooped up with folded flour tortillas. A soupy bowl of beans came with it, and a side dish of some mashed, yellow-green substance. Guacamole, he had been told. Avocado, Wally Gower had informed him. Again with the ever-present tomato, garlic, onion and chiles. It had been flavored with some pungent, green herb and it tasted delightful. Smoke had just finished wrapping his lips around another bite of it when a loud crash and the sound of breaking glass summoned him from the office. From the knot of excited onlookers in the street, he learned the disturbance came from La Merced, one of the more un- savory saloons in town.

Smoke headed that way at once. He had to shove his way through a cluster of brown-faced spectators who crowded the boardwalk and entranceway. Three steps led to a grime-coated tile floor. Again, Smoke had to grab shoulders and heave men out of the way. This time, he noted that the faces wore expressions of anxiety and concern. He soon learned the reason.

A quartet of white thugs worked systematically at breaking up the place. Their erstwhile leader snarled at the bartender, who cringed in the far corner of the back bar. "You damn greasers like to have poisoned two of my men last night. We're takin' over this town, so you might as well get an idea of what happens to folks who put funny powders in drinks for the Quinn gang. You under- stand? *¿Comprende?*"

Bobbing his head frantically, the barkeep, who knew not the least word of English, and could not understand a thing being growled at him, covered his eyes as a wrought-iron legged chair went hurtling toward the mirror behind the bar. The big plate of glass shattered into a million shards on impact. The complaining hard case yanked a jug-eared, slightly built fellow from his chair and flung him after. Two of his henchmen turned to check out the disturbance between them and the doorway. In the next instant, Smoke came face-to-face with them. Neither ruffian suffered from being slow. As one, they balled fists, and the nearer one drove a hard- knuckled hand toward the face of Smoke Jensen.

18

Smoke Jensen jerked his head to one side and let the fist whistle past. Then he brought one up from the cellar that connected with the brute's jaw. Teeth clopped shut, and the yellowish whites of his eyes showed as his pupils rolled upward. Smoke closed in and gave him two hard shots to the heart for good measure. Then he felt a sharp jolt as the second thug caught him in the gut. Smoke took a back step and braced himself.

At once, the brawler came on. Smoke let him get in close. Then he flexed his knees, fired his best right cross and put shoulder and hips into it. The outlaw's boots left the floor. Squalling like a cinch-galled horse, he pitched face first across a nearby table. The legs broke and went four directions, as did the stacks of coins and bills. By that time, the first one to assault Smoke had recovered himself enough to launch another attack.

He came in low, intent on taking Smoke off his feet. Smoke stood his ground and, at the last instant, smartly raised his right knee. Face met knee and the face lost. Blood flew in a shower from a mashed nose. Three teeth snapped loudly, and more crimson ribbons streamed from the damaged mouth. The legs stopped churning and the eyes gradually crossed. The would-be tough dropped two feet in front of Smoke Jensen. Which left the other assailant to tend to.

Smoke turned to face him as the member of the Quinn gang put himself back on his boots. He had lost his cock-sure smirk. His eyes glazed, he took an unsteady step toward Smoke Jensen. Blindly, he tripped over the broken table and sprawled again on the green baize. One of the men, who'd had his game disrupted and his winnings scattered, boxed the outlaw's ears. Which got him up right smartly. He spat a curse at Smoke Jensen and came on.

Smoke snapped a right-left combination to the head, then lowered his point of aim to work on the chest and gut. His elbows churned back and forth while he delivered short, punishing blows. When the ruffian's guard disappeared entirely, Smoke took a quick back step and launched a solid left jab that rocked his opponent to the toes. He spun half left and shuddered while still erect. Then he wilted like a stalk of grass before a prairie fire and thudded on the floor. Seeing the pair so hastily dispatched, the leader and his remaining henchman went for their guns.

Smoke did not even change stance. His right arm already across his body for counterbalance, he simply grabbed at the butt of his second Colt and hauled it from the horizontal leather. He snapped back the hammer and tripped the trigger. By that time, and much to his later regret, the subordinate section leader of the gang had cleared leather. He had not, however, leveled his weapon when a hot poker jabbed him in the belly and his six-gun discharged into the floor. Beside him he heard his underling utter a boast he knew could not be fulfilled.

"I got him! I got him—got him!"

What he *got* was the center of the forehead of a big black bull that hung on the wall behind Smoke Jensen, as the bullet of the last mountain man smacked into his chest and burst his heart. Smoke crossed the short space between him and the dying man and kicked the Colt from his grasp. Then he turned on the gut-shot leader.

Plucking the Merwin and Hulbert from his numb fingers, Smoke observed, "You won't survive that. So, I'll let you go. I have a message for Paddy Quinn. Tell him to keep the hell away from town or I'll bring down a fire storm of hurt on him."

Gasping, the hard case observed, "You've got a mouth on you. Who are you?"

"Smoke Jensen."

"Awh . . . shit, shit, shit." With that, he passed out.

Smoke turned to the customers. "Will four of you bring those two to the jail. *La carcel, ¿comprende?*"

Volunteers nodded their heads eagerly. They roughly grabbed up the unconscious hard cases and dragged them from the saloon. Smoke faced the bartender. "Whatever money you find on those two, I'll add what I get from the others to help offset damages."

One vaquero at the bar translated. It brought a beaming smile from the worried brow. Smoke had earned his gratitude.

On a small mesa to the west of town, Whitewater Paddy Quinn listened to the sound of gunfire in Taos. All of his section leaders sat horses around him. All except Slim Vickers and three of his henchmen. From what he had learned from one of the seven who did report on time, Slim had remained behind to teach a lesson to some greasers who had poisoned some of them the previous night. Now, hearing the gunfire, Paddy Quinn beckoned to one of the hard cases who waited farther away with many of the gang. The man walked his horse up.

"What do you want, boss?"

"Baker, tell me about this poisoning, will ye?"

Baker looked embarrassed. "Awh, well, boss, it wasn't poison for real. Jist some green beer. It was right skunkey. Bunch of us wound up squirting through the eye of a needle at ten paces. Two of the boys got sick. Threw up over everything."

"Where did this happen?"

Baker frowned. "Some place called La Merced. Don't know what it means."

Paddy gave him a patronizing smile. "It means, 'the mercy.' Though I don't reckon ye got much mercy from them, eh, bucko?"

"That's right, boss."

"Sure an' what did Slim have in mind to do about it?"

Surprised that Quinn would take it further, Baker blinked. "Uh—well, ah, he and three of the boys was gonna go back and bust up the place. Kick some greaser butt."

"He say anything about shootin' them?"

That set Baker back. "Uh—no. Jist wanted to cause some damage."

Quinn's face went hard, his eyes narrowed and he gazed at the distant town. "Then it's that damned Smoke Jensen doin' the shootin'. An' I've no doubt that the boys will not be comin' back. I don't."

"Rider comin'," called out one of the outlaws.

Slim Vickers came on slowly, slumped in his saddle, one arm supporting him on the neck of his horse. When he drew nearer, Quinn saw that the man's face had turned a ghostly white. A green tinge surrounded his mouth. Then he saw the red stain on Slim's belly.

"Awh, saints above. What's happened to ye, darlin' boy? Where's the rest of the boys?"

"Two's in jail. One's dead. An' Smoke Jensen has done killed me." With that he fell off his horse and into eternity.

"Awh, damn Jensen's black heart." Quinn threw up his hands. "Nothin' for it, then. We'll be leavin' now, we will. Spread out, boys. An' hold back until the rest of the lads arrive. When they do, we'll be takin' our positions. This time it will be a regular siege," he told them. "Ye have your assignments. Ye are to pursue them and show no quarter."

* * *

Merchants and townsmen alike turned out to not be so hot for the prospects of standing off a siege. Feeding all of the volunteers became a problem long before Don Diego Alvarado and his vaqueros reached town. Several other ranchers had brought cowboys in to supplement the defenses. The opposition became even more vociferous when the new undersheriff strode through town with a bundle of posters, which he attached to the door of every cantina and saloon.

"What's the meaning of this?" one unhappy saloon owner demanded. "You can't take the opportunity away from us to make a nice profit."

Smoke Jensen stared at him with disdain. "The last thing we need is a lot of boozed-up men with guns on their hips. We won't have time to round up drunks when Quinn and his gang get here. The flyers mean exactly what they say. You will restrict yourselves to the sale of beer only. Any violators will have their establishments locked and spend the duration in jail. It would be a good idea to limit your customers' intake, also. I've known men to get fallin' down drunk on good, strong beer."

Bristling, the owner offered defiance. "You ain't no dictator. What if we refuse?"

Smoke snorted. "Are you volunteering to be the first to get locked up?"

Short and stout, with the flabby muscles of a man unaccustomed to hard work, the bar owner gauged the look in the eyes of Smoke Jensen and rightly read his expression. "Well—ah—well, no. I reckon I'll do what you say, but I don't have to like it."

"No, you don't." Smoke moved on.

When that task had been completed, Smoke had to hurry to the town hall for a meeting he had scheduled with the women of the community and the restaurant owners. In the public meeting room, Smoke stepped to the lectern and addressed the gathering.

"Ladies, we have a good fifty outsiders in town. None of them have the facilities to feed themselves. And there will be more coming. I have been assured that the eating places in town cannot handle the increase except on a continuous operation basis. What we need to do is set up a cookhouse here at city hall. I'm asking for volunteers to cook and serve."

Abigail Crowder, wife of the Taos fire chief, raised her hand. When Smoke recognized her, she stood to ask her question. "Where will we get the food?"

"I have spoken with Mr. Hubbard at the general store. The city will purchase all supplies from him. There will be no charge for the meals. If you give of your time, it won't empty the city treasury, what there is of it."

Another woman stood. "How long will this go on?"

Smoke frowned, scratched at his jaw. "Hard to say. At least two or three days. The mayor and I have sent a message to Santa Fe. We're asking the governor to call out the militia. But, politicians move slowly. Troops under arms move even slower. We'll be on our own for a goodly while."

She had another question. "Will there be enough to eat?"

Smoke nodded reassurance. "I reckon so. For the volunteer fighting men, I suggest you concentrate on fixin' what there's the most of. Such as corn bread, biscuits, potatoes, rice and beans. Hubbard has dozens of barrels of those. Plenty of pickles, too. If you can come up with some chickens from home, it would help. Now, if you'll step over here, Mr. Dougherty, the town clerk, will sign you up, put down the times of day you want to work."

Small columns of outlaws streamed down off the mesa. They spread out, and those tasked to the detail made ready to close off the roads. Others waited two miles from Taos to set up roving patrols to prevent anyone from sneaking out of town from houses on the outskirts. What Paddy Quinn did not know would soon prove to have fateful consequences for his plans.

Less than ten minutes earlier, twenty-five young Tua warriors, with Santan Tossa in the lead, had ridden into Taos and assembled outside the sheriff's office. Their faces were set, emotionless, the stereotypical Indian visage. At the direction of their tribal police chief, they filed into the office and came out with far more animated expressions. Each of them clutched a rifle or a shotgun. Faces of horror flashed through the Mexican and white residents of Taos when they saw this. Enough so that Santan Tossa went inside and spoke briefly with Smoke Jensen.

Smoke came outside and went among the troubled citizens of Taos. He spoke briefly and earnestly to small groups. "They are here to fight Quinn's gang. They can't do that with bows and arrows. If more of you had volunteered, it would not be necessary."

One indignant, pudgy man in a banker's suit protested hotly. "It's not our fault. You can't blame us. We're not lawmen. It's your job to protect us."

Such whining complaints quickly wore thin Smoke's sparse layer of patience. After the third such outpouring of whining self-justification, he snapped hotly. "And if you had the brains of a gnat, you'd realize that is exactly what I am doing."

"The governor will hear of this," a voice warned darkly. The banker had slunk back to launch another feeble barb.

Smoke laughed in the man's face. "Not until you can get out of town, he won't."

Diego Alvarado, along with two of his sons, Alejandro and Miguel, at the head of thirty-eight vaqueros, thundered up the long slope from the high desert flats where Rancho de la Gloria was located. All of the cowboys had heavily armed themselves. Twin bandoliers of rifle cartridges crisscrossed their chests. Obrigon .45s rode high in holsters on their belts.

Eight of their number cast frequent, nervous glances at their saddlebags, which had been packed full of crudely made grenades. The hand-thrown bombs were made of wine and tequila bottles, tightly packed with black powder and horseshoe nails, then fused and stoppered. The prospect of using them excited some of the more reckless among the vengeance-hungry vaqueros. Ahead waited the men who had murdered their *compañeros* and stolen their pride when they had stolen the cattle they tended. This would be a day for *El Degüello*. No quarter would be given. In the heads of some of the older ones echoed the brassy refrain of the "Cutthroat Song," which their grandfathers had played outside the defiant walls of the Alamo. That these *ladrónes* they rode to fight were gringos only sweetened the revenge. Five miles from Taos, Diego Alvarado signaled a halt.

"Alejandro, Miguel, here is where we will divide into three groups. Miguel, you will take ten men and ride directly down the road to town. Alejandro, take fourteen and circle a short way to the north. Not more than half a mile, mind. I will take the rest and go to the south. When Miguel and his men open fire, we will sweep down on the *bandido* scum and kill them all."

Alejandro and Miguel made their selections and drew the men apart. After signaling to their father, Diego stood in his stirrups and waved a gloved hand over his head. *"¡Adelante, muchachos!"*

With an enthusiastic, shouted cheer of encouragement, the indomitable company of vaqueros thundered off to bring the force of destiny to the unsuspecting outlaws.

Three members of the city council came bustling into the sheriff's office while Smoke Jensen was spooning a plateful of beans into his mouth. From the fiery flavor, Smoke judged that the women cooks had found a ready and willing source of chile peppers among the Mexican households. A florid-faced man in a brown suit and matching derby hat spoke for the politicians.

"What is this we hear that you have actually armed the Indians?"

Smoke chewed and swallowed his most recent mouthful and gestured with the spoon. "Yes, I have."

"Why, that's outrageous. And, it is totally unacceptable."

Smoke shook his head. "No, it's not. Think about it, gentlemen."

Agitation darkening the rosy color of his face, the spokesman yapped at Smoke. "We *have* thought about it. We do not intend to be massacred in our beds or our own homes. We demand—"

Smoke raised a hand to silence him. "Let me acquaint you with some very real, although unpleasant facts of life. When the gang and its hangers-on get here, Paddy Quinn will have between forty-five and seventy highly capable gunfighters at his command. The Tua warriors have come here and are willing to defend your town for you. They can hardly do so against such odds with weapons out of the Stone Age. The mayor agreed with me that we should properly arm them, and that has been done."

"Why were we not consulted about this?"

Smoke Jensen smiled coldly. "To save time. Politicians, from the White House on down, believe that they can talk troubles to death. We could be arguing over arming the Tuas until winter came."

The councilman cut his eyes to his associates and fired his last barb. "Banker Elwell tells us that you refused to notify the governor."

Smoke lowered his gaze a moment. "I—ah—stretched the truth a little when I spoke with the banker. In the letter requesting the militia, I informed the governor of our decision. The mayor assured me it was all right to arm the Indians for—how does the territorial constitution put it?—'the purpose of hunting game and for the defense of the common good.'"

Defeated, and hating it, the spokesman snapped at

Smoke. "For a man with so low an opinion of politicians, you can sure quote law like one."

Grinning, Smoke affected to preen himself. "A man of many talents, wouldn't you say?"

Shocked at this effrontery, the senior councilman's eyes bulged. "Well, I never!"

"Nope. Reckon you haven't."

Smoke's mockery sent them to the door. Heads held high in indignation, the delegation had only reached the porch when they collided with Wally Gower and three other town moppets of about his age, who surged past them, into the office. "They're comin', Sheriff Jensen. The Quinn gang's closin' in on town. It looks like there's enough of them, they're gonna ring the whole place."

19

When the news the boys carried got out, it quickly changed a lot of minds. First to scurry into the sheriff's office was the banker, Elwell. "You're the undersheriff. Do something," he bleated. "We need all of the protection we can get."

Smoke Jensen could not resist a final tweak of this whining hypocrite. "You've changed your mind about arming the Tuas with modern weapons?"

"Yes—yes, anything. Just save us from those vandals out there."

"Well, then, I'd suggest you go home, get your rifle, and help us."

Elwell eyed him with suspicion. "Sheriff Jensen, I've not fired a rifle in years."

Smoke gave him a grin. "It's like ridin' a horse, Elwell. You never forget." To Santan Tossa he suggested, "Let's go out and take a look at the new arrivals."

What they found, as they made their rounds, stunned even the usually unflappable Smoke Jensen. Instead of the expected forty-five to seventy outlaws, Smoke counted fully two hundred border trash, drifters and genuine hard cases spread out around the town. All of them seemed to be cold, grim-faced, hardened killers. Smoke turned to a deputy who stood nearby nervously fingering his Winchester.

"Hardly what we counted on, is it? I want you to go back into town and get those volunteers to speed up filling sandbags. Tell them I want stacks built to line the outer walls of all wooden buildings to the height of a kneeling man. Then come back here and take charge."

The lawman gulped and broke his fixed stare at the outlaws. "Right away, Sheriff." Grateful to be away from there, if only for a few minutes, he hurried off.

Then Smoke advised Tossa and all the men within hearing, "Now all we have to do is wait and find out what the enemy has in mind."

Back at the Sugarloaf, Mary-Beth Gittings worked industriously to load the valises they had brought into the fancy carriage. Her sons, red-eyed from yet another switching, dragged their own packed luggage from the house. Her face drawn, and tight-lipped, she remained ominously silent as she walked past Sally Jensen, who stood on the porch and watched. Sally's face revealed a poorly restrained expression of pleasure.

When the last piece had been loaded, Mary-Beth advanced on Sally, fists on hips, her face a study in self-righteous indignation. Her cheeks burned, not only with her umbrage, but from humiliation. She had allowed this woman to dictate to her how she should deal with the minor infractions her darling children committed. She was the first to admit they were not perfect. All children did naughty things from time to time. But to *spank* them? To viciously punish and degrade them—and one's self—in such a barbaric fashion? It would have never occurred to her that when on another person's property, and under their roof, one should abide by their rules. She should have never listened to Sally, her angry thoughts continued. Especially after she learned what she knew now.

It had come out only an hour ago, while she once

again reluctantly put the switch to the boys up in the room they shared. Wailing in hurt and fright, their bottoms a cherry red, they had sobbed out how that monstrous creature had threatened their lives. Horrified, Mary-Beth had decided on the spot to leave. Now she let all her outrage boil out.

With a visible effort, she restrained most of her dudgeon as she addressed her hostess for the final time. "I never believed that such a dear old friend would be so shamelessly protective of such an ill-bred child."

Her patience exhausted, Sally glowered back. "What is it this time, Mary-Beth?"

Mary-Beth let it spill out. "Why, it is about murder. My precious sons revealed to me not an hour ago that Bobby threatened to hang Seth and Sammy when they ran away."

That banished the last of Sally's sense of obligation. "Mary-Beth, don't you recall that after all they had stolen horses. Horse thieves are hanged out here."

Sally might as well have smacked Mary-Beth in the middle of her forehead. Shock silenced her to a small squeak. Then she hoisted her skirts and turned away. Briskly she walked to the carriage and boarded the driver's seat. She picked up the reins and snapped them. Without a farewell or a backward look, she and her troublesome children rolled down the long lane. At the last moment, only Billy Gittings turned back and gave a friendly, forlorn wave to Bobby Jensen.

Soberly, Bobby returned the gesture. The next instant, Sally and Bobby fell into one another's arms in relief and joy. "They're gone. They're finally gone," Sally shouted happily.

For the defenders of Taos, the wait to see what Quinn had in mind proved a long one. Both sides restlessly eyed one another from across the separating distance. Tenseness increased among the besiegers when the faint drumming of many horses came from the southwest. Paddy Quinn and a dozen of his immediate subordinates lingered on the far side of a bridge that spanned a narrow creek in a deep, red rock gorge. They conversed quietly there with the men assigned to operate the roadblock. It was toward them that a party of eleven men, dressed as vaqueros, cantered in mid-afternoon.

Quinn trotted forward a few lengths and raised a hand in a gesture to halt. "Turn back. No one enters town without our leave."

Several seconds went by before their identity became clear to Quinn. Then he shouted over his shoulder. "B'God, it's that Diego Alvarado's outfit. Turn about, boys, an' give 'em hell."

Miguel and the vaqueros had anticipated that. At once their weapons blasted in a volley. They fired again, and three of the outlaws left their saddles. Paddy Quinn barely escaped with his life. Bullets cracked past his head, and one grazed the shoulder of his mount. He turned first left, then right, only to see a swarm of more cowboys appear on both sides of the road. Determined to salvage what he could of his subordinate leaders and the men, he put spurs to his horse as he shouted to his underlings.

"Follow me! It ain't worth it; let 'em in." Then he cut off at an oblique angle between the hostile forces.

At once, the vaqueros converged on the road and cantered into town in a column three wide. Diego and Alejandro waited at the side until the last of the cowboys got through. He halted six of them.

"Stay here and keep the road open," Diego commanded.

One of the younger vaqueros looked nervously over his shoulder. "*Sí, patrón*. But you saw what they did when we rode in. There are so many of them."

Diego nodded. "They cannot all come against you. They are here to close the town. When some of them come back, use your rifles. Keep them at a distance."

With that Diego rode on into town. He stopped at the

sheriff's office and was greeted by Smoke Jensen. "It's good you're here, Diego. How many men did you bring?"

"Thirty-eight, and two of my sons."

Smoke laughed and wrung Diego's hand. "Make that three. Pedro insists he is healed enough to take part. He wants a rifle."

Diego nodded his understanding. Then he asked the question foremost on his mind, "How many of them are there?"

"By my count, close to two hundred."

Diego frowned. "That is a formidable force."

A smile bloomed on Smoke's face. "We have nearly as many, thanks to you and our Tua friends. Come, I'll show you how we're set up."

Smoke Jensen set off on a tour of town, explaining the defenses to Diego Alvarado. They had covered two sides of town when a flurry of gunshots broke out.

Being run off from the barricade rankled some of the gang. A dozen of the outlaws on the east side received a blistering lecture from their section leader on holding their place at all costs. Being of the criminal class, they saw any orders, especially those couched as criticism, as an affront. It made them restless, and eventually their patience wore out.

One hothead gave his opinion. "I say we can take that town full of sissies just by ourselves."

Another slightly more intelligent one disagreed. "Those Mezkin cowboys are in there now."

"Don't matter. Mezkins is dumb like Injuns. They think it's the noise that knocks a man down, so they don't aim."

A third piece of trash had news that slowed them for a while. "These must; they done knocked two of the boys outten their saddles."

"Lucky shots," the first insisted. He kept on for another ten minutes, until he had them all convinced.

They trotted their horses to the east road and passed

through the blockaders without restraint. Then the reckless hard cases spurred their mounts to a gallop and, with six-guns out and ready, rode like a whirlwind into Taos. They met immediate opposition. A hail of lead came from the second-floor windows in buildings near the center of town. Rifle fire, they soon learned to their regret. Two of the frontier trash left their perches and sprawled in the dirt of the street. A third gritted teeth and clapped a hand to a hole in his shoulder.

From closer at hand, more guns sought out the survivors. Bullets clipped through the air around them. For all that the defenders had been instructed to take good aim, the fact remained that there was more air out there than meat. Nine of the outlaws managed to reach the Plaza de Armas, which they proceeded to ride around, firing into the building fronts. They had made half the circuit when Smoke Jensen and Diego Alvarado arrived on the scene. The situation changed abruptly.

"That shooting is coming from the Plaza." Diego Alvarado announced something that Smoke Jensen already knew.

"We'd best get there the fastest way," the last mountain man opined.

Diego pointed to an alley that cut through several blocks at a sharp angle "Take this *callejón*."

They set out at a fast trot, both men with six-guns in hand. At the far end, Smoke could now see the fountain in the center of the square. A horseman obscured his view a moment as he rode by in the Plaza de Armas, firing into buildings as he went. Another followed, then another. One block to go. Smoke held his fire as another of the Quinn gang—he figured it could be none other—rode by the alley mouth. In another three seconds they came out into the open.

"Here's a couple of 'em," a strange voice brayed from behind Smoke Jensen.

He crouched and whirled in the same move. The Colt in his right hand bucked, and the outlaw who had called to his friends took a bullet in the right side of his chest. To Smoke's other side, the Obrigon in the hand of Diego Alvarado belched flame, and a .45 slug struck another bandit in the gut. His eyes bulged, but he kept coming. The odd, foreign-looking revolver—the barrel, cylinder and frame had not been blued—in his hand raised to line up on the chest of Diego Alvarado.

Diego fired again and put his bullet in the brain of the man with the 11mm Mle. '74 Saint Etienne, French-made six-gun. He died before the shock of his first wound faded. The heavy, soft-gray steel weapon fell from his hand. Immediately more of the outlaws came at them. By then, a scattering of defenders had reacted to the sudden appearance of the enemy. The volume of fire raining on the intruders grew rapidly. It soon had an effect.

Three more went down, and Smoke Jensen found himself nearly run over by a riderless horse. He jumped to one side, tripped over the body of a hard case, and fell to the red tile walkway around the base of the fountain.

"I've got you now," a triumphant voice shouted from above Smoke.

Instantly, Smoke Jensen rolled to his left and brought up his Peacemaker. He fired the moment he saw a human form. By the sheer perversity of chance, the slug struck the front of the outlaw's revolver cylinder. The thug screamed and dropped his now useless weapon while Smoke rolled again. This time, Smoke took better aim.

"Dutch!" the dying man screamed, in spite of the hole in his throat. "He got me, Dutch. Did me good." Then he groaned softly and fell across the neck of his mount. The frightened horse carried the corpse away from the plaza.

Smoke rounded the base of the fountain, forced to dodge bullets from both sides. Inexorably the numbers mounted. Suddenly Dutch Volker found himself and only two others cursing and firing defiantly at the defenders. He opened his mouth and bellowed loudly enough to carry above the tumult of gunfire.

"Get out of here! We're all that's left."

Swiftly, they clattered away through a low screen of powder smoke. Diego Alvarado, his face grimed with black smudges, walked over to where Smoke Jensen stood with the loading gate of his .45 Colt open for reloading. "If they are all as stupid as those were, we should have an easy time, ¿no, amigo?"

Smoke gazed at the litter of the dead. "I wouldn't count on it."

Soft shafts of yellow lanced through the wrought-iron barred windows set high in the outer wall of the second-floor master bedroom. This side of the Satterlee hacienda outside Santa Fe faced the south. It provided a slight, though noticeable, temperature advantage during the winter months. Clifton Satterlee selected articles of clothing from a large armoire, which he handed to an Indian woman servant, who diligently folded and packed them into a large carpetbag.

Satterlee spoke aloud to himself as he decided on his wardrobe. "I think something elegant, perhaps a morning coat. For the formal capitulation of Taos nothing less would do." A soft rap sounded on the open door, and he looked up.

His majordomo stood there, a sparkle of expectation in his ebony eyes. "A rider just in from Taos, señor."

The expression on the face of Satterlee reflected that of his servant. "Show him up."

In two minutes the official greeter of the house returned with a smiling Yank Hastings. The young outlaw did not dwell on formalities. "Ever'thing's goin' fine, Mr. Satterlee. Paddy Quinn says there's no need for you to hurry up there. We'll have 'em flushed out by tomorrow morning. That's his guarantee."

Satterlee stretched his thin lips to even narrower proportions. "Mr. Quinn may well want his hour in the sun, but I have no intention of being denied my triumph. I will be ready within the hour. You will accompany me and my personal retinue to Taos at that time."

Sundown lingered only a quarter hour away. Rich orange light bathed the bowl in which Taos lay. It painted the red, yellow, and brown buttes, mesas and volcanic mountains in muted shadow. Following the ill-thought-out charge of the hotheads, the gang had settled down to strengthen their stranglehold on the town and its occupants. On the three sides not influenced by the creek and its deep gorge, the bandits edged in close enough to be well within range of their weapons. They opened up in a fury.

Windows became the first targets. Every visible pane ceased to exist in a wildfire storm that lasted twelve minutes. By then, the town custodian, whom no one had thought to inform to the contrary, had begun to light the street lamps. They quickly became the objects of punishment for the outlaws.

Glass flew into the street first, followed by thin streams of kerosene. It did not take long for one burning wick to be dislodged from the body of a lamp and fall into a pool of the flammable liquid that formed at the base of the post. Flickering blue at first, to be reduced to yellow-white, the flames swept the length of one block, then a second. At once the alarm sounded at the fire station, and volunteers had to abandon their fighting positions to answer the call. Always a curse, fire could reduce the city as surely as the outlaws who had caused its release.

Chief Ezekial Crowder directed his firemen from the shelter of a doorway. Bullets from the gang continued to be a hazard. One young fire fighter suddenly dropped his length of hose and yowled as he grabbed at his ear. Blood trickled between his fingers.

"At least it ain't like fightin' a structural fire," Crowder observed to Smoke Jensen, who had come at the first alarm. "So far, that is," Barnes amended.

His volunteers quickly spread out to beat down the flames. To Smoke it appeared the very earth burned. Black smoke vaulted the sky above town, and the outlaws cheered and shouted in derision. Gradually, the blazes subsided. After ten hard minutes the last one went out.

Encouraged by the diversion the fires had created, half a dozen scum charged the vaqueros who had been holding the west road. One of the Mexican cowboys reached to the saddlebag at his feet, grabbed up a bottle and used his hand-rolled cigarette to ignite the fuse that protruded from the cork in its mouth. When it began to sputter, he counted to three, stood and threw it out the open window.

It turned end-for-end four full times before it exploded violently at shoulder level in the midst of the gang members. All six screamed piteously and went down in a heap. That quickly changed the minds of those who thought of joining them. The effect on those who had witnessed the grenade became obvious as the fire it had caused began to dwindle. The last shots came from the outlaws only minutes after nightfall.

Half an hour later, Smoke Jensen finished off a piece of pie, sent over by one of the restaurants, and licked his lips. "I think that ends it for today. Diego, I'd keep a few people on the lookout for any effort to test our strength. The rest can get a little sleep, at least until an hour before daylight."

"And you, amigo, what will you be doing?"

Smoke gave him a wicked grin. "I'm going to go out and raise a little hob."

20

Smoke Jensen chose to leave town by way of the road controlled by the vaqueros from Rancho de la Gloria. The ranch hand on watch gave him a silent salute as he crossed the bridge on foot. Thick coatings of burlap muffled the hooves of his stallion, Cougar. They would remain on until Smoke slipped past the pickets of the outlaw army. So skilled was the last mountain man that when the vaquero lookout who watched him depart blinked, Smoke had completely disappeared.

It did not take long after that for Smoke to find targets for his night's mischief. Silently he wormed his way in among the outlaws at one camp fire. One look at his gunfighter rig and they accepted him as one of their own. He was offered coffee, which Smoke accepted.

"Thanks, I needed that. Maybe it'll settle my nerves."

"What are you gittin' at—er . . . ?"

Smoke dropped into the loose grammar and dialect of his mentor, the old mountain man called Preacher. "They call me Jagger. An' what I'm gettin' at is that there's Injuns in among the folks in town."

"Naw," another hard case disputed. "They're Mezkins, Jagger. You've jist caught a case of the spooks."

Smoke played the trump in his rumor hand. "Mezkins wearin' moccasins, loincloths and floppy shirts? Hair down to their shoulders? Believe it. I've seen 'em myself. They're all sharpenin' scalpin' knives."

A shiver passed over his audience. Smoke added more to their unease. "There must be as many fightin' men in thar as out here."

The doubtful one again challenged his statement. "Not accordin' to Whitewater Paddy."

Smoke cracked a grin. "Mr. Quinn don't know ever'thing. I've seed 'em. There's Injuns, an' Mezkin cowboys, and a whole lot of townies."

Smoke answered a string of troubled questions with inventions calculated to fan the blaze of fear he had introduced. After ten minutes of yarn spinning, Smoke drank off his coffee, came to his boots and drifted on.

"I'm makin' the rounds, checkin' if anyone needs anything," Smoke explained at the next fire. Using the names he had acquired at the first gathering, he deepened his cover. "Are you Zeke? Well, Rupe told me to tell you howdy for him. He's holdin' his own. 'Cept for what he found out about the Injuns in Taos."

Zeke eyed Smoke. "What's this about Injuns?"

Smoke launched into his tall tale about scalping. Then he added another log to the overloaded wagon. "That's not all. A feller who's been in close to town tells me that this Smoke Jensen has put up a hundred-dollar bounty on every one of us who gets killed."

Zeke denied that at once. "I don't believe it. Nobody, especially a rovin' gunfighter, has that kind of money."

Smoke ignored him. "Somethin' more about those Injuns. Jensen's armed them with rifles and shotguns."

"No!" Agitated, Zeke came to his boots. "Ain't no way them townies would stand for that. It's fools' work givin' guns to Injuns."

"Makes no never-mind. That's what I saw with my own eyes. Injuns runnin' around with Winchesters. An' that's not all of it. Not by half." Smoke went on to add yet another burden to the worried outlaws. Then he quietly left the uneasy souls to these imaginings.

After three more such visits, Smoke decided that his rumors would take sprout and grow with satisfactory speed. Crouched low, he worked his way in among the horses of those who ringed the town between roads. With a cautious hand, he reached for the cinch ring of one animal. He kept the other on the nose of the animal to calm it.

Ever so slowly, Smoke eased the leather end free of the ring and loosened the cinch. Next time the owner tried to straddle his mount, he would wind up with a lap full of saddle. Smiling to himself, Smoke completed the task and moved on to another critter to do the same. He repeated the loosening of cinch straps a dozen times, then switched tactics.

Along the west side, he fitted front hooves into black leather hobbles on ten other horses. He started to come upright from the last one when a voice challenged him from the darkness. "What are you doin' here?"

Smoke had a ready explanation. "Cleanin' the frog on the right forehoof of my horse. On the way out here he come up lame. Figgered it wouldn't do for us to jump up a fight and me unable to ride."

"Good thinking." The speaker moved closer. "Say, I don't think I—"

Prepared for that, Smoke had already slid his left-hand Colt from its pocket and gripped it tightly around the cylinder with his left hand. He swung the weapon now and connected the butt with the outlaw's temple. The alert section leader went down without a sound. Smoke bent and checked him, then tied the man's wrists and ankles and dragged him off toward the rear. His night vision in perfect condition, Smoke sought a place to stash his burden.

He found it in the form of a small ravine. He lined up

the bandit parallel to the gully and rolled him down, out of sight. During his brief search, Smoke had come upon a secondary ring of camp fires. These had not as yet been ignited. He carefully marked their location for later attention. For now, he moved on to find more who had straggled away from the picket line.

Nate Carver had his mind on a glass of whiskey, a hand of winning cards, and a pretty bit of fluff to sit on his lap. He eased his cartridge belt upward and unbuttoned his fly in order to relieve himself. While he fumbled with one stubborn button, visions of the sort of celebration he would have once this was over danced behind his eyes.

That whiskey would sure taste good. His mouth watered at the thought of it. And a nice big steak, well done, the way he had learned to eat it in Texas. And four of the stupidest fellers to ever hold pasteboards in a poker game to play against. Yeah. And then that tingling feeling that came every time a feller walked up them stairs with a floozy on his arm. The small room, the soft bed, the tender flesh. His self-distraction prevented him from sighting the ghostly movement against the lighter darkness of a star-lit horizon. All too late, he sensed another presence an instant before Smoke Jensen smacked him on the side of the head.

Nate would have rather died than be found by his friends in the condition that resulted from sudden unconsciousness and a full bladder. Smoke Jensen trussed him up and set him in the center of a collection of large, fat, barrel cactus. There were bound to be more, Smoke told himself.

Ten minutes later, Smoke found the reason for the second ring of fire pits. An outlaw wearing a cook's apron gathered dry mesquite branches and stacked

them beside a chuck wagon. Well beyond rifle range, this
would provide a safe place for breakfast. Smoke quickly
thought out a way to spoil the meal for them. Ghosting
in on moccasined feet, he closed with the belly robber.
Smoke's lips thinned to a grim line of disapproval when
he saw the curly gray hair on the head he intended to
thump. A feller his age should know better than to run
with outlaws.

Smoke's regret was not tempered by mercy. He eased
up behind the unsuspecting rascal and put him to sleep
with a solid blow from his Colt. Quickly he grabbed the
man and eased him to the ground. He pulled another
prepared strip of latigo leather from a pocket and
bound the bean burner's wrists. Then he pulled off the
man's boots and removed a sock. After binding the
ankles, he stuffed the dirty, smelly wool stocking into an
open mouth, careful to remove a poorly fitted set of den-
tures first, and used another pigging string to secure it
in place.

"Time to get to work," Smoke muttered to himself.

He went directly to the rear of the chuck wagon,
where the oversized tailgate/worktable had been lowered into place. He opened the drawer that contained
about five pounds of salt. This he poured into a bowl for
the time being and refilled the receptacle from the sugar
bin. The salt then went in to replace the sugar. A quick
search under a rising moon located an ant hill. Using a
tin plate, Smoke scooped up a generous number of the
busybody insects and delivered them to the flour barrel.

Half a dozen road apples, from the team of mules that
pulled the wagon, completed his sabotage when he
dropped them into the liquid that covered the corned
pork. Then he hoisted the supine cook over one shoulder and carried him off a goodly distance to where he
would not be found for some time. Someone else would
be fixing breakfast for the Quinn gang. Someone Smoke
felt confident would not have the skill to recognize the

change in the ingredients. That attended to, he began a round of the prelaid fires.

Into each of ten, he inserted a capped and fused stick of dynamite. Being careful to cover them well with dirt, he replaced the kindling and larger wood, then faded off into the night. He reflected on what he had done and counted it a good night's work.

Clifton Satterlee fumed over the delay. A wheel had broken on his surrey not thirty miles north of Santa Fe. Fortunately there had been a posada close by. One that did not have vermin swarming in the mattresses and climbing the walls of the kitchen, he noted grudgingly. The food had been good, for a change. Not the excellent meals his cook prepared, yet flavorful and generous in quantity. Much against his best instincts, Brice Noble had come with him. They sat now at a small table in the alcovelike cantina off the lobby of the inn. Noble poured for both of them from a green glass bottle of Domeq Don Pedro brandy. Not so good as his preferred cognac, but it would do, Satterlee considered.

Taking a sip, he spoke to Brice Noble. "This delay is inexcusable. A spare wheel should be brought along at all times."

"It's your carriage, Cliff." Noble did not mention that the damage had been done as a result of Satterlee's insistence that they travel at the fastest possible speed.

Satterlee cued on his partner's tone. "Meaning?"

"You are the one who has to order a spare being lashed on the surrey."

With a snort, Satterlee took a long pull on the amber liquid. "I hate people who ooze practicality." Abruptly he changed the subject. "We may have some difficulty with some of the people in Taos. They are a stubborn lot. But our time is running out. Quinn has assured me he has rounded up enough gunfighters and rough types to overcome any objections. We'll have about two hundred men."

Noble winced. "That's going to cost a lot of money."

"Yes, but necessary. We may have to take the town by force." He paused, sighed heavily. "Although I would prefer not to resort to that. It might affect our credibility when it comes to filing for new deeds. No matter what, we will have Taos, and we will log that Indian land. That is all vital to our project. I think I've had enough of this." He nodded to a quartet of mariachis playing to a Mexican couple at a corner table. "I'm going to retire. Hastings has assured me that they will have the wheel fitted by morning. Good night, Brice."

Smoke Jensen returned to Taos, linking up with the route he had used to depart only at the last moment. His keen night vision, augmented now by a hazy full moon, allowed him to pick out the significant differences from when he had left town. Seven darker lumps stood out against a background of twinkling pinpoints of light in a black velvet sky. Slowly they resolved into human figures. All faced inward toward the community they invested. Smoke had already dismounted. Now he clapped a hand over Cougar's muzzle and eased the big Palouse off the roadway. He ground reined his horse and slid off into the night once again.

One of those who attempted to reestablish the road-block under cover of night had taken a position some fifty feet from the verge of the road. He had hunkered down, the stock of his rifle used as a prop. He constantly cut his eyes from side to side and up and down to enable him to better see what lay across the deep gully and its creek that divided him from the outermost houses. He had no way of knowing that Alvarado's vaqueros knew to do the same and had picked out his position to within an inch. Had he known so, it would not have done him any good. He lost consciousness before they could do anything about his presence.

Smoke Jensen eased up behind the gunman and

slammed the butt of a Colt Peacemaker into the side of his head. With a soft grunt, the outlaw fell over onto the sandy red soil. Smoke quickly tied him and moved on.

Another of Quinn's ragtag army sat cross-legged with his back against a low palo verde. Smoke Jensen found him and decided upon a little trickery. "Hey," he whispered harshly. "Over here. We've got a problem."

Almost dozed off, the response sounded quarrelsome. "What's the matter. Ground too hard?"

"Come here. An' be quiet."

Roused from his near snooze, the outlaw came to his boots and duck-walked over. "Now, what's this problem?"

"I am," Smoke told him before he clouted him on the temple with the barrel of one .45. The thug went rigid and then dropped face first to the ground.

Smoke moved on in an instant. He suddenly realized that he had allowed himself to grow overconfident when a voice growled at him from the side. "Hold it right there."

Moving slowly, so as not to startle the speaker into shooting, Smoke faced his challenger. "What do you mean? I was only goin' down to bum a smoke offa Hank."

Suspicion thickened in the outlaw's voice. "There ain't no Hank with this outfit, an' I ain't seen you before." He beckoned with the muzzle of his rifle. "Come over here an' let me get a look at you."

Smoke complied, easing his left hand around out of sight. When he got within a long arm's reach, he stopped. The distrustful hard case peered closely at Smoke's face. "Nope. Never saw you with the gang before. Who are you?"

Smoke came out with his Greenriver sheath knife in his left hand and, with a short lunge, drove it horizontally through the costal region between the fifth and sixth ribs on the left side. The pointed tip penetrated the heart and sank the blade deep into the pulsing organ. Then Smoke jerked the haft to rip sideways. The man died without a sound. Smoke maneuvered to hold the dead man between him and any outlaw bullets and called out loudly to the defenders across the way.

"*¡Oigan, vaqueros de la Gloria! Ayudenme!*"

He got his help right away as the Mexican cowboys opened fire on the hard cases they had previously located. Smoke gave a shrill whistle, and Cougar trotted toward him. Quickly he flung the body away from him and swung into the saddle. With heels drumming into his sides, Cougar jumped to a fast canter and sprinted across the bridge and into the shelter of the buildings on the outskirts of Taos.

Smoke had thoughts only for sleep. But he found a delegation waiting for him at the sheriff's office. The mayor, Fidel Arianas, and Dr. Walters occupied chairs, along with Santan Tossa and Ed Hubbard. All except Tossa wore worried expressions.

Arianas opened the session. "How long do we have to hold them off?"

Smoke studied on that. "Three or four days, however long it takes for the militia to get here."

Arianas turned pale. "*¡Chingada!* There's not maybe fifty hombres in the militia. And that's on a good day. This *ladrón* has four times that many."

"Not anymore. I took care of a few. And tomorrow's sure to do in more."

Dr. Walters addressed a more serious problem. "We cannot hold out for more than four days. There is not enough food. There are too many mouths to feed."

Smoke frowned. "Make sure the vittles at the town hall get served only to the fighting men. The townspeople will have to fend for themselves."

Horrified at that prospect, the mayor thought first of votes. "The people will not stand for that. They'll blame me."

Smoke Jensen cut hot, angry eyes to the politician. "They'll have to live with it, if they don't want Paddy

Quinn campin' on their doorstep." He had not the slightest concern over the mayor's reelection possibilities.

Dr. Walters had another idea. "What about the water supply? If they poison the creek we have only a few cisterns, fewer wells."

Smoke looked to Tossa for a solution. "Can you have some of your warriors slip out of town and make sure Quinn's men do not put anything in the water?"

Santan Tossa smiled. "That will be easy. They will never be seen."

"Then that's settled. Reduce rations all around and guard the water that is in town. No matter how this goes, we'll all have to tighten our belts to survive. And . . . you can expect another attack in the morning. I reckon those scum will be spoilin' for a fight."

21

Four o'clock in the morning was entirely too dang early to get up and get around, the swamper for the missing cook complained as he trudged through the darkness toward the chuck wagon. All around him, the tiny flames twinkled as men struck lucifers to ignite their fires. They would boil their own coffee. It was up to him and old Snuffy to turn out the grub. Where was Snuffy? he wondered as he reached the wagon and did not find the belly robber anywhere. By now he usually had a lantern going and the first rollout of biscuit dough ready to cut.

"Snuffy! Where are you? Come on, we're fallin' behind."

Right then, at a fire pit not far away, flame hit the split and frazzled end of a length of fuse. It sputtered and hissed gustily, consumed the powder train that ran down its middle, and reached the detonator cap. A bright flash drew the swamper's eyes as a stick of dynamite let go with a tremendous roar. An instant later a shower of dirt and burning kindling mushroomed over the fire ring nearest the chuck wagon. Concussion knocked men rolling. One, who had leaned over, blowing gently to encourage the flames, died instantly.

Five seconds later another buried stick let go. Then a

third. The sound of the eruptions echoed off the walls of buildings in Taos. Reverberations had not died out when a fourth fire ring erupted in a gout of dirt. A fifth followed on its heels. By then, the swamper had dived to the ground and hugged red-brown clots of earth in a forlorn hope that a similar fate would not overtake him. Light the cook fire? Not very damn likely.

Two more blasts shattered the predawn quiet. An eerie silence followed. Then the swamper heard the cries and moans of the injured. Gradually his heartbeat began to slow. Then an anguished shout chilled him anew.

"Don't light that! Nooooo!"

BLAM!

No, there was no way he would light that fire. Two more explosions quickly dotted the *i*'s and crossed the *t*'s of that decision. No matter what Snuffy might say, he would absolutely, positively never even strike a match.

Smoke Jensen stood in a second-floor window, an old pair of brass army field glasses to his eyes. Ignited by the exploding dynamite, tufts of prairie grass had burst into flame, along with mesquite bushes and greasewood. The conflagration illuminated the disordered ranks of the enemy enough to let him clearly see the results of his night's work. It turned out to be better than he had expected.

Those outlaws already awake and not injured took to their horses. Shouts and curses blistered the air when some of them put a boot in a stirrup and wound up flat on their backsides. Several forked their mounts only to pitch face forward to the ground when their hobbled beasts jerked to sudden stops. Some rode off in the direction of Raton without a backward glance. Yet other hard cases ran around in confusion, their horses scattered in fright by the explosions.

More men helplessly stood in place to shout curses

and shake their fists. Dust thrown into the air by the dynamite explosions began to settle and obscure the entire scene. Acrid smoke from the explosives hung in undulating waves over the former fire sites. The others who had crowded into the room with him were laughing and slapping one another on the back. Smoke Jensen felt no such elation. Men had died, and others had been maimed by his actions. If it served to break the resolve of the outlaws, well and good.

"What happened to them?" Diego Alvarado asked Smoke.

Smoke lowered the field glasses. "That's what I'm here for anyway, isn't it? I prepared a little wake-up call for them."

Don Diego studied Smoke's handiwork in awe. "It looks . . . devastating."

"Who was it said something about omelets and eggs?" Smoke asked aloud.

He shifted the glasses again as a pearlescent ribbon silhouetted the jagged mountain peaks to the east. There. He had found him. Paddy Quinn stood on a knoll, the reins of his horse in one hand. His expression was one of disbelief. What next? he seemed to be asking himself. If need be, Smoke Jensen decided, he would show Quinn what.

"Begorrah, there's a black-hearted bastard at work here," an enraged Paddy Quinn exclaimed as Garth Thompson approached to report on their condition.

"You'll think it is Old Nick himself when I tell you where we stand right now."

Quinn cut his eyes to Thompson. His black orbs, which usually twinkled in harmony with his perpetual smile, had become flat mirrors. The beaming expression had melted away. "What is it yer sayin', boy-o, what is it?"

Garth had never seen his boss like this. He noted the black smudge of unshaven jaws, the little mouth set in an angry slash, high forehead furrowed, the muscles of his head so rigid that his small ears literally twitched. To Garth, Quinn looked ready to explode like one of their fire pits.

"We've had fifteen men killed. There's another twenty injured. Twenty-five men just plain rode off. I don't reckon they'll be coming back. Old Snuffy, our cook, and his swamper have plain disappeared."

A foul stream of curses gushed from Paddy's mouth. At last he curbed his fury. "By damn, this is the doing of Smoke Jensen. I've got to talk to whoever is in charge in Taos. He's got to curb his mad dog. And, he's got to see reason, he does. Even with our losses, we've enough men to wipe out the entire town. There's other places to live, an' men start over all the time, they do." Paddy went on for a good five minutes, as though rehearsing his presentation to the leader of the defenders. When he wound down, he issued his orders to Garth Thompson.

"Rig a white flag. Then ride down there and tell them I want to meet and talk with whoever is in charge. We'll meet after break—awh, hell, we don't have a cook, ye say. How am I gonna get some breakfast?"

Smoke Jensen and Diego Alvarado rode out to the meeting with Paddy Quinn later that morning. As they swung into their saddles, Smoke offered a word of caution. "I think it would be wise to have some of your vaqueros keep a close eye on every hard case in rifle range of our meeting."

Diego cut a knowing eye to Smoke. "You suspect that Señor Quinn will not honor his own flag of truce?"

"That's putting it mildly. I'll keep watch on Quinn. You do the talking."

Smoke's arrangement worked out excellently. Paddy Quinn knew Diego Alvarado from previous encounters and naturally addressed him as the leader. He chose to ignore Smoke Jensen, whom he also recognized. The snub was wasted on Smoke.

"Don Diego, it's good to see you again, it is."

Diego's black hair and mustache and chiseled features gave him a sardonic appearance. "Somehow I doubt that. What is it you want, Quinn?"

"Ah, no time for pleasantries, is it? A busy man ye are, no doubt. Well, then, we might as well get to it." Quinn paused and drew a deep breath, which he sighed out before he continued. "There's no denyin' that ye hurt me some. An' Mr. Satterlee will be sore distressed over that, an' that's a fact. But, it's also a fact, it is, that we've the strength to wipe out any resistance ye might choose to put up. So, me fine grandee, I've come to discuss the terms of your surrender. Not just the town, but that grand ranch of yers."

Diego Alvarado swallowed the rising anger to request in a cold, grave tone, "In return for what?"

Paddy Quinn leaned back in the saddle, as though considering that question, then produced his usual cherubic smile. "Now, Mr. Satterlee was perfectly willing to pay fair market price for all the property he desires. But . . ." His expression changed to the mask of deadly fury witnessed earlier by Garth Thompson. He nodded toward Smoke Jensen. "Then the devilment wrought overnight by this hired cur of yours changed all that, it did. So, Señor Alvarado, here's what we'll be havin'. All hostilities will end immediately. We will be allowed into town at once, without hindrance, to select which properties Mr. Satterlee desires."

To Paddy Quinn's surprise, it was Smoke Jensen who answered. "You'll be dancing with the devil before that happens."

Quinn masked his reaction and raised an arm to make a curt gesture. Two of his henchmen appeared over a low rise. Between them they held Martha Estes. They brought her forward until Smoke could plainly see the fear in her eyes. Quinn openly gloated over his prize, his voice a velvet purr.

"So, then, unless we are allowed into Taos, and the people are lined up eager and ready to sign over their property to C.S. Development Company, a division of C.S. Enterprises, Miss Martha here will be slowly killed right out here before your eyes."

Smoke Jensen's face took on a rock-hard stillness, his amber eyes and expression thunderous. "I sincerely doubt that's true. Clifton Satterlee would not be at all pleased."

Quinn appeared not at all affected by that judgment. To further prove he did not bluff, he made another signal. Four houses on the edge of town, which belonged to some of the poorer Mexican farmers, suddenly burst into flames. The dry thatch of their roofs burned rapidly. Women and small children ran screaming from their fiery homes. In the distance, the fire bell began to clang. Smoke and Diego looked on, unable to do anything.

Paddy Quinn watched with them for a while, then turned his horse and spoke over his shoulder. "You have one hour." Then he posed a question for Smoke Jensen. "Tell me, Smoke Jensen? How does it feel to at last meet your better?"

Smoke Jensen's flat, level gaze pierced Paddy Quinn and fixed him in place. "I don't think I have."

For a long, tense moment Paddy Quinn did nothing. Then he turned about and rode swiftly away without another word.

Smoke Jensen looked up from the lists of preparations that had so far been completed. A delegation of some eight local merchants stood in the sheriff's office. He clearly read the fear on their faces. Smoke erased the frown that had creased his brow and forced a smile.

"Something bothering you gentlemen?"

He noted that they were among those he had rated as the most timid among the businessmen of Taos. They fidgeted now, like schoolboys caught in some naughty act. One ran an index finger around the interior of his celluloid collar. Two shifted their feet in an uneasy manner. All eight clearly wished to be elsewhere.

"Come on, no need to hold back."

Charlie Lang, the haberdasher, cleared his throat and bobbed his Adam's apple. "Well, ah . . . we—that is, it's gotten around that we have an hour before those brigands just come in and take what they want. Is that true?"

Smoke shook his head. "No. We have an hour before they supposedly murder a young woman before our eyes and then come in and take what they want."

"Oh. That—ah—that makes a difference."

Smoke's face registered his discontent. "Mr. Lang, I was trying to be sarcastic. I chose the wrong words. The facts are that they cannot take this town no matter how hard they try. A lot of them are along out of curiosity. They have no real loyalty to Paddy Quinn or Clifton Satterlee. When they get a taste of our firepower, a lot of them will drift away. More than twenty of them ran out this morning before sunup."

"What about the young woman?"

Again, Smoke made a negative gesture. "Quinn will never kill her, not even hurt her in a serious way. He believes she is still the lady friend of his boss. With all the gunfighters he commands, Quinn would never buck Satterlee."

Lang persisted. "Why is that?"

"Mr. Lang, do you pay your employees at the start of the week or at the end?"

Charlie Lang frowned. The question puzzled him. "Why, at the end of the week, for all that it matters."

"My point. You don't pay them until they have performed the work for which they are being compensated. I firmly doubt that Satterlee has paid Quinn, and won't until the job is done. If Quinn and Satterlee got at odds, and Quinn didn't get paid, he'd have a whole lot of angry, broke gunhawks to contend with."

Lang thought on that awhile. "That makes sense. Even

so, we've been talking about the danger we're in, what those outlaws can do to us. We have families, investments, roots in the community. We don't want to risk harm to our wives and children and lose everything we have. This Clifton Satterlee has offered to compensate us fairly for our property. It seems wise for us to accept what he is proposing."

"Not anymore. Quinn says our resistance has changed all that. Satterlee is going to take what he wants, and that's all of Taos. As to protecting what you have at stake, I suggest that all of you grow a pair of stones and fight for what's yours."

Lang and three others began jabbering as one. "But some of us will get injured." "We'll be killed." "We have a right to be protected."

Smoke Jensen's disgust spilled over. "Listen to me you yellow-bellied rabbits," he thundered. "You are going to have to fight for your rights; we'll be too busy protecting the town as a whole. Here's my final word. Not a one of you will give in to such cheap intimidation. If I need to, I'll put a Tua warrior in every store, eatery and saloon to prevent your surrender. Now, get out of here."

Paddy Quinn rode to the abandoned adobe farmhouse where Martha Estes had been imprisoned. Following his instructions, his underlings had lashed her arms to a chair and left her sitting at a table, with only a crumbling wall to stare at. Quinn entered and stood between her and that unpromising vista. At once, Martha's gorge rose, and she began to unload onto him all her disgust and loathing.

"You are the most disgusting, foul, misbegotten piece of human refuse I have ever laid eyes upon. Your every act shames your mother and father."

She stopped for a breath, and Paddy seized the opportunity to get in a word of his own. "My mother, God rest her soul, is dead these twenty long years. An' me father is a drunk, who would not feel insult if someone crapped in his hat."

Eyes narrowed in her rage, Martha spat, "When Clifton discovers how you have treated me, he'll have you horsewhipped."

"Ye've got the right of it, lass. He's not got the balls to do it hisself." Realization that Jensen's taunt had struck home made her reminder even more unwelcome. "It's well an' good, it is, that ye know I'll never be for carryin' out me threats against you. That was for those dogs from town. Let them be worrin' over it. But, between you an' me—ah, an' Lord, there's somethin' I'd love to have between you an' me, there is—before this is over, I intend to get to know you better. *Intimately* better, if ye catch me meanin'?"

Martha twisted her face into an expression of disgust. "I'll see you in hell before that happens."

His smile bright as ever, so disarming it did not lend credibility to his words, Paddy Quinn spoke lightly as he started for her. "Will ye now? An' what's to stop me? All I need do is hoist them skirts and have at you with a will."

A sudden clatter from a carriage outside halted Quinn. He stopped, then took two hasty back steps. The next moment, Clifton Satterlee stormed through the askew doorway. His face flushed, Satterlee pointed a glove-covered forefinger at Quinn.

"That lout of yours out there tells me that you have Martha Estes in here as a prisoner, trussed up like a Christmas goose."

Paddy gestured to his prisoner. As though jerked by a string, Satterlee took two steps toward the young woman, then turned on Quinn. "Release her. *At once!*" Then to Martha, "My dear, this is inexcusable. I'll have you freed in a moment. And I promise you nothing like this will ever happen again. Where is Lupe?"

Martha turned her cobalt gaze on Clifton. "She's . . . being held someplace else."

Ice formed around the words of Clifton Satterlee. "Quinn, you will finish untying this young lady; then you will go and fetch her maid. And be certain that she has with her everything needed to restore Miss Martha to her usual loveliness."

Paddy Quinn had recovered himself enough to bark back. "She ran away from you, did you know that? I didn't send men to take her, I didn't. She went off with none other than Smoke Jensen."

Satterlee cut his eyes from Quinn to Martha. "Is that true?"

"Yes and no. I left on my own. I encountered Mr. Jensen on the road, and he was to escort me here to Taos." Hurrying to get it out before her nerve failed, Martha added, "I felt so terrible when I learned that the jewelry you gave me had been stolen. And that they were sacred objects to the Indians here. I wanted to do what I could to make amends."

Satterlee's anger found a new source. "Lies. Jensen must have told you that. It is not true. Trust me in that."

Martha clenched her jaw a moment, then braved it out. "I talked with a young Indian policeman who identified the necklace I wore . . . when they visited in Santa Fe."

"A copy perhaps," Satterlee suggested.

Martha held her own. "They do not make copies."

Satterlee took another tack. "Come, my dear. Let's put all that behind us. I am so relieved to find you safe and sound."

"Not so safe, nor so sound, if that one had his way," Martha challenged.

Clifton Satterlee rounded on Quinn again. "I thought I gave you an order. Now do it."

"You may regret this, Mr. Satterlee," Quinn muttered softly while he undid Martha's bonds.

Satterlee winced as though the threat had hit home. In that instant, after her release, Martha bounded upright and made a break for the door. Before Satterlee could react, Quinn passed him in a flash and snagged Martha by one arm.

"Not so fast, me fine colleen."

Martha did not resign herself so easily. She clawed at Paddy Quinn, scratched his cheek and neck, kicked him in the shins and pounded one small fist on his chest. While she struggled, Clifton Satterlee took it in with an astonished, bemused expression. Martha tried to knee Paddy in the crotch, and he hurled her against a wall.

All fight left her as she slammed painfully into the adobe blocks. Shoulders slumped, she faced the two men like an animal at bay. Her chest heaved from her exertion, and her face had turned a pale white. Clifton Satterlee studied her with new eyes.

At last he spoke. "Perhaps I have been hasty. I may have misjudged you, Mr. Quinn. Yes, I think I far underrated Martha's spirit. It seems that for the time being, you will have to detain her forcibly if she persists in such unbecoming activity."

Paddy Quinn touched fingers to his cheek. They came away bloody. Then he saluted his employer with a tap to the brim of his hat. "I'll see to it right away, that I will." Before departing, he added, "When that is done, there are some changes I want to discuss with you as to the taking of the town of Taos."

22

Shortly before the hour deadline, Smoke Jensen came to Santan Tossa with a suggestion. "I want you to gather your warriors. Have them start to drum and sing, do a war dance out in plain view of Quinn's gang."

A huge grin spread on the mahogany face of the Tua. "We haven't done a war dance in fifty years. This will be a true pleasure. We'll make it look very bloodthirsty indeed. Lots of howls, leaping in the air, swinging war clubs and knives." He went off, gleefully listing loudly the terrorizing features they would use.

Twenty minutes later, a drum began to throb in the outskirts of Taos. Tua warriors started to prance and stomp in a circle around a large fire. High, thin voices chanted the challenge to fight and die to all who could hear. Knife blades flashed in the sunlight. The drum beat louder. Some among the outlaws became visibly uncomfortable. Several exchanged knowing glances. They had heard the rumors about scalping.

Some few did not want to test it further. Two drifters, who had joined up for the fun the siege promised, went for their horses. They rode off five minutes later. Five minutes later, three more, who were not part of the gang, held a whispered conference, nodded agreement and left for other parts.

A grinning Santan Tossa waved a lighthearted farewell to Smoke Jensen as Smoke eased himself into the gorge that contained the streambed and set off to locate Martha Estes and her maid.

Smoke followed the creek upstream to the southwest until well past the ring of outlaws. Then he led Cougar up out of the ravine and mounted. Carefully he worked his way back toward the siege lines. He left Cougar behind a screen of young palo verdes and proceeded afoot. Bent double, he presented a far diminished profile to any eyes that might look outward, instead of toward town. There would be few places where Martha might be kept, he reasoned. With silent determination, he set about eliminating those.

Ten minutes went by. Smoke found himself on a small produce farm. No doubt the Mexican owner sold to the general store in Taos, and to others who happened by. Yes, there, beyond the work sheds, barn and house, a palapa had been erected over a stairstepped set of shelves. Baskets of peppers and fresh vegetables lined them. Two small boys, under the age of thirteen or so, kept watch and called out to passersby.

Making little sound in his moccasins, Smoke eased his way up to the side of one shed. The sound of splashing water came from within. Women's voices came from inside, chattering in Spanish over the latest gossip. Smoke's command of the language, slight at best, had not improved over years of non-use. Even so, he made out a number of juicy items.

"Raquel is going to have a baby," one woman revealed as she energetically sloshed a bowl of red and green jalapeno peppers in a tub of water to remove the redbrown dust.

"How can that be?" asked a much younger, more innocent voice. "She is not even married."

"*Sí, esto es verdad.* She has no husband, but she has a baby."

"Padre Domingo says that is a sin." Smoke could almost see the blush her words produced.

"That is true, little one. And you will promise your mother that you will never, ever do what it takes to make a baby . . . until you are safely married."

Another woman brought a change of subject. "I hear that Juanita Sanchez is going to marry that Guerrero boy."

"Which one?" several asked.

"Mateo, I think. Or is it Raul? No, it is Enrique."

"Carlos Guerrero has nine sons. How can you tell which one?"

A titter came from the youngest. "It's not Ricardo. He's only ten."

A superior sounding voice discounted that. "What difference does that make? My sister, Esperanza, was married at twelve."

A snippy voice followed a nasty laugh. "Everyone knows she had to. It was that Dominguez boy, although she married Sancho Valdez."

A wounded squeal came from the defender of early weddings. "Cow."

"Pig."

"*¡Bruja!*" her target spat, then repeated, "Witch!"

"Ladies, please," a matronly woman commanded. "We are here to work, is that not true? Someone hand me some of those squash."

Grinning, Smoke moved on. Small wonder that men who owned businesses preferred not to hire women. The metallic screech of metal against stone directed Smoke to another shack. The farmer sat under a thatch palapa, working a peddle-power whetstone to sharpen a machete. Smoke coughed softly to attract the man's attention.

"*¿Sí, señor?*"

"Have any of the *ladrónes* around Taos come around here?" Smoke asked. When the man shook his head in the negative, Smoke tried another. "Have you seen any of them taking a young woman somewhere?"

Another shake of his head, then, "*¡Ay, sí!* Early this morning, I was turning water into my corn. Two men rode over toward the old Olivera place. They had a woman with them. She did not look happy."

Smoke nodded in satisfaction. "That's the one. Thank you, señor."

Then Smoke asked for and was given directions to the Olivera farm. He headed that way on foot. He had covered half a mile when he came upon the first of several layers of lookouts. Smoke skirted the man easily and continued on. The second one proved not so simple to evade.

He sat his mount, alertly searching the surrounding terrain. From time to time, he stood in his stirrups and peered beyond low obstructions. Smoke, clad in buckskin, hugged the ground. The man's diligence and regularity became his undoing. After carefully timing the outlaw's routine, Smoke was ready when a missed gaze beyond the low brow behind which Smoke waited signaled a change. He came up and moved out in a split second.

Habit had outweighed diligence. The man had his head down, intent on rolling a cigarette. Smoke leaped and landed on him like a stone statue. Tobacco flakes flew everywhere. Dragged from the saddle, the outlaw landed heavily with Smoke on top. Rancid breath shot out of his twisted mouth. His lungs empty, it took only a hard right to the jaw by Smoke Jensen to put him asleep. Smoke quickly tied him and hurried on.

Another watcher lounged in the doorway of a partially fallen in adobe house. Smoke froze and sank to the ground. For five long minutes he studied the man who leaned against the doorframe. He looked bored. He also looked sleepy. Another minute passed, and the thug abruptly jerked awake, stepped out of the shade and paced to each corner of the building, Winchester held at the ready. He looked around the wall and returned to his position. Once more he slouched.

Such kind were dangerous, Smoke reasoned. If the hunch hit him at the wrong time, he might see someone sneaking up on him. Smoke inched his way behind a rock ridge and circled widely around the crumbling structure. He came at the adobe building from the rear.

Through a small, high window he had a clear view of the interior. Across the single room, he saw a large loft, obviously where the family slept when they lived here. In the middle of the room he noted a small table. Seated at two sides of it were Martha and her maid. They had been tied tightly to their chairs. To one side, Smoke observed Paddy Quinn and two of his men in the room conferring quietly. The bad news became immediately obvious.

There wouldn't be time enough to take out Quinn and his fast guns and free both women. This small farm lay too close to the ring of outlaws. Any exchange of gunfire would draw two dozen gunmen in seconds. He could not free them, yet he had a firm belief that Satterlee would not want her harmed. What happened next reinforced that attitude. Quinn's voice raised suddenly, and Smoke listened carefully to each word.

"You're right, Huber. These two are poison. I think we can get away with it if we do it that way, I do. We just take 'em out in the desert and lose them somewhere."

At once, Martha snapped hotly at him. "Clifton will have you gelded if you actually go through with killing me. You heard what he said when he had you bring my maid here."

That was news to Smoke. The criminal overlord was here now. That gave him some fresh ideas. Quietly he slipped away, headed back for Cougar and a ride to town.

Never one to take strict notice of exact time, Smoke Jensen found himself eying the big, octagonal face of the Regulator wall clock that hung on the wall of the sheriff's office. When the hour deadline arrived, he strode

out to where Quinn had confronted them earlier. It did
not surprise Smoke when he found none of the outlaws
present. Particularly, Smoke noted, no torturers and no
Martha Estes. In the next instant, he learned why.

Rifle fire broke out on two sides of town. With shouts
and curses, the outlaw gang opened an attack on Taos in
earnest. Smoke could not understand why the entire
force that ringed the defenders did not press the en-
gagement. He needn't have speculated. Smoke had no
sooner than reached the line of houses that defined the
city limits than riders thundered down the slope where
he and Diego had met with Quinn. They opened fire as
the range closed.

Immediately, Smoke ducked behind a low adobe wall
and drew a .45 Colt. Two .44 slugs slammed into the
outer face of the brown mud bricks, which sent a plume
of dust upward to obscure Smoke's vision. He triggered
a round, and a hard case cried out in pain, his right arm
limp and useless. That concentrated more fire on
Smoke's position. He could not stay in such an exposed
place for long, Smoke reasoned.

Sheriff Hank Banner sat propped up in bed by rolled
blankets and plump pillows. At his insistence, Dr. Walters
had rolled the bed over close to a window. Now he stood
in exasperation at his patient's request.

"I'll do no such a thing, Hank Banner," the physician
snapped, his well-scrubbed hands clasped in front of
him.

"Awh, come on, Adam. We've got the fight of our lives
goin' on out there, and I ain't in it. Hell, man, even
you've got a six-gun strapped on."

"That's to protect my patients and my medical equipment," Dr. Walters responded testily.

"You gave Pedro Alvarado a rifle. All I'm askin' is you
get me one, too."

Unmoved by the argument, Adam Walters answered

primly. "Pedro is thirty years younger than you, Hank, and he's ambulatory. Besides, how are you going to operate a Winchester from that bed?"

Bushy eyebrows knit over his nose, Banner grumped at the doctor. "Easy if you'll give me a rifle and open the damned window. I mean it now, Adam. I can see out of both eyes now, and things ain't so fuzzy I'd shoot one of the town folks. I'm the sheriff, and by damn, it's my duty to help defend the people out there."

Dr. Walters knew that Hank was right. But he was his friend, and Adam Walters did not want to see Hank Banner taking unnecessary risks in his weakened condition. While his thoughts roamed over that little dilemma, Dr. Walters heard a light smack and the musical tinkle of falling glass. The bullet cracked loudly when it struck the wall opposite the window.

"Goldag it, Adam. That does it. If they're shootin' at me, I've got the right to shoot back."

Sighing, Dr. Walters turned from the infirmary and entered his treatment room. From there he proceeded to the office, where he picked up a Winchester and a box of cartridges. He returned to the room where the sheriff continued to fume at the attackers. Adam's face wore a sheepish expression.

"Here. And try not to shoot yourself in the leg." The doctor busied himself with opening the sash. From the end window, which faced the alley behind the building, a rifle barked in the hands of Pedro Alvarado.

For all the fury of their resistance, small groups of Quinn's outlaw band penetrated the defenders' barricades. Six of them from the west side of town headed directly for the center. They made their approach by way of one of the radiating alleys that formed an X based on the Plaza de Armas. To reach their goal, they had to go past the window where young Pedro Alvarado waited with a ready Winchester. The moment one of them came into view, he immediately regretted his hastiness.

Fiery agony spread in his leg as Pedro put a round into his hip. The outlaw fell at once and painfully crawled, crablike, toward the shelter of a doorway. Pedro fired again, ending the thug's movement forever. As his life ebbed from him, the hard case faintly heard the voices of his comrades.

"Up there."

"Yeah, I see him. In that window."

Funny, the dying rogue thought, *I didn't hear any shots.* He did not hear the return fire as his fellow outlaws opened up and darkness engulfed him.

Up in the infirmary, Pedro Alvarado flattened himself on the floor as a rat-a-tat of slugs punched through the thin wall. Glass shattered in the window above him. The moment a lull came, Pedro popped up and sighted on one of the five. The .44 Winchester recoiled smoothly, and the target clutched his chest and slammed back against a wall. Pedro got off another round before he had to dive for the floor again.

Ian MacGreggor held his own from his second-floor room in the hotel. He had been on town patrol duty during the night and had returned to grab a few hours' sleep only to have the attack break out after only forty minutes' rest. Over his sights, he saw one hard case, who appeared to be directing the actions of a dozen others in a push to breach the defenses to the south of town. A long shot for a rifle, but Mac retained the confidence of youth.

He elevated his aim to the maximum and fired. After what seemed a terribly long time, the section leader jerked in his saddle, then slowly folded forward at the waist. He clung to his horse for a moment, then dropped away to land in a puff of dust on the hard ground. Mac levered another round into his Winchester and sought another target. He found one much closer than he would have liked.

Two hard cases ran out of the mouth of an alley and randomly discharged their weapons upward toward second-floor windows. Mac pulled a quick bead and let fly another .44 slug. One of the outlaws continued to run forward while the other did a crazy little jig and crashed blindly into a rain barrel. He died before he hit the tile walk.

Mac charged his rifle again and sighted on the remaining gunman. The Winchester bucked, and Mac remembered this time to shove three fresh cartridges through the loading gate. He ejected the empty and chambered a loaded one. If this kept up, they could easily reduce the enemy by half, he speculated.

Someone else had figured out the same thing. Shouts to pull back went from one outlaw to the next. Slowly they began to withdraw from town, yet they continued to pour a withering fire on the defenders from a distance outside Taos. Whitewater Paddy Quinn sought out his second in command.

"We'll give it a little time, then go back again. I want to get that bastid Smoke Jensen in me sights, an' that's a fact."

Garth Thompson did not sound so eager. "I've heard he is hard to kill. So far, I have no reason to doubt that. How many did we lose?"

Quinn raised a hand and swept the hillside. "That's what I want you to find out, boy-o. Didn't seem to me that half the lads what went in there came back. With losses like that, we can't keep this up for long. Whether Mr. Satterlee likes it or not, we may have to use fire to drive those stubborn folk out."

"He'll have a fit if we do. But, I agree with you. We can't let them whittle us down like that much longer. When do we go back?"

Quinn rubbed a powder-grimed hand across his brow. "Find out where we stand an' we'll give it an hour."

* * *

Ezekial Crowder and Ed Hubbard had taken positions on the south side of town, close to Smoke Jensen. They looked first to the sky when they heard a distant rumble. When they found it to be clear and bright, they lowered their gaze to observe the ominous approach of a large body of outlaws. They exchanged a worried glance and tightened the grip on their weapons. Over the growing thunder of hooves, they could hear the voice of Smoke Jensen, low and calm.

"Steady . . . hold it . . . let 'em come in real close. Make every shot count."

Smoke knew it would not happen that way. Excitement or fear would make the inexperienced men fire carelessly. They would rush their aim and no doubt jerk the trigger. It would only get worse when the outlaws opened fire. Some, though, he knew would make good account of themselves. Like young Mac, who had shouted to him during the brief respite.

"Hey, Smoke, I got three of them. Those two down there and another on his horse outside town."

"Good shootin'," Smoke praised. He continued on his way to check the other defenses. His inspection gave him the impression that some twenty outlaws had gotten inside the town. Perimeter defenses had to be shored up. He had arranged for that, though only just in time.

They were going to have to keep the gang from entering town this time, Smoke thought as he watched the outlaws close once again. A few seconds later, Ed Hubbard proved a better gunhand than expected when he cleared two saddles in rapid succession.

"Did ya see that?" Hubbard called out, surprised by his own success. He took aim again.

With a loud crash, the hard cases opened up. It drowned out Ed's third shot, which hit Dutch Volker in the side. It was a severe enough wound to put him out of the action. With a blistering backward look and a hot curse, Dutch steered his mount away from the conflict. He would get patched up and come back, Dutch thought.

Smoke Jensen had other ideas for him. Careful aim with his .45-70-500 Winchester Express paid a dividend to Smoke. For enough time to make it count, the head of Dutch Volker sat like a hairy ball on the top of the front blade sight. The upright post rested in the notch of the rear, buckhorn sight. Smoke squeezed the trigger. Volker's head snapped forward and back as the bullet bore through his brain and exited the front, taking with it his entire forehead. A fountain of gore splashed on his horse. Without a controlling hand, it went berserk.

Crow hopping and squealing in fright over the smell of blood and brain tissue, the animal cut crossways to the advance, scattered several other riders and at last dislodged its odious burden in a thicket of mesquite. Already, Smoke Jensen tracked another outlaw. The volume of defending fire increased from other points as Smoke concentrated on his aim. He discharged a round that missed one hard case by a finger's width and drove into the shoulder of the man behind him. Smoke risked a quick glance toward Hubbard and Crowder while he cycled his lever action.

Both men so far remained calm. They took time to aim, worked the action of their rifles in a controlled manner and shoved fresh cartridges into the magazine between shots. Hubbard spoke up loudly enough for Smoke to hear him above the rattle of gunfire.

"You're doin' all right for a fireman."

Crowder grinned. "So are you . . . shopkeeper. I'd sell my soul for a shot of whiskey and a cool beer."

"If I was the devil, I'd take you up on that." Hubbard broke off to fire his Winchester again. "Got another one," he commented.

"The way they're comin', this could last until sundown," opined Zeke Crowder.

Hubbard blinked and swallowed hard. "It had better not."

* * *

Sheriff Banner thought much the same as Chief Crowder. From his vantage point he watched the huge gang swirl around Taos. Here and there, one would slump in the saddle or fall to the ground. Not nearly enough, though, the lawman concluded. He watched as three of them charged a barricade made of two overturned wagons.

Their mounts easily cleared the obstacle, and he had one of the men in his sights before the hooves touched ground. An easy squeeze and the sheriff's rifle fired. His bullet drilled the outlaw through the chest. Quickly Banner worked the action and sighted in on another. Before he could fire, one of Diego Álvarado's vaqueros dashed into the street. He carried a large yellow and magenta cape. Swiftly he unfurled it and billowed it out into a fat curve; the skirt flapped in the breeze his motion created.

At once the horses sat back on their haunches and reared. One rider fell off; the second barely hung on. And then not for long. Another rippling pass put the animal in a walleyed frenzy. The rider had all he could do to regain control. While thus occupied, Sheriff Banner shot the hard case through the heart.

Fierce fighting continued through the afternoon. Smoke Jensen made periodic visits to the defenders positioned on the outer edges of Taos. He always had a word of encouragement and usually replacement ammunition. Braving the chance of a bullet, the older boys of the town, organized by Wally Gower, brought food and water to the fighting men. The fury promised to go on forever.

When night fell, the gang withdrew, much to the relief of everyone. To their immediate discomfort, the defenders of Taos soon discovered that the enemy had not gone far enough so that anyone could escape.

Smoke Jensen's words were not greeted with enthusiasm when he made his dark prediction. "They'll be back tomorrow."

23

"They're comin' back!"

Early the next morning the shouts of the lookouts roused the wearied protectors of Taos from uneasy sleep. Too many of the townspeople moved with a lethargy that they would soon regret. Caught between their homes and fighting stations, most looked on in numbed horror as the outlaws easily penetrated the thin defenses and streamed into town.

"We ain't got a chance this time," one less courageous townie wailed.

"We're gonners for sure," the faint-hearted barber took up the cry.

Smoke Jensen would hear none of it. He seemed to be everywhere at once as he worked to rally the resistance of the battle-tired people. "Quit your whining," he growled at the timid souls. "Take your weapons and form up in the streets. We can stop them easier when they don't have room to maneuver."

"Say, that's right," one of the more imaginative townies declared. "We can trap them between the buildings. It'll be like shootin' fish in a water trough."

Smoke moved on, praising the idea over his shoulder. "That's the idea. Get to it." Smoke's confidence rose more when he came upon the more reliant among the defenders.

Those Tua warriors not on water watch were the first to respond. Santan Tossa stood on one side of the Plaza de Armas and directed his fighting men to vantage points on the roofs of buildings. Unaccustomed to the Spanish tile roofing material, one of the Tua men put a moccasin on a loose one and all but fell.

"Be careful," Tossa cautioned. Then he produced a fleeting smile at that choice of words in the face of an all-out assault by men determined to kill them all.

On two sides of town, Don Diego's vaqueros labored valiantly to keep more of the trash from entering Taos. The dapper senior Alvarado shouted encouragement to his cowboys. "*Buena suerte, compañeros.* Shoot their eyes out."

Gradually, men caught by surprise on the west side of town began to calm and take better stock of their situation. Smoke Jensen quickly exhorted them. "This isn't the end of it. Not unless you want to go belly-up. Get some backbone, dammit. All of you there, quit milling around and form up to drive and trap those who got past the barricades in the center of town."

Slowly they began to respond. As the first remotivated men spread out, more joined them. Before long they had enough to ring the business district and began to close in. From the moment of the first encounter, the fighting grew more fierce with each passing minute.

Smoke Jensen soon saw that the outer defenses had been completely breached. The vaqueros fought valiantly as they retreated street by street from the pressure put on them by the Quinn gang. Here and there they managed to rally as those facing them turned out to be drifting bits of frontier trash with no deep-set loyalties. That sort crumbled rapidly, especially when confronted with a revival cry from the Mexican cowboys.

"Con nuestra Señora, Santa Maria de Guadalupe! Maten-los maten!"

Even Smoke Jensen developed chills down his spine the first time he heard it and translated the words. *With our lady, Holy Mother of Guadalupe! Kill them, kill!* He had to admit it had a galvanizing effect. The vaqueros swarmed back down the street, a wall of death with six-gun, rifle and knife. At one point, a saddle tramp who had become over-whelmed by their ferocity dropped to his knees and began to howl like a dog. It did him little good. He got his throat slit anyway.

On the next street over, the vaqueros put a full dozen to flight. Horses surged into one another and spilled two riders to face the advancing fury of the Mexican cow-boys. They screamed a long time as they died.

Paddy Quinn shoved his way into a cantina to catch his breath and reload. He found Garth Thompson there ahead of him. Whitewater Paddy flashed a big grin. "We're doin' fine. Another half hour and the town will be ours."

Thompson looked at him in consternation. "Are you kidding? We have men dying out there by the handful. It doesn't make sense. These townies are fighting back like mad men."

"Awh, Garth me bucko, yer not seein' clear, yer not. Most of those who are being killed are not part of the gang. What that trash is here for is to soak up bullets for us, it is. Let's go upstairs where we can better see what's really happenin'. Ye'll be surprised how good it's goin', ye will."

Two blocks down, in a narrow alley, three of Quinn's men found the situation more like Garth Thompson saw it than their boss. Seven Tua warriors rounded the corner and started toward them. Clearly they had heard

the rumors started by Smoke Jensen. The trio cut their
eyes to the Indians and began to run in the opposite direction. Not a one made an effort to fire a weapon.

"Lou, Lou, we gotta get out of here. They're gonna
scalp us."

Lou looked ahead and paled. The rear of a building
closed off their escape route from the narrow alley.
"We're trapped," he wailed.

The others saw it, too. Unnerved by his belief in the
scalping story, one of the outlaws turned his gun on himself. His body had hardly hit the ground when Santan
Tossa and his brother Tuas opened fire. One of Quinn's
men jerked spastically, staggered two paces to his left
and keeled over. The other got off a shot before Tossa
put a bullet through his screaming mouth.

"They were cowards," the Tua policeman pronounced
over the cooling corpses.

Gradually the tide turned. The shock of their earlier
failure began to wear off, and the men of Taos ceased in
their headlong flight from the threat of the gunmen.
They turned back in twos and threes in one place, half a
dozen in two others. Instead of two men fighting a des-
perate rear guard, while the others fled, the mass of
harried men turned about and lashed out at their enemy.

At first it did not look like much. Then an angry growl
raced through the defenders, until it became one voice.
Five of the gang rounded a corner, laughing and firing
blindly. Halfway down the block a solid mass of growling,
snarling men began to run toward them. A high, clear
cry raised above the roar of their discontent.

"Fire! Open fire!"

A ragged volley crackled from the weapons in the
hands of shop keepers and clerks, bank tellers, and
wheelwrights. A stream of lead scythed into the startled
outlaws and they began to die. Two of the gunhawks
wisely opted to flee. One made it to the corner they had

rounded half a minute before. The other one took two faltering steps along his escape route before he fell over dead.

Throughout town the spirit of defeat disappeared as he died. Shouting, the defenders charged in a massive counterattack. Determined men soon swept the byways of Taos of the dregs of humanity who had attacked them. The only resistance that remained centered around the saloon named Cantina del Sol. Smoke Jensen reached that strong point in the vanguard of the revived defenders.

Curly Lasher and eight relatively capable gunfighters had been stationed outside the cantina to protect their leaders. He and his underlings listened to the shift in mood among the defenders with growing apprehension. When four of them rounded the corner with a determined stride, the outlaws realized that the seeming ease of their capture of the town was an illusion. Weapons already in hand, the townsfolk had the advantage when the hard cases reached for their six-guns.

Curly had time to shout only brief advice. "Spread out!"

Gunfire roared in the confines between two-story buildings. Two of the outlaws went down. Curly Lasher took cover behind a watering trough and traded shots with the aroused residents of Taos. That lasted until Smoke Jensen and six vaqueros rounded the other corner and closed in on them.

"Make for the saloon," Curly yelled to his surviving men.

Curly backed up the steps to the portico over the entrance to the cantina. A quick check showed that the others had preceded him. He had almost disappeared through the glassbead curtain that screened the doorway when Smoke Jensen stepped out into the center of the street and pointed his left index finger at the outlaw leader.

"Curly Lasher, you yellow-bellied piss ant, come out and face me like a man."

* * *

Smoke Jensen had recognized Curly Lasher the moment the man came to his boots and started for the cantina. Although quite young, Lasher had a respectable reputation as a gunfighter. He was reputed to have killed ten men in face-downs in Texas and New Mexico. Rumor had it his total number of kills included three for-hire assassinations and a dozen ambush shootings. At the age of twenty-three, he was about as good as they came these days. But not in Smoke Jensen's book.

The way Smoke saw it, it was time to cancel Curly's pay book. After issuing his challenge, Smoke waited now, ignoring the random bullets, fired by Lasher's henchmen, that cracked into the ground near him. A second stretched interminably long, then another. Smoke counted to five before Curly waved a grubby, rumpled bit of cloth out the opening to La Cantina del Sol.

"You make those others stop shootin' at me an' I'll face you, Jensen. Hell, you're an old man. You can't be much good anymore."

There it was again, *old man*. Smoke's expression grew grim. "We'll see, won't we? And have those back-shooting gun trash with you holster their irons."

Another second went by. "You heard him, boys. Put 'em up." A nervous giggle escaped Curly. "This is between Smoke Jensen an' me."

With that, Curly Lasher stepped out into the street. He looked formidable enough, except for the muscle tic that twitched his left eye. Smoke Jensen side-stepped to line up with Curly Lasher. Curly's hand hovered over the butt-grip of his Smith and Wesson .44 American. He nodded evenly to Smoke.

"Your play, Jensen."

"No, you go first. I want this to be fair."

Another giggle burst from Curly's throat. "Fair? Hell, Jensen, you better be pickin' out your coffin right now."

"You reckon to jaw me to death? If so, it'll be like ol' Samson, eh? Killed with the jawbone of an ass."

That tripped Curly's hair-trigger temper. "Goddamn you, Smoke Jensen, kiss your tail goodbye."

Curly Lasher drew then, confident that he had beaten Smoke Jensen by a good half second. Not until a stunning force slammed into his chest did he realize how terribly mistaken he had been. His lips formed a perfect *O*, and his legs went rubbery. Enormous pain spread through his body, followed instantly by a frightening numbness. Try as his brain might to send signals to his heart, they never arrived. A fat, 230 grain .45 slug had destroyed that vital organ.

His eyes rolled up in their sockets, Curly discharged a round into the street and fell in a crumpled heap. In the moment after he fired, Smoke Jensen moved. He waved at the astonished townies to follow him.

"Come on, let's get in that saloon."

"B'God, that was fast," Warren Engals muttered. "I never seen his hand move."

"Neither did that cocky gunhawk," Buell Spencer snorted in satisfaction.

Mid-morning came and went. Still the fighting lingered, as Smoke Jensen and five of the men from town entered La Cantina del Sol. Theirs could hardly be called a conventional means of entry. Smoke sent four vaqueros around to the rear to make a show of breaking in through the service door. He gave them enough time to be convincing, then dived low through the front doorway. Smoke hit the floor and did a roll, to come up with his Colt blazing. He got immediate results.

One hard case slammed into the bar, his back arched to the point of breaking his spine. Smoke fired again and the bones cracked. The outlaw dropped to flop on the floor like a headless chicken. A townsman and one of

Diego's vaqueros entered behind the last mountain man.
Flame gushed from the muzzles of their six-guns.

Another hard case died in their hail of lead. A third
had dived for cover behind the bar when Smoke first entered. He popped up now and shot Ransom Clover
between the eyes. The feed store proprietor died on his
feet. But not before Smoke Jensen sent the killer off to
eternity with a similar wound. Terrible discordance came
from the upright piano in one corner as another thug
hastily fired a bullet at Smoke's back.

Smoke ducked and spun on one boot heel. The
muzzle of his Peacemaker tracked with him, and he
squeezed off a round the moment the back shooter
came into view. Hot lead punched through thick leather
and then did awful damage to the hip bone of the man.
By then, Smoke had cocked his .45 and put a second
slug into the chest of his assailant. Restricted by the
muslin safeguards suspended below the ceiling, viscous
layers of powder smoke undulated in the room, obscur-
ing the whereabouts of other enemies.

Ears ringing from the enclosed gunfire, Smoke made
for the stairway. There had to be some reason why a fairly
reliable gunfighter like Curly Lasher and eight men had
been guarding this place. He had reached the first riser
with a boot toe when another of the gunmen appeared
at the top of the stairs. Smoke acted at once.

So close to the wall, the force of his gun blast nearly
ruptured Jensen's eardrum. Yet he did not even flinch as
he recocked his six-gun and sent another .45 round wing-
ing upward to seal the fate of the hard case who menaced
him. Hit twice in less than half a minute, the outlaw staggered back and rammed slack shoulders into the wall of
the upper hallway. Smoke paused at the landing and
called back to the ground floor to one of the vaqueros.

"Juaquin, come up here with me." When the slender,
boyish-faced cowboy reached the top of the stairs, Smoke
gave terse instructions. "Stay here. Watch my back."

Smoke set off to search the rooms in the rear portion

of the second floor. Someone of importance had to be up here, his gut feeling told him. He readied himself at the first door, cocked his leg and plated a boot beside the doorknob. A loud crack followed and the panel flew inward. Following his six-gun, Smoke entered the room in a crouch.

Empty. He turned on one heel and started for the next. His explosive entry caught two outlaws with their backs to him, taking shots at Taos residents in the street below. The slam of the door against the inner wall brought one around in a blur of movement. His eyes went wide as he gazed at Death with a outstretched hand. The six-gun in that hand fired a second later, and reflex drove the bandit backward to crash through the window, taking both sashes with him as he fell to the ground. The second hard case wisely released his revolver and threw up his hands. Smoke Jensen stepped up close and rapped him on the skull with the barrel of a Colt. That left three more rooms to check.

The next proved even more empty than the first. It did not even have furniture. Smoke moved on to the next in line.

His vicious kick surprised Garth Thompson and Paddy Quinn in the act of reloading. Thompson swung his six-gun up first and fired at Smoke. The man from the Sugarloaf had already fired a round which ripped into the body of Garth Thompson a fraction of an instant before the outlaw's bullet punched a neat hole in the left side of Smoke Jensen's waist. It burned like hell fire, but it did not even stagger him. Thompson tried to fire again, not realizing he looked at his target with a dead man's eyes.

His bullet cut air beside Smoke Jensen's left ear as the legs of Garth Thompson gave way. Smoke gave him a safety round and turned his attention to Paddy Quinn.

Stunned by the swiftness of action by Smoke Jensen, Paddy Quinn only belatedly closed the loading gate of his Colt Peacemaker. Instinctively, he knew he did not have time for a shot. Not if he wanted to continue living. Instead, he diverted his energy to his legs and sprinted past the wounded Jensen out into the hall. Smoke bit back the pain that burned in his side and turned in pursuit.

Out in the hall, Paddy Quinn raced toward the far end of the building. A window in the center of the corridor there bore a sign above it that read *Escalera de Incendios.* "Fire Escape" for those who could read Spanish. Smoke Jensen pounded down the bare board floor behind Quinn. The outlaw leader made better time.

Without a break in his stride, Paddy Quinn threw his arms up to cover his face and hurtled through the glass partition. Fragments of the sashes clung to him as he hit the small, square projection that served as a platform for a ladder. Legs still churning, Paddy cleared the railing in a single bound and dropped out of sight before Smoke reached the shattered window casement.

Quinn landed flat-footed and hard on the packed earth below. Pain shot up his leg from a broken heel bone. His horse, and those of Thompson and another hard case, had been tied off at the rear door earlier in the day. So unexpected and precipitous had been his arrival from above that the vaqueros sent to break in the rear stood in immobile surprise while Paddy limped to his mount, retrieved the reins and swung into the saddle.

Smoke Jensen sent a bullet after Paddy Quinn as the latter called out to his men. "Pull back. Get clear of town. We've lost it for now."

24

His face twisted in anger and contempt, Clifton Satter-lee rounded on Paddy Quinn. "What do you mean you had the town taken, and then got pushed out? How can that happen?"

Whitewater Paddy's answer came low and meek. "Smoke Jensen. That's how it happened. He killed Garth, he did, an' he near to finished me in the bargain. He found out somehow where we were and came after us with some of those Mezkins."

Satterlee paced the confined space in the ruined adobe farmhouse. "Better that you and a dozen like you die than that I lose Taos."

Stung by the insult, Paddy's eyes narrowed. "Pardon me, Mr. Satterlee, sir. There's no denyin' yer smart an' all that. But, truth to tell, your chances of takin' Taos without me are somewhere between slim an' none, they are."

Face florid with his fury, Clifton Satterlee raised a fist as though to strike the gang leader and bellowed up close in Quinn's face. "Then get out there, gather up what men you have left and go back. And keep on going back until their resistance crumbles. Brice, you're going with them."

Brice Noble gaped at his partner. He knew himself to be good with his guns, better than most of the petty criminals in Quinn's gang. Yet, he realized he was not any sort of gunfighter like Smoke Jensen. The man was entirely too good. "You're not serious. What could I possibly do?"

Sarcasm dripped from Satterlee's words. "You could be like a famous general. An inspiration to the men."

"That's uncalled for. There's simply no reason for me to go there."

Satterlee turned even nastier. "But there is . . . because I insist. Now, get going, Quinn, and bring me back a town on its knees."

Shortly after noon, the gang came back to Taos. Those in the lead met with a shower of wine-bottle grenades. The black-powder bombs exploded with sharp cracks and bright flashes. The shards of their containers, and the scraps of metal within, whizzed through the air. Many pieces bit into vulnerable flesh, both equine and human. One went off so close to two hard cases that both of them and their horses were disemboweled. Their shrieks of agony engendered pity even among those they attacked.

Soon their distressed wailing faded under the tumult as the fighting rose toward a crescendo. Paddy Quinn had centered nearly all of his men on one side of town. Only a few snipers and riders kept the defenders on the other three sides occupied. As the volume of fire increased at the center of the offensive, a voice rose from the assailants.

"They broke! They broke! They're running."

It was quickly picked up. The shouts merged into a roar as the allies could no longer withstand the onslaught. Outlaws poured into the gap in the line and spread out through the streets of Taos. Pushed to the forefront of the vanguard, Brice Noble found himself the first to enter the small town. When the resistance melted away his confidence soared. This might be easier than he had expected. His horse trotted down the narrow avenue toward the center of town.

At the Plaza de Armas, Noble found a tall, broad-shouldered man directing the fight. He forcefully snatched demoralized residents off their feet and shoved them into a position from which they could engage the invaders. His calm demeanor told Brice Noble that if they were to succeed, this man must be eliminated. He edged closer and formed the words of a challenge as he raised his revolver to accomplish that. Off to the side, someone yelled the gunfighter's name.

"Smoke! Smoke Jensen. I've got ten men here ready to fight." Then, sighting Noble, he pointed out the menace, "Look out, Smoke!"

Smoke Jensen turned his cold gaze on the man who sought to kill him. He backed it up with the muzzle of a .45 Colt. Instantly, fear eroded his guts, and Brice Noble swallowed his provocation. He lowered his right arm and released the six-gun. It dropped to the grass with a thud while Noble raised his hands over his head.

"I surrender. I've not fired my weapon. Don't shoot me, Mr. Jensen."

"Get down." Smoke's command moved Noble with alacrity. He swung a leg over and dismounted while Smoke walked up to him "Who are you?"

"I—I'm Brice Noble, a business associate of Clifton Satterlee."

"Umm." Smoke swung from the belt line. His hard fist connected with the lantern jaw of Brice Noble. When the arch criminal crumbled, Smoke reached out and caught a townsman by one arm. "Drag this piece of dog dung to the jail."

Diego Alvarado sought a single man among the outlaws. His wide experience in fighting a variety of enemies told him that the majority of these vermin would flee if they lost their leader. Smoke Jensen had killed Garth

Thompson that morning. That left only Paddy Quinn. He left Alejandro and Miguel in charge of the vaqueros and started off to locate the gang boss. Mayor Arianas, an old friend, approached him as Diego crossed the Plaza de Armas.

"Diego, I am astonished at the valor of the Tua warriors. They fight for us as though this was their town."

Alvarado gave him a wry smile. "They know that if Taos falls, their pueblo will be right behind. Satterlee wants everything around here. I, for one, am grateful for their aid."

"As am I, amigo." Arianas paused a moment, uncertain of the propriety of his question. "May I ask, where are you going? Most of your men are on the east side."

"Don't worry, my friend. I am looking for Paddy Quinn. When I find him, I am going to kill him and end this madness."

Arianas clapped Diego on one shoulder. *"Buena suerte,* then."

"Gracias. I can use all the good luck I can manage."

Diego Alvarado strode off, headed north. As he went by the flight of granite steps that fronted the church on the plaza, he automatically crossed himself and cast a reverent glance at the impressive structure. Suddenly the bells began to toll. Padre Luis threw wide the tall, oak doors and stepped out onto the wide flagstones at the top of the stairs.

"Men of Taos, rally your strength. Fight for your freedom," he exhorted the confused and demoralized defenders who huddled in the plaza. "Remember your women and children. Drive out the invaders."

A gunshot cracked across the plaza, seemingly louder than all of the others. Father Luis jerked at the impact and swayed, a large red stain spreading on the shoulder of his cassock. Diego Alvarado looked in the direction from which the shot had come. Seated on his horse was the man he sought. Paddy Quinn had a smoking six-gun in his hand and a nasty sneer on his face.

"Easy for you to say, priest. You who hides behind his own skirt," the apostate outlaw snarled. Oblivious to Diego Alvarado, Paddy Quinn started to raise his revolver for another shot.

Diego Alvarado filled his hand with his Obrigon .45 with all the smoothness and almost the speed of Smoke Jensen. He cocked and fired in one even motion. The bullet took Quinn in the belly. He winced, but seemed otherwise unaffected. His icy black eyes turned on Diego.

"So, cowherder, you defy me one last time, is it now? The priest can wait. This is between you an' me, bucko."

Before the last word left his mouth, Quinn fired the Colt in his hand. The slug cut a deep, painful gouge across the top of Diego's left shoulder. Then Alvarado fired the Obrigon again. His aim off because of his wound, he nailed Quinn in the right thigh. That proved enough to unhorse the gang leader. He fell and sprawled on the cobbles that paved the street in front of the church. Immediately Paddy Quinn learned how mistaken he had been in shooting the priest.

Rather than demoralizing the residents of Taos, his blasphemous act served to electrify the defenders. A great roar of outrage filled the plaza from Protestant, Catholic and pagan alike. Suddenly the peons, who did not possess firearms, swarmed over the fallen outlaw. Sunlight glinted off the well-honed edges of their machetes. Their arms rose and fell in a steady rhythm while Paddy Quinn shrieked and screamed his way into oblivion.

Blood streaming from his own wound, Diego Alvarado hurried to the injured priest. "Padre, you are hurt. I will get the doctor."

Gentle brown eyes settled on Alvarado. "Care for your own wound, Diego. God will tend to my needs."

Diego would not back down so easily. "Dr. Walters can give Him a lot of help. Let me take you inside. Then I will go for the doctor." Diego Alvarado cut his eyes to the mutilated corpse of Paddy Quinn. "He has answered for his crimes here, now I hope he burns in the hottest corner of hell."

Word quickly spread about the demise of Paddy Quinn. It restored the fighting spirit of those who protected Taos, especially when they learned how and why he had died. It proved to have the opposite affect on the outlaws. Leaderless, and with no assurance of being paid, the hangers-on deserted in droves. Harried by the emboldened townsmen, they streamed out of the city and made tracks toward Raton. The first two dozen to desert opened the flood gates.

Fighting continued for another twenty minutes while the headlong flight reduced the number of outlaws by more than half. Three of Quinn's subordinate leaders held a hasty meeting in the shelter of an adobe house on the west edge of town.

Yank Hastings came right to the point. "We have to get out of here. Those gutless cowards have left us in a fine fix."

Vic Tyson nodded, his face a grim mask. "Tell us something we don't know."

Hastings faced the sarcasm without a reaction. "The boss was right about puttin' all our force on one place. We got in, didn't we? I say we can do the same to get back out."

"Then what?"

"We run like hell for someplace else, Vic."

"What about our share of the loot?"

"There ain't gonna be anything to share. We can rob a couple of banks if we need money. Only I ain't stayin' around here any longer. You with me?"

"We'll do it," the other two agreed.

It did not take long. Hungry for revenge, the guardians of Taos roamed from building to building, street to street. Those outlaws who offered resistance they gunned down. The wiser ones they drove ahead of them. Smoke Jensen and Diego Alvarado led two thirds of them, Santan Tossa the remainder. Within half an hour the streets had been cleared.

"Now what?" a tired, powder-grimed Diego Alvarado asked over the top of a tubo of beer. A thick bandage bulged under his coat.

"Do you think they will be back?" Alejandro Alvarado queried.

Smoke Jensen had been thinking along those lines. "There's always the chance that they will. Though I hope not. We've lost fifteen men killed, and twice that wounded. If there's none of them left except the original gang, they can overwhelm us, given the right leader. To keep that from happening, I reckon to go out late tonight and cut off the head of the snake. That'll end it once and for all."

Alejandro looked eagerly at the big man. "I want to go along."

A smile spread on Smoke's face. "Welcome you'll be, Alejandro. Now, let's drink up and get something to eat. We need to rest before going out there."

Vic Tyson's concern over losing their pay proved baseless. While the remains of the gang fought its way out of Taos, Clifton Satterlee and his bodyguard, Cole Granger, rounded them up and persuaded them to listen. Reluctantly, others joined the gathering.

"Listen to me, men. We have to control Taos in order for our development scheme to succeed. You will all be rewarded. And most generously, I might add. In fact, I will offer you a bonus of one half your original share if you will agree to do what must be done. You will remain here, deny the people in town any contact with the outside. Cut off their food supply. Shoot any armed man you see on the streets. In short, maintain the siege until more men can be recruited and sent here to make the final push." Satterlee paused and let his gaze sweep over the assembled outlaws. "Do you understand what I'm saying?

The whole project now depends upon you. You have good leaders in Yank Hastings, Vic Tyson and Coop Ellis."

Coopersmith Ellis flushed slightly at that praise. Satterlee continued his harangue. "What I want is for you to do this. Return to positions well out of rifle range, and encircle the town again. Concentrate on the roads. Roving patrols can take care of anyone who tries to slip away across the fields. That's simple, isn't it? When enough men reach here for another attack, go at it with a will. Don't let anything stop you."

His stirring words brought a ragged cheer. But not enough to change Satterlee's mind on a matter of some considerable importance. When the remotivated gunmen started out to take their new positions, Clifton Satterlee huddled with Cole Granger and explained what he had in mind.

Darkness had covered Taos three hours earlier when Smoke Jensen and Alejandro Alvarado left town to spy out the enemy. It had taken that long for the gang to settle down. Some of them still had strong reservations about staying there. Several voiced their opinions loudly while Smoke and Alejandro slipped quietly through their line, headed for the adobe ruin where Smoke had earlier seen Martha.

"I think this is damn foolishness," one tough spared no effort in informing those near the fire where they prepared a meal and a pot of coffee.

"Biggs is right," another put in. "Without Whitewater Paddy, we've got no one to stand up to this Satterlee. Who says he'll for real pay us when it's over?"

"I'm glad you agree," Biggs included the man. "I say we walk our horses out of here right now, hit the high road to Santa Fe and don't look back."

"Hell yes. Those Injuns could be out there, sneakin' around with their scalpin' knifes right this minute."

"Don't even mention that," a third hard case replied. "It gives me cold chills."

Smoke and Alejandro crept on in the moonless night. When they reached the spot where Smoke thought the building should be, they found nothing. Smoke motioned for Alejandro to separate from him and look for the adobe. Quietly, both men went about finding the place.

Smoke located it first and saw that the farmhouse was unlighted. Had everyone gone to sleep? Somehow he doubted that. Moments later, Alejandro joined him, having made a wide, half circle. Smoke leaned close and whispered in the young ranchero's ear.

"I want to get a look inside. But if you were to ask me, I'd say the place is deserted. No light, no guards."

Smoke's speculation proved correct. He cautiously entered the structure through a crumbled rear wall. There he quickly discovered that Martha and Lupe no longer occupied the chairs. The table where they had sat had been overturned. He saw no sign of Clifton Satterlee either. Back outside, Smoke suggested they check along the line of fires where the watchers remained at the roadblocks.

A careful search among them revealed no sign of Martha Estes, her maid, or Clifton Satterlee. When they approached the last of the barricades, Smoke suddenly realized that Alejandro's appearance would give them away. Smoke made an abrupt signal that told the youthful *caballero* to wait outside the firelight and cover him while he went in to talk with the outlaws. Alejandro disappeared into the night, and Smoke continued to the fireside.

"Quiet as a graveyard," Smoke observed as he walked up.

"You coulda picked something better to say about it," grumbled one of the saddle trash. "What you doin' here?"

"You've got coffee goin', I smelled it. So, here I am."

His earlier jitters forgotten in light of no forays from town, the outlaw chuckled. "Pour yourself a cup."

Smoke took a blue granite tin cup and filled it.

"Where's the big boss? He was so hot for us stayin' here," Smoke probed casually.

A low curse answered him. "Didn't have the grit to stay here himself. A little while after that pep talk, he took the women an' Granger and they high-tailed it outta here. Off to Santa Fe, I reckon."

One of his companions spoke up in support of Satterlee. "He's goin' to get more men. Remember what he said about sending us some fresh blood?"

"Yeah. And blood is what it'll be, you ask me."

Smoke let them talk for a while, then drained his coffee and handed back the cup. "Thanks for the brew. I'd best get back to rovin' from place to place or someone will have a hissy."

"Yeah, that's right. So, you're with Vic Tyson's crew, eh?"

"Yep. For better or for worse. See you fellers."

Reunited with Alejandro Alvarado, Smoke Jensen and the ranchero made a rapid return to town. On the way, Smoke weighed the alternatives facing him. Not unusual, he did not like any of them. Back in the sheriff's office, he sent loungers to summon a war council. This would be a long night, Smoke knew.

"There's nothing for it but that I go after them," Smoke announced after relaying what he had learned beyond the town.

Mayor Fidel Arianas nodded thoughtfully. "I can understand that. But how are you going to go about it?"

Smoke Jensen had his answers ready. "First we have to break this siege. They are mighty spooked over two defeats in one day. And we've not attacked them at night before. What we are going to do is organize an assault force from the local volunteers and Diego's vaqueros and wipe out their roadblocks, scatter the patrols around the town and plain raise a lot of hell."

Diego Alvarado's eyes glowed. *"Muy bien, amigo.* Naturally, all of my men will volunteer."

Smoke shook his head. "We only need half of them. Someone has to hold the fort. Gather five groups of ten each, and meet me in the Plaza de Armas in half an hour. One bunch will take each road out of town. The fifth will make a sweep of the roving patrols. Tonight we're going to kick hell out of these scum."

Thirty minutes later, grim-faced men gathered in the plaza. All were heavily armed. Every man had a horse. Smoke quietly gave them their assignments and moved out himself with those going after the mobile pickets. When everyone had gotten into position, they watched the hands on one of the clocks located on the four sides of the church steeple. The minute hand closed on 10:45, and the deadly bands moved out.

Three hundred yards from the roadblocks they urged their mounts to a gallop. Weapons out and ready, they opened fire at seventy-five yards.

With Quinn and Thompson dead and Satterlee gone, the attack quickly became a rout. Already demoralized by the turn of the day's events, the outlaw trash had little heart for a fight. Muzzle flashes in the night, followed by the crack of bullets and roar of weapons, undid even the most courageous among them. Men seemed to be shooting at them from all directions. Riderless horses ran past, and those securely picketed whinnied in the mad desire to join their fellows.

"To hell with this, I'm gettin' outta here," the hard case known as Rucker spat as he ankled over the ground to his horse.

He slipped on a bridle and swung up bareback. No time for the niceties. Too many guns out there. He drummed his heels into the flanks of his horse and broke clear of the melee behind him. His mount nearly ran into the chest of a big, gray, spotted-rump 'Palouse. Veering at the last instant, he caught a glimpse of the rider.

"Oh, God, Smoke Jensen," he wailed aloud.

Then Smoke shot him.

In twenty minutes the last of the vermin had been exterminated or surrendered. Diego's vaqueros herded them back toward town. At the jail, Smoke confronted the leaders of the resistance. "Thank you all for what you've done. You've saved your town. The end of this is up to me. I'm going after Clifton Satterlee. Mac, Alejandro, I'd like you to come with me. We'll take about twenty-five men to handle any opposition Satterlee can muster. Even with them, it's gonna be mighty hard to end this."

25

Smoke, Alejandro and Mac rode out of Taos at the head of a twenty-three-man force. Even pushing to the limit, they would not reach Santa Fe until early morning of the next day. Smoke used the time to review how they should go about cornering Satterlee. His options were limited; that he accepted. He had no way of knowing how many gunhands Satterlee might have at the large estancia outside the territorial capital. Whatever the count, he wanted to keep the number of injuries and deaths small among his volunteers. Most of all he wanted to give Mac a chance at building a satisfying life for himself. All such considerations aside, he wanted to end it quickly. Could he count on the sheriff in Santa Fe?

That question remained with him as they rode through Española. False dawn caught them still two miles from Satterlee's lair. To Smoke that answered his preoccupation with the sheriff. They simply did not have time to ride past the road that led to the ranch and into Santa Fe. They would have to do it on their own.

Half a mile from the estancia, Smoke halted his small force and informed them of what they would do. "Mac, I want you to take charge of everyone but Alejandro and myself. Take on any gunhands Satterlee has at the ranch and keep them busy. Alejandro and I will go in to find

Martha. Also to get Satterlee." Then he added with a crooked smile, "If something happens to let us open the gates for you, we will."

"I want to go with you, Smoke," Mac protested.

"Not this time. Keep in mind, youngster, that you are only fifteen years old. I'm not going to coddle you, but I want you in a responsible position, doing something that has to be done. Something that keeps you out of the center of most danger."

Mac blurted his objection. "But I want to be there, to help."

"Hell, boy, you're gonna get shot at anyway. Why make it worse?"

Grudgingly, Mac saw his point. "I'll do my best, Smoke. Count on it."

Alejandro nodded silent approval. He couldn't help but like this boy/man. "I think my father will find it impossible to continue his food production without you, young Mac. We want you around to make our gardens more productive."

Mac flushed and put on a foolish grin to hide his elation at this praise. "Yes, sir—uh—Alejandro. Do they—ah—ever call you Alex?"

Alejandro flashed white teeth in his olive face. "Only my gringo friends. So, I suppose you can, too."

Smoke concluded his strategy session. "Let's get to it, then. Mac, circle wide around and hit the place from the rear. Once you have their attention, we'll come at 'em from the front."

A short while later, Mac and his mixed force invested the walls around three sides of the hacienda. Under cover of darkness, Smoke and Alejandro approached the front gate in the twelve-foot wall that surrounded the compound. Smoke had a little surprise that he had not mentioned to the others. With the battle raging around them, he quickly went to work sheltered by the inset of the massive portals.

"Alejandro, gather up all the big rocks you can find. Bring them here."

Diego's eldest son went to work with a twinkle in his eyes from sight of the cylindrical sticks in Smoke's hands. By the time Alejandro returned for the sixth time, Smoke had attached a bundle of five sticks of dynamite to the center of the gate, where the crossbar would be.

"Mix some mud," Smoke commanded as he bent to place more dynamite against one of the hinges.

Alejandro found water in a horse trough and plenty of desert soil right where they needed it. He carried the liquid in his hat to make a quagmire under the sheltering lip above them. When he thought he had it right, he stopped to watch Smoke packing rocks against the charge on the hinge.

"Smoke, it is ready."

Studying the consistency of the mud, Smoke passed judgment. "Thicker. Make it sticky."

When it reached the desired texture, Smoke began to pack it around the explosives in the middle of the gate, then poured more over the rocks. That completed, he cut his eyes to Alejandro. "We'll let that dry awhile."

The volume of gunfire rose and fell as the outlaws traded shots with the men from Taos. It served well to keep attention off Smoke and Alejandro. After ten minutes, the surface had returned to its natural color, and cracks began to appear in the mud. Smoke nodded approvingly and bent with a lucifer in his hand.

"You light that one and I'll get this. Then we get out of here . . . fast."

With the fuses sputtering, Smoke and Alejandro ran from the gateway and flattened their backs against the wall to either side. Three minutes went by, and then a tremendous roar shattered the sporadic gunfire from within the hacienda. Dirt and acrid smoke billowed out of the arched opening. Splinters of flaming wood mingled with them. The ground shook, and Alejandro smelled the nauseous fumes of the burned dynamite. In the numbing silence that followed, Smoke and Alejandro heard a shrill shriek, followed by an enormous crash.

"Let's go," said Smoke tautly.

Quickly they rounded the corners that had sheltered them. Alejandro's jaw sagged at sight of the damage the explosives had wrought. One side of the thick gate hung askew. The other lay flat on the ground, blown out from the bottom. Smoke jumped on top of it and ran into the courtyard. They met with no resistance until they reached the main entrance to the hacienda. Two dumbfounded thugs with bestubbled jaws stood inside. They gaped at the damage until the figures of Smoke Jensen and Alejandro Alvarado filled the range of their vision.

"Lutie, it's him. It's Smoke Jensen," babbled one.

"Then git him, Frank, git him."

Each man made the fateful mistake of reaching for his six-gun. Smoke beat them both, with Alejandro not far behind. The Colt in Smoke's hand bellowed, and Lutie doubled over, shot through the liver. Frank fired a round before Alejandro ended his life with a bullet in the head. Side-stepping the dying men, Smoke and Alejandro pushed on into the house. Cole Granger and three men waited for them in the inner courtyard.

"There they are," shouted one piece of human debris as Smoke became visible at the inner opening of the corridor.

Smoke, the .45 still in his hand, shot him through the heart. Two others dived for cover behind the cheerily splashing fountain. Granger dropped behind a huge clay olla that held a stunted banana tree. From there he triggered a round that ripped along the left ribs of Alejandro Alvarado.

Face grimaced in agony, the young grandee spun to one side and leaned back against the wall of the arched corridor that connected the front door to the patio. "Go on, Smoke. I'll be all right."

Alejadro extended his right arm along the wall and took

aim at a pale face that appeared above the lip of the fountain. Biting his lip, he squeezed his trigger. The slug
slammed into the edge of the marble basin. Water and
stone chips showered into the air. The face disappeared, an
irregular hole in the center of its forehead. At once, Smoke
was on the move.

He bounded to his left and dropped behind a long,
earth-filled planter. Three slugs pounded into the opposite
surface. Smoke inched along to the end and hazarded a
quick look. Granger had come to his boots, peering across
the open garden in a attempt to get a sight on Smoke. It
would be all too easy.

Smoke raised his arm and fired at the center line of
Granger's body. The bullet smashed into Granger's belly,
and he staggered backward. Smoke came to his boots and
jinked off another direction. He learned that he
had miscalculated Granger's strength a moment later
when Alejadro shouted from behind him.

"Smoke, look out!"

Cole Granger fired his six-gun with less than acceptable
accuracy. A hot tunnel opened in Jensen's left arm an instant before he discharged his Colt and put another bullet
in Cole Granger's chest. To his surprise Granager absorbed the punishment and turned his gun on Alejandro.

This time he wavered unsteadily so that the slug struck
the stucco-plastered, adobe wall before it plowed into the
chest of Alejandro Alvarado. Cursing his bad luck, Smoke
raised his point of aim. He fired at Granger's face and
blasted the life out of his assailant. Quickly he bound his
arm and chaged his empty Colt for the freash one. Then
Smoke began to search for the final hard case.

Sagged to his knees, Alejandro called out to Smoke
"He's gone. Ran out to the others."

"What about you?" Concern rang in Smoke's voice.

"It's . . . not bad. Go on. Find Satterlee and get the girl
to safety."

Smoke Jenson started for the stairway that led to the
second floor. Behind him a door flew open. Smoke spun

on one heel and snapped off a shot. Another of Satterlee's henchmen died. Halfway up the stairs, he paused to look back. Alejandro sat spread-legged against the wall, his face pale, but his breathing regular. The bullet must not have reached his lung, Smoke speculated.

He took time then to reload, then ascended to the open-sided hallway that ran around the upper story. Now the search turned serious. Smoke stepped to the first door and kicked it in. A starled hard case turned from the window where he had been exchanging rounds with Mac and the attackers, who had swarmed into the compound through the damaged gate. Smoke shot him in the shoulder, took his weapons and locked the door behind as he left. The next two rooms were empty. Smoke worked his way out into the open.

From below, Alejandro spoke to Smoke, his words light and breathy. "I can cover you from here."

Smoke nodded and went on. The next door he found locked from the inside. His .45 Peacemaker at the ready, Smoke lined up and kicked the center panel beside the lock case. It hurt like hell. Made of stout manzanita, the door did not yield. Smoke kicked again, with the other foot. Wood splintered in the frame. Dimly, from behind and below, Smoke noted the arrival of Mac and some of the vaqueros. They swarmed through the courtyard as Smoke lashed out with his boot a third time. The door flew open to reveal a frightened and startled Lupe and a bulldog-faced hard case.

"Down," Smoke shouted to the maid.

She dropped without hesitation. Smoke popped a cap on the outlaw at close range. The slug pierced a forearm and entered a vulnerable chest. Smoke shot him again, and the thug's six-gun flew upward out of his hand. It discharged when it struck the ceiling. The bullet went through the thin plaster and exited the building by way of the tin roof. A stunned expression washed over the dying gunman's features, and he fell face-first to the floor.

Smoke pointed to Lupe. "Stay here."

Footsteps pounded in the stairwell as Smoke faced the next door. It was also locked. Smoke reared back for a good blow with his boot as Mac and three of Diego's cowboys ran toward him.

"We got 'em all, Smoke. Most just gave up."

"Stay back," Smoke cautioned. Then he slammed his boot sole against the door.

It happeded in a blur. Smoke saw a thick-shouldered gunman facing the door and fired instinctively. The lout dropped his revolver and clasped his belly with both hands. Smoke shot him again. At once her looked to his left.

With a long-legged stride, Clifton Satterlee moved across the carpet toward ta wide-eyed, visibly shaken Martha Estes. He had a .44 Colt Lightning in his left hand. Too, late, and knowing it, Smoke swung his Peacemaker toward Satterlee and fought to gain time with his voice.

"Don't move!"

"Stop where you are." Mac's voice broke as he stormed into the room, eyes fixed on Satterlee.

Satterlee swung his Lightning away from Martha and fired double-action. His bullet hit Mac in the notch of at the bottom of his throat. Quickly, Satterlee shot again. This .44 slug punched through Mac's right lung and ripped out his back. Instantly, Clifton Satterlee grabbed Martha Estes and pulled her in front of him. Driven backward by the agony of his wounds, Ian MacGreggor stumbled into the corridor. He teetered on the bainister for a precarious moment. Then his legs went out from under him, and he caught himself with his elbows.

Smoke did not have time to check the youngster and knew it. He faced Satterlee, who now held the muzzle of his Colt to Martha's temple. "I'll kill her. So help me, I will. Holster your iron and get out of my way. Let me go and she won't be harmed."

Reluctantly, Smoke complied. Then he heard a miserable groan from Mac, and his eyes narrowed to furious slits. "You're a dead man Satterlee. There's no way you are getting out of here."

Satterlee cut his eyes to a large carpetbag on the floor. It bulged with his portable wealth. Two finely wrought pieces of Tua jewelry spilled from the open top. "I'm taking that and her and leaving."

Smoke eyed the loot and returned his attention to Satterlee. "You killed that boy for nothing, Satterlee. More than for any other reason, I'm going to kill you for that."

Clifton Satterlee forced a nasty chuckle. "Not likely, Jensen. I've worked too hard for that." Again his eyes shifted to his ill-gotten gains. "You make a try and the girl dies."

Suddenly, Martha Estes moaned and uttered a huge sigh. She went limp in the arms of Clifton Satterlee. The instant her head fell away from the gun barrel, Smoke Jensen drew with blinding speed and triggered a round. The slug hit Satterlee at the top of his nose and pulped the empire builder's brain. He did not have time to send a signal to his trigger finger. He flew away from Martha Estes and sprawled across the bed.

At once, Martha straightened and opened her eyes. A big smile adorned her face. "I thought you might do that," she told Smoke a moment before she rushed to him and gave him a big hug.

Gently Smoke disengaged her. "You're safe now, Miss Martha. I'll arrange for passage to your home. Now, if you'll excuse me."

Smoke stepped out into the hall and gazed down at the bloody, sweating, pale-faced Mac. Ian MacGreggor worked his throat, and his lips moved. He spoke in a low, wheezy voice. "I—I guess I'll not be needing that gardening job."

Something stung Smoke's eyes, and he blinked rapidly. "That was fool thing to do, Mac. But you did save a girl's life. I'm proud of you." No reason to hide the obvious from the boy. "I'll see that your family gets your pay."

"Th—thank you, Smoke. It was—was an honor to fight at . . . your side." That said, Mac heaved a mighty sigh and died.

Eyes wet and burning, Smoke Jensen turned away to

discover that Don Diego Alvarado and his remaining vaqueros had arrived. Smoke went to his friend. "Alejandro took a couple of bad ones."

"Yes, I saw. What about you?"

"I'll live. But . . . Mac didn't make it. I'll have to see that the Marshal's Office sends his pay to his parents."

"It's a beatiful day," Martha Estes opined as she joined the two men.

Still deeply moved by the death of Ian MacGreggor, Smoke looked across the early morning vista. The rising sun cast a pink hue on the white caps of the Sangre de Cristo range. No matter the cost, peace could return to Taos and the Tua pueblo. He nodded to Martha.

"Yes, it is right nice day." *She's right, it's beautiful,* Smoke mused. *Almost as beautiful as the Sugarloaf.*

Sally and Bobby Jensen greeted Smoke's triumphant return to the Sugarloaf with unbounded joy. After a long, energetic embrace, Smoke looked around and then kissed Sally on one cheek.

"It doesn't look like anything has changed. What did you do while I was gone?"

Sally pursed her lips, fought to banish her sour memories, then answered. "I had a visit fron an old school friend."

"That's nice. Did you have a good time?"

"Like heck," Bobby put in. "Her kids sure are a bunch of brats." In spite of Sally's sharp look, Bobby went on. It's the truth. And you're always after me to tell the truth, Smoke. An' to be man enough to stand up for it."

Smoke put and arm around each of his family and started for the porch, hugging them tightly. "So, tell me about this friend of yours, Sally. And don't forget the brats."

BATTLE OF THE
MOUNTAIN MAN

1

Smoke Jensen rode his big Palouse, Horse, into Big Rock, Colorado, just as the sun peeked over the mountains to the east. As Horse cantered down dusty streets, Smoke's eyes flicked back and forth, checking alleyways and shadows for potential trouble. Though his days as one of the West's most feared gunfighters were behind him, old habits died hard, and old enemies seemed to live longer and outnumber old friends.

As Smoke passed the jail, Sheriff Monte Carson stepped through the door and tipped his hat. "Howdy, Smoke. Gettin' an early start this mornin'?"

Smoke smiled at his old friend and pointed back over his shoulder at a buckboard following him. "Got to set an example for these young punchers, Monte. Otherwise they'd sleep half the day away."

Monte grinned and glanced at the wagon. Pearlie, foreman of Smoke's Sugarloaf ranch, was riding slumped over, his hat pulled down over his eyes, snoring loud enough to be heard over the creaking of wheels and the clopping of horses' hooves.

Sitting next to Pearlie, leaning against his shoulder, was Cal Woods, Pearlie's second in command at the ranch. His hat was also down and his eyes were closed. Though he wasn't snoring, he was obviously asleep, too.

Monte chuckled. "Good thing those broncs know the way to town, Smoke, or them boys'd be in Denver by now."

Smoke nodded and reined Horse to a stop in front of the general store next to the jail. He stepped out of his saddle and tried the door, finding it still locked.

He shook his head. *Guess everyone but Monte and I are sleeping in this morning,* he thought. He climbed back up on Horse and called out, "Cal, Pearlie, wake your lazy butts up and I'll treat you to some breakfast over at Longmont's."

Pearlie opened one eye and peered out from under his Stetson. With a prodigious yawn, he nodded and nudged Cal awake. "C'mon boy. Food's callin' an' the boss is buyin'."

They left the buckboard in front of the store and ambled over to the Silver Dollar Saloon, following Smoke.

When they brushed through the batwings, the three men found Louis Longmont sitting at his usual table, drinking coffee and smoking a long, black cigar. The ex-gunfighter smiled and waved them over to his table. Even at this early hour, he was, as usual, dressed impeccably in a black suit and a starched white shirt with ruffles on the front, a black silk vest, and a red cravat around his neck.

Louis looked like a dandy, but he was in fact one of the fastest guns in the West. He was a lean, hawk-faced man, with strong, slender hands and long fingers, his nails carefully manicured, his hands clean. He had jet black hair and a black, pencil-thin mustache. He wore low-heeled boots. A pistol hung in tied-down leather on his right side; it was not for show alone. For Louis was snake-quick with a short gun. A feared, deadly gun hand when pushed. Just past forty years of age. He had come to the West as a young boy and made a name for himself first as a gunfighter, then as a skilled gambler. He was well educated and as smart as he was dangerous.

Smoke and Pearlie and Cal pulled up chairs across from Louis, who waved a hand at a young black waiter. "Tell Andre to scramble up some hen's eggs, burn three steaks, and make a fresh pot of coffee. These punchers look hungry."

Smoke's eyes flicked around the room in an unconscious search for danger, automatically noting three men sitting at a corner table on the far side of the room. Though it was barely dawn, two of the men had mugs of beer in front of them and the third a glass of whiskey.

The cowboy drinking whiskey sported a fancy double-rig of hand-tooled holsters containing pearl-handled Colts, and wore a black silk shirt and black pants tucked into knee-high stovepipe black boots. He had red hair and a red handlebar mustache. His hair was slicked down and glistened with pomade, and the corners of his mustache curled up, held in place with wax. His companions both wore pistols hung low and tied down on their thighs with rawhide thongs.

Smoke inclined his head toward the gunmen and said to Louis, "Trouble?"

Louis smiled and tipped cigar smoke from his nostrils. "They think they are. The one with the fancy rig calls himself the Arizona Kid." He paused to chuckle. "The big one on the left, the one with the shaved head, says his name is Otto, and the other one's name I didn't catch."

Louis paused while the waiter placed three mugs of dark, steaming coffee in front of them.

Pearlie built himself a cigarette and stuck it in the corner of his mouth, in unconscious imitation of his idol, the famous gunman Joey Wells, whom he had met and fought alongside the previous year.*

"They were here drinking all last night," Louis continued, glancing in the direction of the gunnies who were staring at Smoke and his men. "Said they heard Ned Buntline was in the area and they wanted to talk to him about writing a book about them."

At the mention of Buntline's name, Cal came fully awake, his eyes wide. "Mr. Buntline is in Big Rock?" he asked.

Louis smiled, knowing Cal's addiction to the penny

*Honor of the Mountain Man

dreadfuls Buntline penned. "He was. He came through here last week, said he was headed into the high lonesome to talk to some of the old mountain men before they all died off. He's planning on writing a story about how they opened the mountains up to the white man."

"Wow!" Cal said. "Maybe I can meet him and tell him how much I like his books."

Louis nodded. "You'll probably get the chance. He plans to stop by Sugarloaf and talk to Smoke on his way back from the mountains." He hesitated. "That's if Smoke will talk to him at all. Smoke isn't all that long-winded, especially when it comes to talking about himself. If Mr. Ned Buntline intends to get any real information from Smoke Jensen, he'd better be real careful how he asks. Smoke has never been all that inclined to waggle his tongue when it comes to men who live in the high lonesome. There are some things that a man has to learn the hard way, not from some blown-up story in a book full of fancy language. Half of it isn't true to start with, a piece of some writer's imagination. I don't think Smoke will be all that excited about telling Buntline what he wants to know." He glanced at Smoke. "Am I right?"

Smoke seemed momentarily preoccupied with the three men in the corner, in particular the one Louis said called himself the Arizona Kid. "There's things ought not to be written up in some book," he said quietly. "A man who takes on high country all by himself learns a trick or two about how to survive. Learning it isn't easy, and I can show you more'n a handful of graves up in those mountains to prove my point."

"Like Puma's," Pearlie reminded. "That was one tough ol' hombre, only he put his life on the line an' his luck jus' plumb played out."

Smoke didn't want to be reminded of his dead friend. "Puma Buck was one of the best, like Preacher. But it wasn't Puma's luck that ran out . . . he went up against long odds, and sooner or later, as any gambler'll tell you, those odds catch up to a man who takes chances." He was still watching the Arizona Kid from the corner of his eye, strangely uneasy, feeling a heaviness in the air, the smell of danger.

Louis noticed Smoke's distraction "I don't think those boys are dumb enough to make a play," he said under his breath, his gun hand close to his pistol. "But if they do, I'll take down the gent who shaves his head. You can have the owlhoot with the double rig. If I'm any judge, he fancies himself as a quick draw, so I'll give you the pleasure of proving him wrong."

Smoke took a sip of coffee, using his left hand to handle his cup. "The one who calls himself the Arizona Kid will be the one to start trouble."

Louis chuckled mirthlessly. "Wonder just where in Arizona Territory he'd like to have his body shipped to? I don't suppose we'll have time to ask."

"I feel it coming," Smoke whispered, "just like a mountain man can feel a chinook wind before it starts to blow."

"I sure as hell hope you're wrong," Pearlie said, "on account I'm sure as hell hungry fer them eggs . . ."

2

Cal added his voice to Pearlie's concerns. "Y'all sure are makin' me nervous, all this talk about a shootin'. Maybe I ain't got so much appetite after all."

Pearlie looked at the boy. "Relax, son. If any two men can handle them three, it's Smoke an' Mr. Longmont. Truth is, either one could most likely handle all three, no matter how tough they claim to be."

Smoke wasn't really listening, pretending to watch a sunrise out the front windows when in fact he was keeping an eye on the three men at the corner table.

"It's my belly that ain't relaxed," Cal muttered.

Right at that moment the Arizona Kid signaled the bartender for another round of beers.

Louis seemed amused over Cal's uneasiness. "My money says when those eggs and steaks get here, you'll lick your plate clean as a whistle."

"Maybe," Cal replied, taking his own quick glance at the men in the corner. "Those boys look like a bad case of indigestion to me."

Smoke still sensed the nearness of danger, a lifelong habit, learning to trust his instincts. There was something about the three gunmen, not merely the way they wore their guns tied down, but something more, an attitude of confidence, even arrogance, on their faces. He drank more coffee, hoping he was wrong about the prospects of trouble.

The bartender brought three beers to the table. Smoke heard one of the men ask who the newcomers were.

"That big feller's none other than Smoke Jensen," the barman replied. "He makes his home right close to Big Rock."

"He came struttin' in here like he thinks he's tough, them big shoulders thrown back."

The barkeep lowered his voice even more. "Make no mistake about it, stranger. He is tough. Plenty of men have tried him to see if he's as mean as his reputation. Some got away with a hole or two in their hides. Some went below ground to feed the worms."

The Arizona Kid was watching Smoke closely now. "You say his name is Smoke Jensen? Never heard of him. Maybe all he's got is that mean reputation."

The bartender glanced over his shoulder in Smoke's direction and quickly looked away. "I ain't no doctor, mister, but if I was you an' wanted to stay healthy, I wouldn't test Mr. Jensen to see if I'm tellin' you the truth." He turned on his heel and hurried away. The Arizona Kid and the gunman named Otto continued to stare at Smoke.

Like predicting winter weather in the high lonesome, Smoke knew what was coming. It was just a matter of time. The Kid wanted to draw attention to himself, perhaps to add to his self-importance if he got the chance to talk to Ned Buntline, to put another notch on his guns.

To keep young Cal and Pearlie out of the line of fire, he said, "Why don't you two go out and see to the buggy team and my Palouse. Won't take but a minute and you'll be done before the food gets here."

Pearlie nodded, like he understood. Cal needed no urging to push back his chair for a walk outside. As the pair was leaving, Smoke turned at the waist to look directly at the Arizona Kid and his partners, deciding there was no sense in wasting time when a confrontation was as sure as the snow in high country now. "You boys got a bad case of the goggle eyes," he said evenly. "Maybe I'm too particular about it, but it sticks in my craw like sand when some gent stares at me. Especially you, the carrot-topped hombre with the mustache, you just gotta learn some manners or somebody's liable to teach you some."

The Kid put down his beer mug and rose slowly to his feet, his back to the wall. "Is that so?" he asked, sneering, both hands near the butts of his guns. "Tell you the truth, mister, I don't see nobody in this room who's man enough to git that job done."

Smoke came to a crouch, then rose to his full height, lips drawn into a hard line. "Then look a little closer," he snarled, as every muscle in his body tensed. "I think it's time you boys cleared out of here. We'll take our little disagreement outside. A friend of mine owns this establishment and I'd hate like hell to be responsible for spilling blood all over his nice clean floor, or putting any bullet holes in his walls. Meet me out in the street and we'll settle this."

"Like hell!" the Kid bellowed, hands dipping for his pistols as Smoke had anticipated all along.

In the same instant, Otto and the other cowboy were clawing for their guns.

Lightning quick, employing reflexes that had kept him alive in much tougher situations, Smoke came up with both hands filled with iron, Colt .44s, working his thumbs and trigger fingers in well-practiced movements, almost second nature to a man who kept himself alive by wits and weapons.

The Silver Dollar Saloon exploded in a thundering series of deafening blasts, becoming a symphony of noise when Louis Longmont added his gunshots to the concussions swelling inside the establishment's walls.

The Arizona Kid was driven back against wallpapered planks behind him, his mouth grotesquely distorted when balls of speeding lead shattered his front teeth. His hat went spinning into the air like a child's top as the back of his skull ruptured in flying masses of tissue, red hair, bone fragments, and brains.

At the same time Otto swirled, balancing on one booted foot while a spurt of blood erupted from the base of his neck above his shirt collar. Another slug entered his right eye, closing it upon impact amid a shower of crimson squirting from a hole below his right ear. Otto appeared to be dancing to an unheard melody for a moment, trying to remain upright on one foot, hopping up and down, dropping his gun to the floor to reach for his throat and eye socket.

The third gunman went backward through a shattering windowpane before his gun ever cleared leather, a .44 caliber bullet splintering his breastbone, puckering the front of his shirt as it sped through his body in the exact spot where Smoke placed it, with as much care as time afforded him.

Amid the roaring gunblasts, someone screamed outside the saloon, but it was the Arizona Kid who held Smoke's attention now as the gunman slid down the Silver Dollar's expensively decorated wall, leaving a red smear in his wake as he went to the floor in a heap, what was left of his mouth agape, dribbling blood down the front of his silk shirt, remnants of teeth still clinging to bleeding gums. A plug of his curly red hair was plastered to the wall above him, sticking there for a curiously long time before it dropped soundlessly to the floor beside him.

Otto teetered on one foot, making strangling sounds, blood pumping from his wounds as he somehow managed to remain standing, hopping for no apparent reason, since he had no leg wounds, merely unable to put his left foot down.

Smoke and Louis stopped firing, watching Otto perform his odd dance steps while gunsmoke rose slowly toward the ceiling.

"He'll fall down in a minute," Louis said, as though he was discussing the weather, or the felling of a tree. "Or should I put another slug in him and be done with it?"

"Hard to say," Smoke replied dryly, holstering his pistols, his eyes on Otto. "He does a right nice dance step. Too bad we ain't got a fiddler."

The thumping of Otto's boot and his choking sounds were the only noises inside the Silver Dollar for several seconds more as Smoke and Louis watched the dying man's struggle. Suddenly, Otto's knee gave way and he collapsed on the floorboards beside a brass spittoon with a soft gurgling coming from the hole in his neck. A dark stain began to spread across the crotch of his pants when his bladder emptied, a sure sign of the nearness of death.

Smoke sauntered over to the broken window, gazing out at the third gunman's limp body. "This one's dead," he told Louis in a quiet voice. "I reckon I owe you for a piece of glass."

"Nonsense," Louis replied. "Hardly a month passes that I don't buy a window or two, after some of my customers get a bit too rowdy. You don't owe me a thing."

Smoke turned to his old friend and grinned. "Yes I do, and you know it. The big guy, Otto, was a little faster than I had him sized up to be. I might have been picking lead out of my own hide if you hadn't been here to back me."

"Nobody is keeping score," Louis said. "We've been backing each other so long I lost count of who owes who a long time ago. I'm not keeping a tally book, but I'll wager it's heavily in your favor. You've stopped a lot of lead from flying in my direction over the years. Now sit down. I'll send someone for the undertaker and then I'll send out those steaks and eggs, if the cook didn't let 'em burn while all that shooting was going on."

3

Sheriff Monte Carson came racing through the batwing doors with his gun drawn, followed closely by Pearlie and Cal. Carson stopped in midstride when he saw the two bodies, and the broken window.

Carson looked at Smoke. "What the hell? I heard all the shootin' an' got here quick as I could."

"A little misunderstanding," Smoke replied, settling into his chair. "Two's dead and the other one's dying. They went for their guns first."

"You didn't need to explain that part," Carson said, putting his pistol away. "I've known you long enough to know you'd never draw on a man first. Should I send for the doctor to attend to that bald feller?"

"He's too far gone for that," Smoke answered, lifting his cup of cold coffee as a signal for a warm-up. "Two slugs, one through an eye and the other through his throat. He'll be dead before Doc can get here."

Carson looked around momentarily. "Louis told me about these three strangers, how they was askin' about Ned Buntline an' drinkin' a helluva lot of whiskey an' beer."

"They're done with their drinking now," Smoke remarked with no trace of emotion, "unless you count the way that big one over yonder is drinking his own blood."

Carson took a deep breath. "I reckon I should be used

to the fact that sometimes things start happenin' early in Big Rock now an' then. Before the last rooster stops crowin' at daybreak we got three dead men to bury. Maybe we oughta change the name of this town to Dead Man's Gulch. Damn, what a mess." He gave Louis a tight grin. "On top of bein' the undertaker's best friend, you've been mighty good for the glass windowpane business up in Denver."

Louis nodded, taking note of the fact that Cal was standing over Otto with a waxy look paling his cheeks. "It's a necessary expenditure in the whiskey trade, Monte. As a businessman, I have to be prepared for a certain amount of fixed overhead. Windows are a part of that figure."

Smoke heard Cal speak softly to Pearlie. "This feller ain't got but one eye. You can see plumb into his skullbone. I swear I'm gonna be sick. Lookee there, Pearlie . . . he's still breathin' once in a while. Jeez. I sure as hell ain't got no appetite now. You can have my steak an' eggs."

"A man dyin' ain't never a pretty sight," Pearlie replied, putting his arm around Cal's shoulder. "Go on outside fer a spell an' catch yer wind. You'll feel better in a little bit."

Cal turned and hurried past Smoke's table without looking at him, embarrassed by the way he felt sick to his stomach, Smoke guessed. Outside the Silver Dollar, curious citizens of Big Rock peered through front windows to see what all the ruckus was about so early in the morning . . . some were still dressed in nightshirts and long johns.

Louis spoke to the bartender as Sheriff Carson stepped over to the doors behind Cal, following him out to fetch the undertaker. "Tell Andre to hurry with that food," Louis said, as though he knew Smoke and Pearlie would be hungry despite what had just happened.

A nervous-eyed waiter refilled Smoke's coffee cup and gave a similar warm-up to Louis's, then Pearlie's.

"Helluva way to start the day," Smoke said under his breath as he brought the cup to his lips.

Louis chuckled and sat down. "I've had worse and so

have you. Sometimes it comes with the territory if a man carries a gun."

Smoke thought of something. "I don't intend to talk to this Buntline. If he asks, tell him I'm not in the habit of talking about old friends, or even old enemies. He'll have to get his information someplace else."

Louis stared thoughtfully into his cup. "I doubt if any of the old-timers up high will talk to him either, if he can find any of them in the first place. I figure Mr. Buntline wasted a trip out here. As you know well, mountain men are a different breed, for the most part. I never knew one who could be called long-winded about what goes on up there."

Smoke recalled his introduction to mountain men and their habits. "Preacher wouldn't talk to other folks about it. Puma could be as talkative as a clam when somebody asked him about the mountains."

Louis glanced at him. "Preacher had a tremendous influence on you, didn't he?"

For a moment, Smoke closed his eyes, forgetting the killings only minutes ago to think back to his upbringing. "More than anyone will ever know," he said. "I reckon it was the little things, not just how to survive in the wilds or how to use a gun or a knife or my fists. It was the way he took things in stride that I remember most. No matter how rough things got, no matter how bad any situation turned out to be, Preacher always kept his head. I never saw him scared. He never let his anger show when somebody crossed him. He was a man of damn few words, but when he talked it was a real good idea to listen. Never heard him say things twice, or ask a man but once to do what he wanted done. I learned real early to pay close attention to everything he told me, that there was a reason behind it. Nothing ever surprised him, either, no matter how bad it was. I used to think Preacher expected everything to go wrong. I was nearly grown by the time I understood that was his way of being ready for the worst."

Louis was studying Smoke's face. "I hear tell no one knows if Preacher is still alive. He'd be an old man by now . . ."

Smoke remembered his conversation with Puma Buck, asking the same question one night before the battle with Sundance Morgan and his gang.* "I asked Puma what he thought one night. He said as long as there was beaver to be trapped up high, or grizzlies on the prowl, he didn't figure it was time for Preacher to cross over. I think that was his way of telling me something he was sworn not to tell, that Preacher is alive up yonder somewhere. Like you say, he'd be getting on up in years by now and maybe it's his pride that won't let him come down to show himself after age has robbed him of a few things, maybe some of his eyesight and hearing, some aching joints or an old wound that didn't heal. I respect him too much to go off looking for him even if he is alive in the emptiest parts of the high lonesome. Knowing Preacher like I do, I know if he wanted to see me or anybody else, he'd come looking for 'em, or send word. I've been thinking about it for years now, off and on. A prideful man is too proud to be humbled by old age in front of anyone else. I've got it figured he's still up there, hunting and fishing, exploring the last stretches of wild country. He's a mountain man all the way through, and his kind don't need people to enjoy what's around him."

"Maybe I shouldn't have brought the subject up," Louis observed, lighting another cigar with a sputtering lucifer. "I didn't mean to open pages in a closed book."

Smoke shrugged. "The book on Preacher isn't closed until I get word he's gone, or find his bones on some high mountain ridge someplace. As far as I'm concerned, he's still up there, having one hell of a good time living the way he wants."

Pearlie walked over, having overheard part of their conversation. "Puma said he'd lay money Preacher was still alive, that night me an' Cal got took to his cabin."

Vengeance of the Mountain Man

Louis gave Pearlie a stare. "I think the subject ought to be dropped right now, Pearlie." He looked toward a waiter with a tray laden with steaming plates. "Here comes your breakfast. If you want, I'll have someone tell Cal his food is ready."

"I don't think the young 'un is up to it just yet," Pearlie replied, "but I'll walk outside an' ask. The boy's seen a right smart share of killin' in his short years, but when he got a good look up close at some of them bullet holes, his belly went to doin' a flip-flop, which ain't the natural place to put no big passel of food. Like invitin' a schoolmarm to ride a pitchin' bronc."

Louis laughed, casting a sideways glance in Smoke's direction. "I know one schoolmarm who's up to the task. Sally can ride a bucking horse as well as any cowboy in this country."

Smoke's thoughts went to Sally. He'd promised her only this morning that they'd winter up in an old cabin high above Sugarloaf for a spell, so they could spend some time alone and perhaps encounter a few of the wandering mountain men still living in the Rockies northwest of the ranch. "She's a good hand with a horse," Smoke agreed. "She's a right decent hand when it comes to handling men, like her husband. I've never laid claim to being the smartest feller in Colorado Territory, but she can out-smart me damn near any time she takes the notion. When she's after something she wants, she can be deadlier than a two-headed rattler. Worst thing is, she lets me think I'm getting my way every time. A time or two I've actually believed it."

Pearlie shook his head in agreement. "Miz Jensen knows how to handle a man, all right. She'll come out the door smilin', like all she wants is to say howdy-do, when what she's really after is a cord of wood chopped or a load of hay pitchforked in the wagon fer the cows. Every time I see her smile at me I feel like I oughta take off runnin', 'cause there's sure as hell some work she wants done." He grinned when his plate of steak and eggs was put before him. "That's another thing 'bout Miz Jensen. She ain't above workin' a man to death with bribes. She'll bake up a real sweet peach pie, or fix a batch of them bearclaws with brown sugar, an' open every window in the house so a man goes plumb crazy over the smell. Sooner or later a hungry feller is jus' naturally gonna be drawn to the house on account of them wonderful smells, an' that's when she springs her trap. She'll git one of them pretty smiles on her face, and start tellin' me 'bout them delicious pies or whatever she's bakin', an' I know I'm caught, trapped like a bear in a shallow cave. Then she'll up an' invite me an' Cal to have a little taste of what she's been cookin', right after we git a load of wood piled up next to the kitchen door. What's a starvin' man supposed to do?"

It was Smoke's turn to chuckle over Pearlie's recollections when it came to Sally, as his own plate was set on the table in front of him. "Pearlie's right as rain. I'm married to a woman who knows how to get what she wants . . . one way or another."

As he was about to knife into his steak, Caleb Walz came into the saloon. Walz was Big Rock's part-time undertaker, when he wasn't in the act of cutting hair at his barber shop. Caleb tipped his derby hat to everyone, glancing at the bodies, a hint of a grin raising the corners of his mouth. "Looks like somebody drummed up a little business for me real early," he said in his perpetual monotone. "Whoever it was, I'm obliged."

4

Ned Buntline had grown exceedingly frustrated over the past few weeks in his unsuccessful quest to interview some of the last of the old-time mountain men. Up on the Yellowstone he had finally been able to track down Major Frank North, leader of the famous Pawnee scouts. North had turned him down cold when he asked for an interview, stating flatly he believed dime novels were trash, a pack of lies, refusing to give Ned even a moment of his time other than to tell him to be on his way. A slap in the face, Ned thought, guiding his surefooted mule up a steep ridge roughly forty miles as the crow flies to the northwest of Big Rock in Colorado Territory. North had to know Ned had been responsible for Buffalo Bill Cody's rise to fame, along with other Wild West characters he'd glorified in his books. It hadn't been necessary for Major North to be so rude about it.

Now, in northwestern Colorado, Ned was trying to track down a few genuine mountain men for a series of stories that would set easterners on their ears. From a list given him by the old scout Alvah Dunning, Ned was searching for men with names like Puma Buck and Huggie Charles and Del Rovare, or the deadly gunfighter turned mountain man named Smoke Jensen. And there were others, a legendary figure known only as Preacher, whom many suspected to be dead of old age by now, one of the most elusive of all the early mountain pioneers, so that little was actually known about him or even what he looked like. Some claimed Preacher was only a figment of lesser men's imaginations, that he never existed at all except in stories told around mountain campfires, a dark hero of sorts with a penchant for killing anyone who intruded into his high country domain unless they crossed these stretches of the Rockies in peace, without disturbing it. But when it came to mountain men with a penchant for killing, all his sources were in agreement. Smoke Jensen was said to be a killing machine in this part of the West, a man not to be trifled with. If just half the stories Ned had heard about Jensen were true, he could be the man eastern readers would devour. Finding him, finding Jensen, was relatively easy, Ned was told. Jensen owned a high meadow ranch called Sugarloaf, having come down from the mountains a few years back to marry a woman from back east and live a quieter life, although as the stories went his existence was anything but quiet. Getting Jensen to talk to him was going to be the trick, according to those who knew about him or had made his acquaintance in the past. Jensen was a man of few words, and words were what Ned needed from him. The proposition promised to be touchy. Difficult.

Following a map given to him by an elderly Indian scout at a settlement named Glenwood Springs, Ned rode his brown mule slowly into higher altitudes, where it was rumored Puma Buck, Huggie Charles, and Del Rovare hunted and trapped. Perhaps with some sort of personal introduction from one of them to Smoke Jensen, he might just get what he came to Colorado to find . . . true stories of the exploits of mountain men. He hoped he might even be able to find out if this fellow they called Preacher actually existed, if he might still be alive and willing to talk.

Still, Ned was haunted by something Major North had told him in those few brief minutes they talked. North had said, "A man's got to *earn* his knowledge of the high lonesome, Mr. Buntline. No real mountain man is gonna hand it to you like a piece of cake. If you go lookin' for a man who knows the mountains, and if you find one, he ain't likely to tell you a damn thing."

Ned wondered if this would turn out to be the truth, making his ride to Colorado Territory a waste of time.

At the top of the ridge, Ned's mule stopped suddenly and snorted, pricking its ears forward. On a mountain slope across the valley, he saw a giant brown grizzly ambling slowly among tall ponderosa pines. Ned glanced down at the Henry rifle booted to his saddle . . . he was an expert marksman and this would be an easy shot . . . until he recalled what the old scout at Glenwood Springs told him.

"If you aim to find yourself a mountain man or two you'd best remember a couple of things."

"What's that?" Ned had asked.

"If they're close by, they'll be watchin' you, to see how you handle yourself. When you come across a wild critter, don't shoot it 'less you aim to eat it or wear its hide to stay warm. Those critters are as much a part of the high lonesome as them mountains themselves. Don't kill nothin' you ain't gotta kill to stay alive."

Ned had digested this bit of news. Hunting only for sport was frowned upon by mountain men. "What's the other thing? You said there were a couple . . ."

The old man had almost laughed. "Learn to sleep with one eye open, son, or you'll be the one who gets a taste of lead. I done told you where to look for ol' Puma Buck an' Huggie Charles an' some of them others. Could be you won't be so happy if you was to find 'em. Depends on the mood they's in, an' how you go 'bout handlin' yourself whilst you're up there. An' watch yourself real close 'round Smoke Jensen. Be my advice you act real polite. If he don't care to talk about his high country days, or tell you 'bout Preacher, you'd be well advised to clear out of Sugarloaf as quick as that mule can carry you."

Ned watched the grizzly, discarding any notion of shooting it simply for the sake of proving he had good aim.

"No sense buying into trouble," he muttered, urging the mule forward with his heels.

Turning north, Ned had ridden only a quarter mile before he caught sight of a tiny log cabin nestled in a grove of pines that overlooked a ravine choked with brush. Even from a distance he could tell the cabin hadn't seen much use lately, or any repairs to its mud-chinked logs. But the cabin was a starting place, and he rode toward it. His mule still seemed uneasy even though he had left the grizzly moving in another direction.

A voice from a stand of pines to his left made his heart stop beating.

"Them's mighty fancy duds you's wearin' fer a man travelin' empty spaces!"

Ned jerked his mule to a halt, looking in the direction of the voice, finding nothing but tree trunks and shadows. He took a deep breath to calm himself. "You scared me. I wasn't expecting anyone else to be here."

"Coulda killed you if'n I took the notion."

Ned felt fear forming a ball in his belly. "I hope you're not a killer, whoever you are. My name's Ned Buntline and I'm looking for a couple of mountain men . . . men by the name of Puma Buck, Huggie Charles, or Preacher."

A dry laugh came from the trees. "Puma's dead. Got killed nigh onto a year ago. Huggie runs traps east of here. As to the feller you called Preacher, ain't but one man livin' who knows where he is, an' that's Preacher hisself."

"Then Preacher really does exist? He's not just a camp-fire tale?"

A silence followed. Ned was still nervous, wondering if he was in the man's gunsights now.

"Maybe he does an' maybe he don't," the voice replied. "You ain't said what you want with a mountain man."

"Just to talk to them. To hear tales about what it's like to live up here. I'm a writer. I write books for people back in the eastern states who'll never see this beautiful country. They love reading my stories about the West."

Another silence, shorter. "What makes you think Huggie'll

talk to you anyways? He ain't inclined to use no over-supply of words."

"I was only hoping he would. I didn't think it would hurt to ask him. No one told me Puma Buck was dead. I'd also planned to talk to Smoke Jensen."

A laugh. "He's worse'n Huggie when it comes to waggin' his tongue. To say he's quiet would be like sayin' a beaver's got fur."

"I thought I'd try. I was warned he was dangerous."

"Fer a man who claims to make a livin' with words you sure as hell ain't been usin' the right ones. Smoke's a peaceable man when he ain't pushed, but he don't take kindly to gents who try an' ride roughshod over nobody. There's men buried all over these here mountains who figured they could take what they wanted from gentler folks who knowed Smoke Jensen."

"I only wanted a chance to talk to him about some of his exploits so I could write about it. If I may be so bold as to ask, who might you be? I can't see you from here."

"If I'd wanted you to see me I'd have showed myself. You got a rifle, an' there's a pistol under that fancy coat. Till I knowed what you was after, I was stayin' right where I'm at. As to my name, there's some who call me Griz. That's short fer a grizzly bear, case you didn't know. I go by Grizzly Cole when I git asked my full handle. I'm acquainted with Huggie Charles an' Smoke Jensen, if it matters, an' I knowed ol' Puma Buck as well as I knowed my own name. But till I know more about who the hell you are an' what you're after, climb down off 'n that mule an' keep yer hands where I can see 'em. You reach fer that pistol an' I swear I'll kill you, mister. Now git down."

Ned was careful to keep both hands in plain sight as he swung down to the ground, holding the mule's reins. He wondered if this might be a piece of luck. Was he having his first encounter with a real mountain man?

5

"I assure you, Mr. Cole, that I mean you no harm," Ned told him as he stood in front of his mule with his palms spread. "I only want to talk to a few mountaineers, the men who opened up this territory."

A shadow moved behind a pine trunk deep in the forest, and there was the brief glint of sunlight on a rifle barrel. A thin figure clad in buckskins came silently between the trees in Ned's direction.

"I kin assure you, mister, that I wasn't worried 'bout you doin' me no harm . . . not the way you rode up here in plain sight like a damn greenhorn. If a bunch of them Utes or Shoshoni was still huntin' white men's scalps, yer hair'd have been decoratin' some warrior's lodgepole tomorrow mornin'. It was the other way 'round when it comes to bein' in harm's way, Mr. Buntline. Any time I wanted, I coulda killed you quicker'n snuff makes spit."

Ned hadn't realized he'd made such a target of himself, yet neither had he expected to run across a mountain man so soon, figuring they'd be higher up in summertime, farther from the closest settlements. "I was told the Indian troubles were over in this part of the Rockies, so I felt I had nothing to fear if I rode out in the open."

The buckskin-clad outline of Grizzly Cole came to the edge of the forest. Ned could see a snowy beard surrounding his face and white hair falling below his shoulders. A rifle was balanced loosely in his right hand, and a huge pistol, probably a Walker Colt .44, was stuck in a belt fashioned from animal skin strips. While not one of his sources on the subject of mountain men had ever mentioned the name Grizzly Cole, Ned had a feeling Cole was one of the old-time mountaineers he'd been looking for.

"That's mostly true," Cole agreed, at last stepping out into slanted sunlight so Ned could see him clearly. "The Utes are at peace with the white man now, an' them Shoshoni don't range this far south no more. But a man had oughta practice bein' careful with his hide no matter how much he knows 'bout a stretch of the country. Things can change real sudden-like."

Ned felt somewhat more relaxed now. It did not appear Cole meant to harm him, not by the way he stood with his rifle lowered and his other hand empty. "Are you one of the early mountain men to come to this region?" he asked.

Cole's deeply wrinkled face twisted with a touch of humor, a grin of sorts. "Me? Hell no, I wasn't one of the first. Fact is, I come real late to this country, after Preacher an' Puma an' a whole bunch of others. I reckon you could say I'm a newcomer to these parts. Hardly been here more'n twenty years."

It was the mention of Preacher's name that caught Ned's full attention. "So there really is, or was, a mountain man by the name of Preacher?"

"He sure as hell weren't no ghost, if that's what you're thinkin'."

"Is he still alive? Would he talk to me?"

Now Cole wore a guarded look, shifting his weight to the other foot. Knee-high moccasins with beadwork and porcupine quills, badly worn in places, protected his feet. "I ain't in the business of answerin' questions. I trap beaver an' hunt a few griz now an' then fer their skins . . . that's where I got my handle, the one I go by. I done told you more'n I shoulda, how Puma was dead, an' where to look fer Huggie." He paused, and it seemed he was thinking. "I'll tell you this much, Mr. Buntline, so it'll save you some time. You ain't gonna find Preacher 'less he wants to be found, an' that's if he's still alive. He'd be close to ninety years old now, if he ain't crossed over the Big Divide up yonder in the sky. He never was a sociable feller, I hear tell."

"But have you actually met him?"

"Nope. Ain't many folks alive who kin say they did. One is Smoke Jensen, only Smoke ain't gonna tell you nothin' 'bout ol' Preacher. Preacher nearly raised Smoke, case you didn't know, an' I've heard it said even Smoke don't know if Preacher is still alive somewheres."

"Why would they cut off all communication between them if they were once so close?"

"Yer askin' the wrong feller, but I reckon it's what Preacher wanted . . . to live out the last of his years by hisself up in these here mountains."

Ned wanted more from Cole. "I've got a sack of Arbuckles in my packs. I'd be happy to build a fire and offer you a cup, just for the information you already gave me, a gesture of friendship or whatever you wish to call it."

Cole frowned, and it appeared he was sizing Ned up far more critically before he agreed to coffee.

"A cup of that Arbuckles do sound mighty nice, but I ain't gonna trade no more information 'bout my friends for it. You git that through yer head aforehand."

Ned nodded quickly. "I won't ask about your friends. You can tell me anything you want about yourself, if you wish to, or we can simply share a cup of coffee and I'll be on my way."

Cole glanced upslope at the old cabin Ned had seen earlier. "Bring yer mule. There's a firepit an' some seasoned wood up yonder. I use that ol' place from time to time, if'n I git caught in a snowstorm come winter. Ain't nobody lives there no more. Used to belong to a helluva mountain man . . ."

"Whose cabin was it?" Ned asked.

Cole gave him a stern look. "I done told you I ain't gonna talk 'bout none of my friends, them that's crossed over, an' them that ain't."

Ned blew steam away from the rim of his cup, all the while examining Grizzly Cole closely. Cole had to be near sixty, with weathered skin and snowy hair, gnarled hands, rheumy eyes that had surely seen so many things Ned needed for his stories about the men who'd first explored these wild mountains. But Cole was not about to be tricked into telling him anything he wasn't willing to say, Ned judged.

"There ain't many beaver left in this part of the lone-some," he said. "Used to be beaver dams every quarter mile on these creeks. They got trapped real hard by men who didn't understand nature. You gotta take some an' leave some, so they'll multiply an' raise a new crop every spring."

"Experienced men like Preacher or Smoke Jensen and Puma Buck wouldn't have trapped them out, so it had to be others who did this to good beaver country."

Cole eyed him. "I done warned you I ain't gonna talk 'bout none of my friends. But you's right 'bout the three you mentioned. They knowed Mother Nature's ways, all right. If'n this high country never saw nobody but their kind, it'd still be plumb thick with beaver an' every breed o' critter there is. That's what put ol' Preacher an' Smoke on the warpath a long time back, when men come up here to change things. Some came with cattle to push other grazin' animals out. Some showed up with cross-cut saws to cut timber. There was a few who didn't bring nothin' but bad intentions. That's a part of what put Smoke Jensen into the gunfighter's trade."

Griz Cole was telling Ned far more than he meant to without realizing it, with a slip of the tongue now and then. "I'm going to ask Jensen if he'll talk to me about some of it. Readers back east would be fascinated."

"The only thing he's liable to tell you is to skedaddle if you ask him about the past. Huggie might talk to you a little, an' Del Rovare can git kinda windy at times, 'specially if his tongue got loosened with a dab o' whiskey. But there ain't none of 'em gonna tell you much, Mr. Buntline. These men ain't city folk with an inclination towards idle talk." He looked off at the mountain peaks around them, toying with his coffee cup for a time. "It takes a man who likes his own company to live up here, an' most of us don't have no hankerin' for outsiders who come nosin' around. Winters git long an' lonesome for some. Me, I like the sound of fallin' snowflakes on pine limbs, the howl of a north wind at night when the fire's warm inside a cabin."

"Do very many mountain men have a woman, a wife?"

"Some. Not many. Womenfolk ain't built for the loneliness or this rough life. There's a few. Smoke's got him a lady who takes to the high lonesome like a bear takes to honey. Sally's built different than most women. Puma used to have him a Ute squaw. Cute little thing. She died of the smallpox back in '59 I believe it was. Injuns ain't got much tolerance for a white man's diseases."

"Did Puma himself die of old age?"

Cole gave him a hard stare. "That ain't my story to tell, Mr. Buntline. You'll have to ask somebody else." He drained a big swallow of Arbuckles from his cup, squatting across the rock-lined firepit from Ned. "I've told you too much already. Much as I enjoyed this coffee, you an' me are done talkin'. If you ride north, maybe ten miles or so, you'll be in Huggie Charles's trappin' range. Now I'll warn you, he can be a real disagreeable feller at times, so don't go tryin' to push yer luck with him. You can say I told you where to look fer him. It'll be up to him if he decides to show hisself, or blow a tunnel plumb through yer head with his rifle. Depends."

"On what?"

"On the mood he's in, an' on how you handle yourself. If it was me, I wouldn't shoot no game or raise no ruckus. Just ride quiet an' mind yer own business. He'll look you up if he's curious 'bout why yer there." He drank the last of his coffee and stood up, wincing, as though he felt a pain somewhere in one of his legs. Then he bent down and lifted his Sharps .52 caliber rifle, holding it by the muzzle. "Good luck, Mr. Buntline. I'm grateful fer the Arbuckles. Don't figure on gittin' what you came here for. Them readers you've got is most likely to have to read somethin' else. Stories from a real mountain man are gonna be mighty hard to come by."

"I'm obliged for what you've been willing to tell me, Mr. Cole, and for the directions." He stood up and dusted off the seat of his pants. "Just one more thing. You said Smoke Jensen is running a ranch now, and I know it's close to Big Rock. That must mean he's given up his old ways, using a gun the way he did in the past."

Grizzly Cole wagged his head. "Yer dead wrong, son. Smoke ain't changed one bit when it comes to gunplay. He's every bit as dangerous as he ever was, a fact yer liable to find out if you press him any. Just last year, he put a feller by the name of Sundance Morgan into an early grave, along with a pack o' his hired guns, *pistoleros* from down around the Mexican border. He ain't given up nothin' fer the sake of ranchin' or anything else, an' if you happen to be in the wrong spot at the wrong time, you can git a firsthand look, if you live to tell about it."

"I'm not looking for trouble."

Cole smiled. "You said you was lookin' for Smoke Jensen. What you ain't understood just yet is them two are the same, if you ain't an acquaintance or a neighbor of his."

"But I'm not here to cause him any trouble . . ."

"Askin' him about the past is gonna put him on the prod. If I was you, I'd find out 'bout mountain men some other way."

Cole turned away from the fire. Ned tossed out the grounds from his tiny coffeepot as Cole started toward a line of trees behind the abandoned cabin.

"Thanks again, Mr. Cole, for everything you've told me. I am in your debt. I'll be very careful while I'm up here."

Grizzly Cole ignored his remark, taking long quiet strides up a grassy slope with his rifle over his shoulder. Ned watched him until he went out of sight in shadows below the pines.

"At last," he muttered under his breath. He'd just had his first talk with a mountain man, and learned a number of things he could use. The heroes he would write about later on would be like Griz, hardened by an unbelievably brutal and lonely way of life into strong, silent types. This initial meeting with a true mountaineer had given him far more than he had hoped. Now it was time to look for more men of Cole's strange breed, until he had enough to make characters come to life on the pages of the series of books he planned to write about them.

6

Smoke let Horse pick his own gait, an easy jog trot that was only a little faster than the buckboard loaded with supplies, to keep him well out in front of Pearlie and Cal and the flour, fatback, sugar, coffee beans, and other necessaries Sally put on her list, along with iron hinges for a sagging barn door, horseshoes and nails, saddle soap and axle grease, and a load of planking to fix a slant-roof cowshed. As the summer ended, all ranch chores needed to be attended to, despite not owning cows or bulls after selling off their herd to the Duggan sisters. This was a winter Smoke and Sally planned to spend alone, more or less, if you didn't count visits with some of Smoke's old friends in the mountains. Pearlie and Cal would be watching the ranch and saddle stock while Smoke and Sally enjoyed time together in a cabin that once was home to Puma Buck, a two-room affair with a dogrun and sod roof, plenty of shelter from the worst storms in a deep mountain valley where wintertime was both beautiful and bitterly cold. In the spring, Smoke planned to head down to New Mexico Territory, along with a handful of neighbors, to pick up a few prized Hereford bulls and a herd of Mexican longhorns in order to produce a hardier breed with more beef. It was an idea they'd talked about for some time, and after a telegram from John Chisum, called the Cattle King of New Mexico, offering them bulls at a good price, the decision was made. It would be a long and rugged drive, coming back north with spooky longhorn cows and the gentler, slower Hereford bulls, but well worth the increase in beef their offspring would produce. Smoke felt good about the notion. And about spending a winter with Sally where he could have her all to himself for a while, enjoying a few months without the responsibilities of ranch work and tending cattle.

Crossing a wooded switchback, Smoke heard a voice coming from a crossing over Aspen Creek down below, a high-pitched voice full of anger. He heeled the Palouse forward at a lope to find out what the shouting was all about, to see if a neighbor or a friend might be in trouble.

When he came to the caprock at the top of the switchback, he saw a sight he didn't fully understand at first. Two men were standing beside a team of mules at the crossing, mules hitched to a wagon loaded with wooden crates and barrels. He didn't recognize either one of them, for they were strangers to this part of the country—he was sure of it, and sometimes finding strangers close to Sugarloaf made him edgy.

Then he saw what was causing the disturbance. One of the men was whipping the mules' hindquarters with a blacksnake whip, and it was evident the mules had balked at the creek, refusing to cross, which was sometimes a trait in certain mules that hadn't been trained properly. The crack of the whip and the men shouting, one of them trying to force the off-side mule to take a step into the stream by way of striking it across the rump with a wood fence stave, got Smoke's dander up.

"Damn fools," he muttered, urging Horse down toward the creek at a full gallop. "Can't stand to see a man whip an animal when it don't understand what it's bein' whipped for . . ."

It really wasn't his affair, and he knew it, but when a mule or a horse got a whipping it didn't deserve or understand, Smoke was likely to take a side with the animal even when it didn't belong to him. At times he wondered about the contradiction, the absence of feeling when men killed each other and the deep sorrow he experienced when an animal suffered needlessly. One mule could have easily been unharnessed and led across the stream so the other would follow on its own . . . but it was apparent these two men knew nothing about mules or their inclinations. If one mule balked at a stream, most often the other did. Smoke was about to offer his help whether it was wanted or not, since these weren't men he recognized as being from these parts.

The men saw him coming and one moved his right hand to the butt of a pistol belted around his waist, quite possibly a very deadly mistake if he'd pulled it out. Smoke pulled down on the big stud's reins when he got within earshot.

"Take it easy on those mules, boys. There's an easier way to get across."

"Who the hell asked you to interfere?" one bearded man asked in a low growl.

Smoke brought his Palouse to a halt. "Nobody," he said in a calm, even voice. "It's just my nature. Can't stand to watch a man whip a mule when the man's got less sense than the animal. I can show you how to get those mules and your wagon across."

"You're a smart-mouth son of a bitch, an' you goddamn sure are inclined to stick your nose in where it ain't wanted, whoever the hell you are."

Smoke gave both men a humorless grin. Then he spoke to the man who had spoken to him. "You're wrong on two counts, mister. I ain't no part of a son of a bitch, and I put my nose wherever I please when an animal's bein' injured. Now, get your hand off the butt of that pistol or I swear I'll make you eat it. If you give me a couple of minutes, I'll have those mules across the creek and you'll be on your way."

The cowboy touching his gun made no move to lift his hand away, and the gleam in his eye was a warning that

Smoke had best be ready for trouble. He swung down, leaving the Palouse ground-hitched, his eyes fastened on the man resting his palm on his gun grips.

Smoke walked toward them, both hands dangling beside the brace of pistols he carried. "Get your hand off that gun or I'll make good on my promise," he said, approaching the cowboy whose hearing needed improvement.

"To hell with you, mister!" the man snapped, closing his fingers unconsciously for a quick pull, a signal to a man like Smoke that the time for talking had ended.

Smoke clawed one .44 free with the speed of a rattler's strike, thumbing back the hammer as he leveled it at the cowboy's belly. He halted a few feet away with his feet spread slightly apart as the cowboy's eyes became saucers, staring down the dark muzzle of Smoke's Colt before he could clear leather. When Smoke spoke to him, it was in a hoarse voice.

"My mama used to say that when somebody don't listen, it can be on account of too much wax built up in their ears." He took a step closer. "She told me the best way to clean out somebody's ears is to jar some of that built-up wax loose." With the same lightning speed, Smoke struck the cowboy with the back of his free hand, a blow so powerful, it sent the man reeling backward until he stumbled into the shallow stream and fell down on his rump in a foot of icy snowmelt gurgling down from the mountain peaks still capped by last year's snow.

"Shit!" the cowboy exclaimed, shaking his head to clear it, scrambling back to his feet with his denims soaked. Only now he had his gun hand held to his face, where an angry red welt was forming, after Smoke had knocked him into the water. He rubbed his sore cheek a moment while his companion merely stood there near the mules holding the fence stave. "You had no call to do that to me!"

"I never ask a man to do anything twice," Smoke replied, his gun still aimed in front of him. "I saw you whippin' these mules and it didn't sit well with me. When a man's dumber than the animal he's tryin' to use, giving it a blacksnake treatment it doesn't understand, I've got plenty of reason to slap the hell out of that kind of fool. I'm gonna get your team across this creek as soon as my ranch hands come over that ridge behind me, and after that's done, you can be on your way. But if I ever see you whip mules like that again, I'll take that same blacksnake and work your ass over with it, same as you done to those poor dumb animals."

The other cowboy spoke for the first time. He was glowering at Smoke, holding the fence stave like a club. "You wouldn't be talkin' so big if it wasn't fer them guns, stranger."

"Is that so?" Smoke asked as he heard Pearlie and Cal in the buckboard rattle downslope toward him. "In that case, since you believe in what you say so strong, I'll take 'em off and we can test your idea." He examined the bearded gent with the club a little closer, making sure he wasn't carrying a gun, finding him to be thick-muscled, big-handed, probably the sort who thought he was tough with his fists.

Smoke turned to the cowboy standing shivering wet in the creek ."Toss that pistol out with two fingers. Pitch it up here. Soon as my boys get here they'll make sure nobody goes for a gun while me and your pardner settle this."

"You ain't got the guts to fight Clyde bare-handed."

"We can fight with feather dusters or claw hammers, for all I care," Smoke replied, watching the cowboy lift his gun out very carefully to throw it near Smoke's feet. He picked it up, then holstered his .44 and removed his gunbelts, placing them in the back of the wagon. He spoke over his shoulder just as Pearlie drove up. "Boys, make sure that other feller stays right where he is while I teach this big fool a lesson."

Pearlie drew his pistol. "I reckon you'll explain after you're done beatin' this poor bastard half to death," Pearlie said matter-of-factly, like the outcome was certain.

Smoke turned to the man with the wood stave. "Not much to it, really," he answered back. "What we've got here is two of the dumbest assholes who ever tried to drive a team of mules. I watched 'em use a whip on this team, and that toothpick the big one is carryin' now. I can't hardly stand to watch men hurt an animal like that. I asked 'em real nice to stop, only they was not of the same mind on it. I'm gonna teach this one how it feels to have the hell knocked out of him with that very same club."

Clyde answered in a snarl. "You gotta come git it first, you cocky son of a bitch. Ain't gonna be easy."

It was Cal who said quietly, "I'm real sure you're gonna regret callin' Mr. Jensen a son of a bitch, mister, not to make mention of what you done to them mules."

"Are you Smoke Jensen?" the other cowboy asked, just as Smoke made a lunge toward Clyde before Clyde was ready for it. Swinging a powerful right hook at Clyde's jaw, Smoke felt his knuckles crack when they landed hard against bone just as Clyde drew back with his fence stave.

Clyde grunted when Smoke's fist struck him, and it seemed a mighty gust of wind lifted him off his feet, snapping his head around so that all he could see was mountains on the far side of the stream. Clyde staggered a few wobbly steps and then he knelt down as if he meant to pray, dropping the club beside him, his arms hanging limply at his sides.

Smoke walked up behind him and picked up the stave while Clyde blinked furiously, trying to clear his head. Smoke took a pair of short steps around the kneeling figure until he stood in front of him. "That's what it's like when a man hits another man in the head," Smoke explained, sounding calm. "And now I'm gonna show you how those mules felt when you were whippin' their asses with this stick."

He swung a vicious blow with the stave, striking Clyde across the left cheek of his buttocks with a resounding whack.

"Yeeeow!" Clyde shrieked, tumbling forward until he landed on his chest with his palms covering the seat of his pants, his face twisted in agony.

Smoke took a deep breath, tossing the stick aside.

"Now you know what the mules wanted to say. Remember how it feels to have the wood laid to your own ass. Me an' my cowboys will cross that team over the way it oughta be done. And I meant what I said. If I ever see or hear of either one of you whippin' a mule again when it ain't necessary, I'll come lookin' for you. Believe me, you don't want that to happen."

Pearlie was already climbing down from the buckboard. "I'll unharness the lop-eared mule an' lead it across," he said as if the remedy was all too clear. "Cal can drive the wagon across as soon as I git to the other side."

Smoke returned to buckle on his pistols as Pearlie went about the harness task, selecting what was obviously the gentler mule to lead it across.

Clyde came to his hands and knees shakily and shook his head again. "You broke one of my goddamn teeth when you slugged me," he complained, running his tongue over a chipped tooth.

Smoke almost ignored him, until he said, "Count yourself real lucky I'm not still breakin' 'em out one at a time. After that wagon gets across, I want you boys harnessed and headed on your way, wherever that is. But don't stay in this country too long or I might change my mind about leavin' the teeth in both of your mouths."

"I've heard of you, Smoke Jensen," the cowboy in wet pants said. "I reckon me an' Clyde are real sorry we said what we did to you."

Smoke gave him a withering stare. "Save your goddamn apologies for those mules. They've each got one coming after what you did to 'em with that club and whip."

He mounted Horse and watched Cal drive the loaded wagon easily across the shallow creek. Smoke waited until Cal and Pearlie waded back and climbed in the buckboard; then he glanced over to the men harnessing the mule.

"Let's head home, boys, so Sally won't be wondering why we're late."

Pearlie shook the reins over his buckboard team. He had a grin on his face. "I'll swear we had a loose hub on

this here buckboard, so she won't have to be told the truth
. . . that you killed two men early this mornin' an' just beat
the hell out of two more over a pair of stubborn mules."

Smoke returned Pearlie's grin as he swung Horse
toward the ranch. "Won't do any good to lie to Sally. It'd
be a waste of good breath. She'll know there was a little
trouble when she looks me in the eye. Damnedest thing
I ever saw, how she knows before I ever open my mouth."

7

Jessie Evans, clear blue eyes shining below a mop of sandy hair under a flat brim hat, turned his stocky torso toward one of his men where they sat their horses hidden in a line of piñon pines above the Pecos River. Bill Pickett was watching a handful of John Chisum's cowboys in the valley driving a herd of market-ready steers upriver, beeves for a government contract with the Apache reservation west of Ruidoso, New Mexico Territory.

"This is gonna be too easy," Jessie said, grinning, some of his front teeth yellowed by tobacco stains. "Ain't but seven of them an' they're range cowboys who can't shoot straight. Let's make damn sure we kill 'em all so there won't be no witnesses who can identify us."

"It don't make a difference to me," Pickett replied, eyelids gone narrow. Killing was a passion with him, Jessie knew, after years of rustling cattle together. Pickett was a raw-boned man who had a preference for shotguns at close range, once stating that he liked to see his victims' faces when he blew them apart, the look of surprise they wore when shotgun pellets shredded their skin. He told Jessie he liked the smell of blood and gunpowder when it got mixed together.

Jessie looked past Pickett to Roy Cooper. Cooper had a big jaw, always jutted angrily, even when he was happy, which was rare unless he was with a woman and a bottle of tequila. "Ready down there, Roy?"

"Ready as I'm gonna be, boss," he said, his deep voice like a rasp across cold iron. He drew a .44 caliber Winchester from a boot tied to his saddle and worked the lever, sending a cartridge into the firing chamber. "I can kill one or two of 'em from here soon as you give the word."

Beyond Cooper, Ignacio Valdez showed off a gold tooth in the front of his mouth. "Ready, Señor Jessie," he said, fisting a Mason Colt .44/.40 revolver. "I gon' shoot hell out plenty sons of bitches when you tell me is time."

Last in line was a reed-thin boy, Billy Barlow, a small-time rustler from the Texas panhandle. Jessie didn't fully trust the Barlow kid yet. There was something about him, the way he didn't look at you when you talked to him. But Jimmy Dolan said to hire shootists to get Chisum's cattle so the Murphy Store would get the beef contracts away from Chisum and John Tunstall, and Jessie had put word out all the way to the Mexican border that he was hiring guns to fight a range war. More and more experienced men were showing up at Lincoln to inquire about the job, and before this winter was out, Jessie could easily have fifty hired guns on Dolan's payroll by the time reservation contracts were up for renewal.

"Let's spill some blood," Jessie said savagely, putting a spur to his horse's ribs, freeing his Colt .44 from its holster in an iron grip. Jessie had long forgotten how many men he'd killed over the years, but it was something he knew he was good at. It had never mattered whether a man had his back turned or if he was facing him when he pulled a trigger. A killer for hire couldn't wait all day long to earn his money.

Five galloping horses charged down a rocky slope toward the Pecos, and toward a herd of eighty steers belonging to John Chisum, with seven cowboys pushing them toward Fort Sumner, and a butcher's block. The thunder of pounding hooves ended a silence in the serenity of the lower Pecos region.

Cooper was the first to fire, a booming shot from the back of a running horse that would be difficult for even the best of marksmen.

At the river's edge, a cowboy on a sorrel gelding yelled and barreled off the back of his horse, turning in midair, arms and legs askew, his cry of pain echoing off the bluffs that ran along both sides of the Pecos.

Valdez fired, more to spook the cattle than with any hope of hitting what he aimed at.

Longhorn steers began to run, a stampede that would only add to the confusion, charging along the grassy banks of the river at full tilt.

Jessie aimed his .44 carefully, knowing full well the action of the horse between his knees would worsen his aim. He waited until his gunsights rested on the chest of a terrified cowboy on a prancing pinto.

The pistol slammed into his palm, barking, spitting out a finger of orange flame. Jessie saw the cowhand jerk upright in his saddle. Runaway longhorns raced past the wounded man as he toppled to the ground, lost in a cloud of dust sent up by churning hooves boiling away from the stampede.

Barlow's rifle roared and a horse went down underneath a cowboy spurring frantically to cross the river. The chestnut collapsed, legs thrashing in shallow water, falling on the cowboy to pin him against a shoal of sand and rocks on the far side of the Pecos.

Nice work, Jessie thought, spurring his horse for more speed as he and his men thundered down the embankment. Maybe he'd been wrong about Barlow.

Pickett's shotgun bellowed, rocking him back against the cantle of his saddle, blue smoke erupting from one barrel. A steer bawled and fell on its chest in front of a cowboy trying to escape the melee aboard a goose-rumped bay. When the steer went down in the pathway of the galloping horse, it tripped the mount and sent its rider flying, as though he'd sprouted wings, into the river.

Valdez popped off three shots as quickly as he could

pull the trigger, sweeping a hatless vaquero off the side
of his running buckskin mare, sending him tumbling
into tall prairie grasses near the riverbank.

"Ayii!" Valdez cried, turning his pistol in another direction.

Pickett's shotgun roared again, this time at much
closer range to a cowboy whipping his gray pony with the
ends of his reins to escape the hail of flying lead.

The man atop the gray did a curious thing . . . he
turned to face the shotgun blast, and when he did his face
seemed to come apart as pellets ripped away his cheeks.
For a moment, there was no sound other than the banging of guns, until the cowboy slid off his charging horse
into a stand of bulrushes growing along the edge of the
water.

Fear-stricken cattle bounded in every direction,
making a noise like honking geese. The herd split into
three groups when trees blocked the longhorns' path.
One bunch ran northeast, and a second charged across
the Pecos, where a shallow spot kept them from having
to swim. A third portion of the stampeding steers went
straight ahead, crushing everything in its way.

Jessie took careful aim and fired at a cowboy abandon-
ing the herd on a piebald gelding, shooting him in the
back between his shoulder blades, driving him out of his
saddle with the force of a sledgehammer blow before his
horse could cross the river.

"Nice shot!" Cooper yelled, levering another round
into his Winchester.

Valdez fired just as Jessie was about to rein south after
a lone cowboy making his escape back down the trail running beside the Pecos. The cowboy slumped in his
saddle, yet he somehow held on to the saddle horn and
continued to rake his spurs into a black gelding's sides.

Jessie swung his horse south . . . there could be no survivors to tell Sheriff Brady about what happened here, or
identify any of the attackers.

Behind him, he heard a gun crack. Pickett and Cooper

would finish off any wounded men. Pickett would enjoy it. Of all the cold-blooded killers Jessie had known, Pickett had less feelings than any of them.

The cowboy on the black horse rounded a turn in the trail and for a moment he was out of sight. Jessie spurred harder, asking his big yellow dun for everything it had. The rhythm of its pounding hooves filled his ears. He stood in the stirrups for a better view of what lay ahead. A grove of cottonwoods lining the river prevented him from seeing the fleeing cowhand for a few moments, until his dun carried him past the trees.

A pistol barked suddenly. Jessie felt something tear the left sleeve of his shirt, followed by a burning sensation moving from his shoulder down his arm. In the same instant he saw the cowboy aboard the black horse sitting at the edge of the cottonwood grove.

"You bushwhackin' son of a bitch!" Jessie cried, aiming his pistol carefully before he triggered off a shot while bringing the dun to a bounding halt.

The cowhand rolled out of his saddle . . . his horse bolted away as he fell. He toppled to the ground clutching his belly with a groan.

Jessie stepped off his horse, walking slowly, gun pointed in front of him, to the spot where the Chisum cowboy lay. Jessie gritted his teeth, for the moment ignoring the stinging pain in his left arm until he stood over the fallen man, casting his shadow over a face twisted in agony, the face of a young cowboy hardly old enough to shave.

"You yellow bastard," Jessie hissed, "layin' for me behind those trees like that. You're gunshot, an' I oughta leave you here to die slow. But you pissed me off when you shot me in the arm, so I'm gonna do you a favor. I'm gonna scatter your brains all over this piece of ground. That way, when Big John Chisum or one of his boys finds you, he'll know we ain't just fuckin' around over this beef contract business. It'll be like a message to Chisum, only I ain't gonna sign my name to it."

He aimed down, cocked his single-action Colt, and pulled the trigger, the bang of his .44 like a sudden bolt of lightning striking nearby.

The young cowhand's head was slammed to the ground, blood shooting from a hole in his right temple. A thumb-sized plug of brain tissue dangled from the exit wound, dribbling blood on the caliche hardpan. A momentary twitching of the cowboy's left boot rattled his spur rowel, until his death throes ended abruptly as blood poured from his open mouth.

"I hope you get a good look at this, Chisum," Jessie said tonelessly. "Maybe you won't be so all-fired interested in the beef business."

He turned away to catch his horse, holstering his gun, examining a slight tear in the skin atop his left shoulder, finding it to be little more than a scratch.

He rode back to the scene of the attack just in time to see Bill Pickett standing over a motionless body, his shotgun pointed down. Pickett glanced over his shoulder when he heard Jessie ride up.

"This sumbitch is still breathin'," Pickett said, "only he ain't gonna be much longer." Pickett thumbed back one hammer on his ten-gauge Greener and calmly pulled the trigger, as if he was merely swatting a fly. The big gun roared, pulverizing the skull and neck of the wounded Chisum trail hand, splattering blood and hair and flinty pieces of bone across a six-foot circle of dry buffalo grass.

Pickett grinned. "Pretty sight, ain't it?" he asked, "like breakin' an egg, only it's got blood in it. Sumbitch hadn't oughta signed on with John Chisum in this war. Folks in Lincoln County better learn whose side to be on."

Another gunshot distracted Jessie before he could offer any comment. Upriver, Roy Cooper was down off his horse, his feet spread apart over another body. Jessie thought about how good it was to have men like Pickett and Cooper riding with him. He knew he could count on either one of them in a tight spot.

"Roy found him one," Pickett muttered, sounding as if he had wanted the job himself.

"Let's get those steers rounded up an' head 'em for Bosque Redondo so we can change them brands," Jessie said, reining his horse away from Pickett's bloody execution spot. Off in the distance he could see Valdez and Barlow trying to gather up one bunch of cattle.

"I ain't gettin' paid to handle no runnin' iron," Pickett said as he rode off.

"We've got Mexican vaqueros to do it," he answered back. "You're the same as me. . . . I'd rather have blood on my hands than cow dung. Don't stink near as bad."

8

The cow camp at Bosque Redondo was hidden in a piñon forest in an empty section of Lincoln County. Pole corrals held steers being branded, made ready for market, most often with a running iron changing brands belonging to previous owners. Jessie knew few questions were asked by the territorial militia, since it was merely a police arm of the powerful Santa Fe Ring, as most men called it, a group of crooked politicians headed by Catron and L.G. Murphy. Jimmy Dolan was Murphy's ramrod in Lincoln County, and in this part of the territory, only John Chisum and a few of his followers were brazen enough to buck the Santa Fe Ring with bids on federal government contracts to feed reservation Apaches. But Chisum was bullheaded about it, refusing to knuckle under or sell to Murphy at a lower price. What was building here was a range war over beef. Folks were beginning to call it the Lincoln County War, and Jessie knew it had only just begun.

He sat in the shade of a thatched ramada, watching vaqueros work the branding irons, sipping tequila, chewing limes, thinking about yesterday's fight. Roy Cooper was in one of the huts with a Mexican whore. Bill Pickett, as he so often did, was cleaning his guns; pistols and rifles, and his shotgun. Jessie was about to doze off when he heard someone shout, "Riders comin'!"

Jessie and Pickett scrambled to their feet, wondering if a party of Chisum riders had come for revenge. But what he saw in a ravine twisting into the camp was only a pair of horsemen, a little man in a battered top hat and a Mexican cowboy. However, both were carrying guns.

Jessie relaxed against a roof support of the ramada without worrying over the two riders. Two men wouldn't stand a chance against so many Dolan men, no matter how skillful they might be with pistols or rifles.

The pair rode up to him and halted sweat-caked horses in a patch of shade from a piñon limb. The man, only a boy by his appearance, spoke.

"We was told you were hirin' a few men," he said, his thin voice almost girlish, lilting.

"Men is what we're hirin'," Jessie replied, "not school-boys who ain't old enough to need a razor."

"I'm eighteen," the rider said, his ears sticking out away from his head in an odd fashion. "The name's William Bonney an' this here's Jesus Silva."

"Like I said, we ain't hirin' no kids," Jessie replied in an offhanded way. "Come back in a couple of years."

"We can shoot," Bonney said. "I already killed a man over in Fort Grant, an' that ain't countin' Indians or Mexicans."

Jessie laughed. "You're full of lies, boy. Now ride on outta here before I lose my patience. If you're lookin' for work, you might try the Chisum outfit. Or there's this crazy Englishman by the name of John Tunstall who's hirin' a few cowboys now an' then. Ask for Dick Brewer. He's foreman for Tunstall an' he ain't much older'n you. Appears Mr. Tunstall ain't opposed to changin' diapers on some of his cowhands."

Bonney stared at him, and Jessie felt a strange sensation when he looked into the young man's green-flecked eyes. He had buck teeth and looked downright ridiculous in an old top hat, but there was something about him . . .

"You may be sorry you didn't offer us any work,"

Bonney said as he turned his horse. "We heard you was needin' good men with guns."

Jessie gave him a one-sided grin. "Like I said before, come back in a couple of years, when you're old enough to grow some chin whiskers."

Bonney and Silva rode off, back down the ravine. Jessie watched them go, wondering.

Pickett had stopped cleaning his Winchester long enough to listen to what was being said. "You might regret that, like the boy said, Jessie," he remarked, going back to his gun cleaning. "I've got a pretty good nose for a man who ain't got no fear in him. That Bonney boy ain't scared of nothin'."

"Maybe he's just too young to know to be scared," Jessie offered.

Pickett shook his head. "Age ain't got all that much to do with it. It's what's in a man's backbone that counts. He sure did look plumb silly in that ol' hat, an' them's the worst-lookin' buck teeth I ever saw. But there may come a time when you wish you'd have let 'em hire on with us. I hope I'm dead wrong about it, that we won't be wishin' we had Mr. William Bonney on our side of this fight."

9

Smoke's chest and arms glistened with sweat as he split the last of yet another cord of wood piled beside the cabin. It had been hard at first, to see Puma's old log dwelling where he and the Ute girl had lived so long ago, until smallpox took her. There were so many memories here for Smoke, and as colorful fall leaves swirled around him, with the coming of winter he couldn't help a recollection or two, of time he spent with Puma in this aspen forest back when they were younger men, and it saddened him some to think of Puma being gone forever. He told himself that wherever Puma was, there would be mountains and rivers and clear streams.

On the ride up to the cabin he and Sally talked about their plans for an improved cow herd, the Hereford bulls and what Sally said was sure to be a way to raise crossbred breeding stock for the future. Smoke even told her about another idea he'd been toying with . . . to buy a Morgan stallion to cross on their mustang and thoroughbred mares, adding strength and muscle and short-distance speed to the offspring. On the way down to New Mexico he planned to inquire about purchasing a Morgan stud. He grinned when he thought about their three-day trip up to Puma's cabin, how infectious Sally's enthusiasm was when she talked about the Hereford crosses. She was a rancher at heart, with a natural gift for handling live-stock, better than most experienced men who made a living off raising cattle. But Smoke's grin was far more than amusement over her excitement when she talked about their future plans . . . it was an unconscious way of showing how much he loved her. He'd decided long ago that Sally had been the best thing that had ever hap-pened to him. She had changed his life and he often wished for the words to tell her how much she truly meant to him.

Smoke rested the axe against the splitting stump and took a look northward. A line of dark clouds was building along the horizon. At these higher altitudes, a storm would mean snow, the first snowstorm announcing the coming of winter. They'd just barely had time to unpack the packhorses, clean out the abandoned cabin and stretch cured deer hides over the windows and rifle ports, repair rawhide hinges on crude plank doors, and clean out the rock chimney. Sally was inside now, fashioning hanging racks for their heavy winter clothing and other essentials, after putting their food staples away on what was left of the shelves Puma had made near the fireplace. They had plenty of warm blankets and a thick buffalo robe given to Smoke by a Shoshoni warrior years back. Last night, Smoke had held Sally in his arms atop that furry buffalo skin, watching her eyes sparkle in the fire-light when he kissed her. He vowed to make this winter with her a special time, away from the day-to-day chores around the ranch which were now being done by Pearlie, Cal, and Johnny North . . . what little there was to do with no beef cattle on the place, only the horse herd and old Rosie, their Jersey milk cow, to attend to. Smoke knew Sally needed the rest as much as he did, not only from ranch work but away from the troubles that seemed to follow Smoke Jensen no matter how peacefully he tried to live now. Trouble had a way of finding him, and he hoped it wouldn't track him down here, in a beautiful mountain valley near the headwaters of the White River, roughly eight thousand feet into the Rockies, where few white men had ever traveled, formerly the hunting ground of the Utes until a treaty with Washington moved them farther west. Here, Smoke could be at peace, spending time alone with his beloved Sally.

Falling aspen leaves showered to the forest floor, a mix of reds, bright yellows, and every shade of brown. Towering ponderosa pines grew thick on the slopes around them. The scent of pine was strong in the air, mingling with the smell of smoke coming from the chimney as Sally prepared their supper. They had plenty of foodstuffs and clothing, and enough firewood for even the most brutal winter, after almost a week of hard labor gathering dead limbs and fallen tree trunks. It had been a wonderful time, as was the ride up with Sally. If it were possible, he loved her more deeply with each passing day.

He heard light footfalls behind him.

"You must be getting old, darling," Sally said, smiling one of her memorable smiles. "I've never seen you needing a rest so often. You used to be able to chop wood all day without stopping to catch your breath every five minutes. I may have to look for a younger man, if this keeps up."

"A younger man would refuse to take all this punishment from a woman, no matter how pretty she was. I'm only slave labor, in your opinion. That would be just like you, to throw me away for a younger man as soon as I've chopped and split all this firewood to keep us warm."

"A younger man could have finished this job in half the time and still had something left for me."

He turned to her, hard muscles gleaming in the sunlight. "I may have a surprise for you tonight, Mrs. Jensen," he told her with mock seriousness. "I may be getting a little long in the tooth, but I can still chop wood all day and make love all night. I hope you feel up to it."

Her smile only widened. "I think I'm developing a headache just now. Maybe another time. Ask me in the spring."

He sauntered over and put his arms around her, staring

down into her eyes. "Be careful, pretty lady, or you might force me to tear your clothes off right now and throw you down on a bed of pine needles. I'm not buying any headache stories."

She forced a frown, giving a halfhearted attempt to pull away from his embrace. "You're an animal. I've known it for years. You only brought me up here so you could use me, and I won't stand for it. I'll scream."

He chuckled. "No one will hear you, except for a few grizzlies or an elk or two. Scream your head off, for all I care. I'm taking what's mine."

"You think of me as a piece of property?"

"My property, and if any younger man lays a hand on you I swear I'll kill him. You can include older men in that same bunch." He scowled.

Sally tried to conceal the beginnings of a grin. "Not only are you an animal, but you're violent, a savage beast. I should have listened to my mother. She warned me about you."

He maintained a stern expression "She did? Exactly what did she say?"

Now Sally was serious for a moment. "She told me that some men are loners, that they can't be tamed or tied to one woman or the same piece of ground for very long. She said it was bred in them, and that I'd never change you from being a solitary mountain man or a drifter."

"She was wrong," he whispered, bending down to kiss her gently on the lips. "She didn't give her daughter enough credit for knowing how to change a man's ways."

She stared deeply into his eyes. "Some things about you will never change, my darling," she told him softly. "You'll always be just a push or a shove away from another fight. You are two different people. One is the gentle man I love so dearly who can't seem to stop showing me or telling me how much he loves me. Then there's the other Smoke Jensen, the man almost everyone in Colorado Territory fears. It's hard to describe, how you can change so quickly. One wrong word, a wrong look, a wrong deed, and you become someone I scarcely recognize. It's not that you can't control your temper. . . . You always seem calm, in control of yourself. But when you get your mind set to go after another man, or a dozen men, for whatever reason, you can't be talked out of it. Not even by me, not even when you know how much it frightens me when I think about the possibility of losing you."

"You worry too much."

"What else can I do when the man I love is putting his life on the line?"

He thought about it for a time. "You can learn to trust me, to trust my instincts for staying alive. Over the years a hell of a lot of men have tried to kill me, for one reason or another. None of 'em got it done, although I've got a nick or two in my hide to show for it. Trust me when I promise you I'll always come home to you."

"It won't stop me from worrying . . ."

He glanced up at the advancing clouds. "There's a storm coming. Probably means snow, this high, and maybe some rain we need for our pastures down at the ranch."

"You changed the subject, Smoke. We were talking about how much it scares me when you go off on one of your manhunts. Like what happened in Big Rock this summer when those three men came to town looking for Ned Buntline. Louis told me what happened. You could have ignored the way they were looking at you. Instead you prodded them into a gunfight."

"They were looking for one anyway. I know I've got my share of faults, Sally, but when some gent challenges me, it's just my nature to answer back. Let's talk about something else, like what we're having for supper. Whatever it is, it sure does smell good."

"Venison and wild onions. I found some wild onions down at the creek when I went for a pail of water. And I've got another surprise. The Dutch oven is loaded. I've got it banked with a pile of hot coals, so it'll cook slowly."

"What's in it?" he asked, his mouth already watering.

"You'll have to wait and see, Mr. Jensen. I told you it was a surprise."

"Those tins of peaches. You made a peach cobbler, didn't you?"

Sally pushed away from him playfully. "I'll never tell, not unless I can find a man who can chop wood without threatening to rip my clothes off."

"Don't tempt me, woman. I may just carry through with that threat."

"You're getting too old to catch me if I decide to run away. Which I just might do. Or I might take my clothes off and lie down naked under a pine tree, if the right man came along. But it would have to be for the right man . . ."

He laughed, and came toward her.

Wind whistled through cracks in the logs. Outside, it was full dark. They sat side-by-side in the soft glow from the fireplace, listening to the wind and the whisper of the first falling snowflakes landing on the sod roof.

Smoke was so full of venison stew and peach cobbler, he was sure he would burst. Sipping coffee, he stared thoughtfully at the flames. "We've got enough money in the bank to buy fifteen of those bulls at Chisum's price, and maybe two hundred head of good longhorn cows. We'll offer a few of the bulls to some of our neighbors. We'll need about ten to service that many cows."

"Everything I've been reading about Herefords makes this seem a sure way to breed cattle with more meat on them," Sally replied in the same thoughtful tone. "They are far better than shorthorns for the type of range we have, and I've read that they are resistant to most diseases, although they are susceptible to pinkeye in warm weather."

"Crossing 'em on longhorns will take some of that out of the calves. A longhorn don't hardly ever get sick, and they can take any kind of temperature extremes."

"I can't wait to get started next spring. Of course, I'll be worried until you get back."

"You're looking for reasons to worry. We talked about that before."

"I know you, Smoke. I don't see any way you can take men all the way down to New Mexico Territory without running into some kind of trouble. Sometimes, I think you look for it."

"That's not true," he complained, sipping more coffee. "I try to avoid it whenever I can."

"I want you to promise me that this spring, you won't let anything happen. Please?"

He felt her snuggle against his shoulder. "I'll promise you I won't let anything happen to me or our cattle. I'll swing wide of a fight whenever I can, even if some bastard is lookin' for one."

Sally touched his cheek, turning his face to hers. "I wish I could believe that," she said, then she kissed him hard before he could insist that he meant every word . . . just so long as nobody pushed too damn hard.

10

A layer of light snow blanketed the valley and slopes above the log cabin when dawn came gray and windy to this part of the Rockies. Tiny windblown snowflakes came across the higher ridges in sheets, spiraling downward where mountains protected the land from blustery gusts. Smoke came out before sunrise, when skies were brightening, to feed the horses. The temperature had fallen forty degrees overnight, hovering close to freezing, and as he put corn on the ground inside a pole corral protected from winds by a three-sided lean-to for their four horses, he shivered a bit in the cold and smiled inwardly. This was weather he understood, and he had a fondness for it. Surviving blizzards back when he was with Preacher had been difficult at first, until he'd learned how mountain men kept warm, no matter how cold it got, with layers of clothing and footgear made from tanned animal skins and fur, and how to prepare for weeks of hibernation like a bear when the elements in high country unleashed their fury. Glancing at snow-clad mountains around him now, he allowed himself to think about those times and Preacher, wondering if the old man might possibly be alive up there somewhere after so many years. Preacher would be against sentiment like this. However, Smoke found himself with a longing to hear that familiar deep voice, to see his grizzled face etched by hard times and adversity. Preacher wouldn't allow it, of course, if he were still alive in his declining years, a man with too much pride to let anyone, even Smoke, see him when age took its toll on him.

Spits of snow blew across a ridge to the northwest, flakes falling gently, almost soundlessly, around him. He inspected the horses: two pack animals, Sally's chestnut mare, and a bay and white Palouse three-year-old, sired by Horse, that he was breaking to mountain trails so it would be bridle-wise climbing narrow ledges, where sure-footedness counted. When he was satisfied they were in good flesh and warm inside the shelter, he turned away from the pole corral to fetch pails of water from the slender stream at the foot of the slope where the cabin sat.

Carrying wooden buckets down to the creek, he was again reminded of Puma. This cabin and valley, the mountains, were full of old memories, and in some strange way it wasn't painful to remember them this morning. A part of him was comforted by those recollections of bygone days. The moments of sadness he felt when they first arrived here weren't with him now. He could remember Puma without feeling lonely for his company.

He came to the stream, brightened by a slow sunrise above thick storm clouds moving across the valley, his boots crunching softly in a few inches of newly fallen snow. There was a crispness to the air he didn't notice as often down at the ranch, a part of the experience in higher country, where most of his life he had felt at home. What had changed his feelings, his love for the high lonesome, was Sally. His whole life had changed because of her, and he'd never been so happy, so content. As he knelt beside the stream, he vowed to keep the promise he had made her last night, to steer clear of trouble whenever he could . . . not because he had any fear of it, of bad men. But because he loved her.

A small brook trout darted away from his shadow, moving downstream. Crystal clear water gurgled over multicolored rocks in the streambed, a sound so peaceful he couldn't help listening to it before he dipped his buckets full. To his right was a deep pool where, as the creek froze over, he would be chopping through ice to get their water, or using melted snow, should temperatures drop and remain low for long periods of time.

Hoisting his buckets, Smoke thought about how different this was from his usual existence, or his more violent past. He gave a grin when he considered it, laughing at himself. His biggest worry now was chopping through ice, instead of chopping off the heads of his enemies. This was truly going to be a winter of contentment with Sally, not his usual fare of seemingly endless ranch work, always vigilant for the possibility of the return of old enemies, worrying about Sally while he was away.

When he entered the warm cabin, he found Sally building up a breakfast fire in the fireplace. Puma had installed two swinging iron cooking hooks, holding cast-iron cooking pots, that could be moved over the flames. A rusted iron frame for a skillet or a coffeepot sat to one side of the fire.

She smiled at him as he was closing the cabin door. "This is so nice," she said, adding split wood to a pile of glowing coals. "I thought I might miss my woodstove, but I was wrong."

Smoke placed the buckets near the fireplace and took her in his arms. "The only thing I would have missed would've been you, if you hadn't come with me," he said gently.

"Nonsense," she replied, pretending to sound serious. "You would have found Huggie and Del. The three of you would have been so busy swapping yarns, you wouldn't have noticed I wasn't there. I know why you wanted to come up here this winter. You get this yearning look in your eye when you've been away from your mountain men friends too long."

"That isn't true," he protested. "I'd much rather be with you."

She rested her cheek against his chest "I believe that

too, and I've never doubted you loved me, but it's something else that brings you up here. You want to keep in touch with your past every now and then. I understand, darling. I know it's not just Huggie and Del and some of the others. It's this place, these mountains and valleys, the quiet, and the beauty of it drawing you back. It's okay. I love this high country as much as you do, in my own way. You don't have to make excuses."

"It wasn't an excuse," he mumbled near her ear. "Seems we never get any time alone."

"We're making up for that now," she whispered, tightening her embrace around his chest. "But I want you to know I will understand when you go off to look for your friends."

Once again, Sally was reading him like a book. He'd been thinking about Del and Huggie for a couple of days without any mention of it. "Maybe after we get things squared away around here we'll go looking for Del. He'll get word to Huggie and a few of the others . . . like Grizzly Cole and ol' Happy Jack Cobb, if any of them are still around, or still alive."

Sally giggled, drawing away to look at him. "Who is Happy Jack Cobb? I've never heard you mention that name before. And why is he happy?"

"That's just it," Smoke told her. "Happy Jack would have to be close to sixty now, an' nobody can recollect ever seeing him smile in the last forty-odd years. Puma named him that, best I remember. He said Jack Cobb wouldn't crack a smile if he was to discover the mother lode up here someday. He wears this frown all the time, like he's mad at somethin', only he isn't. It's just his natural expression."

She stood on her tiptoes to kiss him. "I'm happy," she said while searching his face. "I hope you are too."

He swallowed when a strange dryness occurred in his throat. "I've never been happier in my life, and that's on account of you being with me."

* * *

They were Shoshoni by the way they wore their hair and their dress, wrapped in buffalo robes, guiding half-starved ponies into the far end of the narrow valley, riding into the brunt of winds accompanying the snowstorm. He pointed them out to Sally as she was going inside with an armload of green limbs from a pine tree for smoking trout he'd caught just before noon. "Appears they're Shoshoni and they're way off their range, this far south. Fetch me my rifle, just in case these boys are renegades." It had been hard to tell, due to increasing snowfall, until they came out of the trees, a good sign in Smoke's experience. Shoshoni warriors looking for a fight would have stayed hidden until they were very close to the cabin. "They smelled our smoke, being downwind."

"I see six of them," Sally said, her voice tight, changing pitch after she counted the warriors. "I thought all the Indian troubles were over up here."

"The Utes are gone. Shoshoni range north of here by more'n a hundred miles in Wyoming Territory. This isn't their usual hunting ground."

"I'll get your rifle. Maybe they're only looking for food and a place to get out of this storm."

"Maybe," Smoke agreed, thinking otherwise. There was no sense in worrying Sally until he found out what the Indians were up to. He put down the snowshoe he was repairing, watching the Indians ride toward him, wondering why they were so far south of their ancestral homeland.

Sally came out with his .44 Winchester and a box of shells, like she too expected the worst. She gave him the rifle and cartridges, shading her eyes from the snowfall with her hand.

"Those calico ponies look mighty hungry," he said, talking to himself more than for Sally's benefit. "Could be times have been hard up north. Buffalo hunters have damn near wiped out the big herds."

"Perhaps all they want is food. We have enough venison to give them—a hindquarter off that deer you shot. The meat's still good. I can roast it, if that's the reason they're here. Or we can give them all of it. You can go hunting again when this storm breaks."

"We'll give 'em a chance to explain," Smoke said, working a shell into the firing chamber, pocketing the extra shells. "You go back inside until I find out. It's real clear they're headed straight for the cabin."

Sally backed away, turning for the door. "I hope it's only food they want," she said again, her voice almost lost on a gust of howling winter wind.

Six mounted warriors crossed the stream and now Smoke was certain they weren't looking for trouble. Their bows and arrows and ancient muskets were tied to their ponies or balanced across their horses' withers in a manner that was clearly not meant as a threat.

The leader halted his black and white pinto twenty yards from Smoke and gave the sign for peace, and true words, closing his fist over his heart. Smoke returned the sign, then he held one palm open, inviting the Shoshoni to speak.

The Indian began a guttural string of words, a language not much different than the Ute tongue, asking if Smoke understood him.

Smoke replied, *"Nie habbe,"* meaning he spoke their tongue and understood.

The Shoshoni began a lengthy explanation of a tragic tale, how his people were starving because of white buffalo hunters on the prairies, leaving meat to rot in the sun this summer, only killing buffalo for their hides. Shoshoni children and older members of the tribe were dying of starvation. A dry spring and summer left little grazing for deer, elk, and antelope, and most of the wild game had drifted south into lands once controlled by the Utes.

"We have deer meat we can give you," Smoke told him in words he hadn't used for years. "You are welcome to make camp here until the snow ends."

"We would be grateful for the meat," the Indian said, his head and face partially hidden by the hood of his buffalo robe. "We have very little gunpowder and shot.

Our arrows have been cursed by the Great Spirit and they do not find their mark on this hunt."

"I will have my wife cook the deer if you want."

The warrior shook his head. "We must take it back to our village for the hungry children."

Smoke gave the sign for agreement, a twist of his right wrist with two fingers extended close together. He turned and walked to the dogrun between the cabin's two rooms, where the carcass of the deer hung from a length of rawhide.

Resting his rifle against a cabin wall, he cut down the deer and carried it out to the Indians. Another Shoshoni jumped off his pony to take it, cradling almost a hundred pounds of raw meat and bones in his arms.

The Shoshoni leader spoke, his voice softer to convey his gratitude. "You will be welcome in our village, White Giver of Meat. We leave you as friends in peace."

"*Suvate,*" Smoke replied, a single word to say the talk had ended and all was well, then he added a few clipped words.

With the deer slung over a pony's rump, the six Shoshoni reined their ponies away from the cabin, riding north up a very steep ridge that would take them into the worst of the winds and snow.

"Tough people," Smoke said under his breath, hearing Sally come out as the Indians rode off.

Sally came over to stand beside him, watching the buffalo-robed men disappear into a veil of snowflakes. "Food was all they wanted," she said. "I'm glad you gave it to them. We have more than enough for ourselves."

"Their leader told me his people were starving up in Wyoming country . . . that white buffalo hunters had killed off most of the herds and Shoshoni children were dying of hunger."

"We've both seen what buffalo hunters can do. It's a shame to see all that meat wasted," Sally said, "especially when Indian children are dying from starvation."

Smoke picked up the snowshoe, thinking out loud. "Our government doesn't seem to mind breaking its word to a few Indians," he replied to her remark. "Never had much use for politicians or the army in the first place. The more I hear about what they're doin' to most plains tribes, the less use I have for 'em."

Sally took his arm. "We've done all we can for them now. You can't change the world, Smoke. The government in Washington is going to continue its policy toward the Indians no matter how we feel about it."

He saw the Shoshoni as they crossed the high ridge in one brief letup in the storm. "I know you're right, Sally. I can't change the world, maybe, but when I see a wrong bein' committed it makes me wish I'd started shooting politicians and bureaucrats a long time ago. I've killed my share of men who carried guns, but there's times when it seems to make more sense to kill the bastards who run this country."

"I'd hoped we wouldn't have to talk about killing at all this winter."

Smoke squeezed her delicate hand. "We won't. If people will just leave us the hell alone."

"Maybe they will," she said hopefully. "Raising good cattle should be a peaceful enterprise. For so many years now I've been hoping your past would be forgotten, so we could get on with our lives together, as ranchers. You're not a gunfighter anymore, and I hope the word spreads."

He turned her toward the cabin, ducking his head into the wind and snow. Sally would never understand that for some men a gunfighter's reputation followed them all the way to the grave, in spite of their best intentions to change.

He had asked the Shoshoni to tell solitary white mountain men they encountered where he was, what part of the Rockies he was in, and that his name meant "smoke" in Shoshoni, hoping Del or Huggie or Griz would come down when one of them learned he was camped in Puma's summer cabin near the White River. Any one of his old friends would know who was staying here. Maybe when this storm let up, he and Sally would have some welcome company.

11

He was wearing his old deerskin leggings, bloodstained in places from previous battles, one clear cold morning after the storm moved south, taking aim at a fat young doe to replenish their fresh meat supply. They had plenty of jerky and smoked fish, but every so often Smoke got a hankering for venison, the tender backstrap fried in a skillet or slow-roasted on a spit above a bed of coals. In a clearing half a mile from the cabin, he watched the doe paw through snow to find grass, unaware of his presence entirely. Sighting down his Winchester, he aimed for the deer's heart, hoping to make it a quick kill, when something to the east alerted the doe to danger, a distant noise or a scent in the wind. She bounded off into the ponderosa forest, leaving Smoke without a clear shot.

"Damn," he whispered, looking east to where the deer had sensed a threat seconds earlier.

Out of old habit, he didn't look at anything in particular, the way Preacher had taught him, waiting for something to move on a snowy mountainside dotted with pines and leafless aspen. Tiny hairs prickled on the back of his neck . . . something, or someone, was up there. Was someone watching him, he wondered, standing in the shadow of a pine, motionless, unwilling to make the first move, thereby becoming a target, hunted rather than a hunter if the danger frightening the deer had two legs. Black bears and much larger grizzlies would be in hibernation by now. Mountain lions hunted all winter, and it could be a big cat up there somewhere, one of the most difficult wild animals to kill because it rarely came close to the smell of men.

He studied the slope, frosty breath curling away from his nostrils in below-freezing cold. Nothing moved.

"If it's a man, he's a careful son of a bitch," Smoke said softly. It could be more Shoshoni hunters, he guessed, another party ranging far to the south looking for meat. With that looming as a possibility he decided to creep backward and make for the cabin to make sure of Sally's safety. While she was more than capable of taking care of herself in most any situation, he couldn't let her face hungry Shoshoni alone. Sally was a hell of a shot with a pistol or a rifle, and she had his Spencer, along with one of his ivory-handled Colts.

When nothing showed itself on the mountain, he backed away to the shadow of another pine and inched from tree trunk to tree trunk on the balls of his feet, heading for the cabin by a route through stands of pine . . . longer, but far safer if he was being watched from the eastern slope, a sensation that lingered as he made his way among dense trees. He was certain now that someone was up there, a sixth sense telling him this was no mountain lion or late-feeding bear.

He was close to the cabin, less than a quarter mile, when he heard a voice that sent him ducking behind a ponderosa trunk.

"You ain't near as cautious as you used to be, Smoke!" It came from a snow-covered ledge two hundred yards away, a shout. "If I'd took the notion, I coulda dropped you a couple of times. I ain't sayin' you ain't still one of the best, but that easy life yer livin' close to town has made you careless!"

He grinned, recognizing the voice now, swinging away from the tree to stand in plain sight, his rifle barrel lowered near the ground. "Show yourself, Del! You've got me cold! I'm a city slicker now!"

A shaggy mane of black hair peered above the ridge, with a beard to match. The man grinned a toothless grin and stood up with a long-barrel Sharps balanced in one hand. "It's damn sure good to see you, Smoke! Been a hell of a long time!"

Del Rovare began a gradual descent off the ledge, his odd bowlegged gait almost a swagger. He was a bull-like man who had learned to move his tremendous bulk across the mountains without making a sound, somehow. His moccasined feet barely made any noise through difficult snowdrifts where most men would have had trouble remaining quiet. Part French, he spoke Ute and Lakota and Shoshoni fluently. His fierce appearance often made outsiders fear him, when in fact he was most often a gentle giant who avoided difficulties whenever he could. But when he was challenged by man or beast, including rogue grizzly females protecting their cubs, he could be deadly, dangerous with a gun, a knife, or his bare hands.

Smoke walked toward him, and when they met in a small open spot between trees, they embraced like the longtime friends they were.

Del grinned again. "I seen you was headed back to Puma's old cabin like you was worried. Don't fret over that woman of yours. She's fine, an' there ain't nobody else around."

"Did you talk to Sally?" he asked, noticing streaks of gray in Del's hair and beard, and a milky spot over the pupil of Del's left eye.

"Naw. Didn't want to scare her none. I jest watched fer a spell an' come looking fer you. She come outside once to gather a load of firewood. She's okay. I came down after I talked to Mo-pe an' his hunters. They told me you give 'em a deer fer them hungry kids they got up in Wyomin'. Damn nice of you. I give 'em six wild turkey hens I shot the other day. When Mo-pe said you was named after a cloud of smoke I knowed right away who it was stayin' here at Puma's summer lodge. I reckon you miss ol' Puma much as I do. Hell, all of us who live up here miss the ol' bastard, even cranky as he was sometimes. A man never had no better friend than Puma Buck if he took a likin' to you."

Smoke turned Del toward the cabin with a motion of his head as he tried to forget about the way Puma had died, in a fight that was Smoke's, not his. "Puma took a killin' that was meant for me," he said, trudging through snow, remembering in spite of himself. "If it had to happen, I wish it could have happened another way."

"You can't blame yerself, Smoke. Puma knowed what he was up against. An' there's another thing. Puma never was himself after his Ute woman passed away. Used to climb up high all by his lonesome an' sit fer days, starin' at the sky like he was thinkin' real hard 'bout her. He'd git kinda choked up if you was to mention her name."

Smoke thought about Sally. "Every man has his soft spots, Del. I've got the best woman on earth and she's changed me, to some degree. I get lonesome when I'm away from her too long, and I never figured that sort of thing would ever happen to me."

Del changed the subject quickly as they crossed over a low ridge. They could see the cabin down below. "I come to warn you 'bout somethin', Smoke. It ain't no kinda trouble, maybe just an aggravation. There's this long-winded feller ridin' a mule all over these mountains. Says his name's Ned Buntline, an' he says he's aimin' to talk to you. He writes books. A nosy son of a bitch too, askin' all sorts of dumb questions 'bout what it's like to live up here, askin' if Preacher is still alive, wantin' to talk to him if he is. I run the bastard off after he come up with too goddamn many questions. But he's lookin' fer you, so I figured I'd better warn you. He's already talked to Griz, an' ol' Griz wouldn't hardly tell him nothin'. He offered Huggie a jug of whiskey an' Huggie tol' him some things he hadn't oughta."

"Like what?"

Del needed a minute to form his reply. "Like where we all figure Preacher is, if'n he ain't dead by now. Nobody's seen him fer years, I reckon you know. But I was up at Willow Creek Pass this summer an' I found a footprint beside a stream. Ain't a livin' soul up there . . . never has been. Too damn high fer most anybody. Air's so damn thin a man can't breathe it right. I wouldn't have gone up there myself if it hadn't been I wounded a big elk bull an' followed his blood sign fer damn near five miles straight up, nearly to the tree line. That wounded bull wanted water, an' when I come to this creek, there it was, a print made by a man with a foot half a yard long. Ain't no such thing as a big-footed Injun, an' Preacher always had to make his own rawhide brush moccasins. Now, I ain't sayin' that footprint was his, but it was fresh, maybe a few hours old, an' it sure as hell reminded me of his tracks."

"He'd be close to ninety years old by now, Del, if it was him."

"Ain't claimin' it was him. Just sayin' how unusual it was to find that big footprint at Willow Creek Pass. I told Huggie 'bout findin' it. A few weeks back, Huggie told me he'd made some mention of it to that book-writin' feller whilst Huggie was dead drunk on that whiskey."

"I suppose Buntline headed for Willow Creek Pass to see if he could find Preacher."

"That's what Huggie claimed when I talked to him."

Smoke wagged his head as they neared the creek. "Preacher is just as liable to kill him as talk, if he's still alive. He won't have changed much in the disposition department. I've made up my mind not to talk to Ned Buntline either. He can find some other way to write his books. I'm spending the winter up here with Sally. Any son of a bitch who shows up who isn't an old friend of mine will get shown the trail out of here in one hell of a hurry."

"Griz told me the bastard was nice enough. I got tired of all the damn questions mighty quick, so I pointed to the way he rode up to my cabin an' said to clear out now. He got right back on his mule an' I ain't seen him since.

It was Huggie who told me Buntline was headed up to Willow Creek."

"If Preacher's alive, he'll handle it. Now let's see what Sally has got cooked up for lunch. She was makin' brown sugar bearclaws in the Dutch oven when I left."

"I'd claim them bearclaws was callin' to my sweet tooth, only I ain't got any teeth left."

Smoke chuckled as they crossed the stream, stepping ever so carefully on a walkway of flat, slippery rocks. "You won't need any teeth for Sally's bearclaws. Damn but it's good to see you, Del. It's been awhile."

"Good to see you too, Smoke. We had some good times, an' a few that was bad when lead was flyin'."

"We'll talk about some of them tonight. Sally cleaned that other room across the dogrun, and we've got plenty of blankets to keep your old ass warm."

"My ass an' everything else is gettin' old," Del replied. "I get these powerful aches in my joints when it gits cold, and can't hardly see nothin' outta my left eye. Got this white stuff over it so it looks like it's snowin' all the time. Makes everythin' fuzzy as hell, too. One of these years I'm gonna have to come down outta the mountains, when I can't see to aim this rifle no more, or climb a mountain without it hurtin'. Till that day comes, I'm gonna enjoy every minute I've got left. I figure I'm goin' blind, Smoke, an' that's about the worst thing that can happen to a man who loves the looks of high country."

"I'd rather lose a leg than lose my eyes," Smoke said on their way to the cabin door. He noticed smoke curling from the chimney and something else, a delicious smell coming from inside that made his belly growl.

Del stopped a few feet away from the cabin. "You might be well advised to warn your woman I ain't had no bath fer a spell. She won't wanna stand downwind from me. If she'll offer me some of them bearclaws, I'll eat 'em out here."

Smoke laughed heartily. "Sally's used to the smell of a man who's been away from bathwater. C'mon inside. From what my nose just picked up now, I don't figure a skunk could get noticed over what that melted brown sugar smells like." He went to the door and pulled the latchstring.

Sally turned away from the crude, hand-hewn plank table Puma had built for his Ute bride years ago. "I see we've got company," she said. "It's good to see you, Del. You're just in time to try one of my little brown sugar pies. Smoke calls them bearclaws because of the way I shape them."

"I'd be plumb delighted," Del replied, showing off his gums before he leaned his rifle against the wall near the door. "I do git a real strong hankerin' fer somethin' sweet now an' then."

Smoke rested his Winchester on its pegs. For the rest of the day and most of the night, he'd be listening to Del's stories about recent happenings in the mountains. Some of them would evoke old feelings, good feelings, about the years he'd spent up here with Preacher. "How about some coffee?" he asked Sally, to get his mind off the story Del had just told him about finding that footprint at Willow Creek Pass.

12

Ned Buntline was sure he was dying, slowly freezing to death sitting at the base of a rock ledge surrounded by snow and wind, unable to build a fire without the matches in his packs after his mule bolted away, breaking its tether rope for no apparent reason as though something had frightened it, perhaps a bear or a cougar Ned hadn't seen or expected to see at these high altitudes. The mule had trotted downslope, and now he was afoot, freezing, without any food or water, or a gun. Or those all-important matches he must have to get a fire going before he died of exposure. Shivering inside his checkered mackinaw, he knew he was only hours away from death. He'd gotten lost looking for Willow Creek, for his map showed nothing, no details of this region, only blank paper and the notation, *Unexplored*. Yet for days he'd felt he was close to the place Huggie Charles had described, even though the man had been half drunk at the time. Following the timberline west, he'd come to the rocky gorge Charles had mentioned, but somehow, after crossing it just as the snowstorm was letting up, the creek and high mountain pass were nowhere in sight. He'd tied his mule for a climb above the timberline to have a better view of what lay below. And that's when the mule had broken free. Ned had been following its tracks in the snow for hours, until his legs and lungs played out. The air up here was almost too thin to breathe, and the bitter cold only worsened his plight. Now, as the sun lowered behind towering peaks to the west, temperatures would plunge, and he would be lucky to survive the night without a fire to warm him.

He wondered now if it had been worth it, to try to find the legendary mountain man known only as Preacher. Looking was about to cost him his life, unless he found his mule. "Damn the luck," he stammered, teeth chattering, forcing himself to rise slowly on unsteady legs. Tracking the mule was his only hope.

Ned stumbled away from the ledge, feeling strangely sleepy, having trouble keeping his eyelids open. Staggering, almost falling in places, he made his way downslope, following hoofprints left by the mule. Lengthening shadows fell away from smaller pine trees below him, only the damn mule's tracks kept moving in the wrong direction, sometimes higher, continually westward, as if the dumb beast could have known its destination. Ned's feet were frozen numb, without any feeling, his boots and socks insufficient to warm them in a foot or more of snow.

Half an hour later, when Ned was certain he could go no further, the tracks suddenly turned down the mountain toward a snow-mantled line of much taller pines that seemed to wind back and forth aimlessly, winding around switchbacks, headed down to lower altitudes. Slowed to a snail's pace, truly staggering to keep his balance while maintaining some forward progress, he floundered toward the closest trees, gasping for breath.

Skies darkened as he entered the pines; however, he could see a small trickle of partially frozen water, a stream coming from a spring hidden in a jumble of rocks. And there were the mule's prints, following the creek downhill.

For a moment, Ned allowed himself to hope, summoning all the strength he had. His mule could be around the next bend in the stream. Dreaming of a steaming cup of

Arbuckles, flames to warm his hands, face, and frozen toes, he placed one foot in front of the other, now and then pausing long enough to use a pine trunk for support and to catch his breath.

As he made his way down, wind whispered among snow-laden pine boughs, occasionally brushing a dusting of snow to the ground. Ned came to a sharp bend in the tiny trickle and pulled up short when he glimpsed a flickering light.

"A fire," he wheezed. He hadn't seen a living soul for days and couldn't fathom who could be up here. Would it be friend or foe? He had no gun, having hung his pistol belt around his saddle horn for his climb this morning.

"I have no choice," he said a moment later, taking short steps toward the distant flames. Whoever it was with a fire in this cold was about to have company . . . he would die anyway from these temperatures unless he warmed himself.

Getting closer, he saw his mule tied to a tree. A fire in a circle of stones near the creek bank revealed nothing else at the moment. A huge boulder covered with a mound of snow sat beyond the dancing flames, but as he drew closer he became puzzled by the white shape atop the giant rock. . . . It was too large and too irregular to be snow.

"I'm a friend!" he cried with all the voice he could muster in the thin air, even though he saw no one near the fire. "That's my mule! If you have a gun, please don't shoot me! I'm unarmed!"

No one answered his call. Had someone simply found his mule and built a fire for him before continuing on to his destination? It seemed unlikely. He struggled faster, eyes fastened on the strange white shape on top of the boulder, until at last he could see what it was when he was only twenty or thirty yards from the flames.

A figure in a white furry robe was perched on the rock, a hood made from the same material covering his head and any detail of his face. A long rifle lay across the man's lap. Ned was too cold and exhausted to care who it was just then, merely hoping the oddly dressed stranger wasn't planning to shoot him.

His knees wobbled the last few steps until he stood at the edge of the firepit. He looked closely at the dark hole in the hood where a face would have been revealed in better light.

"Who are you?" Ned asked, teeth rattling so loudly he was almost unable to hear his own voice, pulling off his gloves to warm his hands above the flickering flames. "I've never seen a robe that color. It looks like buffalo fur. Was the buffalo a rare albino?"

"You sure as hell ask a bunch of questions for a man who's damn near froze solid," a deep voice replied. "Any fool can see a man like you don't belong up here. Get warm. Boil some coffee if you've a mind to, then get on that mule an' clear out of here without askin' no more stupid questions."

"It isn't that I'm not grateful for what you've done," Ned replied, as some feeling returned to his fingers and feet. "I was only curious as to who you were, and why you'd help me."

"Felt sorry for you, Tenderfoot. I been watchin' you fer a couple of days. You ain't got the know-how to be up here, so take some advice afore your next fool mistake gets you froze till the spring thaw. Get back to the flatlands where you come from an' don't come back."

Ned wasn't quite sure what to say, or if he should say anything. "I'm a writer," he said, to explain. "I was looking for a mountain man they call Preacher. I intend to write a series of books about the real pioneer mountain men. Alvah Dunning told me about this Preacher fellow, and so did Major Frank North of the Pawnee scouts. Everyone seems to know about Preacher, only there are some who say he's dead now."

"Maybe he is."

"Did you know him?"

"Ain't none of your affair."

"Please don't be offended. My readers back east would love to know more about this famous mountain pioneer."

"You can write about some of the others."

"Not many of them will tell me anything. I found out one of the last of the early pioneers, Puma Buck, is dead. I was hoping he would tell me a few tales."

"He wouldn't, even if he was alive."

"You knew him?"

"Ain't none of your affair."

Ned looked down at his boots, wondering who the man was in the white robe. . . . He couldn't see his face. "My last hope, if I can't find this Preacher fellow, is a man named Smoke Jensen. I was told he used to be a mountain man before he took up ranching close to Big Rock, and that he knew Preacher better than any of the others."

A silence followed, long enough to be meaningful, but what did it mean and how could he find out? "Would you care for a cup of coffee? I have some Arbuckles in my pack."

"Nope. You ask too damn many questions to be good company over a cup of coffee." Now the white-robed stranger stirred, swinging off the rock. He stood for a moment looking at Ned, even though Ned couldn't see his eyes. He seemed bent as if with old age, stooped over, although it was hard to tell because his robe was bulky, touching the ground so even his feet and legs were hidden. "Boil your coffee an' head back where you come from quick as you can, mister, afore somebody, or these mountains, up an' kills you."

Before Ned could ask for his name again, the man whirled and walked away into the darkness beneath the pine canopy shadowing both sides of the stream.

"Thanks again, mister!" he called out.

There was nothing but silence and the soft crackle of flames for an answer. Ned knew he would always wonder who the benevolent stranger in the albino buffalo robe was. . . . He owed the man his life.

13

Jessie Evans liked all six of the Mexican *pistoleros:* Pedro Lopez, Jorge Diaz, Carlos and Victor Bustamante, a half-breed by the name of Raul Jones, and a fat Yaqui Indian simply called Tomo. All six were experienced gunmen and Jessie needed every good gun he could hire, since word had come that Big John Chisum was looking for men who could handle themselves. What was being called the Lincoln County War was now shaping up to be a deadly fight, if things continued the way they were. Cattle were being stolen on both sides. Jessie was ready to teach a few more Chisum riders a permanent lesson, while the territorial governor turned his head at the request of Catron and Murphy. Dolan said they might even burn down John Tunstall's store some night, to teach him to keep his nose out of the cattle contract business. Jimmy Dolan knew how to fight a war, how to win at any cost, and he had Murphy's money behind him to get the job done.

Jessie turned to Bill Pickett as sundown came to their camp at Bosque Redondo. "Let's test those new Mexican boys tonight. We'll ride over to Chisum's cow camp on the Ruidoso River. If we gather up about fifty head of steers, an' kill a few cowboys while we're at it, Dolan's liable to give us all a pay raise. We'll tell those *pistoleros* to shoot as many men as they can."

"Sounds good to me," Pickett replied, tipping a bottle of tequila into his mouth. "I was gettin' bored, sittin' 'round here, freezin' our asses off, waitin' fer somethin' to happen. I say we make somethin' happen ourselves. There's another thing I been thinkin' about. That goddamn high an' mighty Englishman, John Tunstall, has been hirin' more men. Mostly green kids, or so I hear tell. Wouldn't be nothin' wrong with shootin' that Englishman, if you ask me. He ain't connected to nobody important in this territory. Killin' him oughta throw a scare into Chisum an' everybody else in Lincoln County."

"I'll ask Dolan about it. All he said was, maybe we oughta burn down his store. Tell those Mexicans to saddle up. You an' me an' Cooper will ride with 'em."

Pickett eased his weight off a bull hide stool on the front porch of the cow camp bunkhouse. "Suits the hell outta me. We ain't spilled no blood since winter started. Time we turned some of this snow red. It gets tiresome, seein' everything white all the damn time."

The mighty roar of a shotgun from the darkness ended with a shrill scream. Loose horses and cattle, bedded down for the night, took off in every direction. A lantern brightened behind a cabin window as men in long johns carrying rifles raced out the door in the pale moonlight, shouting to each other.

Another withering blast of shotgun fire erupted from a spot behind a split rail fence, lifting a hatless cowboy off his feet in mid-run, bending him at the waist with the force of speeding lead pellets entering his chest and belly.

A rifle cracked from the corner of a hay shed, dropping a Chisum ranch hand in his tracks, groaning, landing in fresh snow with his feet thrashing as though he meant to keep running while he lay on his back.

More guns roared from a loose circle around the cabin, and more men fell in the snow, yelling, crying out for help or lying still, dead before they went down.

Jessie leaned against the fence in the dark without firing a shot, watching Pickett, Cooper, and his Mexican gunmen in action, keeping a quick tally of the bodies. Eight men, then a ninth, collapsed in a hail of bullets. Terrified longhorns broke out of one corral, snapping rails like kindling wood, bolting toward freedom and an escape from the banging of guns. As the last of the Chisum riders fell, Jessie turned away from the fence to get his horse.

All gunfire stopped abruptly. Somewhere near the cabin a cowboy moaned. Pickett or Cooper would take care of his suffering in short order, along with any others who might still be alive.

"Let's round up those beeves," he shouted. "We'll gather as many as we can an' clear out. Somebody across the river is liable to have heard the noise."

He mounted a nervous sorrel gelding and held its reins in check until all his men were in their saddles . . . all but Pickett, his absence explained when a shotgun bellowed near one of the cowsheds.

Nine Dolan riders spread out to collect over a hundred head of longhorn steers. Jessie knew it was time to get the running irons hot again, changing brands before Sheriff William Brady went through the motions of investigating what would look like a massacre tomorrow morning. A serious escalation of the Lincoln County War had just taken place a few days before Christmas, a warning to John Chisum that the government beef contract business could be a little risky here in the southern part of New Mexico Territory.

14

It was very close to the beginning of April when Sally took a look at the sky one morning, then at the snow-filled valley with a slight frown on her face. She turned to Smoke as he was using a whetstone on his Bowie knife blade.

"It's time to go, my darling," she said. "This has been one of the most wonderful times of my life, but we can't hide up here forever. There's work to be done at Sugarloaf. By now the snow is melting down there. You've got to hire some extra men to help bring cattle up from New Mexico. Some of our neighbors who want Hereford bulls may ride along. I suppose I'm getting restless, but something tells me it's time. You've seen your friends, and we've had all these months of peace and solitude. Our staples are running low. As much as I'd love to stay here with you for the rest of my life, we can't. We have a ranch to run."

For weeks he'd been experiencing the same strange sensation, that it was time to leave, almost like an itching feeling, only it occurred inside, somewhere in his chest or in the back of his brain. He hadn't wanted to say anything to her. She seemed so happy here and happy with their closeness. "I agree," he said, sheathing his heavy knife. "I've really been thinkin' about the Herefords, and maybe finding a Morgan stud. We may still hit some bad weather if we start out early, but it'll be slow movin' those cattle so many miles. Some of that is still renegade Apache country, so we'll have to watch our herd real close in a few spots."

He stood up and cast a sweeping look at the snowy mountain peaks around them. "I'll hate to leave here. I reckon there'll always be a part of me wanting to stay in this high country from time to time." He smiled at her. "Especially with you. But like you said, we've got a ranch to run and miles to travel to make our plans for the future work out. We can start packing gear today and leave at first light tomorrow. It'll be slower, going down with all this snow on the ground. We should be back at Sugarloaf in four days."

"It'll be good to see Pearlie and Cal and Johnny," she said after a bit. "I didn't realize I'd miss them so much. I guess they're like a part of the family, almost. When I saw you with Huggie and Del, or Grizzly this winter it made me happy to hear you talk about what it was like to be one of them. You seemed to really be enjoying yourself."

"I was," he answered truthfully. "It was good to see them again, to talk about old times. I was sorry to hear Happy Jack got killed by that grizzly last spring, but a mother with cubs can be one of the most dangerous animals on earth. Griz Cole knows bears better'n anybody, and he said Happy Jack never did give 'em enough room. Carelessness caught up with him, I reckon. And none of 'em knew for sure what ever happened to Preacher."

She placed her hand in the crook of his arm. "Still, this was the most peaceful winter we ever spent together, and I'm so grateful for that. I'll always remember it, and how gentle you can be. The only time you used a gun was to hunt fresh meat, and I'm grateful for that too."

"Maybe I've changed," he told her. "Let's get started with that packing. Won't be as much to carry going down, so our pack animals will have an easier time of it."

She smiled and kissed him lightly. "I love you, Mr. Jensen."

"I love you too, Mrs. Jensen. Maybe I didn't realize just how much until we spent this peaceful winter together. It made me realize just how important you are to me."

She tilted her head, still smiling. "Maybe you have

changed your ways, darling. Those are some mighty sweet words coming out of your mouth this morning. Maybe the old Smoke Jensen is gone for good, so I won't have to worry so much . . ."

Pearlie and Cal and Johnny shook hands with Smoke and Cal gave Sally a hug, still being part boy despite a fast growing up riding alongside Smoke in a few tight spots.

"Everything's plumb satisfactory," Pearlie said. "Only had this one aggravation all winter long."

Smoke's expression clouded. "And what was that?"

"That feller Ned Buntline showed up, wearin' this derby hat like he belonged in Saint Louis or somewheres. Asked to talk to you. I told him you was gone fer the winter."

Cal's face brightened. "He told me all about how he writes those dime novels. And you ain't gonna believe this! He wants to write one about you!"

Pearlie wagged his head before Smoke could disagree. "I went an' told him he'd be wastin' his time, that you wasn't gonna tell him a damn thing. He acted real disappointed. Then he told us this crazy story, 'bout some feller up near Willow Creek Pass who wore this albino buffalo robe. Buntline said he never saw his face or got his name, but he told us that feller saved his life when his mule run off. Built a fire so he wouldn't freeze to death, and tied his mule up fer him. Buntline said he was an ornery cuss. Wouldn't answer a single question 'bout who he was or how come him to be way up there. Downright unusual, fer a man to own an albino buffalo skin. Ain't seen but two my whole life, an' they was way off, wild as deer."

Smoke turned northwest, looking at the distant peaks outlined against a clear sky. Had Ned Buntline accidentally run into Preacher up there somewhere? He was reminded of the story Del had told him about the unusual footprint at Willow Creek Pass, not real proof of anything. Buntline's story might only be the product of a fertile imagination of the type he used to write his books.

He spoke to Pearlie. "Ride to the neighboring ranches, the Walker spread and Bob Williams's place. Ask them if they want to ride with us down to New Mexico Territory at the end of next week to pick up those Hereford bulls."

"We leavin' that soon?" Pearlie asked. "It's still a touch on the chilly side."

"It's a long trip, and comin' back with those gentle bulls will be slow," Smoke answered. "We'll leave next Friday, and anybody who wants to ride along with us is welcome company."

"I'll ride to the Williams place," Johnny offered, as Cal was helping unload the packhorses. "One thing, Mr. Jensen," he added, glancing over to Sally as she went in the house with an armload of winter clothes. "While I was in Big Rock the other day, Mr. Longmont said he read somethin' in the Denver newspaper, that there was big trouble down in New Mexico. Folks are callin' it the Lincoln County War, an' you said Lincoln County was where we had to go to meet Mr. John Chisum an' pick up them bulls. Mr. Longmont said there was dead bodies all over the place, an' it might not be a safe place to be."

While this wasn't particularly good news, Smoke said, "It isn't our war, Johnny. We'll stay out of it. If we can."

Pearlie chuckled. "I never did know you to avoid no kind of war. If there's any killin' goin' on wherever we's headed, I'm dead sure we'll get in on our share of it."

Smoke didn't want any danger discussed in front of Sally. "Don't say any more about it, Johnny, not when Sally's in hearing distance."

"Yessir. I mean, no sir, I won't."

"It's because she worries too much," he explained, unsaddling the bay Palouse colt.

Pearlie muttered, as he stripped the saddle off Sally's mare, "Maybe it's because she's got good reason to worry. This outfit ain't exactly famous fer ridin' the other way when lead's flyin'."

15

They made up quite a group riding south along the base of the Rockies, following a cattle trail that would take them to Durango before they crossed over the New Mexico line. Cal and Pearlie and Johnny, then Cletus Walker and Bob Williams, along with a seasoned cowboy from the Williams ranch by the name of Duke Smith. Smoke left Tinker Warren to help out at the ranch and watch over Sally while they were away. He trusted Tinker, and the old man could shoot straight if he had to, which was just as important as his cowboying skills when Smoke considered he was there to protect the most important thing in his life . . . Sally.

"Snow's already melted in this low country," Pearlie said, "an' here it is only the middle of April."

Cletus Walker offered his opinion on the subject. "Ain't near as pretty this far south, an' it sure as hell ain't as good grazin' land." Cletus was a stocky man in his fifties, a good neighbor and friend, although he and Smoke rarely saw each other, his spread being over ten rugged miles east of Sugarloaf.

"It's warmer," Bob Williams remarked, a lanky bachelor who ran cattle in lowlands south of Smoke and Sally, "but I'll agree with Cletus that this is junk land compared to what we've got. There ain't hardly enough grass most places in this valley to keep a jackrabbit alive."

Duke Smith, not much older than Cal, said, "It's damn sure different all right. I never rode this trail afore, but I been up the Goodnight twice. Believe me, if you figure this part of Colorado ain't got much grass, wait'll you see the Goodnight down in the south part of New Mexico. You can count the blades of grass an' not run out of fingers in some of them stretches along the Pecos."

Cal had been unusually quiet for several days after they left the ranch. He rode silently beside Smoke as though his mind was on something else. "Down along the Pecos is where they's havin' that big fight, accordin' to Mr. Longmont. Lincoln County is where he said most of it was, an' that's right where we're headed. They's callin' it the Lincoln County War, if you'll remember."

"It isn't our fight," Smoke told him. "We're buyin' cattle and that's all. No sense getting yourself all worked up over it, Cal. I promised Sally we'd ride a hundred miles in the wrong direction to stay out of trouble."

"It'd be the first time," Pearlie observed dryly. "Seems we make a habit outta ridin' a hundred miles to look fer a fight on occasion."

Cal swallowed, seeming edgier than Smoke had ever seen him. "Just so nobody starts shootin' at us before they know we ain't on either side."

There were times when Cal reminded Smoke of himself as a boy growing up, when he was known by his given name, Kirby Jensen, in a bleak part of southeastern Missouri at the edge of the Ozark Mountain range. He remembered too how his Pa, Emmett, went off to war and how lonely he felt, trying to scratch a living out of thin soil to help support his Ma. It was after the war when he and his Pa rode west, running into the filthiest-looking old man he'd ever seen, dressed in greasy buckskins, calling himself Preacher and never anything else. It was another step toward manhood for Kirby Jensen, and a chance meeting where he earned the nickname Smoke early on, a meeting and a friendship that had changed Smoke Jensen's life forever. And now Cal was becoming a man, one step at a time as it must always be, learning lessons that would keep him alive, as well as making him a man who could be a trusted friend and perhaps, later on, a deadly adversary. Cal had the basics, the things it took inside—courage and true loyalty to those who stood by him. His uneasiness now over the trouble in Lincoln County was just his way of preparing himself to stand and fight beside Smoke and the others if the need arose.

Smoke recalled his frontier education with Preacher, his own early fears, until Preacher taught him how to stay alive . . . and how to kill when necessary. With those skills came confidence, along with experience. While Preacher had been a hard taskmaster at times, he explained that it was necessary, that life-and-death struggles are unforgiving, usually allowing no mistakes. It had been hard to live up to Preacher's expectations, without understanding it was a rite of passage into manhood in a land filled with sudden violence and harsh conditions. More than any other single thing, Preacher had taught him to rely on himself.

Smoke wondered if these memories were coming back because of the footprint Del had found at Willow Creek Pass, and the story Ned Buntline had told of encountering a solitary mountain man up there who handed Buntline his life. That would be just like Preacher, to help a tenderfoot in trouble and then abandon him as quickly as he'd arrived. Or was Smoke merely trying to comfort himself with the thought that Preacher was still alive up in the high lonesome, living out his final years?

Leading a string of spare horses, Duke pointed to a distant line of trees wandering back and forth to the south, stretching across the far horizon. "That looks like a river way off yonder," he said.

"It's the San Juan," Cletus told him, before Smoke could say it. "Means we're gettin' mighty close to the New Mexico Territory line. Durango oughta be off to the west a few miles."

Smoke settled back against the cantle of his saddle, hearing the bay Palouse colt's hooves squish through melting snow and mud with some satisfaction. The young horse was proving itself to be like its sire, Horse, a solid trail pony with endurance and an easy gait, with enough stamina to outlast most other breeds in this part of the country. Crossing their mares on a good Morgan stud, he and Sally could raise tough cow horses with early speed at shorter distances.

"We'll also be ridin' into Apache country," Bob warned as they neared the river. "Time we loaded our rifles an' the rest of our guns."

It was wasted advice for Smoke Jensen. He couldn't remember a time when his guns weren't fully loaded, or being reloaded for another round of gunplay. An empty gun was about as useless as a three-legged horse.

He noticed neither Cal nor Pearlie were checking their weapons, and Johnny North did not so much as look down at his pistol or rifle. Sugarloaf riders learned to be prepared for most anything at any time. Otherwise, they didn't stay on the payroll.

Smoke smiled when he thought about Sally. If she happened to be wearing a dress, underneath it, strapped to her leg, she kept a short-barreled Colt .44. And if she rode the ranch in a pair of denims, she wore a gunbelt just like the rest of the cowboys, with a Winchester booted to her saddle. For a gentle-natured schoolteacher, she could damn sure shoot straight with a handgun or a rifle.

Above the river, on a twisting road that would take them to Santa Fe, then farther south, they were climbing into the San Pedro Mountains toward El Vado Pass two days later when Smoke sensed danger, a feeling he would be hard-pressed to describe, a tingling down his back resembling a chill. Although for now he saw nothing to arouse his concerns, the sensation was there just the same.

"Keep your eyes open," he said over his shoulder. "Maybe it's nothing, but my nose smells trouble up ahead."

"That's enough fer me," Pearlie remarked, pulling out his Winchester, resting it across the pommel of his saddle. "I never have knowed how you could smell it comin', but I'll take an oath you've done it more times than I care to remember. Jerk that smoke stick, boy," he said to Cal, "an' git yerself ready to use it. Johnny, if you like the sweet smell of this air, you'd best git ready to fight fer your next breath of it."

"I don't see a damn thing," Cletus said, squinting into the sun's glare off melting snow on slopes leading toward the pass.

"Neither do I," Smoke told him. "I just figure it'll be a good idea to stay watchful."

Bob and Duke drew their rifles, levering shells into the firing chamber, resting the buttplates against their thighs as their horses carried them higher. Cletus remained unconvinced for the present, leaving his rifle booted.

"Could be all you smell is a skunk," Cletus argued, when nothing moved on either side of the pass.

"Maybe," Smoke said softly, his experienced eye roaming back and forth across steep slopes dotted with smaller piñon pine trees and still barren aspen, it being too early in the spring for new leaves. "Skunks come in several shapes. I'm lookin' for the two-legged variety. They've got a different smell."

The sounds of hooves filled a silence. Smoke left his rifle in its boot, opening his coat to be able to reach for both Colts in case he needed them in a hurry.

Then he saw the source of his concerns, five or six Apache warriors by the cut of their hair, brandishing rifles, rounding a cutbank near the top of the pass. They rode to the crest of the trail and halted their multicolored ponies, fanning out, blocking the pathway of Smoke and his neighbors.

"Son of a bitch!" Cletus exclaimed, pulling his Winchester free. "How the hell did you know, Smoke?"

Smoke halted his horse without answering Cletus, judging the distance, measuring how much drop a slug would take reaching an Indian more than three hundred yards away. A .44 caliber rifle cartridge held a considerable amount of gunpowder, properly loaded with the maximum number of grains, but unlike a Sharps, its range was far more limited and the bullet had a tendency to fall at shorter distances, requiring a higher aim and a piece of luck.

Only now, Smoke unbooted his Winchester, when it became all too clear the Apaches were after their horses and money, blocking the roadway through El Vado Pass. He chambered a shell. "I'll aim over their heads once," he told the others, "a warning shot to convince 'em we're willin' to fight our way through if we have to. Maybe we can scare 'em off. We've got 'em outnumbered. I'd be willing to bet these are young renegades, not older warriors with a lot of fighting experience. Let's hope they back off."

Aiming well above the warriors' heads, he triggered off a booming shot that echoed off the slopes. The result was not what he expected.

All five Apaches jumped their ponies forward, shouldering rifles, racing down the trail to engage the enemy. Smoke took it in stride, levering another round. "Start droppin' as many as you can, soon as they're in range," he said, placing his rifle sights on a warrior's blanketed chest. He heard war cries and the thunder of unshod hooves.

Smoke fired, feeling the Winchester slam into his shoulder. The Apache disappeared from his sights almost instantly, performing a backflip off the rump of his galloping pinto.

Cal fired before Smoke could aim again, and to Smoke's surprise a squat Apache warrior toppled to the ground, rolling in snowmelt slush and mud, arms and legs like the limbs of a limp rag doll, until he tumbled to a halt at the base of a piñon pine.

"Nice shot," Smoke told the boy, when only three Indians remained in the reckless charge.

"I allowed fer the drop like you showed me," Cal said as he worked another cartridge into place, his horse prancing underneath him following the explosion so near its ears.

A fierce war cry ended the instant Smoke pulled the trigger and an Apache tossed his rifle in the air to reach for his throat while he was falling backward. Before anyone could fire another shot, the last two Indians swerved their ponies around, drumming heels into the little horses' sides to race back up to the top of the pass.

Without a word, Smoke urged his Palouse forward, keeping one eye on the fallen warriors and the other on the pass. When he came to the first downed Indian, he saw a pulpy round hole in the Apache's neck and a circle of blood growing around his head. He would be dead in a matter of minutes.

The Apache Cal had shot had a mortal wound near his heart, and while he was still breathing slowly, his life would end soon. Cal rode up just then, peering down at what he'd done.

"Jesus," the boy whispered, losing some of the pink in his cheeks. "Looks like I killed him."

The others rode up to inspect Cal's handiwork.

"You done yerself proud, boy," Pearlie said. "Couldn't have done no better myself at half that distance."

"You sure as hell can shoot, son," Bob said. "I had you figured to be a little bit on the young side to have any nerve, but I was damn sure wrong."

Smoke gave Cal a nod, all that was needed to praise him for the time being. Later, he would tell the boy how steady his aim and nerves had to be to make that kind of shot at a moving target from two hundred yards away.

Riding further up the trail, Smoke gazed down at his first victim briefly. A bullet hole ran through the warrior's side, exiting near his backbone. "This one's gonna die slow. Maybe, if his friends come back for him after we're across this pass, it'll be a lesson to them."

Pearlie was grinning, looking at Cal. "I'm right proud of this young 'un. His color ain't all come back just yet, but fer that kind of shootin', I'm gonna overlook a little bit of change in his face. Damn nice work, son."

16

Jessie Evans had promised he would put a stop to that damn Englishman's interference. John Tunstall was complaining to the sheriff, the territorial governor, and almost everyone else about cattle rustling in Lincoln County, and the killings, even though there was no real evidence as to who was responsible. Witnesses were hard to come by. But when Jimmy Dolan said he wanted the Englishman taken care of right then, after another complaint had reached Sheriff Brady this morning, there wasn't anything to do but get the job done immediately.

Today, riding with two new gunmen he'd recently hired, Tom Hill and Billy Morton, they were headed to Tunstall's ranch to scare him out of the country or silence him. Jessie would have been more comfortable bringing extra men with him; however, word had it that Tunstall had only five or six green kids working for him and with Dolan screaming his head off to put the Englishman in his place, either headed back to England or in a six-foot hole in the ground, Jessie decided the three of them could handle it rather than ride all the way out to Bosque Redondo to pick up a few more shooters. On the road to Tunstall's ranch, Jessie told Billy and Tom what he wanted done.

"Look for any excuse to kill him," Jessie said, "an' if any of them wet-noses reach for a shootin' iron, blow 'em away. We gotta get this done right. Jimmy's mad-der'n hell about all them letters Tunstall's been writin'."

"Why do we need an excuse?" asked Billy, a narrow-eyed man who had a reputation in West Texas as a backshooter. "Let's just ride up to the house an' kill the son of a bitch. Mr. Dolan don't have to know. We can say he went for a gun."

"There may be too many witnesses," Jessie replied. "If we have to, we'll take him off somewheres at gunpoint an' do the job where nobody's watchin'."

"It don't make a damn bit of difference to me," said Tom Hill, another Texan who made his living in the gun-fighter's trade. "Unless he's got himself surrounded by some good men with a gun, I say we just shoot the sumbitch an' be done with it, so we can earn our money."

Jessie saw no need in planning it until they saw what they were up against at Tunstall's place. "We'll wait till we get there to make up our minds. Don't worry none 'bout his cowboys. I've seen a few of 'em. Hardly more'n school-boys. John Chisum is another matter. He's payin' top wages for men who can shoot. He aims to turn this into a killin' contest. Dolan told me Buck Andrews is on Chisum's pay-roll now, an' so is Curly Tully. Them two boys is dangerous as snakes. I've knowed Buck for years, an' when he sets out after a man, he'd best be real careful. Curly can be worse'n Buck, if the money's right. Curly ain't scared of no man on earth, an' he ain't opposed to killin' a man in his sleep if he gets the chance. Chisum's got plenty of money behind him, an' that's what's gonna make this dangerous as hell. Soon as Chisum gets an army of shooters behind him like he's doin' now, all hell's gonna break loose."

Billy looked behind them, resting his palms on his saddle horn while his horse trotted down the two-rut lane leading to Tunstall's place. "Don't none of them names scare me," he said in an offhanded way. "A man's just a man when the shootin' starts."

Tom grunted and nodded once, sighting along the horizon as he spoke. "Billy's right. Just show us the bas-tards you want killed, an' we'll do the rest. Couldn't help but notice you got Bill Pickett on your payroll. Now there's what I call a crazy mean son of a bitch. I was with him on a little job up in Fort Worth a few years ago. Didn't know who he was back then. We was hired to help clear some hard cases out of a saloon in Hell's Half Acre, when the law wouldn't do it on account of they was scared of 'em. Pickett come in the back way with that scattergun, an' when he started shootin', wasn't much left but blood and shredded meat all over the floor. Hell, I was half scared he was gonna shoot me, the way he was blastin' lead all over the place. Buck Andrews an' Curly Tully are bad men with a gun, but they ain't never run into the likes of Bill Pickett."

Jessie knew all too well how dangerous Pickett could be, and along with Roy Cooper, Ignacio Valdez, and the *pistoleros* he'd hired from below the Mexican border, Chisum would be up against so many killers, he wouldn't have time to bid on any beef contracts. And while he never said so publicly, Jessie knew he was a match for any of them, including Pickett. . . . He'd tested his guns against some of the best in El Paso and Juarez, Laredo, and other tough border towns.

Crossing a gentle rise in the prairie, Jessie signaled a halt when he saw a buggy and five mounted men coming toward them. The cowboys were pushing a herd of loose horses. He recognized John Tunstall at once, even from a distance.

"Yonder he is, the feller drivin' the buggy. This is as good a place as any, boys. Fill your fists with iron an' we'll charge straight toward 'em, throwin' lead. That'll scare off his young cowboys, an' we'll shoot Tunstall right here."

Tom and Billy drew pistols. Jessie pulled his .44 and dug spurs into his horse's sides. Firing a few rounds in the air long before they were in range, Jessie led his men toward John Tunstall and five riders. . . . Even from here Jessie could see three of them weren't carrying guns.

Two cowboys swung off, spurring for the top of a rock ridge to the east. The others milled back and forth for a moment near the buggy, then they rode off to the south as hard as they could ride, leaving Tunstall alone in the middle of the road.

Jessie grinned as he bore down on the buggy. This was going to be even easier than he'd thought. Tunstall's men deserted him without firing a shot, proving they were the young cowards he had known they would be.

The Englishman reined his buggy to a halt. He carried no gun Jessie could see. He watched Jessie and his men gallop up without showing any sign of fear. Tunstall wore a brown suit and a bowler hat, his usual attire. Jessie pulled his mount to a stop a few yards from the carriage.

"What was all the shooting about, Mr. Evans?" Tunstall asked as he looked at their drawn pistols. "You have frightened my men and scattered our horses. Please explain your actions."

Jessie found it hard to believe Tunstall could be so calm in the face of three armed men who were his enemies. "Your boys did scatter like quail, Tunstall. Don't appear they've got much in the way of backbone."

"I ordered them to leave, to keep them from being injured if this were a robbery."

"Ain't no robbery," Jessie told him. "You've been complainin' to Sheriff Brady an' to Governor Wallace an' the soldiers at Fort Stanton about cattle rustlin'. You've wrote a bunch of damn letters accusin' Mr. Murphy and Jimmy Dolan of bein' behind it all. Somebody's gotta stop you from writin' all them goddamn letters, Tunstall, accusin' the wrong people, makin' 'em look bad when they ain't done nothin' to you. You took the wrong side in this here cattle war, Tunstall. John Chisum is a goddamn thief an' a liar."

Tom was looking at the rocky ridge. "Two of them yellow-bellied bastards are watchin' us from up yonder. Me an' Billy could ride up there an' run 'em off."

"Ain't gonna be necessary," Jessie replied, thumbing back the hammer on his Colt. "Mr. Tunstall just pulled a gun on me. Got no choice but to defend myself." He aimed for Tunstall's chest and pulled the trigger.

The sharp report startled Tunstall's buggy horse—it lunged forward as a small hole puckered in his suit coat a few inches above his heart, the bullet's force pinning him to his buggy seat for a few seconds. Billy grabbed the buggy horse's bridle to keep it from running off.

Tunstall slumped forward clutching his chest, blood pumping from his wound. He mouthed a few silent words, hands tightening around his reins in a trembling grip.

"That oughta be the end of them letters," Jessie said as he swung down to the ground. "Hold my horse," he told Tom. "Let's see if Mr. Tunstall is packin' a gun."

He found a small-caliber revolver hidden inside the Englishman's coat. "Lookee here, boys. Mr. Tunstall was armed. Even though he's the same as dead right now, he's gonna fire a couple of shots at us."

Jessie aimed the pistol at the ground, firing twice, again spooking the horses. Then he placed the revolver in Tunstall's right hand and pushed him back against the buggy seat.

"Now then," Jessie said, grinning a one-sided grin with no humor in it. "What we got here is a case of self-defense, an' you boys can testify Mr. Tunstall's gun fired two times."

"I seen it with my own two eyes," Tom replied casually.

"I was lookin' right at him when he tried to kill you," Billy said. "Plain and simple, Jessie. You didn't have no choice but to defend yourself. I'll swear to it on a stack of Bibles as high as your head."

"Only thing to worry 'bout," Tom said, glancing back to the ridge, "is them two. They seen what happened."

Jessie climbed back on his horse. "Too far away. Nobody can be sure who they saw, or exactly what happened from so far off."

"We can ride up there an' kill 'em," Tom suggested. "I see one wearin' an old top hat looking down at us now."

Jessie looked at the ridge again. "I remember him. He came to Bosque Redondo lookin' for a job with us. I ran him off 'cause he was too young. Seems like he said his name was William Bonney."

"If we ain't gonna kill 'em, let's clear out," Billy said. "No tellin' who else might come along."

Jessie gazed down at John Tunstall. Tunstall was still able to breathe, although now blood was coming from his mouth and nose in rivulets. "We did what we set out to do. Jimmy's gonna be real glad to hear Mr. Tunstall won't be writin' no more of his damn letters."

Tom and Billy swung their horses away from the buggy, but they waited when Jessie sat his horse. Jessie stayed a moment longer, watching blood pool on the floorboards of the buggy.

"What's wrong, boss?" Tom asked.

"Just thinkin'. I say it's time we quit messin' around. I say we kill every son of a bitch who does business with Mr. John Chisum, no matter who it is."

"Suits me," Billy remarked. "I thought that's what we was gettin' paid to do anyways."

"Murphy ain't got enough starch in him," Jessie said. "If he wants to end this war real quick, he'll just turn us loose to burn a little gunpowder."

"One of us oughta keep an eye on John Chisum's ranch," Tom suggested. "Anybody who shows up to buy cattle, we kill 'em. Won't be long till word spreads that it's dangerous, buyin' beef from Chisum."

Jessie thought about it. "That's one hell of a good idea, Tom. I'll ask Jimmy. The first sumbitch who comes to Chisum's spread buyin' cattle, we kill 'em soon as they get out of earshot of the ranch."

Billy was watching the ridge. "I still claim we'd be a lot smarter to ride up there an' kill them two."

Jessie wagged his head. "Leave 'em be. Sheriff Brady ain't gonna believe 'em anyways."

"Whatever you say, Jessie. You're the boss."

Jessie led his men away from the buggy at a trot, in no real hurry to leave the scene. Down deep, he knew he had just put out one of the major fires causing trouble in Lincoln County, and when word of it reached Chisum and some of his friends, this cow war would soon be over.

At the top of the rise, Jessie looked backward. The two cowboys who rode for Tunstall were riding their horses carefully down to the buggy. "That oughta teach 'em a lesson," he said under his breath, kicking his horse to a short lope.

17

Smoke took Cal aside while the others sat around their fire eating beans and fatback. Cal had been behaving strangely since he'd shot the Apache, riding along in what appeared to be a moody silence. As soon as Smoke got the boy off in the dark, he gave him a questioning look.

"What's eatin' on you, Cal?"

Cal couldn't look Smoke in the eye, gazing up at the stars for a time. "I reckon it's rememberin' that Indian I shot back yonder, Mr. Jensen, remembering what he looked like with that big hole in him . . . knowin' I done it."

"Killin' a man is never easy," Smoke said gently. "Sometimes it's necessary. Those Apaches were coming after us, and if one of 'em had gotten off a lucky shot, one of us might have been killed. You did what you had to do in order to save your friends and that's part of accepting the responsibility of being a man."

Cal shoved his hands in the front pockets of his denims. "I wasn't scared or nothin' like that. I reckon I hadn't oughta admit it, but it sorta made me sick when I seen what I done. I wish I could be more like you, Mr. Jensen. I've seen what you done to bad men, like them boys who rode with Sundance Morgan. I seen how you stay calm, like it don't rattle you none when you kill somebody."

"It comes with time, Cal. You have to make up your

mind that it's them or you, or your friends. Some men seem to have a natural gift for fightin', like some others have a gift with breaking horses."

"It never did bother you right at first when you killed a man?"

He thought about it a moment. "I suppose I'd already made up my mind that it had to be done, that there wasn't any other way. There's some men who need killin'. They break the law and bring harm to other folks who can't defend themselves. I never went out lookin' for a man to kill. Seems like they always found me, one way or another, and I've been willing to oblige 'em when it was a fight they wanted."

"You're the best at it I ever saw, Mr. Jensen, but to tell the truth I don't think it's my natural callin'. You taught me how to shoot, an' how to look out for myself. I'm real grateful for that. When I looked down at that dyin' Indian, somethin' in my head said maybe it was wrong, even though he had a rifle an' he was shootin' at us. I can't explain it proper . . ."

"Some men ain't cut out for killing, Cal. You know how to do it when it's necessary, and that can be a good thing, so you can defend what's yours if somebody tries to take it. I think you realized for the first time how final death is, after you took another man's life. Understandable, to feel that way. It may keep you from becoming a killer yourself, unless you've got a good reason to kill."

"But you've killed plenty of men and it don't seem to bother you none. Leastways, you don't show it."

Smoke turned back toward the fire. Cal would understand the incident today, given time. "I never killed a man who didn't ask for the opportunity. The Apache you shot knew it could turn out either way . . . he'd lose his life, or you'd lose yours. He took a gamble, a calculated risk, and he lost. You did yourself proud, and you may have saved a friend's life because of it . . . even mine if the Indian had gotten lucky."

"I hadn't thought of it quite like that," Cal said. "Maybe it wasn't so bad after all, what I did today."

Lincoln Township was a little place, two stores and a blacksmith's shop and a few smaller businesses, a two-story courthouse near the Rio Hondo, surrounded by the Capitan Mountains. When Smoke and his cowboys rode into town on an April afternoon, the village was in an uproar, and it wasn't long until Smoke learned from a blacksmith that two funerals were about to commence.

"Billy Bonney an' some of his friends gunned down Sheriff Brady an' his deputy, George Hindeman. It was retaliation for the murder of John Tunstall, pure an' simple. Billy the Kid, as they call him, led the attack. The governor is puttin' out a warrant for his arrest, along with them others. We's fixin' to have two funerals today, the sheriff's and his deputy's."

Smoke didn't care to hear all the details. "Can you give us directions to John Chisum's ranch?" he asked.

"East of here. It's called South Springs ranch an' that's where you'll find him. It's a day's ride. Can't miss it. It's on the west bank of the Pecos River."

Smoke gave the town a final look. People were standing in groups talking among themselves as two funeral wagons waited at the end of the street near the courthouse and a tiny church. "Thanks," was all Smoke said, wheeling his horse eastward to ride out of Lincoln. The shootings weren't any of his affair.

Pearlie had a twinkle in his eye when he looked at Smoke, then he spoke to Cal. "Like I said not too long ago, young 'un, where there's trouble, you'll usually find Smoke Jensen. Either it comes lookin' fer him, or we ride smack into it. First thing a man learns when he rides for the Sugarloaf brand is to keep his guns cleaned an' loaded. I knowed things was too quiet this past winter. Ain't hardly spring yet an' here we are, square in the middle of a range war."

* * *

John Chisum was a towering figure at six-foot-four in boots, with a square jaw and slitted eyes, with suspicion in them when Smoke and his riders arrived at South Springs ranch. There were men wearing guns near the barns and corrals, a seedy-looking lot for the most part, paid shootists if ever Smoke laid eyes on one. It seemed every one of them was watching Smoke and his men ride in to the ranch.

Smoke swung down and walked up to Chisum, offering his hand. "Name's Smoke Jensen, from Big Rock, Colorado Territory. I wrote you awhile back and you sent me prices on some Hereford bulls."

Chisum's expression changed to friendliness. "Of course, Mr. Jensen. I remember now. You were interested in a dozen to fifteen young bulls, as I recall. I quoted you a price of two hundred dollars each and the offer still stands." He turned to a pockmarked gunman leaning against a porch post. "It's okay, Buck. Tell the boys they can relax an' go back to work. These men are invited guests." He looked back at Smoke. "Tell your men to turn their horses into an empty corral an' then come to the house. I'll offer you coffee or whiskey or both, an' a bite to eat as soon as Maria can get the stove going."

"We're grateful. It's been a long ride," Smoke said as he gave his horse's reins to Pearlie.

Chisum frowned a bit. "Did you run into any difficulties on the way down?"

"A handful of renegade Apaches gave us a try a few days ago, but we handled it."

As Smoke was climbing the porch steps, Chisum gave the hills a sweeping glance. "In case you haven't heard, we're having our share of problems in Lincoln County, only it isn't Indians who are causing it. Cattle rustling has gotten so bad I've had to hire guards to watch my herds. There've been a number of killings, and I've lost almost a dozen men. A rancher friend of mine was murdered in cold blood, and just yesterday our sheriff and one of his deputies were gunned down. The army post over at Fort Stanton won't do anything to stop all this killing, and I fear it will only get worse. The territorial governor, Lew Wallace, may be our only hope of ending what amounts to all-out war."

"We've heard a little bit about it," Smoke said, following Chisum into a big log house decorated inside with mounted cattle horns and colorful Indian blankets nailed to the walls. Leather chairs sat around a massive fireplace and Chisum pointed to one as he went to a cabinet for a bottle of whiskey and glasses.

"You were lucky you didn't ride into a cross fire," Chisum said, pouring Smoke a shot of whiskey, "and I'll warn you to be careful heading back with any cattle you buy from me. We've got rustlers and gunmen riding all over the county stealing cows and killin' folks." He glanced down at Smoke's pair of pistols. "I can see you and your men are well armed, but you'd better know how to use the iron you're packing."

"We can handle ourselves, I think," Smoke replied before he tasted his drink, finding it to be good sour mash, not the cheap watered stuff.

"Glad to hear it," Chisum said, settling into a chair. "If you're lucky, you won't run into any troublemakers."

"Never was real lucky in that regard," Smoke told him, "but if trouble comes our way, I know what to do with it."

Chisum chuckled, reading Smoke's face closely now. "I'm a pretty good judge of men, Mr. Jensen, and I don't figure that's any exaggeration. Some gents send out a warning to other men by the way they carry themselves. While we don't know each other, I'm pretty sure I'd hate to tangle with you if you got mad."

Smoke grinned. He took an immediate liking to Chisum. "I'm looking forward to seeing those bulls. And if the price is right, I'd like to buy about two hundred young longhorn cows to cross 'em on."

Chisum nodded. "I'll give you your pick of my longhorn heifers for twenty-five bucks apiece."

"That's a fair price if they're in good flesh. We've got to drive 'em a long way, so they'll need to be in good trail condition."

"You'll be well satisfied," Chisum assured him, downing his drink in a single gulp. "A Hereford is a good cross on a longhorn. More meat, and the calves are almost disease free. The Hereford breed is the thing of the future in the cattle market, as far as I'm concerned."

"My wife's been reading up on 'em and she says the same thing," Smoke said. "We're just hoping they take well to colder country."

"They do, and they can handle the heat in summer. If they have faults, it's that they're short-legged creatures, so they don't trail as well as a longhorn, and a purebred Hereford is subject to pinkeye in hot weather sometimes."

These were some of the same things Sally had told him about Herefords. Smoke was glad to find that Chisum was being honest about his bulls. He decided Chisum would make a good neighbor and friend, if they lived closer. Chisum would be a good man to ride the trails with . . . he had character. "Soon as the boys get a drink in 'em, I'd like to see those bulls," he said.

Chisum stood up and poured another round. "I'll tell Maria to get the stove hot and fix something for everybody to eat. We can go down to the barns and look at those bulls anytime you're ready."

18

Billy Barlow came galloping up to the log cabin at Bosque Redondo on a lathered, winded horse. He jumped to the ground, seemingly out of breath himself even though his horse had done all the traveling.

"Could be trouble, Jessie," he said to Jessie Evans. Billy had been assigned to watch the Chisum ranch for cattle buyers, and to see if Chisum was hiring any more gunmen.

"How's that?" Jessie asked.

"Seven riders leadin' spare horses just showed up at Chisum's. I had my field glasses on 'em when they come along the road from Lincoln. They was all carryin' guns, plenty of 'em, an' I'm pretty sure I know who one of 'em is."

"Who is he?" Jessie asked, not really interested since he didn't trust Barlow's judgment in these matters.

"A feller from up in Colorado Territory by the name of Smoke Jensen."

"The name don't mean nothin' to me."

"Maybe it oughta. I spent a little time up there workin' on a ranch. Smoke Jensen is one bad hombre with a six-gun. Up in them parts damn near everybody knows him. He's a killer, Jessie, an honest to goodness killer. He's got about the meanest reputation a man can have, an' there was six more rode in with him."

Jessie leaned forward on the bench where he sat watching men change cattle brands in the corrals. He didn't figure Barlow was good enough with a gun to know much about gunmen. Since William Bonney and some of his friends had ambushed Sheriff Brady and Deputy Hindeman, he'd been thinking of a way to strike back. It was a cowardly way to kill two men, hiding behind a fence until they came into range, gunning them down without warning. Bonney and his young friends were calling themselves Regulators now and someone said they were wearing badges authorized by an old justice of the peace, Judge Wilson. Their badges didn't mean a damn thing, and Bonney and his green companions were nothing to worry about, but if Chisum was importing more professional gunmen like Curly Tully and Buck Andrews, this was another matter. "I'll send Roy Cooper an' six of them Mexican *pistoleros* back with you. You show Roy who this Jensen feller is. If Jensen an' his pardners leave the Chisum ranch for any reason, Roy'll know what to do. Saddle a fresh horse an' tell Roy I want to see him. Before this Smoke Jensen causes us any trouble, we'll kill him. It's as simple as that."

Barlow seemed uncertain. "I wasn't jokin', boss, when I said this feller is dangerous. Maybe you oughta send some more men with Roy."

"I'm runnin' this outfit," Jessie declared angrily. "You tell Roy I want him, an' tell them Mexicans to saddle horses up as quick as they can. Show Roy who this Jensen feller is . . . point him out through them field glasses when you get a chance. That makes eight of us an' seven of them, and as far as I'm concerned, Roy is better'n any three men with a gun. Maybe Jensen's just passin' through. No need to get yourself so worked up over one man's reputation."

Barlow backed away in the face of Jessie's anger, leading his horse toward the corrals. Jessie leaned back against the cabin wall, pulling a cork from the neck of a tequila bottle.

Bill Pickett appeared to have been dozing at the other end of the porch with his hat over his face. But as Jessie took a swallow of tequila, Pickett sat up straight, watching Barlow as he went looking for Cooper.

"Barlow may be right," Pickett said. "Maybe you oughta send more men. I'll go. Hell, I ain't shot nobody in so long, I plumb forgot what it's like to see a man die. All we're doin' is sittin' around this stinkin' cow camp waitin' for somethin' to happen."

"I don't put much stock in what Barlow said about this Jensen bein' a real shooter. Maybe Jensen just stopped by the ranch to say howdy. Either way, if he leaves Chisum's, Roy'll make sure he don't go noplace else. Barlow ain't all that good with a gun himself, so ain't no reason why he'd know if a man was one of the best. You stay here. We'll go lookin' for that Billy Bonney an' his friends in a day or two. If we kill 'bout a half dozen of them so-called Regulators, it'll help square things for what they did to Sheriff Brady an' Hindeman. We can't let a thing like that go unpunished, or afore you know it every son of a bitch in Lincoln County will be wearin' a badge."

"Well, damn," Pickett muttered, leaning back against the wall with his hat over his face. "I was tryin' to remember if I'd ever killed anybody named Jensen before, which I ain't. Not that I recall anyways. There ain't always time to ask a feller's name before you blow him to pieces."

"Be patient, Bill," Jessie said. "You can kill that Bonney kid instead."

Down at the corrals, men were running back and forth leading horses to the saddle shed. Roy Cooper came ambling up to the cabin with his rifle balanced in his palm.

"Barlow said we's supposed to head fer Chisum's an' blow hell outta some owlhoot named Smoke Jensen," he said.

"Barlow claims he's a shooter," Jessie said, "from up in Colorado Territory. Him an' six more just rode in at Chisum's place. Take those five Mexicans ridin' with Pedro an' see if you can kill this Jensen an' his pardners, if they leave the ranch. If they stay, keep an eye on 'em. Find out what Chisum's up to. If he's hirin' more guns, we need to know."

Cooper frowned. "This ain't no way to fight a war, Jessie. Hell, we've got damn near thirty men as it is. How come we don't ride over to Chisum's an' kill him an' every last one of them sons of bitches?"

"Orders from Dolan. We kill 'em off a few at a time an' it don't make so much ruckus. Just take care of Jensen an' his men till we get word from Dolan that things have changed. I figure them kids killin' Brady and Hindeman will touch off the boys up in Santa Fe. They've got the purse strings, so we do what they say. After all, Roy, you ain't no different from me. We're only in this for the money . . ."

"This Jensen's as good as dead," Roy promised, wheeling away from the porch.

Jessie felt better about things now.

19

Smoke rested his elbows on a corral pole admiring a group of curious, stocky young bulls with sorrel bodies and white heads, a pair of short, curved horns, and more meat than he had ever seen on a cow.

"They're more than I expected," he told John Chisum, wishing Sally could see these impressive specimens of beef cattle for herself right now. "They carry more muscle across the hindquarter all the way up their backs to their chests. If the crosses are even half this good, it'll mean a bigger profit for every calf we sell."

"I'll show you some of the crosses when we ride out in the pastures," Chisum said. "You won't be disappointed. You're looking at the future of the cattle business."

"I'd like to see those crosses," Smoke said, pulling away from the fence. His men were lounging on Chisum's front porch after a delicious meal of beefsteak, tortillas, beans, and rice. "My boys and neighbors look damn near foundered after all that food. You and me can ride out to look at the crossbreds while my bunch recovers from Maria's good cooking."

Chisum grinned. "Let's saddle a couple of horses," he said as they turned for the barns. "I've got a bunch of crossbred steers close to the house in a pasture north of here. It's less than a half hour ride."

"Sounds good to me," Smoke replied, thinking of pastures at Sugarloaf filled with white-faced cattle in a few years. "Just so you'll know, I'll take fifteen of those bulls. A few are for my neighbors, who aim to start the same breeding program. If you got no objections, we'll pick the bulls and roughly two hundred longhorn heifers tomorrow morning. I brought cash, so you'll be paid on the spot."

"Then we've got a deal," Chisum said, offering Smoke his hand as a way of sealing their bargain.

The crossbreds all had white faces. Some were brindle in body color, while others were spotted like many longhorns, or a solid black or brown. The steers they saw were long yearlings, born last year, and they carried more beef than Smoke had imagined. Riding across a narrow, tree-studded valley turning green with spring grass, they rode among the gentle cattle without disturbing them. At the far end of the valley, a pair of Chisum cowboys kept watch over the herd. Smoke noted they were carrying rifles and pistols as if they expected trouble.

"Your cowhands go heavily armed," he said. "Too bad you're havin' all these problems with rustling. Seems to me like the law would step in."

Chisum's jaw went tight. "The law 'round here is mostly a bunch of crooks wearing badges, taking bribes from powerful men up in the territorial capital at Santa Fe. They looked the other way when I got robbed, for the most part. Now and then they go through the motions, investigating any rustling. That leaves it up to me to protect my own interests if I want to stay in business."

"So you've hired your own gunmen," Smoke observed. "I guess it makes sense if it's the only way."

"I feel I've got no choice, unless our new governor takes some action. Things have gotten so far out of hand it isn't safe to ride my own land any longer. These rustlers get more brazen as time passes, when nothing official is done about them. I'm hoping all that will change this summer. But if it doesn't, I intend to fight fire with fire. I've hired two experienced manhunters . . . Buck Andrews and Curly Tully. If I lose one more cow or one more ranch hand, I'm sending them after whoever is responsible. I'm through sitting on the fence waiting for the law to come to my rescue. I'm taking things into my own hands."

"That'd be my way of handlin' it," Smoke agreed as they rode to a pine-covered ridge at the north end of the valley. "I'm a real firm believer in takin' an eye for an eye."

"You'll need to watch the cattle you purchase from me very closely until you get out of this area," Chisum warned. "They won't spare your herd if they think they can take it."

Now it was Smoke's jaw tightening a little. "Let 'em try," he said quietly as they neared the trees where the last groups of crossbred steers grazed peacefully.

It was a sudden glint of sunlight on metal up on the ridge that made Smoke twist in the saddle, one hand reflexively going for a holstered Colt. "Watch out!" he snapped, eyes glued to the spot. "Somebody's up there with a gun."

Chisum wheeled his horse for the closest tree. "Get to some cover!" he yelled, wasted breath since Smoke was already heeling his borrowed horse in the same direction.

Almost at the same instant, a rifle cracked somewhere above them. A piñon branch snapped above Smoke's head just as they rode into the pines.

"Stay here an' draw their fire!" Smoke bellowed, jerking his other pistol free, caught up in a rush of white-hot rage over the attempt to drygulch them.

He drove his spurs into the ribs of Chisum's bay gelding, beginning a full-tilt charge toward the top of the ridge without knowing how many men he faced. . . . At the moment he didn't give a damn. Smoke was hell-bent on teaching a bushwhacker some manners as he reined his galloping horse among the trees upslope. He heard a pistol bark behind him. . . . Chisum was drawing their fire with his big Walker Colt .44.

Smoke saw a man kneeling with a rifle to his shoulder, hiding behind the trunk of a piñon. Steadying his pistol, despite the gait of a running horse underneath him, Smoke snapped off a quick shot at fifty yards.

A splash of crimson flew from the rifleman's left ear as he was turning toward the sound of a speeding horse. The bushwhacker's rifle discharged harmlessly in the air as he spun away from the tree with blood squirting from his skull.

Another movement caught Smoke's attention, a stocky Mexican in a drooping sombrero turning a rifle in Smoke's direction. As the Mexican readied for a shot, Smoke fired a roaring pistol shot aimed at his chest.

The Mexican staggered backward, dropping his Winchester to clutch his breastbone, where a dark red hole suddenly appeared in his soiled white shirtfront. Drumming his spurs into the bay's sides, Smoke raced toward another shadowy shape in the dense pine forest, bending low over his horse's neck, aiming as best he could with the bounding strides of the bay throwing his gunsights off a fraction.

The outline of another Mexican gunman became clear enough for a tricky shot and Smoke took it, hearing the roar of his .44 fill his ears, a wisp of blue gunsmoke curling past his face.

A sombrero-clad figure jerked upright next to a thick pine trunk, reaching for his shoulder, moving into plain sight just long enough for Smoke to fire again. A cry of pain filled the forest around them as Smoke pulled his bay to a sliding stop at the edge of a piñon thicket, leaping to the ground before the horse came to a complete halt. . . . He had no way of knowing how many more men were hidden along this ridge, and now it was time to hunt them down individually, stalking them until he was certain no one else was there.

The third man he'd shot slumped to the ground, groaning. Off in the distance, maybe a hundred yards further down the ridge, he heard voices, men yelling to each other in rapid Spanish, at least two more gunmen who would pay dearly for trying to ambush him and Chisum.

Smoke crept forward, both pistols at the ready, his anger slowly cooling to a more calculated revenge. Moving on the balls of his feet, he advanced toward the sound of voices. His horse trotted back downhill to escape the noise of guns. Darting from tree to tree, never knowing where another attacker might be, he heard the drum of pounding hoofbeats coming from the back side of the ridge, a lone horseman escaping the battle, apparently running out of nerve.

Soundlessly, he stepped across beds of fallen pine needles, keeping to the shadows wherever he could. Now all was quiet along the ridge. . . . The voices had stopped.

A moment later, he heard another horse take off at a gallop, and he wondered if the last bushwhacker had pulled out, until he caught a glimpse of a running man, a Mexican wearing a sombrero, carrying a rifle.

It was a difficult target, requiring Smoke to steady his Colt against a tree trunk. When he fired, the report echoed back and forth throughout the pines, accompanied by a yell as the potbellied Mexican went facedown, legs still pumping, trying to crawl.

Staying behind trees, Smoke hurried over to the wounded man, who left a blood trail over dry pine needles and yellowed winter grass beginning to turn green near its roots. The Mexican had a flesh wound across his ribs. Before Smoke knelt beside him, he gave the forest a close examination, until he was satisfied they were alone.

He put the muzzle of a Colt against the Mexican's right temple and spat out a question. "Who sent you? You've got just one chance to answer before I scatter your brains all over this ridge."

"Jessie," the Mexican hissed, clenching his teeth against the pain. "Jessie . . . Evans."

Smoke didn't recognize the name, although it wouldn't

have mattered anyway. "You ain't hurt all that bad, Pancho, or whatever your name is. Get on your horse an' ride back to this Jessie Evans. Tell him if he ever messes with Smoke Jensen or any of my friends again, I'll come lookin' for him and I'll kill him. I want you to make that real clear. My friends and me are ridin' back to Colorado with a herd of cattle in a couple of days. If I lose so much as one cow or one bull, I'm gonna come lookin' for Jessie. There won't be no place in New Mexico Territory that's safe from me if anything happens to my cows or my friends. I've got no stake in this range war, but I'll goddamn sure take a hand in it if one more shot gets fired in my direction, or if I lose a single head of livestock. Understand, Pancho?"

The Mexican nodded, glancing sideways to the gun Smoke held to his head. "Sí, señor. I will tell Jessie."

Smoke wasn't quite satisfied yet. "I killed three of your partners just now, an' put a little gash across your ribs 'cause you were lucky. Don't count on bein' lucky the next time. Tell Jessie Evans what I said."

"Sí, señor. I swear I will tell him."

"I imagine Evans figures he's pretty tough, pretty good with a gun. He can go on believin' that if he wants, only be sure an' tell him he's never crossed paths with Smoke Jensen before. If he does it again, I'll fill him so goddamn full of bullet holes he won't have to take his pecker out to piss, 'cause he's gonna be leakin' all the time."

"I will tell him you are one bad hombre, señor. I have seen this . . . for myself."

Smoke lowered his Colt, lifted the Mexican's pistol out of his gunbelt, and took his rifle before he stood up cautiously to check his surroundings. Then he spoke to the Mexican again in a voice like ice. "I don't really figure it'll do any good to give Jessie that warning, but I'm doin' it anyway, just in case he's got more sense than most. Men who think they're tough usually have to be proven wrong. You can tell him Smoke Jensen is just the man who can get that job done. If it's a fight he wants, I'm the man he's lookin' for."

John Chisum lowered his pistol when he saw Smoke riding down to the cattle pasture. He waited until Smoke rode up to him to speak. Both Chisum cowboys guarding the herd had ridden up to the north end of the pasture with guns drawn.

"I heard all the shooting," Chisum said. "You must have scared them off. I stayed put, not knowing whether I'd be in your line of fire. When these boys rode up, we were about to head up this slope, when all of a sudden, the shooting ended."

"You'll find three dead Mexicans up there in those trees," Smoke said. "I reckon somebody oughta bury 'em an' notify their next of kin. I wounded another bushwhacker and we had a little talk before I let him go. He told me he works for a man by the name of Jessie Evans. . . ."

"He's the ramrod of Jimmy Dolan's gang of rustlers," Chisum said bitterly, "only I can't prove a thing and nobody in official circles will look into it. Evans is a paid killer from down in Texas someplace." Chisum stared at Smoke a moment. "You said you killed three of them all by your lonesome?"

Smoke began reloading his pair of Colts. "Mexican *pistoleros,* by the look of 'em. I've tangled with their kind before."

"You must be one hell of a gunman yourself, Mr. Jensen. I'd like to offer you a job, if you're interested."

"My guns ain't for hire," he replied, closing the loading gate on an ivory-handled .44 before he holstered it. "But I did send Jessie Evans a little message, by way of his wounded sidekick. I told him if one more bullet came at me or my men, or if I lost a single cow on my way back to Colorado, I'd come lookin' for him, and that I'd kill him."

"Evans won't scare easy," Chisum declared.

Smoke gave the crossbred steers another look as he

said, "I wasn't meanin' to scare him, Mr. Chisum. I meant every goddamn word. Whoever this Jessie Evans is, he'll be a dead son of a bitch if he tests me on it. Now, if you're ready, let's take a look at those young longhorn cows you're offering for sale."

20

Billy Barlow glanced over his shoulder as his horse ran up a steep incline. Another horseman was gaining ground on him. Was it the broad-shouldered crazy man with two pistols, he wondered. He relaxed some when he recognized Pedro Lopez racing away from the scene of the shooting, the same as Billy had done when it became clear the man who rode with Chisum had no fear, no sense, like a locoed bronc, the way he'd charged up that mountain with both guns blazing.

Billy slowed his horse to a walk at the top of the climb to scan the trail behind Pedro. The lunatic with two guns was not following them. He waited for Pedro to catch up.

Pedro's horse was floundering under the punishment of spurs when Pedro rode up beside Billy.

"He ain't followin' you?" Billy asked, looking again at their backtrail, finding it empty.

"No," Pedro gasped, looking back himself. "*El hombre loco* is too busy killing Jorge and Carlos and Raul. This son of a bitch be *muy loco*, to come at us like that."

"He ain't just loco," Billy said. "He can goddamn sure shoot."

"*Verdad*, it is the truth," Pedro wheezed. "He come straight at us like *un idiota*. I never see a man so foolish as him before today."

"It's like he wasn't afraid of our guns at all."

Pedro mopped his brow with a bandanna, glancing back again to look for dust or any sign of the stranger. "I see Roy Cooper ride off very fast when this *idiota* come up the hill. He ride to the east. I don't understand. Cooper is loco himself, but he is also mean with a gun. But he don't stay when this stranger come shooting. He run away, like he know this hombre don't be right in his head."

"I didn't see which way Cooper went," Billy said. "I was too busy lookin' out for my own ass. That guy, whoever he is, can't have a lick of sense to charge us like that all by himself with just two pistols. He's either dumb as a rock, or nearly the meanest bastard who ever stood in a pair of boots."

"Maybe so Cooper go back to get him when he think we all go away," Pedro suggested.

"I ain't so damn sure," Billy replied. "Maybe Mr. Roy Cooper ain't as tough as we think he is. He lit out of there like his tailfeathers was afire."

Pedro shrugged. "Who can say? I see Cooper shoot those cowboys in the night like he enjoy it."

"Maybe he don't enjoy it so much when somebody's shootin' back at him."

"Señor Jessie be plenty mad when he hear this," Pedro said, as though he were speaking to himself.

"Then let *him* face this crazy son of a bitch. We'll tell him he'd better bring Pickett an' every spare gun he's got if he aims to kill that big bastard. I got a feelin' this guy ain't gonna be easy to kill."

"Is the truth," Pedro muttered, looking over his shoulder yet another time. "I don't see Victor. Maybe so this hombre kill him too."

"You're right about one thing," Billy added as he urged his horse to a lope. "Jessie sure as hell ain't gonna like this when we give him the news."

Roy Cooper lay on his belly in tall grass near the mouth of the valley, putting his rifle sights on the square-shouldered cowboy who came at them earlier. He was riding beside Chisum and his ranch hands like a man who didn't have a care in the world. Roy knew the others were either dead or they'd deserted him, which was typical of Mexican gunmen—short on courage when things got tight.

The range for his Winchester .44 was still too great to be sure of the shot, and thus Roy waited, holding his rifle against his shoulder, doing his best to keep the barrel from catching sunlight that might warn the riders below of his presence. He was sure he could take down the newcomer when the distance was right.

The stranger's head turned toward the grassy hilltop where Roy lay, but only for a moment. "He didn't see me," Roy whispered. Then the stranger did an odd thing. . . . He got down off his horse and walked into a line of trees while the others halted to wait for him.

"He needed to piss," Roy told himself. "He's too bashful to pull his pecker out while everybody's watchin'. Maybe I can get him when he walks out of them pines. . . ."

Time seemed frozen, although it did seem to be taking the stranger a hell of a long time to let his water down. Roy was motionless, his rifle aimed for the spot where the stranger went into the trees, judging his chances of a quick kill with just one slug.

Minutes passed. "Maybe he's takin' a shit," Roy wondered softly. The others, including Chisum, sat their horses in clear view as though nothing was wrong, never once looking up at Roy's hiding place.

A sound behind him, something brushing against the grasses, made him turn. Then a towering figure blocked out the sun. The glint of a huge knife blade flashed.

"Son of a . . ."

A blinding pain entered Roy's rib cage, along with a noise like snapping willow limbs. Cartilage was torn from his sternum by a single slash of a razor-sharp knifepoint. He heard himself scream, staring into a face twisted with hatred above him, and just as quickly, the scream died in his throat when a second swipe of the blade went across his windpipe, slicing through cords of muscle, ligaments, and skin.

"Die slow, you backshootin' bastard," a grating voice said quietly.

Roy's backbone arched, and he struggled to bring his gun up at the same time until a heavy boot landed on his wrist, knocking the rifle from his hand.

"You've got no balls, pilgrim. You're just another yellow son of a bitch who can't face the man he aims to kill. I've known half a hundred like you. I don't know your name, but it don't matter who you are. What you are is dead, only not yet, not till the ants feed on you for a spell, until your blood runs all over this hill."

Pain shot through Roy's body from head to toe and for a moment he was sure he would lose consciousness. He made a second attempt to sit up, choking on his own blood, strangling when it entered his windpipe.

"Wish you could live long enough to tell this Jessie Evans he's messin' with the wrong man. But you won't. You'll be dead in half an hour, maybe less."

Roy saw winking stars before his eyes, but he could still see the twisted face looming over him.

"Bleedin' to death is a helluva slow way to die, mister. I hope it don't hurt too awful bad. But if it does, think about all the cows you stole that wasn't yours, or the men you killed who never had a chance. Think about those things while you're dyin'. You ain't got long."

Roy fell back on the grass, unable to breathe at all now.

"Adios, cowboy, whoever you are," the same voice said as Roy slipped slowly into a black void.

Jessie watched two men ride in at a hard gallop with a vague sense of apprehension. He recognized Barlow and Lopez by their horses. "Somethin's wrong," he told Pickett.

Pickett came up from his bull hide chair, squinting in the sun's glare, cradling a shotgun in the crook of his arm.

"It's that Barlow boy an' Pedro Lopez. They's after their horses with a spur mighty hard."

"Wonder where Roy is," Jessie said. "It ain't like Roy to let 'em split up . . . 'less there's been trouble."

Billy and Pedro galloped their winded mounts up to the cabin, and Barlow was the first to speak.

"We got real problems," Barlow said, dropping to the ground in more of a hurry than Jessie felt was warranted. "This stranger showed up at Chisum's. We had it all laid out to kill him, only he come at us like a nest of hornets. He rode right up the ridge where we was hidin' an' started shootin' like a bullet was never gonna hit him. Roy Cooper took off in the other direction soon as it happened."

"Is true, Señor Jessie," Pedro agreed, climbing down from his lathered horse. "This stranger, he don't be afraid of nothing. He ride his horse toward us while we be shooting, and he don't act afraid."

Jessie stood up. "Where the hell is Roy?" he asked with a note of impatience. Roy Cooper had never run away from any man that Jessie knew of.

"He run away, just like Billy say," Pedro said. "He ride off like he be scared of this hombre."

"Nonsense. Roy ain't afraid of nobody."

Billy shrugged. "Can't explain what he did no other way, boss. He jumped on his horse an' rode east as fast as that brown gelding could travel."

"What happened to the others?" Jessie demanded.

"Maybe so all are dead," Pedro answered. "This big hombre, he come up shooting with two pistolas, one in each hand. He no be afraid of our guns."

Jessie's attention was distracted by another rider coming in at Bosque Redondo, a man slumped over his saddle like he was in a great deal of pain.

"Who's that?" Jessie asked.

Pedro looked over his shoulder. "It is Victor Busta-mante, and there is blood on his shirt."

"Ain't nobody gonna convince me Roy Cooper took

off when it was time for a killin'," Jessie stated. "See what the hell that Mexican has to say . . ."

Victor Bustamante rode his grullo gelding up to the cabin with obvious pain twisting his face. He stopped his horse in front of the porch. Blood was leaking from a wound across his right side, covering his right pants leg.

"I have . . . this message for you . . . Señor Jessie," he said in clipped, breathless words.

"What kind of goddamn message?" Jessie wanted to know, as he grew impatient with this latest bit of news.

"This hombre . . . he call himself Smoke Jensen. He say he gone kill you. . . . He say he come looking for you if we don't stop shoot at him."

Jessie's sun-etched face crinkled. "Who the hell is Smoke Jensen? I never heard of him."

"He be one *malo hombre*," Victor replied, still holding his side, wincing. "He kill Raul and Jorge real quick. Then he kill Carlos and he shoot this hole in me."

Jessie stiffened. "The son of a bitch said he was gonna kill me?" he asked in a voice that boomed all over the clearing where the cow camp was hidden. "You mean that arrogant son of a bitch had the nerve to say that?"

"Sí, Señor Jessie. He say he want me tell you how he kill you if anybody shoot at him or his compadres again. This be what he say to tell you."

Jessie glanced over at Pickett. "Who the hell is Smoke Jensen?"

"Never heard of the bastard," Pickett replied. "I'll go saddle a horse an' we'll see if he's as tough as he says he is."

"Where did this happen?" Jessie asked Billy.

"North of the Chisum ranch by maybe ten miles."

"An' you claim Roy took off runnin' when it happened?"

"Yessir. That's sure the way it looked. Roy jumped on his horse and rode east as fast as that pony could travel. Last we saw of him, he was headed for the Pecos River."

"That ain't like Roy. Maybe he was gonna ride a circle around 'em."

"It sure as hell didn't look that way, boss. Soon as Raul

an' Jorge got killed, Roy took off. He never fired a shot at this Jensen feller."

"Roy ain't no coward."

Billy shrugged. "Maybe he just knowed it when he was outgunned. That Jensen never wasted a bullet. He killed Raul so quick it was like they was standin' two feet apart. Then he shot Carlos an' Jorge, all of 'em from the back of a runnin' horse. I took off right after that, when I seen there wasn't no stoppin' this Jensen. He ain't no ordinary man."

Jessie scowled. "You ain't nothin' but a yellow son of a bitch, Barlow. Get your gear an' clear out of here. I'll have your wages ready."

Pickett lifted his shotgun and started down the porch steps two at a time. "I'll saddle a horse an' round up Ignacio, Billy, an' Tom. Let's see if this Jensen is as tough as he claims to be."

Jessie gazed across the corrals. "Tell those boys from up in Arkansas to ride along with us. Chisum may have hired himself a fancy shooter, only we'll see how good he is when the odds are against him. That one-eyed feller from Arkansas says he can hit a sparrow on the fly with a Sharps rifle. We'll let him show us how good he is."

Pickett ambled off toward the corrals, in no apparent hurry to get things started. Jessie looked at Billy. "Get your gear out of the bunkhouse, Barlow. You're finished with this outfit, an' if I ever lay eyes on you again, I'll kill you myself." He turned his attention to Victor. "Have somebody fix you a bandage for that scratch. Then get mounted on a fresh horse so you can show us where all this happened. Jensen could be dead by now, if Roy caught up with him. One thing you can bet on—Roy Cooper didn't run from no kind of fight."

21

Smoke heard horses coming up the hill as he wiped blood off his Bowie knife on the dying man's pants leg. Standing out in plain view, he knew Chisum and his cowboys could see him now, and they were riding up to see what had brought him here. . . . He'd only said to wait for him until he took care of a little unfinished business, without telling them a man was lying in ambush for them on this hilltop, just out of rifle range. Again, he'd seen a flash of polished metal in the sun as they were riding out of the valley, and he knew what it meant. There wasn't time to explain.

"What happened, Mr. Jensen?" Chisum asked just before his horse snorted, scenting blood as it trotted toward Smoke.

"We had another surprise waiting for us," Smoke replied as he sheathed his Bowie, "another gent who thought we'd ride right past his hiding place so he could shoot us down."

Now Chisum saw the body lying in a patch of tall, bloody grass near Smoke's feet. "Damn," he said, swinging off his red sorrel to get a better look.

One of Chisum's cowboys said, "That's Roy Cooper, another one of Dolan's hired guns. A feller told me Cooper had a real bad disposition, that he was a sure enough professional killer."

Smoke took a last look at Cooper. "He should have chosen another line of work. It's just one man's opinion, but it don't seem he was all that good at it."

Chisum was staring at Smoke with a bit of slack in his jaw. "You killed him with a knife. How come you didn't use a gun?" he asked. "You must have slipped up behind him."

Smoke walked over to the bay a Chisum cowboy brought up the hill, taking its reins. "He was real busy watchin' what was in front of him. It's a mistake a lot of men make before they wind up on Boot Hill."

Chisum watched Smoke mount his horse, still not quite ready to believe what he'd seen or heard. "For a big man, you sure as hell get around mighty quiet. It's hard to slip up on a man from behind like that. And all you had to do was shoot him. You'd have been within your rights, seeing as he was trying to kill us with a rifle."

Smoke was far more interested in the beefy carcasses of Chisum's crossbred Hereford steers right then, the incident with Cooper already pushed from his mind, even though the gunman was still alive, still breathing shallowly. Smoke gazed across the valley, thinking of cattle like these carrying a Sugarloaf brand. "I've got no choice but to agree with you, Mr. Chisum. Herefords represent the future of the cattle business out west. A longhorn's tough, and they can get by on poor pastures, but they don't carry the meat these crosses do. In a couple of years, I hope to have steers like those yonder ready for market."

Chisum shook his head and mounted his horse. "You're quite a puzzlement, Mr. Jensen. On the one hand you seem like a very knowledgeable cattleman, but when the shooting starts, you behave like a seasoned Indian fighter, or a trained soldier."

Smoke turned his horse toward the valley floor. "Sometimes a man has got to be a little of both," he said, "if he aims to hold on to what's his."

* * *

The night was clear and chilly, near forty degrees, as Smoke and Pearlie and Johnny and Bob Williams stood at the corral fence examining Chisum's Hereford bulls in the light of the moon. Cal and Cletus and Duke were inside the house enjoying another piece of Maria's chocolate pie.

Bob seemed a bit doubtful. "They look too short-legged to suit me," he said, "but they've damn sure got the meat on 'em. I reckon it's the crosses that count. Until a rail-head comes close to Big Rock, we've still got to drive our cattle to market a hell of a long way. A short-legged cow ain't gonna cover much ground in a day. But I'm ready to try a couple of bulls. That pretty little wife of yours done a lot of convincin' when we talked about Herefords last fall. Put me down for two of them young bulls." He glanced over to Smoke. "I sure hope we make it all the way home with 'em, Smoke. After what them two cowboys of Chisum's told us this evenin' about all the shootin' you did up north of here, I'm wonderin' if us or these cattle will ever see Big Rock country."

"There's always a risk, Bob," Smoke told him. "I never once got up in the mornin' with any guarantee I'd see the end of the day."

"I like our chances," Pearlie said, chewing on a piece of straw. "I ain't sayin' it's gonna be easy, but I still like our chances of gettin' home with these here stumpy bulls. One thing they ain't gonna do is outrun no horse."

Johnny North offered his opinion. "It's outrunnin' lead we have to worry about, with all these hired guns on the prowl."

Smoke heard a noise near the bunkhouse. Four of Chisum's men were unloading dead bodies wrapped in canvas tarps from the back of a wagon, arranging four corpses in a neat row near the front porch. "We'll make it," Smoke said tonelessly. "Let's get some shut-eye. To-morrow I'll pick out two hundred head of young cows for me and Sally's new herd. Then we'll be on our way."

Pearlie turned away from the fence, yawning. "It's been

a spell since we had a roof over our heads. I'm gonna sleep like a baby tonight in one of them rawhide cots."

"I'm ready to turn in," Johnny agreed. "Cal's gonna have a bellyache if he ain't careful. I never saw a boy his size eat so much in one sittin'."

Pearlie nodded as the four men ambled toward the bunkhouse. "I done told that boy he's got worms. Can't nobody eat that much without a bellyful of worms helpin' him."

Smoke gave the outlying black hills a passing inspection as they headed for bed. He wondered if the gunman named Jessie Evans had gotten word of what had happened to his crew of killers today. While he didn't know anything about Evans, he was certain a shootist with a reputation on the line wouldn't take any advice from a stranger . . . not until someone convinced him otherwise.

22

Boyd, Jack, and Lee Johnson were tobacco-chewing brothers from northwestern Arkansas, on the run from the law and Hanging Judge Isaac Parker's unyielding rope justice in his judicial district. Judge Parker had been known to hang three men at the same time, a fate the Johnson brothers had hoped to escape by coming to New Mexico Territory. Boyd, eldest of the three, had but one eye, having lost the other to an Arkansas Toothpick knife similar in size to a Bowie. Along with the Johnsons came two cousins with similar reputations. Dewey Hyde was wanted for murder, in both Arkansas and Mississippi. Marvin Hyde had warrants out for him in Missouri charging him with murdering a Methodist minister for what was in the collection plates on a Sunday morning. As a gang, they were considered a blight on the citizens of Arkansas by Judge Parker, who ordered a squad of United States deputy marshals to chase them halfway across Indian Territory. But individually, none was more dangerous than one-eyed Boyd Johnson, a burly man with a thick red beard and deadly aim with a rifle. When Boyd and his followers answered Jessie's call for experienced men who knew how to use a gun, it was a natural place for the Johnson brothers and the Hydes to show up.

As the hour approached midnight, Jessie led fourteen

mounted men into the hills west of John Chisum's South Springs ranch, all heavily armed. Jessie was still puzzled by the disappearance of Roy Cooper. . . . It just wasn't Cooper's nature to turn tail and run. Roy was utterly fearless in any kind of fight, whether it be with guns or knives or fists. Cooper wouldn't have left the scene of a shoot-out without good reason, a plan of some sort to exact his brand of vengeance against this owlhoot named Smoke Jensen for taking the lives of Carlos, Jorge, and Raul. What Victor described, with Jensen charging recklessly into their guns, had to be nothing more than blind luck. Or stupidity. No man with all his faculties charged single-handedly into the teeth of seven riflemen behind cover. Those were the actions of a madman.

When they could see the ranch down below, Jessie held up his hand for a halt. A light was burning behind the windows of Chisum's main house. The bunkhouse was dark.

"We'll throw a circle around 'em," Jessie explained, making a motion with his hand. "Catch 'em in a cross fire. Get as close as you can to that bunkhouse, 'cause that's where his paid guns are more likely to be. Pour lead into them windows an' kill every son of a bitch who comes out them doors. . . . There's one at the back leadin' to the outhouse. I'll take four men an' make a circle 'round the main house. Soon as the shootin' starts, Chisum will come runnin' out. One of us will get him an' that'll be the end of this cattle war for good."

"What'll Dolan say?" Tom asked. "He told us all we was supposed to do was rustle a few cattle an' kill a few cowboys if they put up a fight. He never said nothin' 'bout killin' Chisum outright."

"I'll tell him it was an accident, that Chisum got in the line of fire. Main thing is to be sure we get this feller Smoke Jensen. It's payback time for him. Victor said he was a real big feller, like Chisum, only he was wearing buckskins. Just be damn sure you kill him, whoever the hell he is. All that tough talk about him comin' gunnin' for me is gonna cost him. I'll cut off his goddamn head an' stick it on a fencepost at Bosque. Be a reminder to any son of a bitch who threatens me."

Boyd Johnson urged his horse alongside Jessie's, a Sharps rifle resting against his leg. "I'll git him fer you, boss. All I gotta do is git him in my sights jest once."

Jessie gave Boyd a sideways glance. "We're about to find out if you're as good as you claim to be. Kill Jensen, an' I'll talk to Dolan 'bout givin' you a little bonus money." He looked over his shoulder. "Take Victor with you so he can point him out in the dark. Just make damn sure you kill the son of a bitch, no matter what it takes." Now Jessie spoke softly to the rest of his men. "Spread out. Billy, you an' Tom an' Bill Pickett come with me. Everybody else covers that bunkhouse. I'll fire the first shot into one of them lighted windows at the big house. As soon as you hear it, start pourin' lead into the place."

Silent riders spread out in twos and threes, beginning a circle around the Chisum ranch headquarters. Jessie led his handpicked men down a grassy embankment, toward a stand of oak where they could tie their horses.

"I'm gonna enjoy this," Pickett said. "Wish it was daylight so we could see 'em bleed better."

Tom Hill spoke up again. "I sure hope Jimmy don't get mad over this. He said he was glad we killed Tunstall, so he didn't write no more complainin' letters. Hope he feels the same way if we kill John Chisum."

Jessie had some private doubts. Dolan wanted a controlled war that wouldn't draw too much attention in the newspapers up in Santa Fe or over in Silver City. But when Victor brought back that message from Jensen, it got Jessie's back up. "Ain't no son of a bitch gonna threaten me like Jensen did," he said. "I'll tell Jimmy that Chisum was hirin' too damn many gunslicks, an' we had to do somethin' about it."

Bill Pickett offered his opinion. "You worry too much, Tom. Dolan ain't payin' us to sit an' whittle on a stick."

They came to the trees and dismounted, taking rifles

and a few extra boxes of cartridges along. Pickett carried a Winchester and his shotgun, one in each hand, as they began a slow walk through the darkness toward Chisum's house, hunkered down to keep from being outlined against a night sky full of stars, in case Chisum had posted any guards.

"No dogs," Pickett said as they neared the house. "Means I can get close enough to use ol' Ten-Gauge Betsy."

Jessie felt his pulse begin to race. Like Pickett, he was looking forward to a killing spree. His men had been idle too long, and until today, when this Jensen started killing a few of his *pistoleros*, things had been too damn quiet to suit everybody at Bosque Redondo. It was hard to keep men who killed for a living content unless they were doing what they were being paid to do.

23

Smoke lay asleep beside an open bunkhouse window when something he couldn't identify disturbed his slumber. Several men across the room were snoring and for a moment he wondered what it was that had awakened him. Cletus Walker and Bob Williams were at the main house talking with Chisum over drinks, talking about the cattle market and some of Chisum's troubles with the Santa Fe Ring and L.G. Murphy and Jimmy Dolan. Smoke had retired early, preferring sleep to conversation after so many days on the trail. But now something had interrupted his sleep, something beyond the window above his bunk.

He sat up slowly, peering out at a moonlit ranch yard and the hills beyond. A vague uneasy sensation warned him something was amiss, yet he was unable to see or hear anything out of the ordinary.

Swinging his legs off the bed, he put on his boots and took his gunbelts from a bedpost, and as an added precaution, he picked up his Winchester, after strapping both cartridge belts around his waist.

He crept to the back door and opened it softly, waiting for his eyes to adjust to the darkness. He was startled when he heard a soft whisper behind him.

"What is it?" Pearlie asked, sitting up.

The pockmarked gunfighter named Buck Andrews

said, "I heard somethin' too, like horses." He swung his legs off the bunk beside Pearlie's to nudge a gunman named Curly Tully, who was in a deep sleep, snoring in the next bunk. "Wake up, Curly. I'd take an oath I heard somethin' outside. Git up and fetch yer guns."

Tully raised his head off the pillow and shook it. "Maybe you was only dreamin'," he said sleepily.

"Wasn't no dream," Andrews told him. "It was horses."

Smoke let his gaze roam back and forth looking for a shape that didn't belong. It was too dark to be sure of anything at a distance. "Might be a good idea if you woke everybody up," he said a moment later, when it appeared something scurried across the crest of a hill behind the bunkhouse, perhaps only a wolf or a coyote. "If this is part of that bunch we tangled with today, they'll be lookin' for revenge. Get these men out of the bunkhouse and have 'em spread out around the corrals and barns. I'll go warn Mr. Chisum that something ain't right out yonder. First of all, it's too damn quiet. That's damn near always a bad sign in my experience. Make sure nobody shoots unless we get shot at first. I'll see if I can find out who it is, or if it's anything at all."

Andrews got up while Pearlie pulled on his boots. He woke Cal up and whispered, "Git dressed, youngun. Smoke says he thinks we may have us some company."

Andrews went down the rows of cots, awakening cowboys, while Smoke edged out the rear doorway, his senses keened. He could almost smell trouble coming on a soft night wind blowing across the ranch.

Moving quietly in the shadow of the eaves, where the bunkhouse roof ended, he made his way to a corner and waited, hidden by the shadow until he crossed the ranch yard to a windmill tower and a water trough, crouching down, unable to shake the feeling that someone was out there in the hills. He could hear sleepy men stirring in the bunkhouse.

He stepped lightly along the front porch and tapped on the door, watching the moonlit hills.

"Who is it?" a deep voice belonging to Chisum inquired, a note of concern in his question.

"Smoke Jensen. I think we've got some night visitors off to the west. Maybe north of us too."

Chisum swung the door open. "I'll get my rifle and wake up the men."

"Buck Andrews is already gettin' 'em up. I told 'em to spread out around the corrals and barns. I'll slip out there to see if it's just my imagination. I told everybody to hold their fire unless someone shoots at us first. And it'd be a good idea to douse that lantern."

Cletus appeared behind Chisum and Smoke was about to leave the porch to scout around.

"What is it, Smoke?" Cletus asked.

"I ain't sure it's anything yet. Just grab a rifle in case we got company."

The lantern inside went out as Smoke crept off the porch to make his way to a split rail fence around ranch headquarters, an open stretch of ground that could be dangerous to cross, yet he was without choices. Hunkered down, he raced across the yard in the bright moonlight, knowing an experienced gunman would see the gleam of metal from his rifle.

A booming shot from a large-bore gun thundered from a grassy hilltop, the wink of a muzzle flash pinpointing the shooter's location. A split pine log on the top rail of the fence in front of Smoke most certainly saved his life from a heavy rifle slug, probably a .52 caliber, as the bullet splintered wood only a few inches from Smoke's face, splitting the dry log almost in half.

He dove to the ground, crawling beneath the bottom rail as fast as he could toward clumps of foot-high prairie grass that would hide him.

"Mr. Evans got my message, no doubt," Smoke hissed between gritted teeth, feeling his mind-set change suddenly, back to the savagery that had been a part of his nature in years past. Now, with a single-mindedness he could never fully explain to Sally, he would become a manhunter on a killing rampage. Something even he wasn't able to comprehend took control of him, his thoughts, his actions, a lust for killing in any way possible, after someone made an attempt to take his life. Until it was over, his mind was a blank, his conscience without a voice, focused only on finding and killing his enemies. Afterward, he sometimes pondered on what it was that overtook him at times like this, when all reason and concern for his personal safety were discarded. All that mattered now was killing, silencing the gun on the hilltop . . . and he was sure there would be more guns out there, waiting for their opportunity to arrive.

Boyd Johnson knew he'd missed. "It was that damn fence," he whispered to his brother Lee. "I'll git the sumbitch next time, soon as he shows hisself."

A rifle cracked from a hilltop north of the ranch, and then a chorus of gunfire erupted from every direction. Answering guns thundered from barns and hay sheds and deep shadows all across the ranch headquarters.

"They was expectin' us!" Lee shouted above the roar of so many guns.

"Shut up, little brother!" Boyd snapped. "You's gonna tell that bastard right where we is!"

Boyd waited, aiming down at the fence where he'd last seen the big fellow, bare-chested, wearing buckskin leggings. "That was him," he muttered angrily. "I had the sumbitch dead in my sights till he come to that goddamn fence. I know one thing fer sure 'bout this Jensen feller— he's damn sure lucky, or he'd be dead as a pig right now."

The crackle of exploding rifles filled the night with sound, making Boyd uneasy. It helped to have keen hearing when a man was stalking about in the dark with a gun, but gunfire was drowning out every other noise, making it impossible to hear footsteps, the snap of a twig, or the brush of grasses against a man's boots.

"How come you ain't shootin', Boyd?" Lee asked, as minutes dragged by without Boyd firing a shot, which caused Lee to keep his gun silent too.

"Nothin' to shoot at yet," Boyd answered. "No sense in lettin' 'em know where we are till we got us a target we know we can hit. Let them others waste ammunition. Remember what Pa told us when we was kids huntin' squirrels—Make every shot count, 'cause gunpowder an' shot is expensive." Scanning the spot where he'd last seen the gent he believed to be Jensen, it was hard to figure where such a big feller could be hiding.

Something tapped him on the sole of his right boot, and Boyd whirled around, focusing his lone functioning eye on the outline of a bare-chested man holding a pair of pistols. "How the hell did you . . . ?" he exclaimed, as both six-guns belched stabbing fingers of yellow flame.

Something cracked against Boyd's forehead, slamming his head to the ground with the force of a mule's kick. He heard Lee let out a scream as lightning bolts of pain shot through his skull in great waves. His vision blurred as he caught a glimpse of the man who had shot him and his brother, and damned if he could explain why the bastard seemed to be grinning just seconds before everything went black. He felt his body floating off the ground and he could not explain the sensation. . . . Bodies didn't float. But he was thankful that now, his terrible pain was fading away.

Dewey Hyde pumped seven slugs through his Winchester in a fit of rage, knowing he'd hit nothing with any of his bullets. Spittle dribbled down into his beard when he forgot to spit with a wad of chewing tobacco in his left cheek, thus he spat and took seven more shells from his pocket, pushing them into the loading gate to fill its cartridge chamber. As the roar of gunfire came from all directions, he wondered idly if Marvin was having any better luck in the ravine below, to the west. This kind of a fight didn't suit Dewey, not when he couldn't see who he was shooting at so far away in the dark.

"Turn around, creep," someone said behind him. "I want to see your ugly face before I blow it off your skull."

Dewey made a quick half turn, swallowing tobacco juice in his haste and fear, bringing his rifle around for a shot at the owner of the strangely calm voice in the middle of a deadly gun battle like this. He saw a squatting figure, muscles bunched in his bare chest, aiming two pistols at him from only a few yards away.

Before Dewey could aim, he heard a noise, an explosion, and in the same instant something akin to a red-hot poker entered the soft flesh beneath his chin—he was sure he could feel fire as it traveled upward, through his mouth and tongue, jarring him the way an iron-rimmed wagon wheel did when it struck a rock. He was scooted backward by the flaming poker entering his brain, and he could feel it tearing through the top of his head. Without truly understanding what was happening, he puzzled over the hot sensation, like fire. How could fire get inside his skull like this?

He lay back as the figure stepped over him, heading down to the ravine where Marvin was shooting. Dewey tried to yell, to warn Marvin, only his mouth was full of blood and tobacco juice and he could feel only the stump of his tongue moving when he tried to speak. He coughed and closed his eyes. Marvin would be able to take care of himself until Dewey could figure out what was wrong. For some reason, in spite of what had just happened to his head, he felt sleepy, and it was sure as hell the wrong time to be needing to take a nap.

Marvin Hyde decided it was time to pull back. Some of the bullets fired from the ranch were coming too close, whizzing over his head by no more than a foot or two. He didn't want somebody to get off a lucky shot that would turn out to be unlucky for him and in all this noise and confusion, Jessie Evans would never know he'd moved to a safer place.

Marvin came slowly to his hands and knees, pulling his rifle along in the grass, its barrel still hot from so much shooting. A few feet more and he was behind the lip of the shallow ravine, where he could stand up.

As he turned around, he came face-to-face with a half-naked man holding two pistols. "Who the hell are you?" Marvin asked, unable to recall this fellow's face as being a member of Jessie's gang.

"Your executioner, plowboy. I'm gonna put a hole through your overalls while you're wearin' 'em."

"The hell you say!" Marvin cried, bringing his Winchester up for a shot.

The roar of a Colt .44 caught Marvin in midswing, before he could get his rifle muzzle lifted. He was torn off his planted feet by what felt like a whistling gust of wind striking his chest. His rifle flew from his hands as he fell backward from the force of it, and when he fell on his back it was as if an anvil had been dropped on his rib cage. He couldn't breathe at all, not a single breath, and when he touched his chest he felt something wet on the front of his bib overalls, then the hole this sneaky stranger had promised.

He saw the stranger hurry off into the darkness, and thought how he needed to warn Dewey. But try as he might, he could not raise his head or suck in enough wind to shout to his brother.

He noticed his legs were trembling uncontrollably, feet twitching as though they had minds of their own. It occurred to Marvin that joining up with Jessie Evans and his gang hadn't turned out to be such a good idea after all. Maybe he and Dewey should have stayed in Indian Territory, or headed north for the Kansas line.

Off in the distance, he could hear the pop of rifles, and it sounded like they were moving away, growing fainter. With all his strength, he tried to draw in a breath of badly needed air, and found again he couldn't. Marvin had always feared drowning in a river someplace, running out of air. How could a man drown out in the middle of a cow pasture?

24

Smoke crept forward, toward the shape of a man lying prone at the crest of a rocky knob, firing down at the ranch in regular bursts, as fast as he could reload a Winchester .44. Smoke had a decided advantage tonight that he couldn't always count on—the noise made by so many rifles firing at once. This made it far easier to slip up behind his quarry, not having to be so careful where he placed each foot.

The rifleman fired seven shells and then paused to load his gun, giving Smoke just the opportunity he needed.

"Turn around. I've got a message for you from Jessie," he said quietly, just loud enough to be heard above the din of guns banging.

A Mexican with a thin mustache looked over his shoulder as he continued thumbing shells into his rifle. He opened his mouth to speak, until he realized he did not recognize Smoke's face in the dark. Then he saw Smoke's pistols.

"*Dios!*" the man cried. "You are not with us!"

"No, I ain't."

"But you say you have a message from Señor Jessie . . ."

"I suppose I should have said I have a message *for* Jessie," Smoke said. "Trouble is, I can't leave you alive to give it to him."

The Mexican seemed to understand at once that he stood no chance of turning his gun on Smoke in time. "*Por favor,* please do not kill me, señor."

Smoke answered softly, in case other members of Jessie's gang were close enough to hear him despite the constant rattle of rifle fire back and forth. "Funny you'd beg for your life when you came here to kill us. If the tables were turned, would you give me a chance to ride off?"

"Of course, señor. It would be the honorable thing to do in this situation, when you have the drop on me."

"You think I oughta give you a chance to aim that rifle at me first?"

The Mexican hesitated, thinking. "I do not believe you would do that, señor."

"Then you're callin' me a liar."

"No, señor. I only say I do not *think* you would be so foolish."

Smoke lowered his pistols to his sides. "Aim it at me. Go ahead. I'll give you plenty of time."

Another hesitation, then suddenly the Mexican squirmed around, sweeping his rifle barrel toward Smoke.

"Long enough," Smoke whispered, whipping his left pistol up, and gently squeezing the trigger so the motion wouldn't ruin his aim.

His Colt barked, jumping in his fist, its echo lost in a wall of noise coming from the surrounding hills and the ranch down below. The Mexican's body jerked as though he'd been startled, jolted by the bullet passing through him at close range. He threw back his head and shrieked in pain, letting his rifle fall between his knees. He sat there a moment, staring at Smoke, then he looked down at his belly, where a dark stain was spreading over the front of his shirt.

"*Madre,*" he groaned, touching the bullet hole in his stomach with a fingertip.

"Your mother can't help you now," Smoke said. "It'll take you awhile to die, bein' gutshot."

"Take me to the doctor in Mesilla!" the Mexican

begged in a high-pitched voice. "Can't you see that I am badly wounded and without a doctor, I will surely die?"

Smoke turned away from the knob. "I might have considered it, if it wasn't for the fact you came here to kill me an' my friends. *Adios, bastardo.*" He strolled away into the deep night shadows, looking for another victim, another paid assassin who came to South Springs ranch seeking a murderer's payday.

A rifle spat flame to his left, behind a thick piñon pine trunk. Smoke crept toward the light on the balls of his feet.

Jack Johnson knelt in matted grass at the base of the tree, with brass cartridge casings scattered all around him. Now and then he saw a muzzle flash wink near one of the barns or a corner post of a corral. He wondered why Jessie Evans would order an attack on such a well-defended ranch. Jack guessed a dozen men were shooting back at them.

"Evans is a fool," Jack mumbled. "Nobody in his right mind would challenge an outfit armed to the teeth like this bunch, if he knew it ahead of time. This could go on all night. . . ." He took aim at a flickering flash of light and fired, knowing he stood no chance whatsoever of hitting anything at this range. A banging series of gunshots answered his bullet, all high or wide of the mark, whining through tree branches above his head.

He wondered about Boyd and Lee, guessing they were as frustrated with this standoff as he was. At least the three of them had found work in New Mexico Territory, no easy task for men with warrants out on them.

Jack doubted anyone on either side had been wounded or killed, what with everyone shooting in the dark at uncertain targets.

A short pause came in the endless gunfire, long enough for Jack to hear someone behind him, figuring it was probably Boyd or Lee. He glanced over his shoulder while he levered another shell into the firing chamber. "Ain't this the worst?" he said to a man coming toward him from the rear, from friendly territory. "Can't see a goddamn thing down there. Looks like somebody oughta decide this ain't worth it, an' call it off."

"Somebody should have," a voice replied, a voice Jack didn't recognize.

Jack offered a simple solution. "Why don't you go tell Mr. Evans this is a waste of time?"

"I'm looking for him now. Where is he?"

"Him an' Bill Pickett an' two more is near the big house down yonder. They was gonna try an' get Chisum if they could."

"Shoot him down in the dark?"

"Hell yes." Jack began to wonder about all the strange questions, and he looked over his shoulder again. "Who the hell are you anyways, an' how come you're askin' so goddamn many dumb questions?"

"My name doesn't matter. What does matter is that you've got only a few seconds to live."

A chilling tingle went down Jack's spine when he realized he'd been talking to an enemy, one of the shooters from down below. With his rifle aimed in the wrong direction, it would take luck and perfect timing to get out of this alive. "I didn't quite hear what you said, mister," he replied, just as he made a springing dive forward toward a smaller tree trunk a few feet in front of him.

A gun roared while Jack was in midflight. Something snapped between his shoulder blades . . . it felt like his backbone had been broken. He landed on his face and chest without feeling any pain, and when he tried to move his arms and legs to crawl to the tree, his limbs refused to obey his commands. He lay there a moment, wondering what was wrong.

"I'll tell Evans what you said, that he oughta call this off," the voice behind him said.

Tiny tremors began in Jack's hands and feet. He saw a circle of light and he began moving toward it despite the fact that his legs were motionless. Somewhere in the night a cricket chirped, the last sound he heard before he was surrounded by an eerie blanket of silence.

Smoke began working his way toward a dark grove of trees to the west of Chisum's house, the logical place for men to take up firing positions if they were bent on killing whoever was inside.

25

Jessie whispered softly to Bill Pickett, "Wonder what the hell is keepin' Billy?" He'd sent Billy Morton to find out what fool was shooting a pistol from hills north of the ranch, when all his men had brought rifles. Nobody with good sense would shoot a pistol from that distance, yet the distinctive sounds of a .44 had come fairly often . . . not always from the same spot.

"I told you somethin' was wrong," Pickett replied, keeping his rifle trained on a shattered window of the house where rifle fire exploded now and then. "They was ready for us. Some son of a bitch warned 'em we was comin'. I figure it was that little coward Barlow, after you ran him off. He probably rode over here an' offered to throw in with 'em, tellin' Chisum we was on the way." Pickett glanced north. "The way I got it figured, one of 'em slipped around behind them Arkansas boys an' now he's takin' potshots at 'em with a pistol. If they're as good as they claim to be, one of 'em will kill whoever it is. That last pistol shot was five or ten minutes ago. Maybe the bastard is already dead if one of them farmers got him. Come to think of it, there ain't been no shootin' at all comin' from them hills lately."

Jessie felt his anger rising. "If I find out that little bastard Barlow warned 'em, I'll kill him myself. I still can't figure what's takin' Billy so long to get back here." As he said it, he saw Billy coming up a draw behind them, moving in a crouch to avoid flying lead. "Yonder he is . . ."

Morton hurried up to Jessie as best he could, keeping down like he was. He sounded out of breath when he spoke quietly to Jessie. "Big trouble, boss. Somebody's sneakin' 'round up in them hills, killin' off them pig farmers from Arkansas. The one-eyed Johnson brother is dead, an' so is the young skinny one. I found that big red-headed guy with the top of his head blowed off, an' it damn near made me sick to my stomach. His brains was all over the place, only the big bastard was still breathin'. I left him layin' there. I got the hell outta there quick as I could, to bring word down to you. At least one of 'em got behind us, maybe more."

"This has to be Barlow's doin'," Jessie growled. "They was ready for us. Hell, they was already spread out all over creation soon as the first shot was fired. I swear I'm gonna kill Barlow. It ain't my way of doin' things to pull away from a fight, but if some of 'em got behind us, we're caught in a cross fire. Spread the word to pull out. Tell Tom to warn the boys over to the south to clear out now."

Pickett turned away from the tree with a disgusted look on his face. "Far as I can tell, we ain't shot nobody tonight. It was them who done all the killin'."

"We rode into a trap," Jessie said, heading for the draw as exchanges of gunfire lessened even more. Keeping his head down, he ground his teeth together while they made for their horses. A double-crossing son of a bitch had done them in tonight . . . he was sure of it.

Pickett seemed reluctant to leave, glancing over his shoulder, scowling in the moonlight. "Wish I'd had the chance to kill at least one of 'em," he whispered. "Don't seem like it's askin' too much to be able to kill just one. I ain't smelled no blood in so long I plumb forgot what it smells like."

"We'll get another chance," Jessie promised. "Lopez told me there's at least a dozen more *pistoleros* headed up from Juarez to hire on with us. Said they'd be here by the end of the week. If Chisum thinks he's heard the last of us, he's goddamn sure in for a helluva surprise."

They reached their tethered mounts just as Pickett said, "I reckon that Jensen feller was all talk. Every one of them yellow bastards kept their heads down so damn low there wasn't nothin' to shoot at. The only thing they did smart was puttin' a few men behind us, an' they couldn't have done that 'less Barlow warned 'em we was comin'."

Jessie mounted, thinking about the warning Victor had brought them from Smoke Jensen, whoever the hell he was, about how if one more bullet flew, he was planning to kill them all, including Jessie. "Like you said, just big talk is all it was. Maybe he got lucky killin' those *pistoleros* like he done. If it hadn't been for Barlow, we'd have killed Chisum an' every one of his shooters tonight. That Buck Andrews an' Curly Tully was supposed to be bad men. Killers. Only, when the shootin' started, they stayed down just like the rest of 'em, includin' that big-winded Jensen feller." He reined his horse around. Shooting in the distance had all but ended. "Tomorrow I'll ride up to the Mescalero reservation . . . see if some of them red-skinned bastards who know how to shoot are interested in makin' a little money. There's always a few renegades lookin' for some excitement." He urged his horse to a short lope, back in the direction of Bosque Redondo. "One way or another, I'm gonna have John Chisum's ass."

They were a few miles from the Chisum ranch when Tom Hill, Billy Morton, Ignacio Valdez, Pedro Lopez, and three more riders caught up with them at a hard gallop. Pedro was the first to speak, after jerking his horse to a halt.

"I see this hombre, Señor Jessie. I only see him one time. Then I hear gun, *una pistola*. I go see where he is, only nobody is there, only Juanito Gonzales, and he is dying. He say this *loco hombre* come from behind where he was shooting and he shoot him. Juanito tell me this hombre ask where to find you, that he have this message for you. It no make sense, Señor Jessie, how this hombre know your name and want to give you a message."

"Jensen," Jessie snarled, curling his lips when he said the name. "It had to be Jensen." Rage welled in Jessie's chest, and he gripped his saddle horn fiercely, trying to control an outburst of unreasoning anger. "That's who got behind us. It was that bastard Smoke Jensen. I never laid eyes on the son of a bitch yet, but I'm swearin' an oath I'm gonna kill him. He's as good as dead. All I gotta do is find him. . . ."

26

Smoke alerted the anxious men spread out across South Springs ranch before he crossed the fence in the dark, fearing a bullet might come flying his way from a nervous Chisum cowboy after a pitched battle like the one they'd just been through.

"It's me, Smoke Jensen! Don't anybody shoot! Looks like they cleared out!"

He heard Pearlie's distinctive voice from a cowshed off to his right. "That's Smoke all right, men. Lower them guns so you don't shoot him accidental."

Smoke went over the fence, his pistols holstered, as Pearlie and Cal hurried up to him.

"How many was out there?" Pearlie asked. "Sounded like a whole damned army."

"Twelve or fourteen," Smoke replied, continuing on his way to Chisum's house. "I scouted around after they left, just to make sure all of 'em hightailed it out of here."

John Chisum met him at the porch steps. He gave Smoke a half grin. "Never heard so much lead flying in my life," he said with obvious relief. "They had us surrounded. Must've been at least twenty riflemen out there . . ."

"More like a dozen or so," Smoke replied. "A few more than that, maybe. I got six of 'em by circling around behind some of their positions. No sense goin' after the bodies till daylight comes."

"You killed six of them?" Chisum asked, relief turning to disbelief when he heard the number. "How in the hell did you do that without getting your ass shot to pieces?"

"They didn't expect nobody to come at 'em from the rear, I reckon."

"You're an amazing man, Mr. Jensen, talking about knocking off half a dozen men like you'd been out picking peaches. Those boys were hired gunmen, not amateurs. Evans and Dolan have sent word all the way to Mexico that they're hiring top shootists to fight on their side of this war."

Smoke shrugged, climbing to the porch. "They didn't appear to be all that experienced, not to me. Maybe I didn't get the cream of the crop this time. But if they come back again, or if they try to stop me and my friends from drivin' our herd up to Colorado, I'll test the rest of 'em. I don't pay much attention to what a man's reputation is supposed to be. Just because some fool hires out to kill other men don't make him good at it."

Chisum wagged his head. "You sure as hell know your business. I wish you'd consider a proposition from me to stay on until this range war is over."

Smoke discarded the notion with a wave of his hand. "I'm in the cattle business, Mr. Chisum. Like I told you before, my guns ain't for hire at any price."

The rancher rubbed his chin thoughtfully. "But you can't deny you know the profession, the gunman's trade. I've seen you in action."

"I've had a little experience with it."

"What made you change? It must have been something of great importance to you."

"A woman," he replied. "My wife broke me of a lot of bad habits, and I don't figure she's done with it yet."

Chisum laughed. "She is certainly an influential lady, even if I haven't met her."

Smoke found himself yearning for a shot of whiskey right at the moment, although he answered the statement. "It isn't so much just influence. When she gets her mind set on doin' things her way, it's mighty hard to change it." He glanced into the house through a broken windowpane. "If all your whiskey bottles didn't get busted, I could use a swallow or two of that good stuff from Kentucky, before I go back to bed."

"I'll have one with you," Chisum said, "and I'll send a bottle out to the men. They've earned it." He turned around and led Smoke inside, lighting a lantern that revealed shattered glass all over the floor. "We were lucky tonight," Chisum added as he went to the cabinet for the whiskey.

"How's that?" Smoke asked, not quite sure what seemed so all-fired lucky about being attacked from all sides.

"Lucky to have you here," he replied. "Maybe this will serve to discourage Evans and Dolan from making any further attempts like this one."

Smoke settled into a stuffed bull hide chair near the fireplace. "I wouldn't count on it," he said quietly, glancing out a window. "Men like those who visited us just now ain't so easily discouraged. They'll be looking for a payday. I'm not much of a gamblin' man, but I'll bet we see 'em again before too awful long. Could be as early as tomorrow."

Chisum handed Smoke a shot glass brimming with golden whiskey as he said, "I sure as hell hope you're wrong."

Smoke tasted his drink, finding it delicious, even though it burned all the way down his throat. "I'm seldom ever wrong when it comes to men with bad intentions," he told Chisum. "I've had more'n my share of experience with their breed."

Riders for Chisum acted as herd-holders while Smoke and John Chisum rode through hundreds of two- and three-year-old longhorn heifers. When Smoke pointed to a good long-backed cow, Pearlie and Cal and Duke cut it away from the main herd to a lower meadow, where

Smoke's selections were being held in a bunch by Bob Williams and Cletus Walker, along with a pair of Chisum cowboys. These young cows were in good trail flesh, making it easier for them to be driven to Sugarloaf without long grazing delays to keep the longhorns from getting hungry.

"You've got a good eye for a mother cow," Chisum told him as they rode through the herd. "You're picking my choice from the bunch damn near every time."

"We've got a long drive ahead of us," Smoke replied, with a nod toward a brindle heifer which Cal immediately cut away from the others, "and I figure picking a longer back will make the crosses better suited for our type of range."

"I've done the same thing myself. We've got no railheads within two hundred miles, so I have to make damn sure what I raise can be driven to market."

"We're in the same boat. Denver is the closest railyard for us, an' that's a considerable drive through mountain country most of the way."

A cowboy from ranch headquarters came riding up as they were picking the last of the heifers. He pulled his horse to a stop and spoke to Chisum.

"We found six bodies in them hills, Mr. Chisum. With the four we got already, makes ten. Them first four is already startin' to stink. It'll take two wagons to carry 'em all the way to Roswell so they can be buried proper. Trouble is, they wasn't carryin' no papers sayin' who they was, so I reckon the undertaker'll have to bury 'em without no name on the marker."

"Take two wagons," Chisum said. "Tell Sheriff Romero they came gunning for us, and that I'll ride in tomorrow and give him a full report."

"Yessir," the young cowboy replied, wheeling his horse for a ride back to the ranch.

Chisum was staring at Smoke now. "Ten men," he said. "You killed ten of Dolan's gunmen without a lick of help from us, in a manner of speaking. I still have trouble believing it . . . how just one man could do all of that."

Smoke didn't care to talk about it, how easy it had been to send ten careless gunmen to early graves. "That oughta be about two hundred head, give or take. Let's drive 'em back to the ranch and I'll pay you for 'em, and for the bulls. We can get a final count while we're drivin' 'em to the corrals."

"After all you've done for me, I'm tossing in ten extra head to help account for losses on the trail. You've been a good man to have backing me during all this trouble, and it's my way of showing gratitude."

"No need for that," Smoke argued. "I did what I did because my friends and neighbors were in the line of fire. This ain't our fight, but when it spilled over, an' bullets started flyin' in our direction, those boys had me to reckon with. We rode all this way to conduct an honest business transaction, an' I damn sure won't stand for nobody gettin' in the way of it, not for no reason."

"I understand," Chisum told him. "All the same, I benefited from it, and I'm giving you ten extra heifers. No reason to talk about it anymore. It's done."

Smoke found he was liking Chisum and his honesty more and more. Chisum would make a good neighbor, and a solid friend a man could count on when the going got tough. "It's your decision, Mr. Chisum," he said, "only I want it understood I never expected payment for what I did."

Chisum didn't answer, swinging off to beckon to one of his men riding herd with Smoke's heifers. "Go back and pick out ten good long-backed heifers to add to this bunch," he said. "Tell Shorty to help you. Bring them up along with this bunch as quick as you can, only make damn sure none of them are cripples. They'll be headed to Colorado Territory in the morning."

27

Pearlie shoveled refried beans and salsa into his mouth with a tin spoon, until his cheeks were bulging. They sat at a long oak table in John Chisum's dining room eating Maria's spicy hot Mexican food, their faces outlined by coal oil lamps overhead.

"I'm gonna miss this cookin'," Cal said around a mouthful of flank steak seasoned with hot sauce, folding a tortilla over a piece of meat heavily coated with *salsa picante.* "We'll be eatin' beans an' jerky plumb to Big Rock, an' I'll be rememberin' what this tastes like."

Bob Williams was sweating from the chili peppers in his food, and he sleeved perspiration from his brow. "This is sure fine eatin', if a man's stomach is made of iron. I'm gonna eat it even if it kills me."

"It'll put hair on your chest," Cletus promised.

"Already got enough hair there the way things is. What I need is another glass of water."

Duke Smith nodded. "Can't put enough water in a man's belly to put this fire out. If it was snowin' outside, I'd run out an' eat a fistful, just to cool my tongue."

Chisum grinned. "Mexican food is supposed to be hot. It isn't any good otherwise."

Pearlie eyed his plate. "If hot's got anythin' to do with it bein' good, this has gotta be the best I ever tasted."

Cal was too busy chewing to offer an opinion at the moment, and he merely nodded, beads of sweat on his forehead, cheeks, and neck.

Cletus lifted the bandanna tied around his neck and wiped away a trickle of perspiration coming from his hat-band while he chewed methodically on a bite of steak. "I've never seen fire on a plate, afore tonight," he said. "Come mornin' there'll be a line at the outhouse half a mile long. That Maria can make fire taste mighty delicious."

"She fixed flan custard to cool everybody off," Chisum said. "That's for dessert."

Smoke listened to all the banter, but his mind was on the ride they would undertake at dawn. He was almost sure Jessie Evans and his gang hadn't had enough of a lesson last night to convince them of their folly. "I want two men riding point on this herd," he said. "I'll be scouting what lies ahead, but in case there's trouble, I want Pearlie and Duke guiding this bunch of cattle until we're well north of Lincoln County."

"You expect trouble," Chisum observed.

"I always expect it. That way, I'm pleasantly surprised if it don't show up."

"It usually does," Pearlie muttered, again filling his mouth with Maria's cooking. "But if any outfit between here'n Big Rock can handle it, it'll be the Sugarloaf crew. Hell-fire, I wouldn't know what to do if somebody wasn't shootin' at us half the time. I'd figure I was with the wrong bunch if we wasn't duckin' lead."

Chisum seemed puzzled. He looked over at Smoke. "You said you were in the ranching business now; however, your men act like they expect problems."

Smoke thought about it awhile as he was chewing. "I guess I've got too many old enemies who won't leave things alone. Now and then a batch of 'em shows up to try an' settle old scores."

The rancher appeared to be mildly amused. "Looks

like after awhile word would spread that you're the wrong man to be trifled with."

Pearlie chuckled. "There's been times when dead bodies did sorta stack up 'round the place. It's been quieter lately, so maybe like you say, word got out that Sugarloaf is the wrong spot to come lookin' for a little bit of excitement."

Smoke finished cleaning his plate. "That egg custard does sound nice," he said, changing the subject. Down deep he felt sure there would be excitement enough driving their cattle back up the trails to Big Rock country.

"One more thing," Chisum said as he got up to tell Maria to bring the flan, "I asked one of my hands to send a telegram to Fort Stanton while he was in Roswell delivering those bodies to Sheriff Romero. I told him to ask Colonel Dudley to meet you along the trail up to Fort Sumner somewhere with a squad of his soldiers, as an escort just in case Evans and Dolan try to rustle any of your cattle. I doubt if Dudley will agree. He's hand in glove with Tom Catron and his Santa Fe Ring when it comes to this beef contract business. I find I'm not only pitted against a gang of paid guns in this range war, but I'm also at odds with the most powerful politicians in the territory. They'll do all they can to put me out of business." He looked down at Smoke. "That's one reason I wish you'd reconsider staying on here for awhile, Mr. Jensen. I have a feeling I'll need all the help I can get . . . men who know their way around a gun."

"Sorry, but I'm not interested. I've got a wife waitin' for me up in Colorado an' a ranch to run. If things were different, I'd stay. As to those soldiers from Fort Stanton, I don't reckon we'll need 'em. I try to make a habit out of handlin' my own affairs."

Chisum nodded and disappeared into the kitchen. Smoke saw a frown on Bob's face.

"After what happened last night, I sure wouldn't mind havin' a soldier escort," Bob said.

"Me either," Cletus added, toying with a spoon.

"Wouldn't be no disgrace to have a company of soldiers ridin' with us part of the way."

"If they show up, we won't send 'em back," Smoke said, more to comfort his friends than anything else. "But you heard Mr. Chisum say it ain't likely they'll show. Apparently the army is backing the other side in this conflict. I never had much high regard for soldiers or politicians."

Johnny hadn't said a word during supper, but he spoke up now, after mention was made of the soldiers. "Don't know 'bout the rest of you, but I was plenty scared last night . . . bullets flyin' all over the place, knockin' holes in the side of that barn where I was hidin'. I couldn't go back to sleep after it was over. I was thinkin' how glad I was to be alive."

Cal was quick to agree, looking at Smoke when he said, "I was feelin' might' near the same way. Not that I ever doubted you'd git us out of that fix, Mr. Jensen, but them slugs sure was comin' close a few times."

Smoke understood both boys' concerns. They were young and inexperienced in the ways of battle. "Leave Evans and his gunslicks to me. The main thing you're supposed to worry about is those cattle, come tomorrow. Just make sure you keep 'em bunched if there's any trouble. Don't let anybody close to those bulls, no matter what happens."

Now Pearlie was eyeing Smoke. "You expect Evans an' his boys to come after our cattle, don't you?"

"It's a strong possibility. I've never met Jessie Evans, but I know his kind. Some men can't learn a lesson but one way, and that's to teach it permanent."

"You aim to kill him, don't you?" Johnny asked quietly.

"Only if he comes at us again. I won't go lookin' for him, if that's what you mean."

It was Pearlie who said, grinning, "He's done come at us once already, which only proves you've gone an' mellowed some in my opinion. If that'd happened a few years back, you'd have gone lookin' fer Mr. Evans by now."

"We came here to buy Hereford bulls and cattle," Smoke reminded Pearlie.

"So we did," Pearlie agreed, as Maria brought a tray filled with cups of caramel-coated custard into the dining room, which signaled an end to all further conversation as far as Pearlie was concerned.

John Chisum had a small fire going in the fireplace due to a night chill, the house being without most of its windowpanes after the shooting. He had given Smoke a bill of sale for the cows and turned down the lantern while they shared glasses of whiskey while the men went to the bunkhouse.

"I'm also interested in buyin' a good Morgan stud to cross on my mares," Smoke said, enjoying his drink, and the peace and quiet.

Chisum wagged his head. "This isn't good horse country yet, not by a long shot; however, I have a friend in Saint Louis who raises purebred Morgans, and you can trust him. His name is Penn Wheelis. I'll give you his address and you can say I recommended him to you. He'll quote you a fair price, and even arrange for delivery by railroad car as far west as Denver. Wheelis is an honest man, and he'll send you exactly what you're paying for if you do business with him."

"I'd sorta made up my mind to look at one before I paid for it, but if you say this Penn Wheelis is honest, that'll be good enough for me. With those Herefords and cows to tend to this summer, I won't have time to travel to Saint Louis."

Chisum sipped his drink thoughtfully. "A Morgan is a good horse for adding muscle to a common mare. The crosses make good cow horses, I'm told."

"I'll take that address in Saint Louis, I reckon."

Chisum got up and went to a rolltop desk, fumbling through a sheaf of papers until he found what he wanted. He wrote down a name and address and handed it to Smoke. "You won't regret doing business with Wheelis. He'll send you a good horse. You've got my word on that."

"That's good enough for me," Smoke replied, tucking the paper into his waistband.

Chisum took his chair again. . . . There was something else on his mind. "I can send Buck Andrews or Curly Tully along with you for part of the way," he offered. "Both of them have made a name for themselves with a gun."

"No thanks, but I'm obliged for the offer. I handle most of my own problems without any help."

"I can see that," Chisum said. "I'm curious about a couple of things. Where did you learn to fight like that? An ordinary man can't kill almost a dozen men the way you did single-handedly without getting a scratch."

Smoke thought about Preacher a moment. "I had a real good teacher, an old mountain man up in Colorado. If I had to try to explain it, I suppose I'd say he had a born instinct for taking care of himself in any situation. He lived alone in the wildest part of the Rockies. He never depended on anyone else. He survived in a place where all odds said he couldn't, goin' up against Indians like the Crows, Blackfeet, the Utes, and the Shoshoni back when the Indian wars were at their worst. After a spell, most tribes got to where they respected him . . . even made friends with him. Some of the Crow medicine men believed he was a medicine man himself, even though his skin was white and his eyes were the wrong color. He earned their respect as a fighting man, and they left him alone to hunt an' run his traps."

"It sounds to me like you were very close to him, whoever he was."

Smoke felt a slight twinge when the old memories came back. "I reckon we were real close, if that's the right word.

He went by 'Preacher.' He told me the last time I saw him his first name was Arthur. I never knew his last name."

"Is he . . . gone now?"

Smoke downed the last of his drink, not wanting to discuss Preacher any longer. "Can't say for sure. He'd be close to ninety by now, if he's still alive. When I left him, it was at his request. He'd been wounded mighty bad and looked for all the world like he was gonna die. He asked me to dress him in his best buckskins an' a sash, which is the way old-time mountain men want to be buried. Then he ordered me to leave that high country for good, to get clear of the trouble brewin' there. He rode off on his favorite mare. That's the last I ever saw of him, an' I believe it was the way he wanted it, so I wouldn't know if he'd lived or died. Preacher had a hell of a lot of pride, an' I'm sure this was his way of sparing me from seeing him pass on, or as mountain men say, cross over."*

"Haven't you ever wondered what became of him?"

Smoke stood up, stretching his legs. "I owe him too much not to respect his wishes."

Chisum got up, a puzzled expression on his face. "What an unusual story," he said, following Smoke over to the front door to show him out.

"G'night, Mr. Chisum," Smoke said, to end any further talk about Preacher or Smoke's beginnings. "We'll be up before first light to get that herd started."

"My men will help you get them started north," Chisum said as Smoke started for the bunkhouse.

"We'll be grateful," he said without turning around, lost in an unwanted memory, of the day Preacher was dressed in his best beaded buckskins, badly wounded from a scrape with men who had tracked him into the Needle Mountains, putting a rifle ball all the way through his hip, a wound that was badly festered by the time he found Smoke.

*The Last Mountain Man

Smoke glanced up at the stars, hoping that some-where those same stars were shining down on Preacher, perhaps at the high mountain pass Ned Buntline told Cal and Pearlie about. Was the man dressed in an albino buffalo robe truly Preacher?

Smoke knew he would never know, and that was the way Preacher had wanted it.

28

Driving half-wild longhorns away from their home range could be tricky business, Smoke knew from experience, and as they put a few lead heifers in motion northward, some tried to turn back. A cowboy had to ride up at just the right time in order to get the animals moving in the right direction.

The young Herefords were another matter. Gentled by being around men feeding them in corrals, they plodded along at the back of the herd quietly.

Smoke leaned out of the saddle and shook hands with John Chisum. "Pleasure doin' business with you," he said, watching Pearlie and Duke lead the cattle north over the very same hills where he'd killed six of Jessie Evans's men.

"The pleasure has been all mine," Chisum replied. "You be careful, Smoke Jensen. Don't let those owlhoots riding for Dolan jump you."

Smoke grinned. "I'm always careful," he said, urging his horse forward to ride around the herd so he could scout the way for several miles before the cattle came.

Dawn had just come to South Springs, casting golden light over tree-studded hills and shallow valleys. Off to the east, the Pecos River was a thin, distant line of deeper green where cottonwoods and grass were nourished by its waters. It was a peaceful beginning, as the heifers and bulls moved away from the Chisum ranch. Smoke wondered how long it would stay this way.

Keeping the Pecos in sight, he led them over grassy meadows where the cows would have plenty of grazing. Once the herd got settled to the trail, the likelihood of a stampede would be less of a worry.

When he'd scouted ahead for a couple of miles, Smoke turned back to see how the herd was moving, and when he topped a rise he could see them strung out in good trail fashion, traveling along at a slow pace, with the Hereford bulls bringing up the rear, an expected outcome since their legs were far shorter and they would have more trouble staying up with longer-strided longhorn cows.

"So far, so good," he said under his breath. The land they were traveling was empty, no houses or signs of civilization in sight as far as the eye could see.

They were passing through what Chisum called the Haystack Mountain range, little more than foothills to a man who knew the Rockies. Water was plentiful in creeks and arroyos. With so much grass and water, the cattle would have an easy time of it until they reached drier regions to the north.

An hour later, Smoke tensed in the saddle when he saw Duke Smith headed his way at a fast trot. Smoke swung his horse to ride to meet him.

"Nothin's wrong," Duke said quickly, when he saw the look on Smoke's face, "but we did see this horse an' rider way off to the west, an' he didn't stay long afore he plumb disappeared."

It could be someone riding to warn Evans of their departure from Chisum's ranch, although he didn't want to worry Duke or the others. "Maybe just a range cowboy out lookin' for strays. But keep your eyes peeled anyway."

"Pearlie said to tell you it didn't look right, how this feller rode off that hilltop so quick, like he didn't want nobody to see him."

"Could just be a coincidence. I'll ride over to the west

a ways, just to make sure. Keep the cattle moving. Some
of those longhorns are a little spooky yet. If one gun
goes off, they'll all break into a run."

"I know the ornery critters right well," Duke declared, as
he turned his horse around. "Ain't no creature on this earth
as likely to run off as a damn longhorn. We'd be tryin' to
round 'em up till doomsday if somethin' scares 'em."

Smoke wondered about the rider they had seen as
Duke rode off to rejoin the herd, riding point. Was Jessie
Evans keeping an eye on them, planning his next at-
tempt at revenge?

Swinging west, Smoke galloped his horse to the highest
hill, where he had a view of what lay beyond. For a time,
he sat his horse, motionless, making no effort to hide himself should anyone be watching. A herd the size of theirs
couldn't be hidden as it moved northward, no matter how
carefully they were kept to low ground, making it point-
less to hide his own presence on the hilltop now.

As far as the eye could see, the land was empty. A red
hawk soared above distant stands of trees, hunting prey,
a sign it sensed no danger from the presence of man in
forests below. A hawk's eyesight and hearing were far
keener than a man's, and it convinced Smoke they were
alone here. For now.

29

Ignacio Valdez came to a decision. Instead of riding back to Bosque Redondo to warn Jessie about the herd moving northward away from Chisum's like Jessie wanted, he would take care of this broad-shouldered stranger called Smoke Jensen himself, and that would please Jessie. The sneaky gringo who'd killed so many of their gang would be dead, and Ignacio would get the credit for it, killing this *loco hombre* who had done so much damage when he snuck around behind them in the dark, like a coward. Ignacio was sure he could take Jensen down. In Chihuahua and Coahuila he'd been the fastest gun in northern Mexico, killing the likes of Luis Ortega, Manuel Soto, and the worst of them all in a pistol duel, Emiliano Zambrano.

He'd killed Zambrano with his first shot when they drew against each other in Juarez, over a woman. Ignacio remembered how much faster he had been, getting off a shot before the famous Zambrano could level his gun. Stories circulated that Zambrano had killed more than a dozen *pistoleros* in gunfights. He'd had ten notches in the walnut grips of the pistol he carried when Ignacio ended his life with a bullet through the heart.

"I can kill Jensen," he told himself as he spurred his bay gelding well to the north of the cattle herd. "He is only a man, and I will be quicker, much quicker. I will cut off his head and bring it to Jessie as proof of what I have done . . ."

He guided his horse down a winding arroyo to a small stream lined with cottonwood trees, lying directly in the path of the herd. Ignacio spent a moment deciding where to hide his horse before he selected a spot to wait for Jensen. Jensen would stop to water his horse, or simply slow down to cross the creek, and this would be when Ignacio would kill him.

Hurrying away from the ravine where he tethered his bay, he trotted down to the stream, where a massive cottonwood trunk would hide his presence. Out of breath, he took off his sombrero and placed it on the ground in the tall grass where Jensen wouldn't see it, before he pulled his Mason Colt .44/.40, checking each load carefully. Ignacio had decided against using a rifle—he wanted Jensen close before he killed him, close enough to see the fear and surprise on his face when he saw the man who would cut off his head for a trophy to give to Jessie Evans.

He peered around the cottonwood, waiting patiently. This would be easy, killing Jensen, he figured almost too easy. It would make up for the lives Jensen had taken in such a cowardly fashion, to creep up behind some of Jessie's men and four of Pedro Lopez's *pistoleros*.

"Adios, Señor Jensen," he whispered, pulling back so that only one eye was visible next to the tree trunk.

Water gurgled softly in the creek, passing over smooth stones on its way to join the Pecos. Ignacio ran the tip of his tongue across his gold tooth, almost grinning with anticipation.

A horse and rider approached the stream. Ignacio recognized Jensen and drew back out of sight, awaiting the moment when he could be sure of the kill. Resting his right palm on the butt of his Colt, he was eager for things to begin. The sounds made by the horse came closer, very close, and suddenly, they stopped.

Ignacio jacked back the hammer on his pistol, so he only needed to draw and pull the trigger when he killed Jensen. He took a deep breath.

He heard a spur jingle when it touched the ground. *He is down off his horse,* Ignacio thought. *All the better.*

And still he waited for the right moment, when the sounds came nearer, making for surer aim.

Quiet footfalls approached the stream. This was the moment Ignacio had been waiting for. He swung around the cottonwood and spread his feet slightly apart.

"Jensen!" he cried, when he saw a tall cowboy wearing two pistols around his waist.

The man froze in his tracks and Ignacio was sure it was fear that made him so still.

"You called my name?" the cowboy asked, both hands relaxed at his sides.

"*Sí,* and I am calling you a yellow coward. You killed some of *mi amigos.* I have come to make you pay for what you did."

"You'd better be good," the stranger said, his voice relaxed and even.

"But I am, señor. Very good. *Muy bueno con una pistola.* I am faster than you."

"I reckon you're gonna try to prove it now."

"*Verdad.* This is the truth. I will kill you for what you did."

Jensen gave him a one-sided grin, unusual for a man who was about to be gunned down.

"Lots of men have tried it over the years. You can see I'm still here."

"But none were as fast as me, señor." Ignacio raised his hand slightly closer to the butt of his gun. "Of that I am quite sure."

"Only one way to find out," Jensen replied. "Reach for that iron you're carryin' and we'll decide this here and now."

Now Ignacio grinned. "You are a fool, señor. *Un idiota.* You do not know who I am."

"I don't give a damn who you are. Just go for your gun and it won't matter about the name."

Ignacio noticed an odd, icy feeling in the pit of his stomach. "I am Ignacio Valdez," he said, "the man who will put you in your grave."

"I've already invited you to try it," Jensen said. "Anytime you're ready."

"You are indeed one *loco hombre*, Señor Jensen. You are too stupid to be afraid."

"What's there to be afraid of? Some Mexican *pistolero* who calls himself Ignacio Valdez?"

"Are you not afraid of dying, señor?"

"It ain't been proven yet I'm the one who's gonna die when we go for our guns. It could work out another way."

Ignacio stared into the eyes of the stranger to these parts, and he wondered about him. His stare was unwavering, and he was so sure of himself.

Ignacio's hand dipped for his pistol. His fingers closed around his gun grips. As he was pulling the heavy .44/.40 from its holster, he saw a sight that made his blood run cold.

Jensen came up with a gleaming Colt .44 in his right hand so quickly, it did not seem possible, and for an instant Ignacio was looking down its barrel, a dark round hole the size of his little finger. No man could be so fast, he thought as his own fist came up filled with iron.

The dark muzzle of Jensen's gun shot forth a beacon of white light that was accompanied by a loud banging noise. Ignacio's finger curled around the gun's trigger, tightening, when it felt like he'd been struck in the ribs by a hammer blow.

The force of the impact drove him backward a half step at the same moment he triggered off a shot into the ground near his boots. He glanced down, seeing tiny tufts of lint arise from a puckering hole in his shirtfront. A trickle of blood came from the hole . . . Ignacio's blood. His ears were ringing from the pair of gunshots.

"*Madre!*" he cried, trying to keep his feet under him when it seemed the earth was tilting at odd angles.

"You were too slow," a voice said in front of him. "I gave you the first pull."

Ignacio sank to his knees, his mind reeling. He barely noticed when his pistol fell from his hand. How could this have happened? he wondered. How could Jensen be faster than Emiliano Zambrano, the fastest gun in all of northern Mexico?

"*Bastardo,*" Ignacio spat angrily, waves of pain spreading across his chest. He looked up at Jensen, and he found the man smiling again.

"It's all in the wrist," Jensen explained, as if he were talking about the proper way to shoe a horse. "Your wrist was too stiff. You gotta learn to bend it some, only I don't figure you'll have the time now."

Ignacio saw himself as a small boy playing beside a creek in Torreón, a creek very similar to this one. He had skipped rocks there as a child. He knew his mind was wandering.

"Adios, Valdez," Jensen said. "That slug caught you in a bad place. You're bleedin' like a stuck hog at butcherin' time right now. I don't figure you'll last long."

"*Bastardo,*" he said again, reaching for his wound with both hands to stem the flow of blood.

"I'd take offense to you callin' me a bastard," Jensen said, "if you wasn't already dyin'."

Ignacio's vision blurred. He rocked forward on his knees and fell on his face, wondering if Jessie Evans had any idea how fast this Jensen was with a handgun . . . faster than any gunman Ignacio had ever seen . . . much faster than Emiliano Zambrano.

30

Two cowboys came galloping over the hilltop, their horses at full speed under the punishment of spurs, pistols drawn as they rode for the creek bank where Smoke stood over the body of the Mexican. Pearlie and Duke slowed their mounts when they could see the trouble was over. Both men pulled their horses to a halt a few yards from the stream.

"We heard shootin'!" Pearlie declared, glancing down at the body. "Don't need no crystal ball to know that's one of Jessie Evans's men."

Smoke holstered his gun. "Said his name was Ignacio Valdez, an' that name should mean somethin'."

Pearlie wagged his head and put his pistol away. "Means it's gonna be hard to spell fer some undertaker when he puts it on his tombstone." He gave Smoke a weak grin. "I figure it's gonna be like this plumb to the Colorado border. I knowed we couldn't just drive them cows peaceful all the way to Sugarloaf the way Cletus was hopin' we could. I told Cletus last night to make damn sure his guns was loaded."

Duke was last to rid his hand of a gun. "We heard two shots real close together."

Smoke looked over his shoulder at Valdez. "He damn near shot himself in the foot just a moment ago. Had his pistol in the cocked position when he drew it. I've known a few gents who did without a toe or two the rest of their lives on account of that same bad habit."

Duke chuckled. "I've never claimed to be much of a gunnie, but it don't appear Mr. Valdez was much of one either."

Smoke turned to collect his horse. "He was fast by most men's standards, I suppose. He just wasn't quite fast enough."

Pearlie frowned. "That hired gun of Chisum's, the one they call Buck, said to watch out fer a feller ridin' with Evans by the name of Bill Pickett. An older feller, Buck said. Pickett is rattlesnake mean, accordin' to Buck, an' quicker'n greased lightnin' with a pistol, only Buck claimed Pickett prefers usin' a sawed-off shotgun."

Nothing Pearlie said caused Smoke any worry as he mounted his bay Palouse colt. "A man with a sawed-off shotgun has to be mighty close to a target, Pearlie. Could mean his eyesight is a little on the bad side. If he crosses the road we're takin' to Big Rock, I'll buy him a pair of spectacles so they can bury him with 'em on."

Duke pointed to the body of Ignacio Valdez. "What you want us to do with that corpse, Mr. Jensen?" he asked.

"Not a damn thing. Let the buzzards and coyotes have a meal out of him. Scout around and find his horse. It won't be far, an' I'd hate to leave an animal tied up till it starves to death or breaks its reins. When Valdez don't show up wherever Evans is waitin' for him, he'll come looking for him. And us. We can be sure of more gunplay sooner or later. Evans will likely bring this Pickett and anybody else he can hire. Like it or not, we've gotten ourselves into the middle of the Lincoln County War, just because we bought a herd of cattle from John Chisum."

"I figured all along we'd have to shoot our way out of here," Pearlie said, wheeling his horse away from the stream and the body. He spoke to Duke. "Look fer that horse whilst I git back to the herd. Ain't nobody ridin' point now an' they's sure liable to wander." Then he noticed Smoke was looking off to the west.

"What's wrong, boss?" Pearlie asked, when he saw a dark look cross Smoke's face.

"I'm thinkin'," Smoke replied.

"Thinkin' 'bout what? If you don't take no offense from me by askin'."

Until right at that moment the attempted ambush by Ignacio Valdez hadn't bothered him. But something changed inside his head in sudden fashion. "Thinkin' about riding back to Lincoln right now to settle this once an' for all, so the rest of you don't have to duck lead all the way out of the territory. I can ask where to find Jimmy Dolan and look him up. I could warn him that if he sends one more gunman after this herd or any of my men, I'll kill him. The more I think about it, the better that notion sounds."

"It could be real dangerous," Pearlie said.

Smoke's mind was made up. A warning was what Jimmy Dolan needed. "You men keep pushing our herd north. Take your time, and don't ride into any tight spots where a bushwhacker could take a shot at you. I'll be back tomorrow. It's time Mr. Dolan found out a thing or two about our intentions."

Pearlie sounded worried. "What'll we do if you don't come back?"

"Keep driving our cows toward Sugarloaf," was all he said as he heeled his horse to a gallop.

The Murphy and Dolan General store sat across from the courthouse in Lincoln. By pushing his horse harder than he wanted to, Smoke arrived in front of the store just before closing time, at five o'clock. When he swung down from the saddle, bone-weary after so many hours of riding, trying to make Lincoln before dark, his legs were stiff.

Smoke entered the store in full stride, walking over to a clerk in a badly stained apron.

"Where's Jimmy Dolan?" he demanded, staring down at the store clerk's face.

"In the back, tallyin' up the day's receipts, only he don't want to be disturbed right now."

Smoke saw a door at the back of the building. "He's gonna make an exception this time," he said, stalking away from the glass-topped counter with his mouth set in a grim line.

He didn't bother to knock, swinging a thin plank door inward as he walked into a small office. A man in shirt-sleeves, with a distinctively pallid complexion, glanced up from a ledger book.

"I didn't hear you knock, mister," the man snapped, making no effort to disguise his anger.

"That's because I didn't," Smoke said, stepping over to the desk where Dolan sat before he drew one pistol with his right hand, leveling it only a few inches from Dolan's forehead. "I'm gonna give you some advice, Dolan," he said, glaring down at the store owner. He thumbed back the hammer on his .44. "My name is Jensen, Smoke Jensen. I bought a herd of cows from John Chisum and I'm takin' 'em back to Colorado Territory. Only I'm havin' this problem with a fool named Jessie Evans. He keeps tryin' to kill me and my cowboys. I've been told Evans works for you in this range war you're having in Lincoln County. I don't give a damn about your war, or who you rustle cattle from, or anything else. I want you to send Evans a message tonight."

"You're a brazen man," Dolan said, looking up at the muzzle of Smoke's gun. "I'll have you arrested for threatening me unless you put that gun away and get out of here immediately."

"You don't understand," Smoke snarled. "You weren't listening to me. Call off this Evans and your gunslingers right now, or so help me I'll come back and kill you."

"That's strong talk, Jensen."

Smoke leaned a little closer to Dolan's face. "It ain't just talk, you dumb son of a bitch. I've already killed eleven of your hired guns. I'll kill every last one of 'em, including you, if anybody messes with me or my cowboys or my cattle again. I want you to understand, Dolan. The next son of a bitch who takes a shot at me is gonna start a game between us, a deadly game where you wind up bein' the first to die. I'll blow a goddamn tunnel through your head big enough to toss a tomcat through, and that'll be just the start. I'll hunt down Evans an' every last one of his gunnies, and I'll put 'em all in shallow graves."

Dolan blinked. "One man wouldn't stand a chance of doing what you claim to be able to do."

"Just try me, creep. You can count on one thing bein' for absolute certain. I'm gonna kill you first if a shot gets fired at me or my friends. You won't be around to know if I can make good on the rest of my promise."

"You're crazy," Dolan whispered.

Smoke wagged his head. "I'm just pissed off. I'm tired of bein' shot at. Tired of having to look over my shoulder to see if any more of your backshooters are behind me. I'm a rancher up in Colorado, but I'm also a real bad enemy to have if you don't pay any attention to what I'm tellin' you."

"I'll go to Sheriff Pat Garrett over in San Miguel County with this," Dolan said.

"I hope you do," Smoke hissed, barely able to control his rage over Dolan's arrogance. "I'll tell him how your boys came gunning for us at Chisum's the other night, and how I killed six of the yellow bastards while they were shootin' at the ranch in the dark. Then I'll tell him how the big-talkin' Mexican by the name of Ignacio Valdez tried to ambush me earlier today, only I killed him too, an' it was easy. Notify this sheriff if you want, Dolan. But remember what I said . . . if just one more bullet comes at us, you'll be as dead as Valdez an' all the rest of your gunslicks."

Dolan swallowed now, and Smoke saw the first hint of fear in his eyes. His message delivered, Smoke wheeled and walked out of the office.

"You may regret this," Dolan warned as Smoke was leaving the store.

Smoke paused in the doorway. "I doubt it. You'll be the one to regret your actions if you ain't been listening to what I said."

"One man can't be all that good, that tough."

Smoke smiled a humorless smile. "One way to find out. Send Evans and some of his men gunning for me."

"I may just do that," Dolan retorted, sounding like some of his nerve had returned.

Smoke kept smiling. "I'll enjoy it, if you do. It's been a long time since I killed more than a handful of men at one time. But I'll enjoy killin' you more than any of 'em, Dolan, because you're a yellow son of a bitch who has to pay to get his dirty work done. Send your boys after me, if you've got the guts for it. But if you do, I'd check on the price of a good casket right after that, and a cemetery plot, 'cause you're gonna need 'em both. And you'll have to hire somebody to dig the hole ahead of time. You won't be alive to attend to your final arrangements."

He slammed the door and mounted his Palouse as the sun was setting on Lincoln. Dolan could have it any way he wanted now, after being warned of the consequences.

31

Cal and Pearlie and Johnny were saddling fresh horses at a stream the next afternoon as Smoke returned from Lincoln. Smoke could see the cow herd grazing along peacefully, and that all was well. He waved as he rode up to the creek, just in time to see Cal pull his saddle cinch and step aboard the back of a gray colt they'd brought along to season it to cow work. Smoke's experienced eye saw the hump in the three-year-old colt's back which Cal had apparently overlooked. Before Cal could get his leg over the cantle of his saddle, the gray downed its head and began to buck.

Cal was dislodged from his saddle during the first unexpected jump. . . . He went sailing over the colt's head as if he'd sprouted wings. Arms and legs windmilling, Cal was propelled into the air, suspended above the stream for a moment before he fell headfirst into the water, sending up a shower of spray.

Pearlie was the first to burst out laughing, just as Cal came sputtering to the surface. Smoke chuckled, knowing it was a lesson Cal needed, to watch for a slight rise in a horse's back before he mounted, a warning that the animal intended to buck as soon as it felt a man's weight.

"What happened?" Cal cried, scrambling to his feet in the shallow water without his hat, blinking to clear his vision. His hat floated slowly downstream, unnoticed for now.

"You got your young ass bucked off," Pearlie replied as he held his belly between fits of laughter. "You looked fer all the world like you was tryin' to fly, youngun, up there with them sparrows an' blue jays. When I seen you way up yonder, I thought I'd just laid eyes on the ugliest buzzard on this earth!" He broke into another series of hee-haws, clutching his ribs.

"It ain't all that funny," Cal mumbled, staggering across slippery stones in the stream bottom to retrieve his Stetson before it floated away. "I just wasn't ready, is all it was. That gray's got a mean streak in him."

Johnny North was grinning. "Wasn't that gray's fault, Cal. You shoulda noticed that hump in his back."

"Wasn't no hump there," Cal insisted, shaking water from his hat, his young cheeks flushed with embarrassment. "It was that damn colt's nasty disposition, is what it was." Cal stumbled out of the creek, his boots full of water, unable to look directly at Smoke or Pearlie for the moment, so deep was his humiliation over being thrown.

"Hell, youngun, you was needin' a bath anyways," Pearlie said, again breaking into a guffaw or two. "If I'd had a bar of lye soap, I'd have tossed it up in the air whilst you was testin' your wings. That way, you coulda scrubbed clean soon as you landed. You done one of the prettiest dives I ever saw in my life just now. Damn near a perfect landin'."

As Pearlie started laughing again, Smoke swung down from the saddle, exhausted by a long night's ride to reach the herd as soon as he could, resting his Palouse more often on the return trip to spare it any bog spavins or other lameness. "It was a right pretty landing, son," he said to Cal, knowing how the boy must feel with an audience for his mistake.

Pearlie fell quiet all of a sudden. He looked at Smoke for a time. "How did things go in Lincoln?" he asked.

"Did you have to shoot Jimmy Dolan? Or was he ready to listen?"

Smoke loosened the cinch on his tired colt. "He didn't pay all that much attention. I warned him what would happen if one more shot got fired at us. He figures I'm bluffing."

"Then he don't know you at all," Pearlie said, serious now. "If he knowed anythin' about Smoke Jensen, he'd know you don't never run no bluff on nobody."

"I'm expectin' more trouble," Smoke told Pearlie. "Dolan is the type who thinks his money will get him everything he's after. He talks big."

"How come you didn't kill him?" Pearlie asked, "Or slap him plumb silly with the barrel of a gun?"

"I'm giving him a chance to think it over. It was probably a waste of time talking to him, telling him what I'd do if Evans and his boys come back. I'm betting they will."

Pearlie shook his head, glancing over to Cal as the boy was pulling off his boots to drain the water out. "Won't be much sleepin' fer this crew from now on," he said. "I can damn near feel it comin' in my bones, like when a blue norther is headed our way."

Smoke cast a lingering look at the herd before he spoke again. "I'm of the opinion your bones are telling you the truth this time, Pearlie," he said, leading his Palouse colt away from the creek to saddle a fresh horse.

32

He gave his name in broken English as Little Horse, then he pointed to seven young warriors standing behind him, introducing one as Dreamer, another as Sees Far, then the others, all names Jessie quickly forgot. He didn't care what these Apaches called themselves.

"Can they shoot straight?" Jessie asked Little Horse.

Little Horse nodded once. "Many time kill white-eyes," he said, balancing a badly worn Spencer carbine in one hand. "We kill more if you pay us money." He carried a rusted Colt in a sash around his waist, along with a gleaming Bowie knife. This Indian in particular was always in trouble with the soldiers at Fort Stanton for running off from the reservation to steal horses and cattle, scalping white settlers in the process. Little Horse had just gotten out of jail at the fort, along with the seven men who came with him, when no witnesses could identify them as the killers of six white farmers in the Penasco Valley last year.

"Get the ammunition you need from that store over yonder," he told the Apache. "Then get mounted an' follow us." He gave Jimmy Dolan a sideways look. "That makes eight more. Ten just showed up last night from Mexico, all good *pistoleros*, accordin' to Pedro Lopez. He knows most of 'em."

Dolan frowned. "I hope they're better than Ignacio Valdez," he muttered. "You told me Valdez was really good."

"That Jensen feller probably ambushed him from hidin' some place or another. It sure as hell wasn't no fair fight if he got Ignacio."

"Just make damn sure you get Jensen at all costs," Dolan said quietly, standing in the road where Jessie and more than thirty mounted men waited, all heavily armed. Townspeople were staring at the gang from all over Lincoln's main street.

"You can bank on it," Jessie replied.

Dolan's expression hardened. "Jensen is a cocksure son of a bitch. He acted like he owned Lincoln County. I wasn't carrying a gun, and yet he stuck his pistol right in my face when he came barging in the store. I want him dead. Nobody sticks a gun in my face like that."

"I'll bring you his head in a tow sack," Jessie promised as the Apaches went inside the store to get cartridges. "I'll have forty men with me, includin' those redskins. There ain't but seven or eight with that herd, includin' Jensen. It'll be over before it gets started."

"Kill them all," Dolan whispered, so that citizens of Lincoln standing nearby wouldn't hear. "Don't leave a goddamn one of them alive to tell what happened."

"It's as good as done," Jessie said, resting a palm on the butt of his Colt. He grinned and aimed a thumb at Bill Pickett. "I've done promised Pickett he can make sure every last one of 'em is dead. He gets a kick out of killin' with that shotgun of his. I'm sure as hell glad he's on our payroll."

"Just get the job done this time," Dolan snapped. "I'm paying good money to get results, not a bunch of empty promises like the last time."

"That was on account of Billy Barlow warned 'em. Soon as we get back, I'll find Barlow an' kill him myself."

"Do whatever it takes," Dolan said, walking away with his hands shoved in his pants pockets.

Jessie mounted his horse, waiting between Pickett and Tom Hill for the Apaches to come out of the store.

"Goddamn Injuns can't shoot," Pickett said with heat in his voice. "None of 'em can."

"Maybe they'll get lucky," Jessie replied. "Little Horse, the one who speaks some English, is tough, an' a dead shot when he's up close, accordin' to Colonel Dudley. They've been tryin' to find something to pin on him so they can hang him, only he's smart. He don't get caught very often. They had to let him go this time because nobody would testify it was him murdered them farmers."

"I hate Injuns," Pickett declared. "After we get done with this Jensen feller, I'll do the army a favor by blowin' off that damn Apache's skullbone."

Jessie shrugged. "When we're finished with Jensen, I don't give a damn what you do. You can kill all those Apaches for all I care. That way, Dolan don't have to pay 'em."

"Sounds good to me," Pickett said.

Jessie noticed Tom Hill's color wasn't quite right after he heard what Pickett meant to do to the Indians. Glancing over his shoulder, Jessie took another look at the ten Mexicans who'd ridden in at Bosque Redondo the night before. All were bearded, hard-faced men with crisscrossed cartridge bandoliers over each shoulder. The *pistolero* who led this bunch was named Jose Vasquez, and he had a certain look about him showing confidence. Pedro said Jose was a *bandido*, and a killer who took great pride in his work.

Jessie thought about Smoke Jensen. For a man he'd never met, this Colorado rancher was sure as hell causing a lot of trouble in New Mexico Territory, a condition that was about to end tonight, or whenever they caught up to him and his cow herd. With the odds being over four to one against Jensen, he would be dead by the time the sun went down tomorrow. Jessie was certain of it, as Little Horse and his Apaches came out of the store to climb aboard their scrawny ponies.

"Let's ride," he said to the men around him, wheeling his horse to the east.

"We can't get there soon enough to suit me," Pickett said as they struck a trot out of Lincoln.

Forty-three gunmen followed Jessie into the hills east of Lincoln Township. The rattle of curb chains, spur rowels, and armament accompanied their departure. Dust curled away from their horses' heels.

Jessie noticed Jimmy Dolan standing on the porch of his store watching them ride off. Jessie promised himself Mr. Dolan wouldn't be disappointed this time when he heard what had happened somewhere along the Pecos River.

33

Bob and Cletus and Johnny rode slow circles around the herd as the cattle bedded down for the night. The day had passed uneventfully, but when Smoke scouted for a place to hold the herd for the night, he selected it carefully, with defense from an all-out attack in mind, deciding upon the middle of a flat, grassy prairie with no trees or brush nearby where a rifleman would be in range. He knew, once the shooting started, the longhorns would scatter in every direction, making for a difficult time rounding them up, even in daylight. Under the present circumstances, it was the best he could do, to stay out in the open so Evans would have to charge them without benefit of cover. Defenders lying in tall bunch grass would have an advantage over men charging across the flat meadow toward the herd.

Pearlie handed Smoke a tin plate full of beans and fried fatback. He had been watching Smoke use a whetstone across the iron blade of a Ute tomahawk he always carried in his saddlebags. "You figure they're comin' tonight, don't you?" he asked.

Smoke began eating, his face more deeply etched by lines in the light of their campfire. "Hard to say, Pearlie. Best thing to do is be ready for 'em anytime."

"They'll come from the west, from the direction of Lincoln, I reckon."

"Most likely." He chewed thoughtfully a moment. "That's why I'm headed that way, as soon as I've eaten. Those trees way over yonder will give me some cover. I'll go on foot, so I can move around quiet. They may come at us from the south if they've been following our tracks. I want you and the rest to spread out around the herd with rifles and plenty of ammunition. Find a spot in that tall grass where you'll be harder to see when you shoot. They'll have to cross a bunch of open ground to get to us, and that'll cost 'em. Those longhorns are gonna run like mad as soon as the first shot gets fired. I'll try to drop as many of Jessie's boys as I can before they get too close. Main thing is to stay down. I don't want anybody to take chances."

"You'll be the one takin' chances," Pearlie observed.

Smoke continued eating. "I'm accustomed to it, Pearlie. I reckon I've been taking chances all my life, so I've had plenty of practice. The most important thing is that none of you take a bullet, and if you can, protect those Herefords. We can buy more longhorns if we lose a few, but those white-faced bulls can't be replaced very easy. Save as many as you can."

Pearlie glanced across the dark prairie. "Evans would have to be a fool to charge us out in the open like this, even if he done it at night, 'less he's got a helluva lot of men with him."

"I expect him to bring a sizable bunch this time. I'll kill as many as I can before they rush you."

"I noticed you's wearin' your moccasins 'stead of your boots tonight."

"Quieter," Smoke said.

Cal had been listening closely while he ate. "I reckon I'm about to git another chance to kill somebody. It sure does a job on my nerves."

"It ain't affected yer appetite any," Pearlie said.

"I'm eatin' because I'm nervous."

"Hell, you eat all the time anyways . . ."

Smoke got up as Duke was coming to the fire after tying his horse to the picket rope. He saw the tomahawk in Smoke's hand.

"I sure hope they don't get that close, Mr. Jensen," he said as Smoke tucked the handle under his cartridge belt.

"That's why I'm headed for those trees yonder," Smoke replied, inclining his head to the west, "so I can keep some of 'em from getting close." He looked over his shoulder at Pearlie and Cal. "I'll see you boys at day-break if nothing happens tonight. Put out that fire soon as everyone's eaten."

Pearlie nodded. "We's all wishin' you good luck, boss."

Smoke picked up his rifle. "You should know by now I never depend on luck, Pearlie." He strode softly into the darkness, his moccasins making no sound.

False dawn came to the eastern sky, making shadows that played tricks on a man's eyes . . . unless he knew a thing or two about shadows in early light. The night had passed without incident, although Smoke continued to circle the herd from a distance, moving from tree to tree, pausing to listen and study the forest before moving on again.

A sound came from an unexpected place, the unmistakable plop of an unshod horse's hoof. He hadn't been expecting Indians, not when Jessie Evans was the enemy. But few white men rode unshod horses in rough country, and the sound of a hoof without an iron shoe was distinctive, easy to recognize.

He hurried toward the sound, dodging from pine trunk to pine trunk, until he crept close to a small clearing, where the outlines of two Apache warriors on wiry ponies moved slowly in the direction of the prairie where the herd was bedded down.

Apache scouts, he thought, by the way they wore their hair under a headband. Smoke continued forward, pulling his tomahawk with his right hand, a pistol with his left.

The element of surprise would be with him if he moved quickly. He crept up behind the pair of Indians, and when the distance was right, he broke into a soundless headlong run.

His first blow with the razor-sharp tomahawk sliced across the back of an Apache's neck, severing muscle and ligaments and tissue all the way down to bone. Jerking his weapon free, he swung at the other Indian just as he was turning to see what had made the wet, chopping noise, then the dull thud of a falling body.

The tomahawk's blade struck the Apache full in the face, entering his cheek and eye socket, splitting bones with a sharp crack. A muffled cry came from the warrior's throat as his pony lunged forward, sending him toppling to the ground with Smoke's Ute tomahawk buried in his brain.

Again jerking the weapon free, Smoke whirled around to dash back into the forest with blood dripping from the ax blade onto his leggings. Where there were two scouts, there could be more. He was certain these were not wandering renegades on the lookout for easy pickings—they worked for Evans, leading his gang to Smoke and his friends. A full-fledged attack was only moments away, coming at dawn, when cowboys who had been vigilant all night would be tired, sleepy, not as watchful.

Smoke knew he had precious little time to reduce the odds against them before Evans led his men charging toward the herd.

The young Apache never heard Smoke's stealthy approach up to his hiding place behind a tree, and when the tomahawk hit the back of his head, splitting it in half like a ripe melon, he did not utter a word or make a sound, crumpling to the forest floor in a growing pool of blood. Smoke knew there were two more Indians watching the herd somewhere . . . he'd found three ponies in a thicket, tied to low tree limbs.

Racing away from his third kill, Smoke saw a shadow move at the base of another oak tree at the edge of the prairie.

"They're makin' it easy for me, spreadin' out like this," he said in a feathery whisper.

Practicing the stalking art he'd learned from Preacher, Smoke came up behind an Apache cradling a Spencer rifle, peering around the oak to see the distant cattle herd. But this Indian somehow sensed something near him as Smoke leaped forward . . . he turned, just in time to see the flash of steel coming at him in a high arc above his head.

The pop of breaking bone ended a total silence in the forest when Smoke's tomahawk cleaved open the Apache's forehead, driving him back against the tree briefly. Then he sank to his knees as Smoke pulled the blade free amid a torrent of blood coming from a wound eight inches deep between the Indian's eyes.

Smoke didn't wait to see the Apache fall. He was running to the south when he heard a muted plop behind him.

He found the last Indian relieving himself behind a bush with his rifle leaning against a piñon pine. There wasn't time to allow the Apache to empty his bladder before he died from a sweeping slash across the side of his throat from a tomahawk severing his head.

Smoke darted behind a tree, listening. Farther to the south he heard the clank of a metal spur rowel.

"Here comes the rest of the army," he told himself. It was unlikely there could be any more killing without gunfire, and the commencement of all-out war.

Smoke trotted back to the fork of a tree where he'd hidden his rifle, passing five lifeless bodies in the soft light of a coming sunrise, the air already thick with the scent of blood.

* * *

A lone Mexican squatting behind a thick tangle of thorny brush gave Smoke one more chance to kill soundlessly. A blow to the head by a tomahawk snuffed out the Mexican's life before he realized someone was behind him. He went over on his face in the briars with blood pumping from his skull, oblivious to the scratches on his bearded cheeks and chin where sharp thorns tore into his flesh.

Smoke paused and took a deep breath. His killing instincts had once again overtaken him, pushing everything else from his mind. But just once, before he took off looking for more victims in the forest, he thought about the promise he'd made to Sally to steer clear of a fight, if he could.

"She'd understand," he whispered. He'd done everything he could to warn Jessie Evans and Jimmy Dolan what would happen if they pushed him.

He moved more slowly now, with light beaming over eastern hills that would reveal his presence. Carrying the Winchester in one hand, a pistol in the other, he'd belted the tomahawk, for it had done all the damage it could before sunrise.

Smoke stepped among the trees, halting often to sweep the forest for any sign of the enemy. When it was safe to continue, he moved south, wondering if Evans had split his forces so that some were already surrounding the herd.

Can't be two places at once, he thought, trotting wherever he could, walking where there was less cover.

Then he saw what he'd been expecting all along, a bunch of mounted men waiting in a draw surrounded by slender oaks. He froze behind a tree to count them.

"A baker's dozen," he whispered. Thirteen men would be hard to tackle single-handed. Smoke knew he had no choice.

34

A pistol in each hand, his Winchester lying between his feet within easy reach, Smoke straightened up behind a bush at the lip of the ravine—as with the five Apaches, these men would get no warning before they died—this was open war now.

He began firing methodically, one pistol, then the other, sending a stream of lead into the gully while the roar of exploding gunpowder filled his ears. Bullets tore through flesh in a steady stream, snapping bone and gristle, piercing organs and muscle. Frightened horses whickered and reared, plunging to be free of the pull of reins as riders toppled down into a mass of churning hooves.

Cries of pain, screams of agony accompanied the gun blasts and the sounds of terrified horses. Taken completely by surprise, the gunmen merely sought an escape from the deadly hail of hot slugs pouring down on them, but as each one made a dash toward freedom, he was cut down, knocked from his saddle by a bullet. Not a shot was fired back at Smoke until both his pistols were empty, and as he seized his rifle, only two unharmed members of Evans's gang remained aboard their horses. One was able to ride into the trees before Smoke could get off a rifle shot, but the second, a heavy Mexican, met his end as he was spurring his horse behind the first to flee. A rifle slug caught him in the ribs, cracking when it penetrated bone while passing into his chest. He fell sideways, with his right boot caught in a stirrup, so that as his horse galloped out of sight he was dragged along in its wake, leaving a trail of blood through the forest.

Smoke was moving before the echo of his rifle shot faded away, hurrying away from the scene, a ravine filled with writhing bodies and motionless corpses.

He raced back among the trees toward the herd, certain that now Evans would order a full charge toward the cattle. As he was running, he reloaded his Colts, cradling his rifle in the crook of his arm.

And as he expected, he heard the rumble of pounding hooves coming from the south and east. Men came pouring from the pines in every direction, spurring their mounts into a hard gallop, and even a quick count revealed there were far more of them than Smoke had anticipated. It appeared that twenty or more riders were rushing onto the prairie, and now the crackle of guns went back and forth almost in unison.

"The yellow bastard hired every gun in Lincoln County," Smoke growled, running faster, hurrying toward a position where he could help Pearlie and Cal and Johnny and his neighbors by firing from the enemy's flank. Until he was in range, he dared not waste a shot, telling Evans and the others where he was.

Answering fire came from Smoke's friends, only a few shots at a time right then. In his heart, Smoke doubted everyone in his crew could make it through a war like this without a scratch, and the thought saddened him momentarily, until blind rage overtook his sorrow.

"I'm comin', Evans!" he bellowed, knowing no one could hear him in the melee, racing along the edge of the forest with a killing fever burning in his brain.

An unexpected bit of good fortune presented itself just as he was nearing a thick oak trunk. Three riders came charging out of the trees with guns blazing, unaware that Smoke was only a few dozen yards away.

Smoke stumbled to a halt and drew a bead on the first rider with a pistol, firing too quickly, shooting high and wide. He triggered off a second shot as all three men turned toward the sound of his gun.

A man in a dirty brown Stetson flipped off his horse when Smoke's second bullet found its mark. Smoke fired again at another gunman, more careful with his aim now. A Mexican with cartridge belts across his chest went down, his sombrero fluttering away while he fell.

The third rider fired at Smoke, a hurried shot from the back of a moving horse. A molten slug screamed high above Smoke's head. Smoke downed him with a booming pistol, watching another Mexican gunman fly out of his saddle with his face twisted in pain.

Three riderless horses galloped onto the prairie, one with blood dripping from its withers, where its owner had bled before he fell.

The rattle of rifle fire became a din, a constant wall of noise as more than two hundred longhorn heifers scattered with their tails in the air, snorting through their muzzles as the stampede Smoke had been worrying about began. He could see the gentler Herefords milling about, but for the moment they stayed together in a tight bunch.

A rifle popped from a clump of bunch grass near the picketed horses. One of Evans's men floated away from his galloping horse with both hands pressed to his face.

"Nice shot," Smoke muttered, shouldering his rifle to begin dropping as many oncoming raiders as he could.

Leading a moving target with his rifle sights, he fired at a cowboy on a speeding pinto. A miss, and it made him angry as he levered another round into place.

"I've gotta get closer," he said savagely.

Two of Evans's men noticed him for the first time and swung their horses in his direction, bearing down on him as fast as their horses could run.

"Thank you, gentlemen," Smoke whispered, taking very careful aim.

His Winchester slammed into his shoulder, and the

report made his ears ring. But mild discomfort did nothing to take away from the satisfaction when a cowboy tumbled into the grass, his horse swerving away from the noise.

Smoke killed the second horseman with a bullet through the crown of his hat, which also sliced through the top of his skull, permanently parting the gunman's hair down the middle before he rolled off the rump of his horse.

"Time to move," Smoke spat, ducking down as he left the tree at a run, heading straight for the middle of the fight.

35

Billy Morton spurred his horse relentlessly to catch up to Jessie, and when Jessie saw him angling across the prairie, he wondered where the others were, the dozen men Billy was supposed to lead into the attack from the southwest. Billy was all alone, and he shouldn't have been. Dodging stampeding longhorns, Jessie motioned to Pickett and the men behind him to continue charging Jensen and his cowboys while he reined off to find out what Billy was in such a hurry to tell him.

Billy hauled back on his reins, bringing his lathered sorrel to a sliding stop when he rode up to Jessie. Jessie saw a look on Billy's face that could only be fear.

"He got behind us again!" Billy shouted to be heard above the bang of guns and the bawling of runaway cattle.

"Who?" Jessie demanded.

"That feller Jensen. It's gotta be him. A big son of a bitch with two pistols. I ain't never seen nothin' like it in all my borned days, Jessie. We was ready to charge out here when this big bastard appeared out of nowhere, both pistols blazin'. He killed everybody! 'Cept me. I was lucky to get out with my skin. One man ain't supposed to be able to do what he did. He killed twelve goddamn men, Jessie, in less time than it takes me to tell it."

Despite the battle going on in front of him, Jessie

stared at the spot where Billy and a mix of *pistoleros* from Vasquez's bunch and Pedro Lopez's gang were supposed to have entered the fight. He couldn't quite make himself believe what Billy had told him just now. "Had to be some others shootin'," he said, as the crack of a rifle close by made him flinch, a wild shot taken by one of the young Apaches galloping by. Sighting the Apache, Jessie wondered where the other Indians were now. Only two of them were out on the prairie doing any shooting, and their leader, Little Horse, wasn't among them.

"Just him, Jessie. I swear to it," Billy said. "Ain't no man on earth can kill twelve men like he done, only I seen it with my own two eyes while I was gettin' the hell away from there fast as this horse could run."

"How come nobody shot him?" Jessie asked, feeling a touch of worry growing in the pit of his stomach.

"Wasn't time. He stood up behind this bush an' emptied both guns as fast as he could pull them triggers. Men was droppin' like flies." Billy looked over his shoulder quickly as a group of terrified longhorns raced by. "That ain't even the worst of it," Billy continued, his voice with an unusually high pitch. "Just when I was comin' to tell you what happened to us, I saw that half-breed, Raul Jones, come ridin' out of them trees yonder with a couple of Pedro's men. Somebody cut 'em down before you could blink. I figure it had to be Jensen."

It wasn't possible, what Billy was telling him, how one man could be so lucky. Or was he that good? He couldn't be, not an ordinary cattleman from someplace up in Colorado.

Now Jessie looked at the fight going on around Jensen's camp and he saw two more of his men fall from their saddles. Pickett and Tom Hill had already swung their horses around when rifle fire from Jensen's cowboys proved too accurate. Pickett was no coward, but out in the open like he was, he and Tom were sitting ducks.

"Maybe this wasn't such a good idea, Jessie," Billy said, "tangling with Smoke Jensen. He ain't the tinhorn everybody claimed he was. The big son of a bitch can damn sure shoot. I seen it for myself."

"I ain't never met a man I backed down from," Jessie growled, with more resolve than he truly felt at the moment, after finding out how many more lives this Jensen had taken, all in a matter of minutes, before the attack had really gotten started. Now he found himself wondering if Jensen had gotten Little Horse and his four scouts. He could see their assault on the cowboys' camp was doing little beyond running off Jensen's herd. "Maybe it wasn't such a good plan to come at them out in the open like this. We'll pull back an' find another way. Ride a wide circle an' tell the men to head north. It's gonna take Jensen awhile to round up these cattle, an' that'll give us time to come up with a better idea. They're headed north to Colorado with this herd, so we'll look for a place north of here to set up an ambush that can't fail."

Bill Pickett and Tom Hill galloped up as Billy was leaving to give Jessie's order to withdraw. Pickett's face was a mask of hatred.

"Half your damn gunslicks ran off before we rushed 'em," he said. "Look out yonder. There ain't but fifteen or twenty of us, an' we come here with more'n forty. So few of us can't get close enough to find anything to shoot at. Them cowboys are all layin' down in the grass where we can't see 'em, an' we're out in the open."

"Some of 'em didn't run off," Jessie said quietly, as most of the gunfire stopped when Billy began motioning men to pull out and follow him northward. "Billy told me Jensen killed twelve men in that ravine where they was waitin' for my signal, an' then he got three more, includin' Raul. He may have killed Little Horse an' our scouts. Ain't seen 'em since before the fight started . . ." As he was speaking to Pickett, he saw a hatless man carrying a rifle running on foot toward the cowboy camp. "That must be Jensen right there. If I had a Sharps buffalo gun . . ."

Pickett saw the running figure too. He squinted to see

him more clearly in the bright morning sunlight. "He's just one man, Jessie. He may be good, but there's always somebody who's a little better. If he done what Billy claimed he did, then he's pretty damn good. Only, I'm promisin' you I can kill him if I get to pick the place, an' the time."

"I'm gonna give you that opportunity," Jessie remarked as a final gunshot popped in the distance. "You can pick the spot. I don't give a damn how you do it. I just want Jensen dead. We'll skirt their camp an' head north, the direction they've got to go to get to Colorado. You can start lookin' for the right place on the way up."

The man Jessie believed to be Jensen disappeared into a tall stand of bunch grass near a group of tethered horses still pawing the ground, prancing as a result of loud gunfire coming from all directions.

"I'll kill him for you," Pickett promised again. "You just let me do it my way."

Unconsciously, Jessie shook his head in disbelief when he got a count of the men Billy was leading north, scarcely more than a dozen. Was it possible that Jensen could have killed so many men himself? It went against everything Jessie knew about paid shootists. Even the best of them in tough border towns like Laredo could barely claim a dozen kills over a lifetime. Jensen had killed at least that many in a matter of minutes.

Tom Hill spoke his mind. "Whoever Jensen is, he ain't got any stake in this range war, really. We could let him ride back to Colorado an' git on with rustlin' Chisum out of business, so don't no more of us git killed."

"Are you turnin' yellow on me, Tom?" Jessie asked.

"Nope," Tom replied with conviction. "I've done my share of killin' over the years, but there's always come a few times when I knowed to toss in my cards an' git out of the game. You ain't asked me, but I've got this funny feelin' about tryin' Jensen again. Never was all that superstitious myself, but I've seen with my own two eyes what this feller Jensen can do. Some men are borned with a knack fer killin'. It comes natural to 'em, same as breathin' air."

Pickett's jaw tightened. "He'll bleed same as any man"

"Maybe," Tom said. "First, somebody's got to git close enough to put a bullet in him. Since he come here, that ain't been too awful easy."

Pickett glared at Tom, as though he'd been insulted by the remark. "Ain't nobody with backbone tried yet. These yellow sons of bitches Jessie hired don't know the first thing 'bout killin' a man, seems to me."

Before Jessie lifted his reins to ride off, he caught a glimpse of an Indian riding out of trees to the west. It was Dreamer, if Jessie remembered right. "Yonder's one of them Apaches. If he speaks any English, I'll ask him what come of Little Horse an' all the others."

"My money says they cut an' run," Pickett growled. "I told you a goddamn Injun ain't worth the gunpowder it takes to kill 'em when it comes down to cases."

The Indian came galloping up on a piebald paint pony. He looked at Jessie for a moment as if trying to think of the right words to say.

Jessie grew impatient. "What the hell happened to Little Horse an' the rest?"

"All dead," Dreamer answered, making an odd slashing motion with his hand across the top of his scalp. "Chop head, like this. Come see."

"I don't need to see it," Jessie snapped, when his grim prediction proved to be true.

Tom swallowed. "I didn't know Jensen used a woodcutter's ax in a fight like this. Most Apaches are mighty damn hard to sneak up on, 'specially fer a white man."

"Let's ride," Jessie said, weary of hearing more bad news. "We'll catch up with Billy an' the others an' then we'll decide what to do."

"I've already decided," Pickett said as he turned his horse to follow Jessie. "I'm gonna kill that son of a bitch myself, an' when I blow his goddamn head all to pieces with ol' Betsy here, you'll see Mr. Smoke Jensen wasn't nothin' but lucky he didn't run into me first."

As they rode around the cowboy camp Jessie wasn't so sure of Pickett's judgment when it came to Jensen. There was a ring of truth to what Tom had said, about some men having a natural gift when it came to killing. He recalled a time down in West Texas a few years ago, when he saw Clay Allison in action. Allison could draw and shoot as quickly as Jessie, and for that reason, Jessie left him completely alone until an offer of a job in New Mexico took him out of Sanderson.

He gave Jensen's camp a last look before he urged his horse into a thin line of trees to the northeast. Jessie couldn't help remembering what Dreamer had just told him, that Little Horse and his Apaches died from split skulls. Tom was right about one thing, that an Apache was hard to slip up on from behind. It was beginning to seem like Jensen was always finding a way to get behind them.

36

Smoke crept up to camp and spoke before he showed himself. "It's me. Is everybody okay?"

Pearlie rose up from his grassy hiding place. "Johnny took a bullet in the leg, but it's hardly more'n a scratch. I tied his bandanna 'round it till we could fix a proper bandage. He's lyin' over yonder next to the horses." He pointed north. "All of 'em cleared out, leastways the ones we could see. Wasn't near as many of 'em as I figured there'd be."

Smoke didn't bother to explain how he'd reduced the odds considerably. "Let's get the horses saddled and round up as many of our cows as we can." He examined the bunched Herefords not far away. "One of our young bulls caught a stray bullet in the neck, and we'll probably have to put him down."

"I seen it up close," Bob called from a spot near the bulls, "an' it's in his brisket. Bullet passed clean through. It don't hardly bleed any now, an' I'm bettin' he'll make it."

"That's good news," Smoke replied tiredly, sinking to the ground to put on his riding boots and place the bloody tomahawk in his saddlebags.

One by one, the cowboys stood up, when it was clear Evans and his men were gone. "We damn sure held 'em off," Cletus said, as Johnny limped over to their blackened firepit with pain written across his face. "'Cept fer Johnny, I'd say we was lucky."

Johnny agreed. "I was also lucky. That slug could have hit me in worse places. I'll mend."

Longhorn heifers were scattered from one end of the plain to the other, while many had run into the trees to escape the loud banging noises.

"We'll be all day gittin' 'em rounded up," Pearlie said, as he carried his saddle to the picket ropes.

Duke was the last to come in from his hiding place in the grass. "I figured they was gonna run over us like a locomotive for a spell. Somethin' must have changed their minds."

Pearlie gave Smoke a knowing look. "I imagine Mr. Jensen can tell us what it was, if'n he's of a mind to talk about it."

"I got a few," Smoke replied, pulling on his boots before he stood up with his saddle and bridle. "Everybody ride careful out there, just in case there's some who ain't dead, or still have some fight left."

Cal's face was ghostly white when he spoke up. "What do we do if we find a wounded man, boss?"

"Leave the son of a bitch right where he is. We haven't got time to be doctorin' men who just tried to kill us. Let 'em rot for all I care."

"I shot one," Cal added quietly, "a big feller in a sombrero with belts on his chest. Makes two so far on this trip. I sure do hope there ain't no more to my credit later on."

"You were doing what you had to do to help protect your friends and the cattle herd, son," Smoke told him. "Don't let it eat on you so hard."

"I'm tryin' not to think about it." Cal lifted his saddle to go to the picket line. "But I seen his face when I shot him. His eyes got big as fried turkey eggs, an' then there was blood all over his face. He dropped the rifle he was carryin' an' put his hands over his eyes just before he fell off his horse. It damn near made me sick all over again."

"I'm bettin' a month's pay you ain't sick enough to

keep from cleanin' your plate tonight, youngun. Don't nothin' make you that belly-sick."

In spite of Johnny's obvious pain, he chuckled. "That's damn sure one thing about Cal, all right. He can eat no matter what."

Cal pretended not to be listening, saddling his horse as quickly as he could.

Smoke was in for a pleasant surprise as the morning wore on, for it seemed the longhorns were willing to gather on the prairie without much urging. Most of them settled quickly and began to graze alongside the Hereford bulls.

As the cow work continued, Smoke thought about the direction the Evans gang had ridden . . . north, making it logical they would try again farther up the trail. He wondered how much convincing Jessie Evans needed.

Pearlie and Duke came trotting over to a grove of oaks where Smoke had just driven out three longhorns, helping him push them toward the main bunch.

"That makes over a hundred an' thirty head so far," Duke said. "This is easier than it looked like it was gonna be when we first got started."

Smoke nodded his agreement as he saw Cletus and Cal bringing five more cows from the east. Two more strays came out of the woods farther north on their own. "Some of 'em are volunteering to come back themselves."

Pearlie shrugged. "Longhorns is the most unpredictable critters on earth. Sometimes they run off fer no reason at all. Other times they won't run if you ask 'em to, an' a few times they stampede an' then come back without bein' asked. The first man who figures out how a longhorn's brain works is gonna make hisself a fortune."

Smoke was keeping an eye on the horizon, and Pearlie was the first to notice.

"You know they'll be back, don't you?" he asked, as the cows took off in a trot to rejoin the others.

"It's likely," was all he said.

"They'll do it different next time," Pearlie assured him a moment later. "They won't come at us straight on."

"Hard to say, Pearlie. About all we can do is stay watchful until it happens."

"It'll happen. You know it as well as me. The way I see it, after they've tried so many damn times, we'll have to kill might' near all of 'em afore it's over an' done with."

Smoke knew there was a great deal of wisdom behind Pearlie's words.

That evening, as Pearlie signaled a pot of beans was ready to eat, only seven heifers remained unaccounted for. Time was more important now than seven cows, Smoke decided, his eyelids heavy from lack of sleep.

He found good news when he climbed down from his saddle at the campfire. The wounded Hereford bull had stopped bleeding entirely, and now it was grazing along with the others, apparently suffering no real discomfort from its injury.

Smoke tied off his horse, carrying his bedroll.

"You gonna sleep or eat?" Pearlie asked good-naturedly.

"A little of both, I hope."

Cletus picked up his rifle. "I already ate all I could stand of Pearlie's beans, so I'll take the first watch along with Cal. Cal's young enough not to need as much sleep as the rest of us."

Smoke tossed his bedroll over a stretch of soft grass before he came for a plate of beans. "Suits me, Cletus. I'll relieve you before midnight. Ride as close to the herd as you can without spookin' 'em. They're still a little jittery after all that happened today."

"So am I," Cal said softly, leaving his beans mostly untouched to saddle the gray colt.

Pearlie straightened up from spooning more beans onto his plate. "Well I'll be damned an' hog-tied. We just witnessed a miracle, boys. That youngun hardly touched his food tonight, an' that's like seein' a man walk on water without gittin' his feet wet."

37

North of the Haystack Mountain range, Jessie led his men to a fork in the Pecos River coming from the west, a shallow body of sluggish water only belly-deep on their horses. Pickett seemed to be interested in a spot north of the crossing, where big rocks and tall cottonwoods lined the river.

"This is it," Pickett told Jessie, while Jose Vasquez and four of his remaining *pistoleros* made it across, followed by Billy Morton, Tom Hill, Pedro Lopez, and the two members of his gang left alive after the fight with Jensen. The last rider to cross was the Indian called Dreamer, who kept glancing backward as if he expected them to be followed.

"This is what?" Jessie asked, still brooding over their resounding defeat yesterday morning at the hands of Jensen.

"The perfect place," Pickett replied, his voice turned to ice. "I'll kill the son of a bitch while his horse is crossin' this river. I can hide in them rocks yonder, an' I'll be close enough to use my scattergun. Betsy'll cut him to pieces at this range. Probably kill his horse too."

Jessie looked things over. "He may get suspicious when he comes to a spot like this where he can't see if anybody's hid on the other side. Might not work like you planned."

"He has to cross here to make sure there ain't no bogs or quicksand that'll trap his cattle. He's a rancher, an' he'll know the risks if he don't test this crossing."

"We can have the rest of the men spread out up and down this riverbank to cover you."

Pickett wheeled on Jessie with fire in his eyes. "That's what was wrong every goddamn time, Jessie. These idiots you hired don't know the first thing 'bout killin' a man out in the open. What you've got is a buncha saloon-raised gunmen who've got no experience bushwhackin' a man who knows wild country. He'll come real cautious down to this river, bein' as careful as he knows how. That's why I'm gonna do this my way, so none of the rest of these fools tip my hand on what I aim to do."

"Suit yourself, Bill," Jessie said. "The only thing I care about is findin' Smoke Jensen dead."

Pickett jutted his jaw. "You won't find nothin' but pieces of him. I give you my word on it. He'll be twenty yards away when he's in the middle of this river, an' that's close enough to shred every piece of meat on his body with a sawed-off shotgun like mine. You leave Jensen to me. The sumbitch is as good as dead right now if he crosses this river."

Jessie wondered. However, Pickett's reputation for killing his victims any way he could made him the perfect choice for this job. Jessie could never have admitted it to anyone, but after yesterday's defeat and the incredible number of men Jensen had killed single-handed, he'd begun to experience twinges of doubt that he could do the job himself. Jensen apparently had some uncanny ability to move around without detection. How else could he have slipped up behind Little Horse and four more experienced Apache warriors, chopping their heads open with some kind of ax, not the sort of weapon the average man used in a war being fought with guns.

"I don't give a damn how you do it, just make sure it don't backfire," Jessie said, as his grim-faced gunmen sat their horses around him, listening to his exchange with

Pickett. Jessie knew the others feared Pickett, and rightfully so. Pickett was a madman, more than slightly out of kilter when it came to killing other men, even as they lay dying from other bullet wounds. Roy Cooper had been much the same in that regard. Only somehow, Jensen had been able to kill him along with all the others that night, and it still worried Jessie some.

Pickett turned back to Jessie. "Tell that Injun to ride back and see how far they are behind us. An' tell the dumb son of a bitch not to let 'em see him. All Injuns are good at bein' sneaky, so tell him to be careful."

Dreamer apparently understood every word. At first he gave Pickett a chilly stare, then he swung his pony around and went back across the river, resting a very old Henry repeating rifle across his pony's withers.

"Dreamer's liable to double-cross us now, after what you just said about him," Jessie remarked, watching the Apache ride out of sight around a bend in the trail.

Pickett made a face. "He won't do it, because he's after a payday. The rotten bastards will do damn near anything to get their hands on enough money to buy whiskey. Never saw an Injun who wasn't drunk, or plannin' to get drunk. That's why you can't trust 'em."

Jessie looked north, where the trail climbed to the top of a ridge between two low mountains. "We'll ride on over that rise yonder an' make camp wherever there's water. Find a spring or somethin', a feeder creek. We'll be listenin' real close for gunshots."

"Won't be but one," Pickett said, "when little Miss Betsy gives Jensen her ten-gauge loads." He drew his double-barrel Greener from a boot tied to the pommel of his saddle, and for a moment it seemed he almost caressed its dark walnut stock while his face visibly changed. He glanced over at Jessie and now a glint flickered in his pale eyes. "This here gun has ended a hell of a lot of men's lives. Only this one's gonna be special, because Jensen thinks he's so goddamn tough an' clever."

"He is clever," Jessie said. "But like you say, he'll die

the same as any other man if a load of double-size buck-shot hits him in the right places."

"He can't be all that clever," Pickett assured him. "A man makes mistakes now an' then. The biggest mistake Jensen made was comin' to Lincoln County at the wrong time. Now he's gonna pay for it with his life."

Jessie reined his horse for the top of the ridge. There was no point in discussing it with Pickett any further. If Pickett was as good as his reputation, and from what Jessie had seen of him in action during several attacks on Chisum's cow camps, all their troubles with Mr. Smoke Jensen would soon be over.

Tom rode up beside Jessie as they were trotting up the ridge to look for water and a campsite.

"This is liable to be one helluva mistake," Tom said under his breath. "I've got a real bad feelin' about it."

"You worry too much, Tom," Jessie said, although he shared some of the same nagging doubts about Pickett's planned ambush.

Tom looked up at a clear spring sky. "I worry when a man's already proved he's hard to kill, an' I'm sidin' the bunch who aims to kill him. Pickett ain't never seen Jensen close before. When he gits a good look, he may change his mind."

"That's damn sure a fact," Billy Morton said, riding along Jessie's left side. "If I live to be a hundred years old, I won't forgit what it was like when Jensen jumped up from behind that bush with both pistols spittin' fire. It was the same as facin' the devil himself."

"Bill Pickett's a proven killer," Jessie argued.

It was Tom who said, "So's this feller Smoke Jensen. I've never heard of him before he came here, but I'll tell you one thing fer sure . . . he's about as mean as they come, and this job ridin' for Jimmy Dolan don't pay enough to be worth gettin' killed. If Pickett don't kill him when he crosses that river, I'm quittin' this outfit fer good. There's gotta be easier ways to make money, an' live long enough to spend it."

494 *William W. Johnstone*

Billy didn't say anything, but Jessie was sure he was of the same mind. "Give Pickett a chance to prove himself before you start quittin' a good-payin' job with Dolan," said Jessie. "There ain't all that much work to be had for a shootist in this part of the West, an' I'm sure as hell not askin' to be taken off the payroll till I know there ain't no other choice."

38

Cattle were strung out for half a mile when Smoke turned to look back at the herd. As they had from the beginning, the short Herefords brought up the rear. Cal and Cletus were riding drag at the back of the bunch. Bob and Johnny held the flank positions, keeping wandering strays driven back, while Pearlie and Duke rode point on either side, aiming lead cows in the right direction. A peaceful day had passed, with no sign of the Evans gang. Smoke had been reading their tracks every now and then, counting horses when the prints crossed barren ground. Between fifteen and twenty men were a day's ride ahead of the herd, judging by the freshness of the tracks, the edges of the clear prints that were still sharp before wind and time had made the dirt crumble.

According to a crudely drawn map he carried in his saddlebags, they were a couple of days' drive from old Fort Sumner, an abandoned army post turned into a small community where sheepmen and Mexican goatherds lived in empty army barracks. The herd was managing fifteen or twenty miles a day, slower because of the short-legged bulls.

Smoke swung his horse away from the trees, where he'd been keeping an eye on the herd's progress. He was staying closer to the cows than before, in part because the tracks left by Evans and his men continued due north, with no sign any of them had turned off to launch another attack or take up snipers' positions when they came to high ground.

Still, Smoke was nagged by the dull certainty that Evans would try again. Arrogant men with high opinions of themselves rarely ever gave up completely, not until someone convinced them they had no other choice.

It appeared to be a small fork leading to the main body of the Pecos River a few miles to the east. Lined with cottonwoods and jumbles of limestone boulders swept aside by previous floods, it looked to be shallow, easy to cross. Smoke sat his Palouse on a high bluff above the river, watching things carefully from a considerable distance before he rode down to test the river bottom for treacherous sand pits and bogs.

Examining the branches of each tree, he was troubled when he found no birds perched on any of the leafy limbs near the crossing. As with most of his experience, reading this sort of sign had been taught to him by Preacher. Most all types of wildlife exhibited behavior that was as good as a signpost, if a man knew how to read it. The sudden flight of birds from a particular spot was a warning to knowledgeable men. The direction a deer ran when it was frightened, sensing danger, was as meaningful as the angry charge of a grizzly protecting her newborn cubs. Even a lowly cricket gave off excellent warnings in the dark, simply by suddenly growing silent when it felt another presence close to its hiding place. The absence of sparrows or blue jays in trees beside the river alerted Smoke to the possibility of danger.

He reined his Palouse around and tied it off in a thicket where it could graze, pulling his rifle, taking a single thin blanket from his bedroll, and wrapping it around his forearm. The sun was almost directly overhead. A soft breeze came from the west; thus he began his approach to the crossing from the east, upwind, in the fashion of all seasoned mountain men stalking prey. He had a possible use for the blanket, a trick, just in case someone was down there gunning for him.

Pickett had grown bored with all the waiting. Last night, as he rested on thin blankets with a pint of tequila for company, his impatience had lessened somewhat. But today his nerves were on edge more than usual. . . . It was this damn waiting, even though he fully understood the necessity of it. If Smoke Jensen was the trained killer everyone else believed he was, he'd be smart and cautious.

He checked the loads in his pistol, a Colt Peacemaker, for what seemed the hundredth time, then he holstered it and after he took off his flat-brim Stetson, he peered above the rocks, where shadows from nearby cottonwoods covered his hiding place. Again there was no sign of a horseman approaching the river. He then clamped his jaw in frustration and ducked back down.

"I'll bet the gutless son of a bitch headed another direction," he said softly, angrily. "He's liable to ride plumb to Nebraska to get back home." Pickett took another swallow of tequila, listening closely for the sound of a horse in the distance.

He'd gone over what he meant to do a thousand times, not raising his head at all when the rider got close, waiting until he heard a horse in the river. Jensen would be looking for any kind of movement, and there would be none until he was in the water. Then he might catch a split-second glimpse of two shotgun barrels flashing in the sunlight just before they exploded, too late for any man to draw and shoot.

"C'mon, you yellow bastard," Pickett whispered, resting his head against a rock, his shotgun held loosely in his left fist with both hammers cocked . . . he didn't want the click of metal to alert Jensen just before he killed him.

He wondered what was keeping Jensen. According to

what the Apache told Jessie, they should be nearing the river by now. He took a bite of jerky and washed it down with tequila. "Hard on a man's nerves, all this waitin'."

He let his gaze wander upriver, then downstream, examining every rock and tree, when suddenly he saw a shadow dart among the cottonwood trunks.

"It's him," Pickett hissed, whirling around to hide himself behind the boulder. Jensen wasn't as clever as Jessie thought. Pickett was sure what he had seen was the outline of a man coming upstream, already on the north side of the river.

He left his horse somewhere, Pickett thought, so he'd make less noise. Peering cautiously around the rock, he aimed his ten-gauge and drew his Peacemaker, ready for anything, every muscle in his body tensed.

He saw the movement again and almost fired at it, until he caught himself. "Not till you're closer, you bastard," he whispered as his grip relaxed on his pistol. Pickett wanted to shred the Colorado cowboy with his scattergun if he could.

Now nothing moved, and only the quiet gurgle of the river passing over stones reached his ears. The second time he saw Jensen he'd been closer, yet not quite close enough for Betsy to do her best work.

"C'mon, turkey," Pickett mouthed silently, as beads of sweat formed on his forehead. He could almost taste the moment when he would kill Jensen, a thickening of his tongue with a slightly sweet taste on the tip. He found himself longing for the sight of a bullet-torn body oozing blood from hundreds of pellet wounds, and he imagined the coppery smell of Jensen's blood. He hoped the first twin charges didn't kill Jensen instantly. . . . It would be far better to stand over him, to see the fear and pain in his eyes just before another shotgun blast tore his head to pieces.

More waiting made him more impatient, until a heavier gust of wind blew down the river, rippling its waters, and at the same time Jensen moved again, darting around the base of a cottonwood, rushing toward him.

Pickett straightened up quickly and fired both barrels of the Greener, jolted by twin explosions that deafened him briefly. He saw the shadow swirl, twisting when a wall of lead struck.

"Gotcha, you son of a bitch!" Pickett cried as he took a step away from the rock, holstering his pistol to reload the ten-gauge for a sure kill when he reached Jensen.

"Not quite," an even voice said behind him.

Pickett froze, twisting his head to look over his shoulder. He saw a man standing beside a rock pile less than twenty yards away. Pickett's mouth fell open.

"You shot a blanket draped over a limb," the man added, an evil grin widening his lips. "But the blanket does belong to me. I'm Smoke Jensen. I reckon you've been waitin' here a long time to ambush me."

Pickett only had one shell in the Greener, and its breech was open. His Peacemaker was holstered. "How'd you get behind me?" Pickett asked, buying time until he could think of a way to get at his pistol without being shot. Both of Jensen's pistols were holstered. . . . He carried a Winchester, muzzle aimed down at the ground.

"To tell the truth, it was mighty easy. I suppose you're the feller named Bill Pickett, on account of that short shotgun. We were told you fancied yourself a man-killer. So far, the only thing you've shot holes in was a blanket."

"You're gonna shoot me in the back, ain't you?" Pickett asked.

"My conscience might bother me, so I'm gonna let you turn around and reach for that Colt. I'll give you plenty of time."

"You're lyin'," Pickett replied. "You'll kill me soon as I move"

Jensen nodded. "I'm gonna kill you either way, but if you want a chance to see how good you are with that six-gun, make a move for it. But do it quick, or I'll just kill you now an' be on my way. That shotgun blast is liable to bring Evans and his men any minute."

Pickett felt he had no selection. He dropped Betsy to

the ground and made a slow, deliberate turn, expecting Jensen to draw a pistol before he could square himself. To his surprise, Jensen remained motionless until Pickett had his feet spread slightly apart and his right hand hovering above his Peacemaker.

"Reach for it," Jensen said, as calm as could be.

Pickett didn't wait for a second invitation. His hand went clawing for his gun.

There was a flash of gun metal in sunlight, then a booming noise.

39

Jessie Evans and Billy Morton were the first to scramble aboard their horses when they heard gunshots, with the others mounting right behind them.

"That was Pickett's shotgun!" Jessie cried, spurring his horse to cover the half mile down to the river crossing as rapidly as he could. "Pickett got the son of a bitch!"

Billy galloped up beside him. "I ain't gonna believe it till I see it!" he shouted back over the clatter of iron horseshoes on rock.

Jessie drew his pistol, just in case, and as if it were a signal, every member of his gang was fisting guns. Riding as hard as they could, they covered the distance in only a few minutes, until Jessie reined to a halt on a knob above the river.

"Yonder he is," Jessie said, as soon as the others came to a stop alongside him. "Pickett wrapped his body in a blanket so's we can bury him."

Billy kept looking up and down the river. "Where the hell is Pickett? I don't see him nowhere."

Jose Vasquez pointed to a distant horseman on a ridge on the far side of the crossing. The figure appeared to be watching them.

"*Quien es?* Who is that?" Vasquez asked.

"Probably just one of Jensen's boys," Jessie answered.

"I'm ridin' down to have a look. You can see Jensen's dead from here, 'cause he ain't moving, all wrapped up in that blanket like he is."

Tom said, "I ain't all that convinced it's Jensen."

Jessie ignored the remark and rode his horse off the knob to reach the river. But as he got closer, he felt something was wrong. He heard the others following him, but at a slower gait.

He rode up to the blanket-clad body and jumped down, in a hurry to set eyes on Jensen's corpse. He knelt and pulled back the dark blue blanket, riddled with pellet holes, and what he saw made him draw in a quick breath.

"It's Pickett," Billy Morton observed without leaving the back of his horse.

Jessie's hand, the one holding the blanket, began to shake. He dropped the woolen cloth quickly and stood up, gazing at the mounted figure far across the river. "That is Jensen," he said with a dry mouth.

"He's prob'ly laughin' at us," Tom said. "One thing's for damn sure—he's gotta be the toughest hombre I ever ran across, an' if Bill Pickett was still alive, he'd be sayin' the same damn thing. You can count me out of this, Jessie. I'm pulling stakes while I still can."

"That goes fer me too," Billy said, looking up at the man watching them from the ridge. "I knowed when he killed twelve of us back in that draw there was somethin' about him that damn near wasn't human. If you're smart, Jessie, you'll let that feller go wherever the hell he aims to go with his cows."

Jessie whirled to Jose Vasquez. "How 'bout you, Jose?"

"I see enough," Vasquez replied. "This man be *muy malo*, one bad hombre. Maybe so he is no man, *un espíritu*. He kill three of my cousins, also many of *mi compadres*. I don't want no more to have fight with him. We going back to Mexico."

When Jessie looked at Pedro, Pedro shrugged.

"Is no good, Señor Jessie. We no can kill him. He kill Ignacio and Roy and now he kill Señor Pickett. He make killing look easy. He kill us also if we don't leave him alone."

Jessie turned back to Jensen, scowling. "Mr. Dolan ain't gonna like it when I tell him."

Tom spoke. "Tell Dolan to try an' kill him hisself. He'll find out damn quick it ain't easy done."

Jessie's jaw clamped angrily. "I wonder who he really is. I can guarantee you he ain't just some cattle rancher from up north."

"*No lo hasé,*" Vasquez said. "It make no difference to me. I only know one thing about him—he don't get no more chances to kill me or *mi compadres.* We go home now."

Billy rested his elbow on his saddle horn. "That don't leave nobody but you, Jessie. We've knowed each other a long time, an' I'm givin' you good advice. Leave that Jensen feller plumb alone or you'll wind up like Pickett an' Cooper an' all the rest."

"He's just sittin' there watchin' us," Jessie said, with his gaze still fixed on the ridge.

"He's waitin' to see what we'll do, I reckon," Tom said. "If we act like we're comin' after him, he won't be sittin' there in plain sight very long."

Jessie's hands unconsciously balled into fists, then they relaxed.

"C'mon, Jessie," Billy said quietly. "Let's git the hell outta here afore Jensen changes his mind."

"It ain't my nature to run," Jessie replied, still frozen to the same spot above Pickett's corpse.

"It's any man's nature to wanna stay alive," Tom suggested. "We got no quarrel with Jensen."

Jose Vasquez was done talking. He gave a silent signal to his men and reined away from the river, riding off in a cloud of dust swirling in the breeze. Pedro and his two remaining men were not long in following Vasquez, swinging their mounts around after the other *pistoleros.*

Jessie's shoulders sagged. He finally took his eyes off Jensen to look at Billy and Tom. "We can't tell Dolan what really happened, boys. It'll make us look like fools."

Billy wagged his head. "The only way we'd look like bigger fools is to stay an' tangle with Jensen again. We can tell Dolan a bunch of Chisum's riders showed up, leavin' us outnumbered. If you agree to leave this Jensen alone, I'll stay on with Dolan's outfit. Otherwise, I'm cuttin' a trail for parts unknown."

"Same goes fer me," Tom said, as Jessie finally mounted his horse.

Jessie gave Smoke Jensen a final stare, then without a word he wheeled his horse around to head back to Lincoln. It damn sure wasn't going to be easy giving Dolan the bad news, and it could cost him a good-paying job as Dolan's ramrod.

40

Approaching the lush green mountains and meadows south of Sugarloaf range brightened everyone's mood. The cattle were fat and had proven to be trailworthy, even the short-strided Hereford bulls. It had been two weeks since the last confrontation with Jessie Evans and his paid guns, a peaceful two weeks of guiding cows across good grazing and plenty of water.

Smoke had all but forgotten about the battles with Dolan's gunslingers, until they neared Sugarloaf. He'd have to come clean with Sally about what he'd done, the men he killed, and he feared making the admission more than he'd ever feared the risks when bullets were flying.

"She'll throw a fit," he said one clear, crisp spring morning less than a dozen miles below Sugarloaf.

"You're talkin' about Miz Jensen, ain't you?" Pearlie asked with a grin. "I understand. I'd rather face the Shoshoni tribe on the warpath than Miz Jensen when she's got her feathers ruffled."

"I'll make her understand," Smoke said without conviction, "even though she'll keep reminding me of my promise to stay wide of difficulties."

"We tried to avoid 'em," Pearlie remembered. "They was just too damn hardheaded, an' wouldn't leave us alone."

Cal came riding up as the herd wound its way through a valley leading to Bob Williams's ranch. "We're home," Cal said with unconcealed excitement. "Means we'll be havin' some of Miz Sally's good cookin' afore too long."

Pearlie made a face. "I see your appetite has done returned to its usual."

"I'm sick of beans an' fatback. A big bearclaw drippin' with melted brown sugar sure would be nice. Maybe two or three of 'em."

Smoke was hoping all had remained quiet at the ranch while they were away. "Before she cooks up a bunch of bearclaws, I'm afraid she's gonna fix me a dish of my own words, when I tell about all the troubles we had."

"You hadn't oughta promised her nothin'," Pearlie said. "I reckon she knows you well enough to know such a thing just wasn't possible."

"She'll have her say-so about it," Smoke said, with all the assurance of experience.

"It'll soften her some when she sees them good bulls," Cal remarked. "That little one with the hole in his chest is doin' just fine. He don't hardly notice it now."

Pearlie spoke again. "Me, I'm lookin' forward to sleepin' in my own bed, 'stead of this hard ground. It's damn sure gonna be good to be back home fer a change."

Smoke looked back at the herd. Some of the Hereford bulls had already mounted heifers coming in season during rest stops. "Next spring we'll have pastures full of white-faced crossbred calves. And I'm gonna wire that feller Chisum told me about down in Saint Louis, and have him ship me a good Morgan stud by rail this summer."

"Sounds like you've got things all planned out," Pearlie said. "Maybe things will settle down now. We've burned a hell of a lot of gunpowder lately."

"For a fact," Cal added quietly. "I still dream about them two fellers I killed, the Indian an' that *pistolero*."

"It'll pass, youngun," Pearlie assured him. "Besides that, if you didn't spend so damn much time sleepin', you wouldn't have time to do all that dreamin'."

Bob Williams and Duke Smith rode up when they came to a fork in the valley leading to Smoke's ranch. "If it's all the same to you, Mr. Jensen, me an' Duke will take a couple of those bulls, an' head for home. I'll bring the purchase money over in a few days, if that's okay."

"You're a neighbor and a friend, Bob. Pay for 'em whenever you get ready."

Bob extended a handshake offering. "Thanks again for takin' us along."

Smoke nodded. "As it turned out, we might not have made it if it hadn't been for the two of you helpin' out with your guns once in awhile."

Bob grinned. "Always glad to help a neighbor," he said as he swung off to pick out two bulls.

As soon as Bob was out of earshot, Pearlie said, "Hell-fire, I never saw Bob or Duke hit nothin' whilst we was shootin'. Bob couldn't hardly hit the side of a barn with a rifle."

"They did the best they could," Smoke replied, not really caring either way. Marksmanship was a low priority when it came to picking good neighbors.

He saw Sally waiting on the front porch as they drove the herd up to the corrals. She smiled a beautiful smile and waved to him.

"Best you put yer lyin' britches on afore you tell her about this trip," Pearlie said, stifling a chuckle.

"I won't lie to her," Smoke replied. "She'd know right off I wasn't telling the truth anyway."

"You can tell her part of the truth. Say we ran into a bit of trouble but it didn't amount to nothin'."

"She'd know," Smoke told him.

Now Pearlie laughed out loud. "Miz Jensen is the only two-legged thing on earth Mr. Smoke Jensen is afraid of."

"That's about the size of it, Pearlie. I wouldn't do anything that might cause me to lose her."

He kicked the Palouse colt toward the house while the

others pushed the cattle toward the corrals. When he got to the front porch, he swung down and took her in his arms.

"I've missed you," he said, kissing her lips. "Have things gone smoothly here?"

"No problems," she told him, smiling. Then her face changed to a serious look. "But I can tell you had a few problems. I can see it in your eyes, and the fact that Johnny's wearing that bandage around his leg."

"There was some shooting," he told her. "I had to discourage some hard cases who didn't want us to get these cows to Sugarloaf."

"You can tell me about it later," she said. "Right now I want to see those Herefords up close."

"I'd rather see you up close for a while," he replied.

She gave him a taunting turn of her head. "That will come later, Smoke, if you behave yourself until the sun goes down."

"I may not be able to wait that long."

"Then find yourself another woman. I'm not that easy, to just take my clothes off when a man comes riding up to ask."

"Even if he's your husband?"

"I'd forgotten I had a husband, you've been away so long."

"I got back as quick as I could."

He held her in a powerful embrace, something he'd been thinking about for several long days on the trail. "You always win arguments, don't you?" he asked.

"We are not arguing. I won't let you take me to bed until I see those Herefords. End of discussion."

"I suppose I should have looked for another woman on the trail."

"Suit yourself, Mr. Jensen. But you won't find another woman who loves you the way I do, and you'll never find a woman who's any better in bed."

He looked down at her in mock surprise. "You've got a very high opinion of yourself, young lady."

"I've earned it, for putting up with you. Now, show me

the new bulls or you may wind up sleeping in the barn tonight."

He let go of her and took her by the arm. "They're just what you said they were. Beefy, and I've seen Chisum's crosses on longhorns. They'll be perfect for the markets."

She squeezed his hand as they walked side by side down to the corrals, where Pearlie and Johnny and Cal were driving the Herefords into a separate pen. She looked at the bulls a moment before she said anything.

"Those bulls are the future of this ranch," she said. "I've never seen so much meat on one animal before."

"Some of them have already bred some of the heifers on the drive up here."

She looked up at him with a twinkle in her eyes. "I'm sure there's much more to tell me about the drive," she said.

"A few minor details," he admitted.

"Like the gun battles you got into, and how many men you had to kill to get them here?" she asked.

"I did have to shoot a couple, maybe more than one or two, but I didn't have a choice."

She stood on her tiptoes to kiss him. "It seems you never have a choice when there's a fight," she told him. "I do wish you'd learn to turn your back on them."

"Somebody might have shot me in the back if I'd done that," he argued feebly, knowing he would have to tell her everything. It was because he loved her so deeply that he couldn't hide the truth from her.

"You can tell me all about it after supper, Smoke. I'll do my best to understand. There's something inside you that won't let you avoid taking a side in things, and I suppose that's also one of the reasons why I love you. Some men would ride right past a one-sided fight. I've come to know you well enough to know you never would." She examined the young bulls again, then she said, "Just remember, one fight you'll never win is a fight with me."